# THE GREEN LADY

# THE GREEN LADY

An Alex Mavros Mystery

## Paul Johnston

CRÈME de la CRIME

This first world edition published 2012
in Great Britain and 2013 in the USA by
Crème de la Crime, an imprint of
SEVERN HOUSE PUBLISHERS LTD of
19 Cedar Road, Sutton, Surrey, England, SM2 5DA.
Trade paperback edition first published
in Great Britain and the USA 2013 by
SEVERN HOUSE PUBLISHERS LTD.

British Library Cataloguing in Publication Data

Johnston, Paul, 1957-
  The green lady.
  1. Mavros, Alex (Fictitious character)–Fiction.
  2. Private investigators–Greece–Fiction. 3. Missing
  persons–Investigation–Greece–Fiction. 4. Suspense
  fiction.
  I. Title
  823.9'2-dc23

ISBN-13:  978-1-78029-034-8 (cased)
ISBN-13:  978-1-78029-534-3 (trade paper)

*All Severn House titles are printed on acid-free paper.*

Severn House Publishers support The Forest Stewardship Council [FSC],
the leading international forest certification organisation. All our titles that
are printed on Greenpeace-approved FSC-certified paper carry the FSC logo.

Typeset by Palimpsest Book Production Ltd.,
Falkirk, Stirlingshire, Scotland.
Printed and bound in Great Britain by
TJ International Ltd, Padstow, Cornwall

To
Sofka Zinovieff and Vassilis Papadhimitriou
with thanks and love

# AUTHOR'S NOTE

I retain a modicum of Modern Greek vocabulary and grammar, so please take note of the following before complaining about poor proofreading:

1) Masculine names ending in –is, –os, and –as lose the final –s in the vocative case: 'Akis, Yiorgos and Nondas are watching the Olympics'; but, 'Aki, Yiorgo and Nonda, turn the bloody TV off!' Some names ending in –os, such as Telemachos, retain the older form –e, as in 'Telemache'.
2) Feminine surnames end differently from masculine ones: Paschos Poulos, but Angie Poulou.
3) The consonant transliterated as 'dh' (e.g. Livadheia, Paradheisos) is pronounced 'th' as in English 'these'.

# PROLOGUE

The girl, fourteen and blonde, her slim form enveloped in a blue polo shirt and tight jeans, was in the middle of a meadow. May Day was warm and the flowers – crown daisies, gladioli, anemones and poppies – were bright and tall in the sea of grass. On the edge of the forest beyond, blossom shivered in the breeze, almond and the brighter pink of *koutsoupia*, the Judas tree. In the distance she could hear the voices of her schoolmates, squealing and shrieking as they discussed boys and how much they hated their parents. She found them dull, not least because she loved her mother deeply.

The girl put the wreath of wild flowers she'd fashioned around her neck then sat down, her head beneath the level of the grass. No one could find her here, she was safe. If they came, she could crawl away and escape. The idea excited her, but there was her mother. She couldn't leave her to face her father. No, she had to go back.

She heard her name being called, first by the other girls and then by the woman who was in charge of the day out in the valley of Mount Elikonas. Her own mother had wanted to come, but her presence had been required at one of the numerous official functions she hated so much. The temptation to disappear overwhelmed the girl again; what would it be like to start her life again? What would it be like to mould your own future? No, she would wait until she'd taken all she could from her father; do as well as she could in her exams; go to university in England or America. She would never come back to Greece, the country where she'd lost everything before she had even begun to grow up.

She got to her feet and put her hand over her eyes as she scanned the meadow and its tree-lined edges. Where were they? The voices were fainter now. Was she going to have to run to catch them up? She started to push through the grass and flowers but found that, even though she was a decent sprinter in the school athletics team, she couldn't make much speed. She breathed in the mingled scents of spring, both from the wreath round her neck and from the still-living blooms among the grass. They were beautiful. Why couldn't she stay here forever?

And then a dark shape reared before her. She felt strong arms fold her up and carry her out of the meadow. She raised her eyes to the sky but she didn't scream. At that point, she didn't know that the gates of hell were opening to receive her.

# ONE

'Those money-grabbing sons and daughters of whores, they've sold the country down Excrement River in a trireme with holes in its hull, the—'

Mavros grabbed the remote control and reduced the volume. Yiorgos Pandazopoulos, sixty-one and built like a sumo wrestler, glared at the TV and went on cursing as the opening ceremony of the 2004 Athens Olympics unfolded in all its kitschy glory.

'Give it a rest, Fat Man. Think of the tourist income the Games have brought.'

'What tourist income?' Yiorgos emptied a bottle of Amstel beer, the folds of flesh around his neck wobbling. 'The fools who've come for the Olympics are staying in hotels owned by multinational groups, drinking foreign fizzy drinks and eating American pizza. The ones who come to Greece for sun, sea and shagging are waiting till the fiasco's over. If anything, there'll be less tourist income this year than last.'

Mavros pointed to the flat boxes on the coffee table in front of them. One contained half of his four seasons pizza, but the Fat Man's peperoni deluxe was represented only by an oily red slick.

'What about those, Yiorgo? They came from a foreign franchise too. Plus the beer's brewed under licence from Holland.'

'Pshaw! We've got to keep body and soul together somehow, Alex.'

In the interests of peace-keeping, Mavros refrained from pointing out that they could easily have eaten local food at the taverna down the road from his friend's flat. On the other hand, the opening ceremony would have been blasting out even louder there, and the idea of the Fat Man spouting bile at other diners wasn't palatable.

'Look at those self-satisfied tossers,' Yiorgos said, as the camera panned along the rows of VIPs – numerous presidents and prime ministers, Greek government representatives, the female mayor of Athens, and other figures less well known to the average viewer. The Fat Man, guardian of the ordinary citizen, as befitted a long-standing member of the Communist Party, knew them all, reeling off the names of members of the organizing committee and of the business leaders who had been involved in the construction of the stadia, access roads, new metro system and other facilities, a.k.a. white elephants. 'Look at them!' he repeated. 'Savoy Road suits for the kleptomaniacs and *ot kewtoor* for their poxy wives.'

'That would be Savile Row,' Mavros put in. He decided against correcting his host's French pronunciation.

The Fat Man glowered, his default facial mode. In the past Mavros would have pressed the point, but now that he was spending most of his time in the two-level flat Yiorgos had inherited, he kept a brake on his tongue. That didn't save him.

'Piss off back to your mother's if you don't like how I talk, Mr Hoity-Toity.'

'Maybe I will.'

'Go on then,' the Fat Man said, seeing the open goal. 'It worked really well last time.'

Mavros sighed and took a swig of beer. He'd been living in his mother's spacious flat in up-market Kolonaki till early spring. Then she decided that she'd recovered sufficiently from her stroke and moved back from his sister Anna's place in the suburbs. He managed two weeks with her, but it didn't work – not least because she had a nurse in every day, who regarded him as the spawn of the devil because of his shoulder-length hair and decidedly non-designer stubble. She was also highly suspicious of his left eye, which was dark blue flecked with brown, and crossed herself frequently. Strange. The combination of his dark blue right eye with its non-identical twin usually captivated members of the other sex. Still, he couldn't have the frail Dorothy being disturbed by the often disturbing people who came asking for his services as a missing persons specialist.

'Or you could grovel to your ex-girlfriend and set yourself up in her place,' Yiorgos said, grinning.

Mavros grabbed a slice of pizza and bit into it. Andhroniki Glezou, known as Niki, hadn't just been his girlfriend. They'd loved each other for over five years and had been through some dangerous escapades together. But things had begun to change after a case in Crete the previous year. Niki had been in danger there, though she stood up to it well. As the months went by she became more needy, never having been hugely self-confident in the first place. She was an orphan and her adoptive parents were dead, leaving her the flat near the sea in Palaio Faliro. Inevitably, the ticking of her biological clock had got louder after she became thirty-five. They'd had several discussions about children. Mavros wasn't opposed to the idea, but he wasn't enthusiastic enough for Niki. One evening, her frustration hit Chernobyl levels and he found himself on the street with his clothes flapping down on to him from the balcony. He'd tried to speak to her on the phone often, but she hung up before he could say more than a couple of words. That had been two months ago and he'd heard from a mutual friend that Niki was dating like there was no tomorrow. That worried Mavros, but he didn't know what to do about it when she wouldn't take his calls.

The Fat Man stopped shouting at the parade of athletes in their curious uniforms and slapped Mavros on the thigh. 'I didn't mean it, Alex. Go and make things up with her if that's what you want. I can't stand the woman, but I know you loved her. Maybe you still do.'

Mavros let that go unanswered. The truth was, he didn't know what his feelings for Niki were. He had loved her even more after they came back from Crete, but months of arguing had taken their toll. Anyway, it didn't really matter what he felt. She'd told him she hated his lack of commitment and that she never wanted to see him again.

'Want some *galaktoboureko*?' There was more than a hint of white-flag waving in Yiorgos's voice. That was the good thing about living with him – no matter how much they yelled abuse at each other, they never held bad feelings for long.

'OK,' Mavros said, well aware that following pizza with the custard-filled fylo pastry would do his burgeoning belly no good. The Fat Man was a skilled cook and thought small portions were for capitalists.

Later Mavros went up to his bedroom, his friend's shouts audible until he put on a Nikos Papazoglou CD. He sat in the sagging armchair and looked at the walls. This had been Yiorgos's room for his whole life, but when Kyra Fedhra died a couple of years back, he'd moved into hers. The tattered Party posters were still there, some of them from the time when the Communists had been banned. Mavros had thought about replacing them with art work of his own – he owned some good framed prints by Moralis, Hadjikyriakos-Ghikas and Tsarouchis – but he didn't want to turn the place into home. Both he and the Fat Man knew this was a stopgap.

Though finding somewhere else would be difficult. Greece had been going through years of unparalleled growth and property prices, both to buy and to rent, were ridiculously high. His mother and sister had both offered to lend him money, but he knew he would never be able to pay them back from his irregular private eye earnings. That adversely affected his *philotimo*, the often exaggerated sense of self-respect that every Greek possessed. The fact that he was half Scots complicated the matter. Dorothy had inculcated in him a Calvinist attitude towards the handling of money, despite the fact that she had been an atheist since she met his father.

Mavros looked at the framed black-and-white photos on the bedside table. On the left was his father Spyros with the hooked nose he himself had inherited, the moustache and the intense stare. He had been a senior member of the Communist Party and had died in 1967, before the military coup that would have seen him sent to a prison island again. On the right was Andonis, Mavros's brother eleven years his senior, who had disappeared at the age of twenty-one when he was already a leading light in the student opposition to the Colonels. He was Mavros's only professional failure. Wherever he delved, there was no substantive trace of his handsome, smiling brother. He didn't know how his mother had managed to bear the double loss. He had been too young at the time and only become obsessed with finding Andonis when he grew up. He would find him, he said to himself, even if it took all his life.

His phone vibrated in his pocket.

'Alexander Mavros?' The voice was female, low and speaking English.

'Alex,' he replied. 'Who's this?'

'Never mind. I have a job for you, it may be the biggest in your career.' The woman paused but he kept quiet, unimpressed by hyperbole. 'Tomorrow morning, nine o'clock. Meet me at the top of Mount Philopappos. Come alone.'

'How will I identify—' The connection was cut.

Mystery woman, Mavros thought, tossing his phone on to the bed. Just what he needed. Nine o'clock? He was very much not a morning person. Then again, he hadn't had a decent job in a month and wasn't in a position to ignore opportunities. The Fat Man didn't want any rent, but Mavros wanted at least to pay his share of the household expenses.

Besides, he couldn't sit inside all the time, especially with the Olympics going on. Not that he wanted to attend the overpriced, often fatuous events, but there was a buzz in the city he enjoyed. Unlike Yiorgos, he hadn't wept when it was announced that the Athens bid had been successful. 'It'll be the ruin of the country,' his friend had said. 'We'll be stripped naked by the jackals of international capitalism, as well as by our own.' He might be right, but why not wait and see? Maybe there would be uses found for the specially built hockey and baseball facilities, even though Greeks knew as much about those sports as Americans knew about cricket.

Mavros set his alarm for seven-thirty, stripped off his sweat-soaked T-shirt and shorts, and had a cold shower. The windows were open, but the temperature was still almost unbearable. The Fat Man didn't have air conditioning, regarding it as a con instituted by big business, so Mavros had to suffer.

That ought to have made his residual Calvinist soul feel good.

'Where is she?'

The man in the mask of burlap struggled for breath.

'What?' the Son shouted. 'I can't hear you!' He poured another bucket of water over the prisoner's head and watched as the heavy material soaked it up. Breathing was almost impossible now and the man struggled against the wire securing his wrists and ankles to the metal chair bolted to the hard earth floor.

'Where is she?' the Son repeated.

The prisoner's heavy head was bent forward, wrapped chin on his throat. He was trying hard to blow the burlap away from his lips.

His captor selected a dental probe from the row lined up on

the table nearby. 'Can you feel this?' he asked, applying the point
to the naked chest.

A squeal came through the burlap.

'I thought you might. So answering my question isn't so hard.
*Where is she*?' The Son pulled back the man's head and put an
ear close to where the mouth would be.

'I . . . I don't . . . I don't know. They . . . they don't . . . tell
us things . . . like that.'

'Really? I thought you were a senior celebrant.' The probe did
its work in another spot.

After the squealing stopped, the prisoner managed a few more
words. 'Yes . . . but I . . . I don't make . . . the decisions.'

The Son, tall and muscular, with his thick hair cut short and
dyed blonde, walked away. Apart from latex gloves and thick
socks, he was naked, as he always was when he extracted information. Sometimes, even with male subjects, he got excited and
there was no point in constricting himself. He went to the sink
and ran water over his head. It was hot, even for August, even
in the hills above Thiva. The ramshackle farmhouse had been
deserted for years and no one came up the rough track. The fields
were untended and there were no livestock on the surrounding
slopes. It was the usual story. When the older generation died
out, their kids, already big shots in Athens with beach houses
and luxury cars, ignored the rural property that had kept the
family going for centuries. It had no value now that farmers,
buoyed by EU grants, lived the good life in the valleys. Like all
Greeks and half the world, they would be watching the idiocy
taking place in the Olympic Stadium.

He opened the door and went outside. To the south the glow
from Athens was visible over the hilltops, but westwards were
only steep mountainsides and, far above them, the sparkle of
long dead stars. How many years would it be before Greece was
a similar burned out ruin? Unlike the Father, the Son was a realist
about his country. He'd never been taken in by the rubbish the
old man spouted about the virtues of army, church and family.
The Father, a security policeman and torturer during the
dictatorship, had been a rancid hypocrite. He'd made big money
freelancing for the Athens crime bosses, who were connected to
the dictators and their henchmen. So much for army, church and

family, especially since the old bastard had pushed his wife down the stairs to her death. The Son had taken steps to make sure nothing like that would happen to him.

The man in the mask was making a curious noise, but the Son paid little attention. He was thinking about his success over the last two years. After being forced to leave Greece – and there would be a reckoning for that – he had plied the trade the Father had taught him throughout the Balkans. There was no shortage of customers. He had also added to his talents, as gang bosses were often more interested in killing their opponents than extracting information from them. He'd become a fully functioning hit man, able to take out people by rifle, bomb, pistol and knife – as well as a few specialities he'd come up with himself. It had cost him a large proportion of the old man's gold to take lessons from a retired Committee for State Security man in Bulgaria, but it had been worth it. Petrov had been a good teacher and he knew his craft, but he had a serious weakness – he drank vodka by the litre. That meant the Son couldn't trust him even with the little he had said about his background. The Father had been a perfectionist, suspending his victims from the ceiling with fish hooks and lines. The Son was more practical. Whatever did the job – such as the piece of burlap he'd found in an outhouse, stinking of goat's cheese.

He closed the door and went over to his prisoner.

'For the last time, *where is she?*'

The man was silent and motionless, his head still forward.

The Son bent over him, his nose twitching. He could smell death better than a master of wine could identify a vintage. He unwrapped the mask and let it drop to the compacted earth floor. The prisoner's eyes were wide open and crimson veined, his lips lacerated where he had bitten through them. He'd succumbed to shock or suffocation, or perhaps had choked on his own blood.

Gathering up the tools of his trade, the Son smiled. No matter. It was obvious the fool didn't know anything. He'd have killed him anyway, though in a more imaginative way. Now he would move on to the next name on the list of worshippers he'd been given. He took the pictures with his camera phone that he'd been ordered to pass on to his employer.

The Son went out to the pickup truck – a battered, five-year-old

Nissan that didn't stick out from the crowd, but packed a hefty punch under the bonnet – and took a plastic petrol can from the cargo space. He doused the dead man with enough fuel to mess up the crime scene investigator's job, even if he was found quickly. Then he laid a trail of petrol to the door, lit a match and dropped it. There was a noise like an ox belching and then the corpse combusted.

'His soul flew past the barrier of his teeth and departed, lamenting bitterly, for the halls of Hades,' the Son said, leaving the door open until the fire was well established and taking a few more photos. He knew he had mangled the lines from Homer's *Iliad*, but he didn't care. The fact that the Father would have broken a stick over him for doing so made him laugh out loud.

# TWO

The alarm woke Mavros from a troubled dream, in which Niki was pursuing him with a large pair of scissors in her hand. He showered and put on a loose white linen shirt and cream trousers. He considered shaving, but dismissed the idea. His stubble wasn't too long and the woman had cut him off.

'Morning,' the Fat Man said, coming out of the kitchen with a tray of *baklava*, sweat streaming down his face. 'How about this for a change?'

'Just coffee,' Mavros mumbled.

'You know that isn't how it works in the holy mother's halls. The deal is coffee and pastry, no negotiation.' Yiorgos went back into the furnace to make the brew. He had leased a run-down café next to the ancient market for decades and Mavros had used it as a makeshift office, mainly because the coffee was the best he'd ever found in the city. The fact that the Fat Man had known both his father and brother also played a part.

'One *sketo* for the half-breed, one *varyglyko* for the chef.'

'That's what you're calling yourself now, is it?' Mavros said, after gulping down a glass of water. 'You should cut down on sugar. Your heart must be thundering like an elephant's.'

'Then I'd get all bitter and twisted like you,' Yiorgos said, straight-faced.

'Ha.'

'Where are you going?'

'Meeting a client.'

'Can I come?'

Mavros headed for the door, grabbing his sunglasses. That was one of the problems with living in the Fat Man's house. He was fascinated by Mavros's business and was always trying to get involved. He had succeeded once, a few years back, and they had both almost lost their lives.

'No,' Mavros said, over his shoulder. 'I don't want you scaring off the lady.'

'Oh, it's a *lady*, is it? I wouldn't want to cramp your style, Mr Cool-as-Michael-Caine-in-linen.'

'Besides, I'm just a parasite on the hide of the capitalists,' Mavros said, parroting his friend's standard gibe about his profession. 'Turn on the TV. You'll be able to abuse Greek athletes doing their best for their country.'

'Sport is—'

'The cocaine of the masses, I know. See you later.'

'Go to the bad,' the Fat Man said, grinning.

Mavros walked up to Ippokratous and caught the bus to the Acropolis. The shabby thoroughfare had been tarted up because the cycling road race would be passing down it. That meant private citizens had got low-interest loans from the city council to repaint their external walls. There were also flags and bunting all over the place, some of them a hangover from the Independence Day celebrations in March. Mavros saw a scrawny cat clawing its way though bags of rubbish in a dumpster. At least it was still alive. There were rumours that the city's stray dogs had been rounded up and gassed, though the council denied it.

The bus turned on to Akadhimias, heading for Syndagma Square. The neoclassical buildings of the national library, university and academy looked splendid, Mavros had to admit. He still harboured a deep love for Athens and there was no question that the Olympics had stimulated regeneration. But, looking at the elderly women in black and the skinny immigrant workers, he wondered how much of that regeneration was only on the surface. No, he wasn't going to become the Fat Man. He still believed the Olympics would do more good than bad. Then a ticket inspector got on and started bullying an old man whose mind clearly wasn't all there.

'This ticket hasn't been cancelled,' the official, a young man with slicked back hair said in an outraged voice. 'You'll have to pay a fine.'

There were murmurs of dissent from the other passengers.

'Name?' the inspector demanded, pen hovering over his penalty notice pad.

Mavros went up to him. 'There's no need for that,' he said. 'Can't you see the old gentleman's confused?'

'That's what they all say. Besides, this is none of your business.'

Mavros caught his gaze and held it. 'Leave . . . him . . . alone,' he said, moving closer.

'You can't threaten a public—'

The young man's eyes sprang wide open as Mavros grabbed his groin.

'I'm not threatening anyone, sonny. Just let him off and see how popular you'll be.' He squeezed harder.

'Very well,' the official said, his voice high and his face red. 'But this is your last warning, sir.'

There was a spontaneous burst of applause from the other passengers. Mavros let the young official go and looked at the old man. He didn't seem to understand what was going on.

'Can I help?' Mavros said. 'Where do you want to get off?'

Cloudy eyes took him in. 'I . . . I don't know.'

Mavros turned back to the ticket inspector, who was preparing a rapid exit at the next stop. 'He needs help. You don't only issue fines, do you?'

The young man stared at him and then nodded meekly. 'I'll hand him over to the route controller in Syndagma.'

'Thank you.'

Mavros watched as the official helped the old man off and led him to the grey kiosk. Mission accomplished.

'Bravo, my son,' said a middle-aged woman in black. 'May the Lord look favourably on you.'

Not very likely, Mavros thought, smiling thanks at her. Although he wasn't a member of the Communist Party, he definitely wasn't religious; but he did believe in doing the right thing, no matter what it took. Maybe that would have rubbed off on the ticket inspector.

He got off the bus at its terminus on the south side of the Acropolis. This perspective was less familiar to him than the opposite side. He used to live over there, with a superb view of the Erechtheion and the Parthenon's perpetual scaffolding, until the rent became too onerous. He still missed his old flat. There had been good times in it, many of them with Niki.

Mavros walked up the path through the pine trees on the slopes of Philopappos. He had strolled there before and knew its history. One of the disputed sites of the prison where Socrates had been held before his state-sponsored poisoning by hemlock was nearby and the hill was also known as the Mouseion because of a temple to the Muses on its flanks. There had been ancient fortifications, part of the great strategist Themistocles's walls, as well as less edifying later military uses. The Venetian general Morosini had bombarded the Turkish-held Acropolis from the hill in 1687, resulting in the explosion that wrecked the Parthenon. Philopappos had also been the apple in the eye of numerous conspirators as an artillery location, the last being the Colonels during their coup in 1967. In the past when he had such thoughts, Mavros's brother Andonis would have flashed before him. Now there was nothing. After years of pleading by his mother and sister, Mavros had finally let Andonis fall into the abyss.

Mavros felt the sweat build up all over his body and cursed the Fat Man's pastries. He needed to get on his exercise bike, but the heat hardly encouraged that. He came out of the trees and looked up at the Tomb of Philopappos himself, a marble tower over ten metres high with friezes and statues commemorating the eponymous grandee from the second century AD. There was a small group of young people in identical T-shirts around the base, and he made out the tones of an American classicist in full lecture mode. As for the mystery woman, not a sign. He skirted the tomb, slipping on the smooth stones, and took in the view. Although there was a heat haze, over the glinting blue sea he could see the triangular peak of the mountain on the island of Aegina and, beyond, the distant mountains of the Peloponnese stepping southwards.

'Mr Mavros.'

He turned and took in a statuesque woman in her mid-forties. She was wearing a loose-fitting grey dress that displayed well-turned ankles, but it was the face beneath the straw hat that seized his attention. It was finely constructed, with almond-shaped pale blue eyes, a narrow nose and unpainted lips, the cheekbones high enough to suggest Slavic or Russian roots. She could have been beautiful, but her expression was infinitely sad and there were dark rings beneath her eyes. Brown hair with blonde highlights hung untended on her shoulders.

'Alex,' he said, extending a hand. She clasped it briefly and then pulled away like a frightened animal. 'You have the advantage of me.'

'What?'

'You haven't told me your name.'

The woman stepped away to the path that led southwards, forcing him to follow.

'How did you know who I was?' Mavros asked, catching up.

'I did an Internet search. You really should consider setting up a website.' She glanced at him. 'Though the number of times you feature in the newspapers probably makes that unnecessary.'

She was definitely English, Mavros thought, the flattened vowels and dropped consonants suggesting her origins were humble. As she walked, he realised that her full breasts were unrestrained by a bra, a serious no-no in the Greek capital. There was a rock at the side of the path and she sat in the shade under it.

Joining her, he said, 'Great view. Wish I could be *in* the water rather than looking at it.'

'You don't recognise me,' the woman said, ignoring his attempt at small talk.

'Should I?'

'Well, I have been on the television rather often recently.'

Mavros studied her profile. There was something familiar about her. He suspected she usually wore make-up and had her hair under control.

'Never mind. Before I tell you what I want from you, I need your assurance that you will tell no one about this meeting or anything said during it.' Her voice was almost a monotone and speaking seemed to require an enormous effort.

'I always observe client confidentiality,' he replied, 'though I reserve the right to share information with trusted associates when necessary.' He didn't have any official associates, but he'd once been burned when a plastic surgeon found out he'd used his sister Anna, a gossip columnist, to dig the dirt.

'Very well,' the woman said, 'but you'll be hearing from my very expensive lawyers if you cross me.'

Mavros smiled tightly. 'This isn't exactly a promising start. You can't force me to take the job.'

'No, I don't suppose I can.' The woman looked towards the sea, her hands with only a simple gold wedding ring on one of the long fingers clasped around her calves. 'My name is Angie – Angela – Poulou and I have lost my . . .'

It was strange hearing herself confessing to a stranger, even though Alex Mavros had the long hair of a priest. She had been required by her fiancé to join the Orthodox Church before they were married. She took the instruction seriously, almost as seriously as learning the Modern Greek language. In six months she'd been baptised into the first and was close to fluent in the second. The wedding had been in the small chapel on the Poulos estate on the island of Evia. A few of her friends from the modelling world had made the all-expenses-paid trip, but she had already lost touch with most of them. Modelling had never been something she took seriously and her full figure had meant that she was restricted to lingerie ads and department store catalogues. She had always assumed something better would come along and it had, in the form of Paschos. The sole heir of Greece's second largest industrialist, he had been handsome as hell, his stocky frame muscular and his black hair glistening. Mum back in East Ham couldn't believe her daughter's luck. She made it to the wedding, drinking far too much champagne and screaming with mirth as she tried to join in the dancing. Three months later she was dead of a cerebral aneurysm and Angie, an only child herself, had no close relatives left in England; her father was a drunk, who'd alienated family and friends and was found dead in the street when she was ten.

So Greece, and especially the huge house in the northern Athenian suburb of Ekali, had become home. Paschos had taken over from his father when he was twenty-nine and now, thirty years later, had made Poulos A.E. the biggest private company in the country, with interests in construction, minerals, shipping and consumer goods. He had lost most of his hair, was three stone heavier than he should have been and spent almost all his waking hours on the phone or in meetings. The last five years had been even busier, as he was vice-president of the company managing the Athens Olympic Games.

Angie couldn't help smiling when she saw the look of recognition on Alex Mavros's face. He had seen her on the television the previous night during the opening ceremony. She was relieved that her boredom – no, worse, her disgust – hadn't been obvious. But he didn't yet know the reasons for that feeling. She told him, but the narrative was disjointed and incomplete. He took the occasional note in a small book.

The fact that she was sixteen years younger than Paschos hadn't worried her at the beginning. She was overwhelmed by her translation to the ranks of the hyper-rich. Her husband didn't talk about money, apart from asking once a year if the monthly allowance he gave her was enough. She refrained from pointing out that it would feed, clothe and house the population of a small country. She had read in the press that Paschos had a personal fortune of over a billion dollars, but she suspected there was even more than that in Switzerland and the Cayman Islands. For the first couple of years, she had thrown herself into a life of extreme luxury, buying the most expensive jewelry, haute couture and shoes. She had three horses, as well as the latest BMW saloon and 4x4. Apart from the estate on Evia, Paschos had villas on Mykonos, Crete and Corfu, as well as properties in Monte Carlo, Gstaad, Manhattan (with a view over Central Park) and Barbados. She herself had spent time and his money renovating an old house on Pelion, with access to skiing in winter and deserted beaches for much of the year. She spent time in all those places, rarely with her husband but with a group of other rich men's wives. None of them seemed to care that she had grown up in a council house – they were dedicated to having the best possible time they could. Many had children, but rarely saw them, hiring the best nurses and nannies. After two years of increasingly empty jetsetting, Angie was relieved when she fell pregnant. Now she had something real to dedicate herself to.

And Lia – Evangelia, after Paschos's grandmother – had given her joy since her birth fourteen years earlier. Unlike her friends, Angie refused to have a Caesarean. She cared nothing about how she would look in a bikini any more. From the moment she held the little bundle with the helmet of black hair in her arms, she knew that life could give her nothing more precious. And her relationship with Lia had remained special as her daughter went through kindergarten and private primary school, and then started the international college two years ago. Lia was one of those rare people who lit up a room. She wasn't conventionally pretty, having inherited her father's rather bulbous nose, but she had presence. That was partly because of her size and shape. When she turned thirteen, she grew tall, almost as tall as Angie, and filled out in the places males of all ages noticed immediately. Lia had taken the metamorphosis in her stride, her moods unaffected and a smile never far from her pink lips. She and Angie used to talk for at least an hour every day. Paschos had never shown anything but distant pride in Lia and never tried to get close to her. Mother and daughter called him 'the visitor', so rarely did they see him. That didn't worry Angie. She knew Paschos had lost interest in her physically before Lia was born and she'd made no effort to attract him back to her bed. He lived his life, she hers.

Except now she had no life. It had been taken away from her and she was an empty shell, a husk the wind could blow away at any time. And the truth was that Lia had changed in the weeks before she disappeared – she'd been less open and was often listless.

Now Angie steeled herself to accompany her husband to events where her presence was essential and she hadn't let him down, but she couldn't go on any longer. She had to do this, she couldn't live without Lia. She needed Alex Mavros . . .

The missing persons specialist looked up from his notebook. 'Let me get this straight, Mrs Poulou.'

'Angie,' she said, in a low voice. Her hands were over her eyes, tears leaking between the fingers.

'Your daughter Lia went missing on Saturday May 1st on the slopes of Mount Elikonas in Viotia. Your husband has handled all questions from the police and enforced a news blackout. There has been no ransom demand or any trace of Lia. And now, three and a half months later, you want me to find her.'

'Yes, but remember what I said. My husband must not hear about your activities. He has forbidden me to hire anyone or talk to the press. I can't even tell my friends. The story is that we've moved Lia to a school in Switzerland.'

'What about the woman who was in charge of the girls that day?' Mavros looked at his notes. 'Maria Bekakou.'

'You can't talk to her,' Angie said firmly.

'But she believed what Lia told her when she called that afternoon?'

'That Paschos had unexpectedly come to pick her up? Yes.'

'Doesn't that strike you as strange? I mean, surely a mother responsible for other mothers' daughters would at least have asked to speak to your husband.'

'Maria isn't a mother. She did ask, but Lia told her Paschos was on an urgent call to his broker in New York.'

'And she reported no hint of fear or coercion in Lia's voice?'

Angie shook her head. 'I don't blame her for not noticing. She had seven other girls to look after and some of them are quite wild.'

'So your husband's initial assumption was that there would be a ransom demand?'

'Yes.' Angie Poulou looked at him through damp eyes. 'I never believed she'd been abducted for money. Something much worse is happening.'

Mavros raised an eyebrow, but she didn't elaborate. 'Had your daughter been different before she disappeared?'

'A bit,' she murmured. 'She was moody and quiet. They have a terrible work load at the college, you know.'

'So I've heard.'

'Find her, Alex,' the woman said desperately. 'I'll give you everything I own. Just . . . just bring my baby back to me.'

Mavros thought about it. Paschos Poulos wasn't only one of the country's most powerful businessmen. He had a reputation for rough practice, including deunionising an aluminium plant whose labour force had been controlled by the Communists. He also knew everyone who counted, both in the government and in the shady groupings that really ran the country. The fact that he'd managed to keep a lid on the police investigation for so long showed how much influence he wielded in that notoriously leaky institution, as well as in the media. Going up against him would be asking for trouble. But he felt for the mother and he couldn't let her suffer unaided.

'All right,' he said. 'I'll do what I can. You need to set up a secure email account and send me everything about your daughter that could be relevant.' He gave her his electronic address, as well as a post box number where she could send hard copies of documents and other material.

'As for your fee,' Angie Poulou said, 'take this. That's my mobile number on the envelope. Please destroy it after memorising. I'll call you from public phones.'

Mavros looked at the fat envelope. 'I'll give you a receipt.'

'No,' she said. 'I can have nothing that connects me to you – for your own safety. Paschos is like a man possessed over this.' She gave a weak smile as she got to her feet. 'Besides, I've met your mother at several functions. I trust you. Please give me ten minutes to clear the area. I managed to talk my driver into leaving me alone for half-an-hour, but he'll be getting hot under the collar now.'

Clear the area, Mavros thought, as he watched her walk away, her shoulders down as if she were carrying a terrible burden. Someone's been reading too much John le Carré. Then again, people *were* devious. He'd never known a client who'd told him the whole story on first meeting.

# THREE

L ady, in your grieving accept these humble offerings of flowers, corn and fruit. Your daughter is gone beneath the earth, but she will return, she must return, the ancient tale has it so. After passing the winter months in Hades' echoing halls, she will find the light of Helios again and you will be reunited.

Goddess, cast your green shroud over the barren soil. Give life to the seeds that lie hidden, waiting for spring's bounty of rain and warmth. Although your pain is great, soon it will be assuaged. We await the maiden's return with restraint, eating humble food and drinking only spring water. But we will celebrate with you when she attains the surface of the earth again.

Great Mother of Fertility, we ask your forbearance. The world is changing and the seasons are no longer as they were. Winters have been harder, the snow on the surrounding peaks and the rain rushing down the watercourses in torrents, taking the precious soil to the wave-crested sea. The summers have become more arduous, the heat killing older mortals and poisoning the canopy of heaven. We pray that your daughter's return will not be unduly delayed.

Be assured, Goddess, that we will perform the necessary sacrifice if the earth's destroyers do not heed our warnings. We are few, but we are united in our faith in your goodness. Already one of our number has been taken and we do not expect to see him again. The enemy is strong and merciless. But so were you in the ancient tale, leaving people to starve and fields to wither. We will maintain our devotion to you until the last, firm in our belief that you will save the land, if only for future generations.

Green Lady, we pour good wine on your altar and raise our hands to praise you. Be assured, our fellow believer will not remain unavenged for long. This is a war that must be won, in your name and in those of our children. As the sun sets over the western mountains, casting its last light on the waters of the gulf, we fall to our knees and rub the precious soil over our bodies and into our hair. We place these figurines, replete with your power, in our dwelling places.

For though the maiden is deep in the underworld, starving and broken by the Death God's dark will, she will rise again. Hail, Potnia, most ancient and revered of immortals. We are your servants now and forever.


When Mavros got back to the flat, he found the Fat Man shouting in front of the TV again.

'Bastard exploiters of the people, thieving desecrators of our history!'

'What now?'

Yiorgos looked round and then pointed at the screen. 'Look at those poxy mascots. They're a parody of our history, a multinational marketing device.'

Mavros nodded without enthusiasm. Athena and Phevos were stylized children with heads as thin as their necks and oversized feet. They had been based on small terracotta sculptures of the goddess Athena and the sun god Apollo, dolls most likely, dated to the seventh century BC. To Mavros, they had always seemed mysterious, far from the realistic forms of the classical period and closer to the prehistoric past. Now they were on everything from hoardings to badges.

'Participation, brotherhood, equality, cooperation, fair play and the eternal Greek value of human scale,' the Fat Man scoffed. 'Whatever that means.'

'I told you to stop memorising the Olympic advertisements. You'll damage your brain.'

'As if anything's equal in this country, as if there's ever been a sense of fair play. The rich steal from the poor and feed them pap like this to shut them up.' Yiorgos caught sight of the envelope Mavros was holding. 'What's that?'

'Er, nothing.'

'Show me or I'll eat all the *baklava*.'

'That'll make a change.' Mavros tossed the envelope on to the coffee table.

The Fat Man ran a practised thumb over the edges of the fifty euro notes. 'Three thousand? What did you do? Rob an Olympic gift shop? If so, eternal glory is yours, comrade.'

Mavros went into the kitchen to get a drink of water. That didn't save him from further interrogation.

'You've got a job, haven't you? From a rich lady with more money than sense.'

'You always say the rich are cunning and devious. Take what you need.'

'A couple of hundred will do.' Yiorgos appeared at the kitchen door. 'Come on, then. Tell me all about it.' His enthusiasm was like a puppy's chasing a ball.

'I can't. It's confidential.'

'Your cases are always confidential,' the Fat Man jeered, 'and you've told me about them all.'

'Only when they're over.' Mavros headed upstairs.

'So that's how it's going to be, is it?' Yiorgos yelled. 'I put you up for free, I feed you and wash your clothes and what do you give me? A big nothing.'

'Oh, for fuck's sake. Let me do some work on this and I'll let you in on it, all right? And since when did you wash my clothes? If I didn't use your mother's washing machine, it would be a spider colony.'

That silenced his friend, who went back to abusing the TV. Mavros had a shower and sat at the table that served as his desk, wearing only a pair of boxers. He opened his laptop and waited for it to boot up. Before it was ready, his mobile rang.

'Good morning, dear.' His mother's voice was slightly unsteady, as it had been since her stroke. Although her Greek was fluent, she always spoke English to her children.

'Hello, Mother. How are you?'

'I'm all right, Alex.' There was a pause.

'Are you sure?'

'Yes, yes,' she replied, with a touch of her old impatience. 'It's just this useless body of mine. I'd like to go and sit in the shade in Dhexameni Square, but Fotini says it's too hot.'

'She's right,' Mavros said, loath to agree with the nurse. 'I've been out and came back drenched in sweat.'

'Lovely,' Dorothy Cochrane-Mavrou, said with a light laugh. 'I wish you'd move back here. At least I have air-conditioning.'

'I'll come over in a day or two. I'm quite busy, actually.'

'Good for you.' His mother's work ethic was still strong. 'I'm editing those unpublished poems of Laskaris.'

Mavros remembered the old communist poet. He'd been part of a case that had nearly cost Mavros and his entire family their lives. 'Any good?'

'Yes. They're mainly love poems to other men, with little or no ideological content. He obviously didn't feel he could publish them when he was alive.'

Mavros suddenly remembered what his client had said. 'Oh, by the way, what do you know about Angela Poulou?'

'By what way?' Dorothy said. 'How has she come under your purview?'

He laughed at the archaic vocabulary, but he was impressed by his mother's sharpness. 'I heard you know her.'

'Let me see. Angie, she calls herself, doesn't she? Paschos Poulos I know more about. He bought one of the main literary publishers and tried to put me out of business. Sold it when he lost interest. Horrible man. His wife, yes, I met her a few times at the usual functions. She seemed nice enough. She does a good job of covering up her proletarian origins.' Despite being the widow of a high-ranking Communist, Dorothy had never completely lost the bourgeois attitudes of her native Edinburgh. 'I always got the impression she'd rather be elsewhere.'

That squared with what Angie had told Mavros – that she preferred to be with her daughter rather than at receptions. 'Ever hear anything about her marriage coming unstuck?'

'Alexander Mavros!' His mother's outrage wasn't entirely an act. 'You should address that question to your sister.'

Mavros smiled. 'How is Anna?' He knew she visited their mother every day – and was unimpressed that he didn't.

'Flourishing. There seems to be an infinite appetite for gossip these days. The build up to these infernal Games has kept her even busier.'

Anna wasn't exactly a gossip columnist, but she was in the know to a disturbing extent about Athenian society and its meretricious vanity.

'I'll talk to her later,' he said. 'When I get a moment, I'll come round one evening and take you down to Dhexameni.'

'Oh, that would be lovely, Alex.' Dorothy's voice was wistful. 'I'll look forward to it.'

'Me too.' He broke the connection. The fact that his mother was getting frailer by the month disturbed him. He rang his sister.

'Is Mother all right?'

'I'm fine, thanks, how are you?' Anna answered acidly. 'And Mother is as well as can be expected. Maybe you should take the short walk round Lykavittos and see for yourself.'

Mavros took a deep breath. 'Sorry. Bad day at work?'

'You could put it that way. At this time of year, I'd normally be on holiday with Nondas and the kids, but thanks to the Games . . .'

'You should swap notes with the Fat Man.'

'No, thanks.' Anna had never got on with Yiorgos, not least because of his wardrobe. She was a devotee of the most chi-chi Kolonaki boutiques. 'Look, Alex, I'm trying to set up an interview with Sebastian Coe. Can this wait?'

'Have you been transferred to the sports desk?'

'Very funny. As a matter of fact, he's a very stylish man and he knows absolutely everyone.'

'I'm very happy for him. Before you go – Angie Poulou.' Mavros could almost hear his sister's ears prick up. She was a newshound of the first order.

'What about her? Don't tell me you're finally going to come through on all those promises of exclusives.'

'I gave you plenty on the Cretan case last year.'

'True enough. All right, so you're picking my brains. Why?'

'No particular reason.'

'Client confidentiality, you mean.'

'No comment.'

Anna laughed. 'What's she got you doing?'

Mavros could tell his sister hadn't picked up anything about the daughter's disappearance. Paschos Poulos's grip was as firm as his wife said.

'Is she what she seems to be?' he asked offhandedly.

'And what's that, exactly? A former Marks and Spencer model from the council estates of East London, who managed to capture the most eligible bachelor in Greece in the late 80s?' There was a hint of antagonism in Anna's voice.

'Don't tell me you were after him?'

'Certainly not. I was already married.' Anna's marriage was famously solid. Nondas was a right-wing Cretan businessman whom Mavros should have despised, but got on very well with. It occurred to him that his brother-in-law might know Paschos Poulos. 'Anyway, rather her than me. Her husband is a horrid piece of work.'

It amused Mavros when Anna used terms of abuse. She had absolutely no talent for it. 'What did he do to you?'

'Oh, nothing. He treats media people like muck and generally steamrollers over anyone who gets in his way.'

'Mother saw him off.'

'He just lost interest. He could have swallowed Persephone

and Hecate Publications in one gulp if he'd wanted to. Mother was lucky.'

'So what about Angie? Is there anything more to her than a rich wife going through the motions?'

'She's crazy about her daughter.'

'Lia.'

'Is that her name? You know more than I do.' That was an invitation to say what he was up to, but Mavros ignored it. 'Well, ever since she had the kid, she made it clear she wasn't interested in anything else. She dropped out of the various elite coteries and stayed at home being the good mother.'

'Not as good as you.'

Anna didn't rise to his attempt at flattery. 'Your nephew and niece are fine, but you could make an effort to visit.'

'OK,' he said noncommittally.

'I think she still rides and I remember hearing that she keeps bees up on Mount Elikonas, but that's about the sum of my knowledge. Can I get back to Lord Coe now?'

'Be my guest,' Mavros said, but his sister had already rung off.

So far, so nothing much. He checked his email and found a message from Angie Poulou, with several attachments. They occupied him for a couple of hours.

Deputy Commissioner Telemachos Xanthakos was responsible, among numerous other things, for homicide in the prefecture of Viotia, immediately northwest of Athens. He was that rare thing, a senior policeman under the age of forty. He also had a degree in classics from the Aristotelian University of Thessaloniki, his home city. He sometimes wondered how he'd ended up in the backwater of Viotia, its industrial eastern section balanced by heavily cultivated land in the plain around Thiva, ancient Thebes, and towards Livadheia further west, where the police and provincial headquarters were. The mountains stood around like great giants, Parnassos at the far west of the prefecture, Kithairon where Oedipus had been exposed to the south, and Elikonas, legendary home of the Muses, in the southwest. With the myths of Semele and Dionysus, Cadmus the first King of Thebes, Pentheus, Oedipus and Heracles, let alone the historical resonances of the ancient city as well as the great battles of Plataea, Leuctra and Chaironeia, Xanthakos had plenty to investigate in his free time. When he'd first been appointed to the force, he had no shortage of that, being secretly gay – Greek policemen were notoriously homophobic – and having no family nearby. At least there was plenty of open space in Viotia for running, his second passion after the ancient world. That kept his two-metre frame slim and, according to his secretary, who he suspected had a hankering for him, 'fit for the ladies'. The problem was his work. Now he was little more than a bureaucrat, reading files, approving budgets and supervising junior officers.

Until today. The deputy commissioner was standing on a hill south of Thiva. Through a narrow valley he could see the fertile valley beneath Mount Kithairon, but the area's links with the Oedipus myth weren't at the forefront of his mind now. Crime scene operatives came out of the charred remains of a stone farmhouse.

'One partially melted body, probably male,' said one.

That much Xanthakos already knew. The switchboard had taken a call from an incoherent man, who was currently leaning against the side of a high-end Volvo. The splatter of vomit at the building's entrance was his.

'So, Mr Matsa,' the deputy commissioner said. 'You drove up here for the first time in two years today and discovered the remains of the man inside.'

The man nodded, his face pale. 'My father grew up here and he came back every winter to hunt till he died three years ago.'

'He was the founder of Matsas Pasta AE outside Thiva?'

'That's right. I run it now with my brother Angelos.'

'And Angelos hasn't been here since your father died?'

'God, no. Angelos hunts women, not rabbits.'

'You have no idea who the dead man could be.'

The businessman stared at him. 'No. How could I?' He looked down. 'He'd been tied to that chair, hadn't he?'

'So it would seem. You don't have any enemies do you, Mr Matsa?'

'If that's an accusation, you can talk to my lawyer.'

Xanthakos smiled. 'Don't overreact. These questions are perfectly routine.'

Stavros Matsas looked up into the cloudless sky and wiped the sweat from his brow. 'Routine for you, perhaps.'

The deputy commissioner caught the eye of the teenage boy in the Volvo. 'Did your son see anything disturbing?'

'I don't think so. He was playing some bloody video game. I brought him up here to see the family roots, but he couldn't give a shit.'

'Did anything unusual strike you as you arrived? Apart from the smoke-blackened building.'

'That's a pretty big "apart from".' Matsas drank water from a bottle. 'Now I come to think of it, there was something.' He stood up straight and pointed to the bend in the rough track below the summit. 'That Judas tree. It was my grandfather's pride and joy. He never expected it to survive the wind up here. Some fucker's driven into it, and recently.'

The deputy commissioner looked at the *koutsoupia*, its yellowed leaves spread across the ground on the near side.

'Interesting,' he said. 'One of my officers will take your statement and you may go.' He walked to the tree, eyes on the track. The ground was drier than a bone in the Sahara and the dust hadn't even retained the recent tracks of the police vehicles. But the trunk of the *koutsoupia* had taken a heavy scrape and there were marks on the dried vegetation around it and the earth below. He waved to the crime scene technicians, then went to talk to the medical examiner, who had just emerged from the roofless building.

'Anything useful?' the deputy commissioner asked, breathing through his mouth to reduce the stench of what was unpleasantly similar to roast pork.

The ME, Frangiskos Priftakis, was a short and laconic Maniate. He took his mask off and breathed in the mountain air. 'His wrists and ankles were bound by wire to the metal chair, and someone had taken the trouble to bolt it to the earth floor – it's as hard as stone.'

Xanthakos nodded. 'Do their penises always swell up like that?'

Priftakis jerked his head back to signal the negative. 'Depends on where the fire is concentrated and how quickly it burns out. Your chemists will be able to tell you more, but I'd say this fire – you can smell the petrol beneath the burned flesh – didn't last long. It certainly wasn't a serious attempt to destroy the body.'

'So what was it then?' the deputy commissioner said, to himself as much as to the ME. 'His teeth are presumably intact.'

'Yes, though who knows how far that'll get you? If he isn't a local, he could have used a dentist anywhere. Or he might be one of the many who never use one. No fingerprints, I'm afraid – the epidermis from the fingers is completely gone. I'd say the petrol was dumped over his head and upper body.'

'Any marks on the body?'

'You'll need to wait for the post-mortem. It wouldn't surprise me if I find something.'

Xanthakos raised an eyebrow.

'There's no sign of clothing at all, my friend. Only the remnants of a piece of burlap, probably from the farm. As the wire shows, the poor guy was tied down. I'd say he was tortured too.'

The deputy commissioner looked southwards to the mountains separating Viotia from the Athenian metropolis. The Olympic Games were in full swing, athletes pounding the track, straining for the tape, heaving weights. He hoped to get down there to see the women's and men's marathons, but he had a feeling that the melted man would not be a solitary victim.

That thought sent him back to his car with a spring in his stride. Life had been dull. Then his phone rang. It was his boss, telling him to be prepared for a call from the Ministry of Public Order and to do whatever he was ordered. He slumped into the seat of his service Nissan, feeling more deflated than an airship with perished seals. It looked like the case was about to be taken away from him.

# FOUR

Mavros had a lot of material, but it wasn't getting him anywhere. Lia Poulou was a good student, according to the scanned school reports her mother had sent as email attachments. Her pastoral tutor was happy with what was called her 'moral development', saying in the last report that she was mature for her years and an example to her contemporaries, though she had become 'rather withdrawn' in the Easter term. She played basketball, went to ballet classes and had passed her Grade Four piano exam. Mavros tried to get an impression of the girl from the photos Angie had sent. She was tall and slim, her hair black like her father's but her complexion as pale as her mother's. In portrait shots, she looked straight into the lens with striking confidence. There were other pictures of her in her school uniform, tutu and sports kit. What struck Mavros most was Lia's stern expression – there were few shots of her smiling and when she did, it was in a restrained way. She reminded him of statues of the ancient gods: austere and composed, but with intimations of dangerous power beneath the surface.

Her mother had written a character assessment which did nothing to dispel that impression. She said that Lia was 'my best friend and helper, the only person I can rely on when things get tough'. Mavros wondered about that. What kind of things got tough for the super-rich? It was notable that Angie never mentioned her husband. He wondered what their relationship was like. It must have been hugely taxing for the mother to be unable to talk about her daughter's disappearance and keep up the façade that she was in Switzerland, especially during the holidays; in her email, Angie said that Lia was supposedly on safari in Kenya with new classmates. It must have been even worse when the person she relied on most was the one missing.

Which led him to Paschos Poulos. Winner of several businessman of the year awards, internationally respected executive with interests in Europe and the Middle East, friend of heads of state and prime ministers – the kind of person the Fat Man called 'the crème de la crap'. It didn't help that the guy looked like a disreputable football club owner, though that was one of the few traditional pursuits of the Greek elite that he had avoided. His hair was thin, his face disfigured by a nose that suggested he drank more than was good for him, and his suits, expensive though they no doubt were, failed to hide his burgeoning paunch. As was the way of his kind, he kept a low public profile, leaving the customary charitable work ('legal tax avoidance', according to the Fat Man) to his wife and attending only the bare minimum of events in the Athenian social calendar. He didn't seem to have any hobbies, though his involvement in the planning for the Olympics made that understandable. He'd fallen from a horse in his twenties and never got back on, and a former employee said he thought sailing was for fools. So why had he taken on the Olympic work, even renouncing the large salary that went with it?

Mavros wasn't an economist, but he knew how the rich in Greece operated: do nothing unless there's something in it for you. A scan of the business pages revealed that Poulos A.E. subsidiaries had been involved in building arenas, roads and the athletes' village, as well as supplying many of the raw materials. His companies had franchises from foreign corporations for a range of Games-related commercial activities and he had even covered the expenses of selected journalists to publicise the Athens Olympics favourably. No matter what the Games ended up costing Greece, Paschos Poulos would be guaranteed a huge profit, but it was all above board – the bid process for contracts had been at least nominally transparent and his companies had prevailed because they were highly efficient. There had been a mini-scandal when three employees who worked in Poulos A.E. headquarters in the northern Athenian suburb of Kifissia had committed suicide in the space of a month, but all had been being treated for mental problems and no blame was attached to the company, despite their families testifying that they had been seriously overworked.

Mavros got up and opened his door. The sound of Yiorgos snoring in front of the TV drifted up the stairs. Going down as quietly as he could, Mavros made himself a sandwich and tiptoed back up. The Fat Man's blood pressure was much worse than it should have been. He took the pills he'd been prescribed reluctantly, moaning about Big Pharma and how the companies reduced people to zombies. Mavros tried to get him to moderate what he ate, but that was a largely futile campaign.

Back to Paschos Poulos. Why had he insisted on a media blackout over his daughter's disappearance? If Mavros had been involved from the start, he would only have resorted to that after preliminary inquiries with her relatives, friends, teachers and other contacts had drawn a blank, despite the risk that one or more might talk. Maybe there had been a ransom demand, but surely Lia's father would have paid up. What reason could he have for keeping things in the dark? Had the kidnappers required that of him? Was he afraid of damaging the image of the Olympics in his homeland or of putting the standing of his businesses at risk? It had been over three months since his daughter had disappeared. Surely he would have been told by the police that it was unlikely Lia would be found alive. Perhaps that was why he had pressed on with his work – but what kind of father would be so cold-blooded about losing his only child?

When in the murky depths – and a case in which he was forbidden to talk to anyone who knew the missing person was about as murky as it got – Mavros had an ace to play, even though it was one that came with a cost. He rang the relevant number and ascertained that its subscriber would be where he usually was in the early evenings. Then he took a 'death in the afternoon', waking from the siesta with the usual unfulfilled dreams and nausea. After taking a shower and putting on a fresh shirt, he went downstairs.

'Look at these wankers,' the Fat Man said, pointing at a pair of Greek wrestlers who had just been eliminated in the first round. 'Their trainers couldn't even get the drug regime right.'

'So cynical.'

'So true. Where are you going?'

'Business meeting.'

Yiorgos looked at his watch. 'With that bastard Bitsos, eh?'

Mavros shrugged. 'Needs must.'

'Make sure you take him a heap of porn.'

'He's got enough of that. Don't burst a blood vessel. Seriously.'

The Fat Man extended an open hand, fingers wide. 'Straight to hell with you, freak.'

'See you there.'

Mavros walked out into the sweltering early evening. Normally he would have walked to Omonia Square, but he hailed a passing cab. Thanks to Angie Poulou, he was in funds.

The cypress trees around the estate on Ekali pointed their green fingers to the bright blue sky as if it were guilty of stealing her daughter. Angie sat on the broad terrace by the swimming pool, a wide sunhat on her head and a towel over her legs. The two street cats Lia had adopted were sleeping in the shade, their front legs entwined. Angie blinked back tears.

What was she doing, taking on a private investigator? Paschos would explode if he found out – and, with the huge web of contacts he maintained, that would only be a matter of time. She didn't care any more. All she had to do was talk to the press and he would be revealed as the schemer he was. Why had she gone along with his insane plan to keep Lia's disappearance secret? In the beginning it seemed to make sense – deprive the kidnappers of the oxygen of publicity – but after she'd got over the initial shock, she should have stood up to him. For all his faults, he wasn't a violent man. He'd never hit her, unlike the husbands of several women she knew, and he did listen to her, although these days she only saw him when they were on parade together.

Angie took a few bites of the salad she had prepared, having given Fidelia, the Filipina cook, the day off, but she had no appetite. She felt empty inside, as if she was wasting away. She couldn't live without Lia. Every possible fate – physical abuse, rape, torture, starvation, the white slave trade, accidental death, murder and more – had kept her awake at night in recent months. The fact that she couldn't tell anyone the truth had given her migraines and driven her to the darkened room she used as a private space. After a week of that, she'd searched for a reliable investigator and found Alex Mavros.

In truth he seemed more maverick than cautious, though the big case on Crete involving a Hollywood film company and a drug-producing village had shown how effective he could be. Besides, what she needed was someone who knew how the system worked while standing outside it. His half Scots half Greek background seemed to have given him that. When they met, she had trusted him immediately.

But who was she fooling? What could one man do, when the best minds in the Greek police had failed? According to Paschos, British and American law and order professionals in Athens for the Games had also been consulted, but had got nowhere. Lia had gone to a place that appeared on no map or screen. Perhaps she'd been beneath the surface of the earth from soon after she was snatched, occupying an unmarked grave that would never be found. Angie wouldn't be able to live with that. She had sworn to herself that if Alex Mavros didn't pick up any traces of Lia, she would go public. That would probably lead to the end of her marriage, but she didn't care. Paschos had shown concern over

Lia only in the first few days. After that, he got back to work and presented his usual implacable face to the world. His efforts to comfort her had been no more than perfunctory.

The cats woke up and started chasing each other around the pool. Angie thought of the countless times she had played and swum with her daughter in this very place. But now the familiar lines of the tiles and stone walls, the canvas canopies and marble benches, blurred into obscure shapes, as if her home and everything she had experienced in it had been illusory – even her husband and, worst of all, Lia.

Only Alex Mavros with his strange left eye could bring Angie back to the world she had known, the world with her daughter at its centre.

Lambis Bitsos, crime correspondent for the left-of-centre paper *The Free News*, was a man of habit. Except when he was covering cases, he occupied a corner table in *To Kazani*, a down-market taverna in a backstreet near Omonia Square. The place had no terrace or roof garden, so in summer it really lived up to its name: the Cauldron.

Mavros pulled out a chair opposite the skinny, balding journalist. 'Jesus, Lambi, how do you cope in here at this time of year?'

'As you see,' he replied, pouring ouzo from a carafe and signalling for another glass and place setting. In front of him was a spread of aubergine salad, octopus with pasta, anchovies, and the taverna's speciality, drunkard's stew, containing pork, sausage and red wine.

'*Bekri-mezes*?' Mavros said. 'How appropriate.'

'I ordered it for you.'

'Uh-huh. There isn't much left.'

'You know me – hungrier than a hyena.'

Mavros dipped bread into the aubergine paste. 'So, how have you been?'

Bitsos took a slug of slightly diluted ouzo and smiled. 'Socialising, are we?'

'If we were doing that, I'd have brought magazines.'

The journalist lifted his battered briefcase. Underneath was a brown paper bag, the garish jackets of the triple-X publications he favoured poking out. 'I'm already well supplied.'

'*Nazi Vampire Lesbians*? Jesus, Lambi, how low can you sink?'

'Very low indeed.' Bitsos grinned. 'Any sign of Niki?'

'Watch it,' Mavros warned. 'No.'

'Pity. I always fancied her.'

'The feeling wasn't anywhere near mutual.'

'That's what made it even more exciting.'

Mavros gave him the eye. 'How are your daughters?'

'All three of them on to their second husbands, as you very well know. I think Ritsa's shagging around, as well.'

'You must be very proud. Do you want more to eat?' He knew the answer. The journalist might have been skeletal, but he ate like a large quadruped. Mavros ordered another serving of wine-stewed pork and a slab of melted cheese. He also opted for the taverna's own wine rather than its brain-melting ouzo.

'Busy?' Bitsos asked.

'Sort of. You?'

'"Sort of", as in you need help from old Lambis?' He laughed when Mavros nodded. 'Me? Haven't you noticed? With the Games on and the cops all over the city in force, the criminals are being good boys. They've put off killing each other to concentrate on fleecing the visitors.'

'I hear the Albanians and Serbs have imported hookers to cover the increase in demand.'

'True,' the journalist said, making space for the new plates. 'But they're keeping a close watch on them and there have been no cat fights.'

'All of which means you must be at a major loose end.'

'Ah, now we get to it. You want me to drop everything and become your sidekick.'

Mavros choked on a piece of sausage. After he'd recovered, he assured Bitsos that wasn't the case. The idea of working in close proximity to the most notorious newspaper ghoul in Athens had little appeal. 'No, I just need a pointer or two.'

'What's in it for me?'

Mavros laughed. '*Now* we get to it. The usual. Exclusive on the story when everything's wrapped up.'

Bitsos started to laugh, an unpleasant sound. 'How many times have you promised me that and failed to deliver, Alex.'

'I gave you an inside angle on the Crete case.'

'True. That makes once.'

Mavros knew he was on shaky ground, given the extreme confidentiality of Lia Poulou's disappearance. 'All right, I will say this. Even if the case is blacked out from above, I'll tell you all about it. Knowledge is power, even if you can't print it.'

Bitsos finally finished eating. He mopped his brow with a paper napkin and lit a foul-smelling unfiltered cigarette. 'We'll see. What's the angle?'

Mavros stifled a groan. A frizzy-haired young man had started setting up a sound system. The last time he'd played, he sounded like Bob Dylan on laughing gas.

'Have you heard of anyone important going missing in recent months?' he asked, with as much insouciance as he could manage.

'Well, there was that ship-owner back in June, remember? His family coughed up a couple of million and he was set free on Mount Olympos with his hands tied to his ankles. Nearly died of exposure.'

'Russians, wasn't it?'

'Right, though I heard a rumour that one of his competitors paid for the kidnapping and was less than impressed when he reappeared alive.'

'Anyone else?'

Bitsos stubbed out his cigarette and lit another. 'With your fine law degree from . . . where was it again?'

'Edinburgh.' Mavros had studied at the university there after going through the Greek primary and secondary system.

'Of course, the Athens of the North – with substantially worse weather. Anyway, you're familiar with the term *quid pro quo*, yes?'

Mavros considered it. On the face of it, Bitsos hadn't heard about his case, but that didn't mean he might not have information that would be helpful.

'A hypothesis only. Rich man. Daughter missing for some time. Kidnapping?'

The journalist put on the gold-framed glasses which were hanging round his neck. 'Interesting, Alex. Very interesting.' He raised his hand and ordered more drink. 'But I haven't heard a thing.'

Shit, Mavros said to himself. What now? If he set Lambis loose with the Poulos name, anything could happen. On the other hand, the hack knew people in all sorts of dubious places. Still, he needed more time to figure the pros and cons.

The singer broke into Theodhorakis's *Sto Periyiali to Kryfo*, mangling the Nobel winner Seferis's poem.

'God, how can you stand it, Lambi? It's hotter than hell and Hades is on lead vocals.'

Bitsos laughed. 'I never liked that old bore Seferis. Come to think of it, Theodhorakis is a wanker too, commie one moment, ultra-nationalist the next. They deserve all they get.'

That was double sacrilege as far as Mavros was concerned, but he kept a grip on himself. 'Tell me, have you ever heard of a rich man's daughter going missing for several months?'

The journalist thought about that. 'Occasionally. They usually turn up in Brazil with their riding instructor or the like. Most of the time, the family pays the cops to put their best people on it and offers a hefty reward. One or both of those does the trick.'

'What about kidnappings that go wrong?'

'You read my reports, don't you? If the crooks are idiots, they can't take the strain and kill the victim to save their skins. Almost always, the body's found and the kidnappers are nailed, either officially or by contract killers.'

Mavros pricked up his ears. 'Interesting. You mean the families have underworld figures on the job as well as the cops?'

'Of course. Would you trust the ELAS, even if you were paying them under the table? A bigger bunch of banana-brains has never existed.'

It made sense. Paschos Poulos would have hired a pro to find his daughter, but he wouldn't have told his wife in case the pressure got too much for her and she blabbed. The question was, who was that individual? Or was it more than one man? And how would he or they react if Mavros's involvement became apparent?

'You're looking very thoughtful, Alex.'

'What? Er, yes. Well, it's been fun as always.' He took out his wallet and put down a fifty-euro note.

'That's it?' Bitsos said, glaring. 'You pick my brains and give me nothing in return?'

Mavros smiled as he got up. 'Nothing? Are you sure, Lambi?' He headed for the door, giving the singer a suggestive look.

Bitsos would start asking discreet questions of his contacts, he was sure of that. If the hack came up with anything, he would tell him more about Lia Poulou.

As he walked through the unusually festive square, the police having moved the junkies, hookers and beggars on in the interests of Olympic harmony, it struck him that he was on a serious hiding to nothing. Then he remembered the look on Angie Poulou's face, the look of utter desperation, decided he would see the case through, no matter how bitter the end was.

His phone rang and he saw it was Bitsos.

'In all the excitement,' the journalist said ironically, 'I forgot to tell you what I heard this afternoon.'

'Spit it out.'

'Some of it'll be in the paper tomorrow, but you might as well know now. The cops in Viotia found someone burned to death in an old farmhouse on the top of a hill in the Kithairon range.'

'So?'

'The victim had been tied to a chair with wire before going up in smoke.'

Despite the heat, a very chill shiver ran all the way up his spine. Could that be Lia Poulou?

# FIVE

The Son had driven overnight to Trikkala in Thessaly, having sprayed paint over the scrape down the pickup's side. He had lost control as he accelerated away from the farmhouse on the hill. It wasn't as if he was afraid of being discovered up there, even though the flames were bright. No matter. On to the next target. The people on his list were being clever, trying to delay him by scattering all over the country. He was prepared to play their game because he knew that eventually one of them would talk. He didn't have the slightest doubt of that.

Trikkala in central Greece was a pleasant and prosperous town built around the River Lethaios, with the Pindos Mountains standing high to the west and, in the east, an open plain leading to the provincial capital Larissa. Beneath the bell tower on the hill were the oldest houses, many of them renovated with grants and cheap loans. Even here, three hundred plus kilometres north of Athens, the Olympic Games had extended their tentacles and there were hoardings and posters all over the place. But the narrow streets of the medieval and Ottoman Varousi quarter were quiet, especially now that night had fallen.

Flicking on a torch, the Son looked at the street plan he'd been provided with. The area was confusing, the lanes often turning into dead ends and street names few and far between. Still, he found the house without difficulty. It had enclosed wooden balconies in the Turkish style and money had been spent on reconstruction. He was reminded of the lakeside town in the far north of Greece where he had grown up. Technically, the Father still owned the house since no one knew what had happened to the old fucker. But he had no intention of going back. It was a place of suffering.

The door knocker in the shape of a thunderbolt was a dead giveaway. There was a convenient ruin across the cobbles and he took up position behind a partially collapsed wall. By two in the morning, he was ready. The only light in the house, on the second floor, had been extinguished half-an-hour earlier. It was time.

The locks were easy enough to pick. The door was solid, but the occupant had made the mistake of trusting the wood rather than reinforcing it with bolts. The Son slipped in, his feet in cheap trainers. His hands were sheathed in latex and his clothes would be disposed of far from the city. The new wooden staircase was solidly constructed and he made it to the second floor without a sound. The door to the bedroom was open and there was a motionless lump on the bed under a sheet. It was as hot as Egypt in Thessaly in the summer and the air-conditioning unit over the window was labouring to maintain a reasonable temperature. It also made enough noise to cover his final approach.

The Son paused at the door, leather cosh in his right hand and silenced Glock 19 in his left. He didn't intend shooting the target, at least not at first. Pain was to be applied before the comfort of death could be allowed. He took a slow step forward, then realised something was wrong. The object on the bed was too still. His left shoulder erupted in a blaze of agony, but he managed to hold on to the pistol while lashing out at the shadowy figure behind the door. There was a gasp and the woman thudded to the floor.

'Bitch!' he said in a low voice, rotating his left arm. He saw a short length of piping by the stunned target. 'You're going to regret that.'

He hauled her to the bed, throwing away the pillows that had been arranged under the sheet. She had been expecting him. Turning on the torch and grasping it between his teeth, he dragged the woman on to the bed, securing her arms and wrists to the frame with pre-cut pieces of wire from his back pockets. He cast the light around and went to the old-fashioned wardrobe that took up half the wall. He saw himself in the mirror on the inside of the door. The crewcut hair, dyed blonde, made him almost unrecognizable from the way he'd been the last time he was in Greece. If anything, he looked like a Serbian mercenary, but he had been given the documentation under a false name to prove he was a Hellene. There were wire coat hangers on a rail, many of them holding up long robes. He took one and straightened it, leaving the hook intact.

Putting the torch on the bedside table, its beam on the target's face, he sat down next to her and blew gently on her partially closed eyes. Soon they opened fully. He grabbed her throat and pressed hard.

'Don't scream or you'll lose an eye,' he hissed, brandishing the coat hanger in his other hand.

'Great Father . . . stand with me in this . . . hour of trial . . .' the woman croaked. She was in her sixties, with long grey hair. He knew her name, but that was of no consequence.

'Your imaginary father's no use to you now,' the Son said, with a harsh smile. 'Only one thing will make your passage to the underworld easier. Tell me where she is.' He released his grip slightly.

The woman gasped for breath and then spat in his face.

The Son carried out his threat and settled down to a long night of torment.

Mavros woke to the sound of the Fat Man yelling up the stairs.

'Courier for you, Sleeping Ugly!'

He stumbled down in his shorts and signed the pimply youth's clipboard. In return, he received a large padded envelope.

'What's this then,' Yiorgos asked, wiping his hands on the discoloured apron he wore over his paunch in the kitchen and grabbing the package from the half-asleep Mavros. 'Looks like a woman's writing.' He turned it over. 'No sender's name and address though. You got a secret admirer?'

Mavros went into the *saloni* and turned down the TV. An elderly female Communist MP was arguing about the cost of the Games on one of the morning chat shows.

'Give me that back, you lump of lard. It's not a *billet doux*, it's work.'

'Not a billy what?' The Fat Man held the envelope above his head. 'As the house owner, I'll have to insist on checking it. For all I know, it could be a bomb.'

'If it is, you're going to make a lovely wall covering.'

'Come on then, take it off me.'

There followed an ungainly struggle, culminating in the package being torn open and its contents scattering over the parquet floor.

'*Malaka*,' Mavros said, looking at the photos, leather gloves and sheets of paper.

'Eh, sorry, my friend,' Yiorgos said. 'Hey, I know that woman. She was on the TV the other day.' He scratched his bald crown. 'She's that bastard Poulos's wife, isn't she? Except she looks a lot more worn down on the box. Who's the girl with her?'

Mavros had a decision to make. He could either gather up the material in a cold fury and stomp upstairs, or let his friend in on the case. The fact was, he could do with someone to talk things over with and, unlike Lambis Bitsos, the Fat Man was trustworthy – decades of operating underground for the Party had made him highly circumspect. On the other hand, Yiorgos had a habit of putting himself in places that Mavros would avoid like dengue fever. Then again, there was the issue of him staying rent-free in the bugger's house. Although the Fat Man didn't necessarily expect payment in non-monetary terms, he would be overjoyed to be a part of the investigation.

'You tell them, Tati,' his friend said, his focus on the television again.

Mavros glanced at the TV. The MP, Tatiana Roubani, was respected across the political spectrum for her outspoken honesty. 'All right, you're in.'

The Fat Man turned to him and smiled broadly. 'Yes!' he shouted, punching the air. 'Ow, that hurt.'

Mavros shook his head, then started picking up the contents of the package. There was a handwritten note from Angie Poulou, her signature an almost illegible scrawl:

> Here are more photos and lists of Lia's friends and contacts. Please be careful if you follow any of them, not that I can think of any reason they would be involved in her disappearance. I'm sure she never had a boyfriend – she would have told me – but I've attached a list of the sons of relatives and friends who she knows. Again, I think it's very unlikely they'll give you any leads, but you know your job. Last night I tried to find out from Paschos what's going on with the police investigation. He told me they were following up some new evidence, but he wouldn't say what that is – apparently it's too early to be sure if it's relevant. I don't know. I feel so lost.

Mavros sat down and waited for his friend to reappear with coffee and pastries. The names on Angie's lists included the scions of some of Greece's richest and most influential families. Setting up surveillance on them would be close to impossible, as they were hyper-careful about security and hired private guards. And he couldn't ring the bell outside their high-walled domains, saying he was investigating the disappearance of Lia Poulou. He thought about the gloves. There were private labs who would run DNA tests, for a large fee, but when did she think he would require that kind of input? After he found a mangled body and kept it hidden from the cops while he confirmed, or at least excluded, its identity? That would be several steps too far, even for him. Then he slid his fingers into the tight gloves and felt a jolt of affinity with the missing girl. Suddenly he wanted desperately to find her.

'So,' Yiorgos said, setting down a tray of coffee, water and great chunks of fresh *galaktoboureko*, 'what's it all about, Sherlock?'

After drinking, eating and drinking again, Mavros gave him a rundown. His friend looked at the lists, shaking his head in disgust at notorious enemies of the people, then frowned.

'I don't get this, Alex. You can't talk to the thief Poulos, you can't interview any of these people, and the cops are out of bounds too. How are we going to find the girl?'

Mavros let the first person plural pass. If the Fat Man wanted to play Dr Watson, good luck to him. At least he was smarter than Holmes's sidekick, if substantially more cynical and less handy with a revolver.

'Did you see anything on the news about a body in a burned farmhouse in Viotia?' he asked, recalling the heads-up Bitsos had given him.

'Yes. The cops' spokesman said it was probably an accident. You know what old people are like with paraffin fires.'

'In high summer?'

'It's cold up in the mountains at night, even now. The body's male, though – he was clear about that.'

Mavros was relieved, thinking of the already grieving mother. But he was also at an impasse, despite only being on the case for a day.

'You know what I think,' Yiorgos said. 'We need to check out the family. After all, most crimes start at home.' He was an avid watcher of the sensationalist true crime documentaries that had begun to flood Greek TV channels late at night. 'Paschos Poulos is capable of anything.'

'Really?' Mavros said acidly. 'What do you base that assertion on, Fat Man? Apart from the fact that he's an exploiter of the working man.'

'And woman. The Party fought the good fight to get a group of female tomato canners reinstated after the management of one of that bastard's companies sacked them without warning.'

'Bravo,' Mavros said, without enthusiasm. 'If you're going to spend your time treating Poulos as a class enemy, we won't get anywhere. Besides, you're not even on speaking terms with the Party any more.' The comrades had taken a dim view of the illicit card games Yiorgos ran in his café; they'd also demanded a cut.

'All right,' the Fat Man said reluctantly. 'More coffee, my lord?'

'Piss off. Have you got any other thoughts?'

'Actually, I have,' his friend said, with a smirk. 'But you'll have to cut me some slack for the rest of the day.'

Mavros shrugged. 'Just don't say anything that might get back to Poulos or the cops.'

'You know I don't move in those circles, Alex.'

That was true. Since Yiorgos had given up the café, he'd only moved in one circle – Mavros's.

Telemachos Xanthakos had been told by a senior Public Order Ministry official to report to a Brigadier Nikos Kriaras, head of the Athens organised crime division and a member of the Olympics security committee. The deputy commissioner had rung him when he'd got back to Livadheia from Kithairon the day before. Kriaras was brusque and overbearing, but seemed to know his job.

'You understand that the country's image cannot be soiled by crimes such as this one?' he said.

Xanthakos had agreed and was told that Athens would handle the media, as well as the prosecutor. He saw the news before he left his spartan flat that morning and had been surprised to see the spokesman say that it was probably an accidental death. The first thing he did when he got into police HQ was call the medical examiner, Priftakis.

'I told them the same as I told you, but they changed it. I'll be doing the post-mortem this morning, if you want to find out what really happened.'

The deputy commissioner considered ringing the chief, but knew it would be a waste of time. The old man's strings were being pulled by Athens the same as everyone else's. He called the crime scene team leader and asked if anything else had come to light.

'Blue paint on the Judas tree. I'm looking for a match, but it'll probably be a pickup – the tracks on the leaves and ground are heavy duty. You know how many vehicles of that sort there are, especially in an agricultural area like this one?'

'No finger or footprints anywhere?'

'Not a thing. The fire would have destroyed all prints and trace evidence close to the body, and there was nothing in the vicinity of the building. Your man – or woman, I suppose – was careful.'

'You think there was only one killer?'

There was a pause. 'Yes, on balance I do, though I wouldn't

stake my pension on it. Two or more individuals would have
been that much more likely to leave traces.'

Xanthakos rang off and went down the hall to the detective
squad. Inspector Christos Tsitas was the only one in, head down
over a report. He and the deputy commissioner respected each
other, but weren't friends. Tsitas was a thick-set forty-five-year-old,
whose interests were football and hunting.

'Have we found any witnesses? You heard the vehicle was blue?'

The inspector nodded. 'I passed it on to the men on the ground.
You saw yourself. There aren't many houses at the bottom of the
road and the killer probably came and went in the hours of
darkness.'

Another one assuming there was only one murderer, Xanthakos
thought. 'Don't you think it would have been hard work for one
person to get the victim in there and wire him to the chair.'

'Not if he was holding a gun on him. Sure, it would have been
harder to carry him in if he was unconscious or already restrained.'
Tsitas gave a loose smile. 'Maybe the killer's taking time off
from the weightlifting down in Athens.'

'Very droll,' the deputy commissioner said. 'I'm going to the
morgue, if anyone needs me.'

'Do you want me to come?'

'No, we're short-staffed enough as it is.'

'Hope the smell of roast pork's died down. Take it like a man,
sir.'

Xanthakos turned on his heel. He was sure Christos Tsitas had
sensed his sexuality, but he wasn't going to let innuendo get to
him. Fortunately, he had a strong stomach.

'Ah, there you are,' Frangiskos Priftakis said through his mask
when Xanthakos entered the autopsy room in full scrubs. They
never had trousers long enough for him and his lower calves
were bare. 'Did you bring the carving knife?'

'That would be medical humour, would it?'

'Suit yourself.' The examiner got down to work, dictating
into the microphone that hung above the stainless steel table.

The deputy commissioner let him drone on, walking round the
table and stopping to examine parts of the body. The wires had
been removed from the wrists and ankles, the fire having made
the flesh shrink around them. The remains were locked in the

seated position. The flesh on the back of the thighs looked rawer than the rest of the upper body.

'Unavoidable tearing,' the ME said. 'We had to remove the chair. His back sustained similar damage.'

'Did the fire kill him?'

'I can't be sure until I've tested the blood and tissue for carbon monoxide levels. But, however it pans out, this is a murder case. You notice how the burning is much less beneath knees. As I said yesterday, the petrol was poured over the victim's head and upper body. What was left of the roof – bamboo, rubble and wooden rafters – caved in and landed on the body. A piece of stone covered his penis, which is why it didn't shrink like the surrounding flesh. Anyway, what you've got to ask yourself—'

'Is why the killer took the risk of burning the body when the wire bonds show that the victim was completely helpless?'

Priftakis nodded. 'Very good. Have you worked a lot of murders?'

'I don't keep a score. Most of them are domestics or revenge attacks. I've never had one like this.'

'Me neither. My guess would be that it's organized crime. With the Games on in the capital, they've got to go further away to do their dirty business.'

'It's possible. I don't see any tattoos.'

'Not on the lower part of the body, no. There's too much blistering and skin loss on the upper areas to be sure. Besides, not all gang members are tattoed, are they?'

Xanthakos shrugged. He didn't have that kind of experience, but no doubt Brigadier Kriaras did.

'I suppose a description of his face is out of the question,' he said, looking at the ravaged features. The lips, nose and cheeks were largely destroyed and the teeth were visible. The eyes had clouded over, reminding him of the Easter goats he'd seen as a boy. His father and uncles had taken bets to see who got to eat the roasted organs.

The ME laughed curtly. 'Well, his teeth are in decent shape, as you can see. Apart from that, who knows? The hair on his calves is black, so there's a good chance that his head was that colour. Then again, he could have been graying.'

'I was going to ask you about age.'

'Again, the calves and feet are the only guide at this stage.

There are quite advanced varicose veins, which points to middle age or later, though there are other factors to be taken into account. Examination of the brain and other organs will give me more of an idea how old he was.'

Xanthakos let him get on his with his work, watching dispassionately as the Y-cut was made in the abdomen and, later, the cranial cavity opened.

'There are small wounds here,' the examiner said, pointing to cuts in the blackened flesh on the chest. 'I think he's been tortured by something pointed – maybe a probe of some sort. Gangland?'

'It's within the parameters.'

After the pluck had been removed and the component organs separated and weighed, Priftakis took the stomach from the bowl held by his assistant to another table.

'Let's see if there's anything recognisable in here.' He used a scalpel to lay open the wall and put his gloved fingers into the shrivelled sac.

'What are those?'

The ME emptied the slimy residue from the stomach and laid out the small fibrous objects he'd found in a row on the stainless steel surface.

'Seven of them,' he said.

'But what are they?' the deputy commissioner asked, squinting at the shrunken remnants. 'Seeds?'

'More than that,' Priftakis said, pointing. 'They're arils, the covers of seeds. And if you ask me—'

'Which I'm doing.'

The ME laughed. 'Patience, my friend. The liquid has more or less gone, but the seeds will still be inside. In my opinion, these would normally be red.' He pointed his finger at Xanthakos. 'And you can eat them.'

'Pomegranate seeds?'

'Very good. Now you've got another question to answer. They were in the stomach rather than the intestines. That means they were swallowed up to three to four hours before death.' Priftakis lowered his mask. 'So there must be at least a chance that your killer made the victim swallow them. Why?'

The deputy commissioner thought about that. 'Pomegranates haven't been in season for months.'

'Maybe the murderer kept the seeds in the deep freeze.'

'How weird is that?'

Back in his office, Telemachos Xanthakos decided to wait for the ME's full report, as well as an update from Inspector Tsitas, before calling Athens. This case was getting stranger by the hour.

# SIX

**M**avros had never felt so confined by a case. He had plenty of information, but none of it was germane to Lia Poulou's disappearance. The Fat Man was still out pursuing his own angle, so he went down to the kitchen and made himself a salad. When his friend was around salads were permitted, but only alongside large pieces of grilled or roast meat, even in summer. He considered eating in front of the Olympics, but couldn't face it – commentators creaming their slacks every time a Greek competitor appeared, advertisements all the time, and a host of sports he couldn't give a shit about.

He sat at the small table in the kitchen and tried to clear his mind. A fourteen-year-old girl, willowy and with a pretty face. According to her mother, Lia didn't have a boyfriend. Was that likely? The culture at the international school was probably more progressive than at state schools. Boys and girls would mix in class and during other activities, and the usual would happen. Then again, there were no boys on the trip to Mount Kithairon. Could Lia have been seeing someone and run off? If so, he couldn't be at her school because Angie would have heard about another disappearance. She could hardly have met someone outside of school hours. The schedules her mother had sent were pretty full, plus she was ferried around by a driver who was also trained as a bodyguard. Paschos Poulos took security seriously. Which made him wonder. How could his client be sure her driver cum muscleman hadn't reported her solitary walk up Philopappos, or even followed her? Maybe she had some kind of arrangement with the guy.

The situation was made worse by the fact that it was August and Lia's classmates were on holiday. Maybe some of them had stayed around for the Games rather than hightailing off to their family houses on the islands or abroad. In any case, he couldn't talk to them. Lia's computer would have been useful, but it had been handed over to the police and never returned. It was likely they hadn't found anything useful, given her continuing absence. Or was there something more to all this?

He shook his head. Anything could happen in Greece, as recently proved by the sprinters who had won medals at the Sidney Olympics. Required to attend drug testing, they had apparently crashed their motorbike and needed hospital treatment; then they had withdrawn from the competition. The whole thing smelled like a rotting rat.

Back in his room, Mavros booted up his laptop and started to go through the lists of names Angie had given him. Was it really credible that the woman in charge of the group of girls back in May would have accepted what Lia said in her phone call – that her father had picked her up – without checking with one of the parents? Answer: no – even though Angie had said that Maria Bekakou and her husband were family friends. He put the woman's name into a search engine and found not her but her husband, Rovertos. He was a lawyer – according to his pretty basic website, a one-man operation with expertise in business law. His photograph showed a handsome face with graying hair swept back. Rovertos Bekakos. The name rang distant bells. He went back to the list of references produced by the search engine. Most were entries in the gossip columns of the less respectable papers, though all that the lawyer and his wife seemed guilty of was attending the most exclusive soirées and dinner parties. Then he found an article from a year back in one of the low-circulation satirical magazines, *Theophrastus*. It was entitled 'Snake in Paradise':

> What exactly has Rovertos Bekakos been doing in Paradheisos? The exceedingly well connected – not to mention exceedingly rich – lawyer has been seen several times recently in the not-so-new town in Viotia. Surely he can't have been sampling the delights of the Corinthian Gulf. The nearby aluminium works render the beaches less than attractive. Perhaps he and his lovely wife Maria, who usually accompanies him, are extending a hand of friendship

to the workers in the village following the Hellenic Mining Corporation's decision to replace two hundred men on high wages with unskilled school-leavers, leaving the former without homes or full pensions. Or maybe the couple has suddenly become aware of the environmentalists who have started campaigning in the area. As one of Mr Paschos Poulos's chief advisers, there is much for Mr Bekakos to get his teeth into in that strange part of the country – the rural bliss ruptured by strip mines and huge machines, the deep blue gulf ruined by pollution. Readers will remember that Mr Poulos stated, when he took over HMC ten years ago, that the company would do more than national and international pollution standards require, as well as honour all existing labour contracts. So who are Adam and Eve in this story? And who is the snake in Paradheisos?

Mavros had initially been deceived by the headline. *Paradheisos* meant 'paradise', but was also the name of the small town that had been built in the Sixties to house workers at the bauxite processing plant three kilometers away. As the photograph accompanying the article showed, the box-shaped houses were white in the sector nearest the beach, yellow in the central area and pink at the rear. He found the town's website and was informed that ordinary workers were allocated homes in the white part, middle management in the yellow and senior management in the pink. He wondered if the architect had read the works of Orwell and Huxley. Social engineering was unusual in a country full of individualists.

But where did this get him? If Maria Bekakou was married to one of Poulos's closest advisors, what connection could she possibly have to Lia's disappearance? There was only one way to find out.

Akis Exarchos was sitting at the bedroom window, the wooden slats of the shutters filtering the afternoon light. The burning sun was on his heavily tanned knees and calves. He should have kept out of the rays – the doctor had told him so after several cancerous growths were removed from his neck – but it didn't matter any more. Cancer had taken his wife Yiorgia a month ago, eating away her womb. They had no children, even though they'd been trying for ten years. Akis, aged thirty-three, felt like an old man. He looked out across the sparkling bay, the usual cloud from the works drifting over the headland. To his left, five kilometres away, the striped blocks of buildings in Paradheisos climbed up the slope, the road that led out of the valley coiling away up the defile beyond. People there worked at the aluminium works, even though they had to leave after their contracts ended. Here in Kypseli, there was nothing. More experienced fishermen than him couldn't make a living. They had to go so far out into the gulf to make a worthwhile catch that there was no time to drive to the inland towns to sell the fish. Nobody in Kypseli would risk eating the fruit of the sea nearby, considering the muck that was dumped in the water during bauxite processing. The huge ships that came to pick up the finished aluminium had been known to leave slicks of fuel oil too.

That was why he had got involved with the ecologists. At first he and the other locals thought the newcomers from Athens were troublemakers, but people were coming round to their way of thinking. Even the beehives that had given the village its name no longer provided much honey. Bees were more intelligent than humans.When they started dying, they left. Yiorgia no longer had that option.

Of course, the mining corporation's representatives had been round, offering money to anyone with a legitimate grievance. A woman with a fake smile had come to Akis's house a week ago. She was very sorry about his wife's death, while stressing there was no link between her cancer and the company's activities. But, in a gesture of good will, HMC was prepared to make a one-time offer of ten thousand euros, as long as he promised never to involve himself in what she called 'misguided conservationist actions'. He wasn't even sure what that meant, but he recognised blood money as quickly as he did the varieties of ever-shrinking fish in his nets. He told her to leave, shouting only when she expressed surprise.

The long-haired, bearded young man and his sandal-wearing woman were right. Kypseli and Paradheisos were a toxic Eden and he wasn't going to take it anymore.

\*　\*　\*

Mavros made preparations. He shaved and then dressed in up-market tourists clothes, consisting of a pair of pale blue chinos his mother had given him and a yellow Bondai Beach T-shirt a friend had brought back from down under. The pièce de résistance was a floppy green hat that almost obscured his eyes, his hair having been tied up and stuffed inside. He looked at himself in the mirror and burst out laughing. If the Fat Man saw him like that, he'd throw him out. A bunch of Aussies – 'convict bottom feeders' – had drunk him out of beer in the café once, argued over the bill and forced him to do what he hated most: call the organs of oppression, i.e. the police. He'd had to bribe them to take action.

Finding out where the super-rich and their acolytes lived was feasible, but cost money – they weren't in the phone book. Mavros could have waited for Angie Poulos to call and asked her for the Bekakos address, but he didn't want to waste time. Besides, Rovertos's website gave his office address, a building on Valaoritou. There were cafés and restaurants on the pedestrianised street not far from Syndagma Square and he would be able to keep watch easily enough, even though the prices were outrageously high in order to discourage the hoi polloi. Before he left, he called an old school friend who ran a car hire firm. Mavros didn't own a vehicle, preferring to walk, or use public transport and taxis. He did a cheap deal for a small Citroen and took the trolley to the end of Alexandhras Avenue to pick it up. He then drove into the centre and parked in a multi-storey near Valaoritou.

Taking up position under the umbrellas of a flash bistro, he ordered the kind of milky coffee he thought would go with his disguise, speaking English. He'd feigned being foreign often in the past – it had often been effective, making Greeks who would otherwise have been on their guard relax and speak openly. He knew what the Bekakos couple looked like from newspaper photos, so he sat back and pretended to read John Fowles' *The Magus* through aviator's sunglasses. He had only to wait half an hour. The street door to the lawyer's office opened and both he and his wife emerged. They paused in the street, kissed each other on the cheek and separated, Bekakos heading towards Syndagma and his wife to the establishment where Mavros was sitting. For once, he was in luck. He gave the woman a few minutes to get settled, then followed her in, taking a table as close as he could get – about five metres away. He'd have liked to be closer as eavesdropping wasn't going to be feasible due to the noise of the customers conversing volubly, but at least he would see who Maria Bekakou met, as well as being perfectly placed to tail her when she left.

The waitress was both stunning and up herself. He mumbled his way to an order of grilled fish, regretting the salad he'd eaten earlier. Keeping his hat and sunglasses on, he looked over to the lawyer's wife. She was in her late forties and he was sure she'd had work done on her face and body. The latter was thin, with small but pert breasts beneath a figure-hugging top, while her short, dyed blonde hair surrounded features that were too tight to be true. She was smoking one of the long cigarettes that were fashionable among Greek women, taking frequent puffs and exhaling quickly. Was she nervous about something or permanently on edge? It seemed unlikely she'd be meeting a lover opposite her husband's place of work, not least because three people had already greeted her warmly. So what was this going to be? A gossip session with a girlfriend?

A few minutes later, Mavros was bending over his sea bream, hoping the person who had sat down facing him at Maria Bekakou's table didn't see through his disguise. He'd have bet good money against Police Brigadier Nikos Kriaras, head of the Athens organised crime squad and a member of the Olympic Games security committee, turning up in the bistro. For a start, Kriaras was notorious for working all hours. He had also put a lot of jobs Mavros's way, usually via contacts in the foreign embassies, though he was a cunning operator who had played dirty more than once. It was impossible to be sure which interest group the brigadier was protecting or promoting at any given time.

Kriaras and Maria Bekakou had kissed each other politely, but there was no sign of emotional involvement. In fact, as Mavros glanced up every minute or so to study them, it seemed they were carrying on an argument in low voices, their lips moving rapidly at the same time and their expressions grim. That was interesting, but also frustrating. Mavros wondered how he could get closer without being recognised. It just wasn't feasible and he called for

another coffee after he'd finished what was an excellent fish –
fortunately, he had a wad of Angie Poulou's banknotes in his pocket.

In the event, Kriaras didn't stay longer than twenty minutes,
eating only a couple of breadsticks and drinking a soda. At one
point, the woman seemed to be pleading with him, her hand on
his besuited forearm. The brigadier stared at her and she took
her hand away. Shortly afterwards, he got up and headed for the
door, without kissing her farewell. Maria Bekakou stayed another
ten minutes before going to the washroom and then settling her
bill. Mavros had already paid his and was ready to roll.

Out on Valaoritou, he had to make a rapid stop outside a shop
the woman entered. She nodded to the girl at the counter and
then pulled out her phone. Five minutes later, her husband reappeared. This time, Mavros was close enough to hear the words
they exchanged.

'He says he is waiting for further developments,' Maria
Bekakou said, her voice harsh.

'That's rubbish,' her husband replied. 'You told him how
important it is?'

'Of course. I even said that Paschos would pay double.'

Rovertos Bekakos looked around, not giving Mavros a second
glance.

'Doesn't he realise they'll kill the girl?'

His wife shrugged. 'The stupid little bitch deserves everything
she gets.'

The lawyer frowned. 'We don't talk that way,' he said firmly.
'All right, I'll advise Paschos. He's got a dinner with the Olympic
hierarchy tonight. He won't be happy.'

Maria Bekakou adjusted her gold-rimmed sunglasses. 'You
think I am?'

Bekakos's eyes were on a smart woman who walked past, a
girl of about twelve by her side. 'What we think or feel is irrele-
vant, my dear. There's far too much at stake for you to start
playing Maria Callas.'

She opened her mouth and then slowly brought her lips together
again.

'That's better,' her husband said. 'Now, go home. I'll see you
later. I take it Phis is up to date?'

'Of course.'

Rovertos Bekakos kissed Maria on each cheek and went into his office, turning to watch the woman and girl as they went further down the street.

Mavros gave Maria Bekakou a twenty-metre start and then went after her. It was his lucky day. She entered the car park where he'd left the Citroen and went up to the second floor. He waited behind the door, watching through the window as she approached a silver Mercedes coupé, then raced up to the level above to the hire car. He was two vehicles behind her at the barrier and managed to stay close as she headed up Akadhimias, turning left at the parliament building.

Three quarters of an hour later, he knew where the lawyer lived. His wife drove to Kifissia, one of the well-heeled suburbs north of Athens, and stopped outside a green metal gate, waiting for it to respond to the device she had pointed. Mavros couldn't see much of the house, but it was large and surrounded by high bushes. He took a note of the address and parked further down the street, watching in the wing mirror. It was always a good idea to wait after people went into their homes, he'd found. This time was no exception.

Five minutes after Maria Bekakou went beyond the green gate, a black BMW saloon with darkened windows pulled up. The electric window came down and a long, pale arm came out and pressed the bell. Then the driver leaned out to speak into the intercom. It was Angie Poulou.

The maiden prostrated herself before the statue of the King of the Dead, avoiding his stern gaze and plaited beard. The temple was smoky and there were tears in her eyes.

'Great Hades,' she said, whispering into the gritty soil, 'grant me leave to revisit the world above your realm. I do not belong here, you brought me without asking my mother's permission even though Great Zeus sanctioned your act. The empty chambers and realms that echo only with the flutter of pallid shades are not for me, a living creature. Allow me to rejoin my brokenhearted mother and spend my days in the light of the Sun God.'

There was a faint rattle and the maiden heard light objects hit the ground around her. She raised her head and saw red tears, the seeds of the pomegranate. The cramps in her stomach returned, this time so pressing that she could not resist. She stretched out a hand and gathered up a few seeds. As she blew the dust from them, she counted seven. What harm could they do? She stuffed the seeds into her mouth and swallowed the bitter, life-giving juice. Immediately she felt stronger and her courage returned.

'Let me go!' she cried, raising her shrouded head to the great god.

His laughter was deep and shocking, his voice a condemnation that would last for eternity.

# SEVEN

Mavros waited down the street from the Bekakos house for over two hours, but his client didn't reappear – even after the lawyer himself arrived in a dark blue Porsche Carrera. Chasing Angie Poulou when she came out and demanding what was going on seemed like a good idea for the first hour, but then Mavros began to have second thoughts. He already knew that the grieving mother hadn't told him everything and her visit may well have been innocent. Perhaps she had no idea about Maria Bekakou's involvement with the police brigadier. Perhaps Paschos Poulos was using his lawyer's wife as a go-between – though why? It wouldn't have been hard for him to establish secure lines of communication with Kriaras, not least because they were both involved in the Games. Could Rovertos Bekakos be playing some dirty game behind his employer's back? And who or what the hell was 'Phis'? Then something else struck him. At first, Mavros thought the lawyer had been watching the attractive woman outside his office, but on reconsideration he realised that Bekakos's eyes had been directed towards the girl.

After delivering the Citroen back to the hire car depot, Mavros went home. He found the Fat Man in an unusually good mood, the scent of cumin-flavoured *soutzoukakia* emanating from the kitchen.

'Meatballs are murder,' Mavros said, looking in.

His friend laughed. 'How many of these tomato-drenched beauties shall I serve you? The usual eight?'

'Later. I'm parched.' Mavros took a large bottle of water from the crate beneath the table and drank half of it down.

'There goes your appetite,' the Fat Man said. 'Still, all the more for me.'

'I had two lunches today.'

'The boy's learning.' Yiorgos grinned. 'Wait till you hear what I found out.'

'Let me have a shower first.'

'Always washing! Your skin's being deprived of its natural oils.'

'It's about time yours was too.' Mavros ducked as a shoe came up the stairs after him.

When he came down, Mavros found his friend in front of the TV, getting through a mound of *soutzoukakia* on rice. In between swallows, he was bellowing at the TV – the usual diatribe about the waste of public money.

Mavros watched the athletes doing their best in the still high temperatures of early evening. It didn't take long for Yiorgos to clear his plate.

'So, what have you discovered, Watson?'

The Fat Man sat back and belched. There was a cardboard file on the table. 'Look in there.'

Mavros did so, finding a thick sheaf of photocopies bearing the logo of one of the Communist trade unions. As he flicked through, he realised they all concerned companies in the Poulos group.

'You *have* been digging,' he said, nodding approval. 'Still got some friends in the Party, then?'

'Of course. How many people do you think I worked with over the decades.'

'A lot, but I thought you'd been black-marked for capitalist activities.'

'Doesn't matter. Once a comrade . . .'

'Hm. Fancy giving me a synopsis of all this?'

'Lazy sod. All right. The bottom line is that the bastard Poulos has been squeezing the work force across the board, despite a huge increase in Games-related activities. When I say work force, I mean the Greek unionised one.'

'So how's he been meeting demand?'

'By bringing in unskilled workers on the minimum wage and using immigrants, many of them illegal. Tosser.'

Mavros remembered what he'd read about the former. 'How come the Party hasn't made a loud fuss?'

Yiorgos shook his head. 'It's not like it used to be, Alex. Deals have been done, favours have been dispensed, funds have been deposited in secret accounts. Tatiana Roubani's one of the few who's been making a stand. You saw her on the box this morning.'

Mavros was saddened. His father would never have countenanced deals and favours with the capitalists.

'Of course, it's all justified by the leadership as a legitimate part of the people's struggle, though oddly enough they don't say so in public.'

'I suppose they know more about their strategic aims than the ordinary member. Anyway, have you got anything specific that might help me –' Mavros saw the Fat Man's eyes narrow – 'might help *us* find the girl?'

His friend picked up another file that had been obscured by his bulk. 'Take a look at that.'

Mavros scanned reports from the branch of the union at the Hellenic Minerals Corporation bauxite processing and aluminium manufacturing plant in Viotia. 'Interesting,' he said. 'I came across a reference to this place earlier today. Yes, Paradheisos – that's the name of the workers' town.'

'Smartarse,' the Fat Man muttered. 'Might have know you'd—'

'No, no, this is useful. What's this about pollution?'

'Seems the company's been dumping all sorts of nasty muck into the bay as well as belching poison clouds into the atmosphere. The union was collaborating with a group of ecologists to prove their case – until the last official two hundred workers lost their jobs.'

'Hang on.' Mavros ran upstairs and found the print-out from *Theophrastus*. 'Look at this,' he said, when he came back into the *saloni*.

His friend read the piece. 'So Poulos's lawyer's been paying people off. That means they must have a case.'

Mavros nodded. 'Interesting how the big newspapers have failed to pick up on the pollution.'

'Interesting? They're in bed with the bastard.'

'You'd have thought the European Union would send inspectors in if the ecologists presented evidence.'

The Fat Man laughed. 'Since when was the EU anything but a friend to big business?'

Mavros looked at the papers again. 'So what are we saying? That the Hellenic Mineral Corporation – part of Poulos A.E. – is playing dirty, literally?' He filled Yiorgos in about Bekakos and his wife, and his client's appearance at their house.

'Kriaras?' his friend said. 'Wherever that dickhead goes, there's trouble.'

'True. Though his meeting with the lawyer's wife might have nothing to with Lia Poulou's disappearance.'

'Got to check it though, haven't we?'

Mavros thought about the girl's mother. He was pretty sure there had been no one else in the BMW. Had she left her driver/muscleman at home? If so, surely her husband would find out – or did he know already?

He had the feeling his client was running rings round him. But why?


The Son was sitting on a hotel terrace in Delphi, looking down at the sea of olive trees in the Pleistos Gorge in the last of the evening light. The port of Itea glowed to his right and, beyond, the gulf was blue-black with tints of red. He breathed in the mountain air and drank his diluted ouzo. He had arrived in the late afternoon and paid for a room in the most expensive place. It wasn't as if he had any shortage of funds.

There was a heap of national newspapers on the table in front of him. None of them had any mention of the body in Trikkala. That didn't mean it hadn't been discovered. He had sent photos again. He wondered what the dead woman's fellow worshippers or the police had thought about his master touch – three perfect, defrosted pomegranate seeds in each eye socket. The message was clear enough to those who knew mythology. With the Games going on, the authorities would take every step they could to protect the country's good name and give the illusion that criminal acts didn't take place in the land of the gods. He had been surprised the burned man had been found so quickly in an uninhabited area. No harm done. The yokel cops in Viotia wouldn't have a clue how to proceed and the Athenians would be keeping a close watch on them. His back was covered.

Although Delphi was in range of Athens for day-trippers, many visitors stayed at least one night to give themselves time to take in the full glory of the ancient site and museum. That meant the small modern town, which had been moved from its location on top of the site when excavations had started in the nineteenth century, was bustling. It was as well that the Son's next victim lived in the upper reaches, away from the tourist haunts. From there, it would be easy to get him to the desired location.

The Son had visited the sanctuary in the late afternoon. He had never been before, even though his school had run outings to many of the country's important historical sites. He didn't go on any excursions as the Father was too stingy to cough up the extra cash. It was curious because the old bastard was forever going on about Greece's illustrious past, as his masters had done, the dictators who were in power between 1967 and 1974. No doubt the Father had been worried some of the teachers would have been on the left and might have filled the Son's head with 'perversions of history'. As he now knew, the Civil War of 1946-9 was no clear-cut struggle between the British and American-backed forces of freedom and the foul Communist brigands. Not that he cared about ideologies. His Bulgarian instructor had said that freedom was an illusion no matter who was in charge, and the average citizen was nothing more than a drone. The Son had made sure he was much more than that.

He found the house without difficulty. The man was in his late fifties, a bachelor, and due to retire next year. No doubt he thought he would be able to worship his gods for the rest of his life. But he would also know that at least one of his colleagues had been murdered, so he'd be on the look out – maybe he'd been sent the photos of both previous victims. The Son, now wearing a black shirt and trousers as well as latex gloves, slipped over the wall at the rear of the property's small garden. The oleanders were thick, giving good protection. There was a single light shining on the ground floor. A squat figure was at the cooker, stirring the contents of a pot. The Son crawled across the hard earth quickly and reached the wall. The windows were closed, the air conditioning running, but that didn't bother him. He took the weapon from his long bag and squatted down by the door. There was no key in the lock, an old-fashioned one that allowed space for the muzzle of the tranquilliser gun. He took careful aim and fired. After a frantic few seconds trying to reach the dart in his back, the man collapsed.

Pleased with the shot, the Son took out his tools and worked the lock. He was inside in under a minute. Now he had ten minutes before the drug began to wear off. His victim wouldn't talk and now he was going to walk to the place of execution, he wasn't going to carry the fool. The Son taped the man's wrists behind his back and placed a strip of the same material over his mouth. Then he had a quick look around the house. Its owner lived on his own, his wife having run off with another man two years earlier. Maybe that had turned him to the worship of the Olympians. If so, they were doing a singularly bad job of protecting him – as with the previous two. On the other hand, these people did know how to keep their mouths shut. This one would feel the blade on hallowed ground. Would that loosen his tongue at the last?

There was a small statue of a robed god in the wall niche usually reserved for Christian icons. The Son didn't recognise the figure. The older male ones all looked the same to him – bearded, stern, their faces intended to provoke awe. This one was a mannequin with as much power as a Barbie doll. The worshipper obviously thought differently. There were bowls containing pieces of dried up meat and fruit beneath the statue, as well as a dark red stain which one sniff told the Son was wine. Hail, whoever you are, he said under his breath. Prepare to lose a follower.

The walk to the top of the sanctuary was easy enough, the now conscious man stumbling along with the tip of the combat knife in the small of his back.

'Open the gate,' the Son ordered.

His victim was a *phylax*, one of the numerous locals who were paid by the state to stand guard over the site. The Son closed the gate behind them and took the keys. Then he jabbed the man forward. Soon they were on the surface of the ancient stadium. The Son knew from the guide book he had read that it was 645 metres above sea level, had been started in the fifth century BC, and tinkered with by the Romans. The track was six hundred Roman feet long and up to eighteen runners could compete at any given time, watched by seven thousand spectators.

'Run!' he said to the guard. 'Run for your life!'

The man started muttering in what sounded like Ancient Greek. The Son had paid little attention to the compulsory lessons at school, earning himself numerous hidings from the Father, so he had no idea what was being said. Then the guard started staggering across the dusty earth. Even giving him a thirty metre start, the Son caught him well before the end. He still wouldn't say anything about the girl's location, sticking to his whiny prayer.

When he had finished, the killer went to the path that led down to the main site. With the help of the strategically positioned lights, he could make out the theatre, the great temple of Apollo with its few upright columns, and the treasuries of the various city-states. It was hard to believe that this had all grown up because of the ancients' need for the ramblings of a drugged old woman – the oracle whose ambivalent words had played such a major role in Greek history. Fortune telling. The Son smiled. He could tell the guard's. Tomorrow his fellow worshippers would be staring at his photographs. The fucker hadn't spoken, though he'd given the impression that he didn't know where the girl was. They were cunning, her captors, restricting that information to a small number of people. It only meant that more of them would die. And if what he'd just done didn't frighten them, he didn't know what would – though he had no doubt he could think of something.

The Son slipped back the way he'd come, stepping over the parts of his victim. If he was lucky, he'd be in time to pick up a foreign woman in one of the late night bars. He had a preference for Scandinavians. They were less shocked by his demands than most.

Mavros was lying on his bed, a fan blasting cold air over him. Although it was past midnight, the temperature was still in the high twenties and he was suffering. His Scottish genes had never been able to cope with killer heat, just as his Greek ones had taken to four years of Edinburgh weather like a duck to confit. The Fat Man was still in front of the TV, watching a dull American cop show that he claimed enabled him to know his enemy better.

At first Mavros didn't realise his phone was ringing – he'd put it on vibrate mode when he was tailing Maria Bekakou. He didn't recognise the Athens number on the screen.

'Oh, hello, you know who this is.'

'Yes,' he confirmed. Avoiding the use of names was sensible, though he assumed his client wasn't at home.

'Have you got anything for me?'

'Not yet,' Mavros replied. 'Let me turn the question back at you.'

There was a pause. 'What do you mean?'

Mavros decided to keep her in the dark initially. 'How close are you to Maria Bekakou?'

'She's . . . she's a good friend.'

'You don't sound too sure.'

'Well . . . after Lia disappeared on Maria's watch, so to speak, Paschos and I decided to put some space between them and us.'

Mavros kept silent. Very few people could resist the urge to talk when they were lying.

'You know, it seemed best. I don't know if you're aware, but Maria's husband Rovertos does a lot of legal work for Paschos.'

He decided to probe. 'And Maria? Is she a lawyer too?'

Angie Poulou laughed softly. 'No, she has a shoe shop in Kolonaki.'

'Would I know it?'

'I've no idea. Are you interested in women's footwear?'

'As a matter of fact, yes.' The pretence made him smile.

'Oh. It's called Heel and Toe, on Loukianou.'

He knew it as his mother's flat was only a few minutes' walk further up the hill.

'So were you talking about shoes when you visited Mrs Bekakou this afternoon?'

'How do you . . .?' His client broke off. 'Have you been following me?'

'No,' he said, leaving her to work out how he knew. 'What were you doing for over two hours with someone you've pulled away from?'

'I don't like being interrogated, Mr Mavros.'

'And I don't like being given the run-around. Here's why I want to know what you and Mrs Bekakou were talking about. An hour or so before you went to her place, she had a meeting with Police Brigadier Nikos Kriaras. I take it you know him.'

'Of course. He's in charge of the search for Lia. But why . . . why would Maria be meeting him? She didn't mention it.'

'I subsequently heard her tell her husband that Kriaras said he was waiting for further developments. And also that your husband said he'd pay double. Are you aware of any of this?'

'No! No, I don't understand.'

Mavros decided to spare her Maria Bekakou's characterization of the female he presumed was Lia as a stupid little bitch who deserved what she got.

'Could you answer my question, please?'

'Which one?'

'What did you and Mrs Bekakou talk about when you were at her house?'

'Oh, nothing of any importance. Honestly. It's true what I said about Paschos wanting me to keep away from them, but I don't have anyone else to talk to. At least Maria knows Lia's missing.'

'Mrs Poulou,' he said, enunciating her surname icily, 'are you sure there isn't anything significant you've omitted to tell me about Lia?'

'Yes, of course.' Then his client stopped. 'You understand that I can't go into all my family's business.'

'Anything potentially significant to her disappearance.'

'I don't think so . . .'

'You're sure she didn't have a boyfriend.'

'Positive,' Angie replied, without hesitation. 'She wanted one, but she also wanted the right one. She'd definitely have told me.'

'All right. From the schedules you sent, I see she has very full days during term time. What about during the Easter holidays?'

'We went to London for a week, but I was with her almost the whole time, visiting friends and relatives, shopping, going to the cinema and so on. Then we were at the villa in Evia for the festivities, again with family and friends always around.'

'Did she spend a lot of time on her computer?'

'No more than any other fourteen year old.'

'Do you know what she did on it?'

'The usual sort of things, I think – the Sims game, fashion sites, music.'

'You *think*?'

'Well, I didn't monitor her, apart from during homework time.'

'So she could have got involved with unsuitable people.'

Angie Poulou sighed. 'You think I haven't considered that –
boys, cults, porn, even paedophiles. But I doubt it. Lia's an
innocent fourteen, trust me.'

Not any more, Mavros thought.

'Besides,' she continued, 'the police would have told us.'

'Would they? I imagine your husband knows Nikos Kriaras
pretty well.'

'With the Games, you mean? Yes, of course.'

'And do you know him well?'

There was a long enough pause to make him prick up his ears.
'No, only from functions. Why?'

'I'm trying to build a picture.'

'That's becoming obvious. Tell me, Mr Mavros, how well do
*you* know Brigadier Kriaras?'

'We have history. If you want me to stay on this case, you'd
better make sure he doesn't find out about my involvement.' It
occurred to him that her husband might have had the phones
near their home tapped. 'Tell me that you're using a public phone
at least two kilometers from Ekali.'

'Don't worry. I'm in Ayia Paraskevi. Paschos is doing a
TV interview.'

'Don't use the same phone again.' He paused. 'One last
question. Where was your driver-bodyguard this afternoon?'

'I . . . I paid him and dropped him off in Kifissia centre.'

'Are you sure he won't tell your husband?'

'As if Paschos would care. He's got far too much on his mind.'

'So he wouldn't be concerned that you were with Maria
Bekakou and her husband?'

'I don't think so.'

'And if Mr Bekakos tells him?'

'You're barking up the wrong tree. Find some other way to
get Lia back.' Angie Poulou rang off.

Mavros lay on his bed, tossing away the notebook in which
he'd been scribbling as they talked. He'd often heard expressions
involving canines and mistaken wooden growths from clients.
They were almost always misleading.

He'd seen how conspiratorial Maria Bekakou had looked,
both with Kriaras and her husband. She was the nearest thing
to a lead he had, not least because she had expressed something

akin to hatred for the girl who had gone missing and because
Rovertos had said there was too much at stake. Meaning what,
exactly?

# EIGHT

B rigadier Nikos Kriaras stepped out of the helicopter at the
far end of the ancient stadium at Delphi and walked towards
the gaggle of uniformed personnel. It was nine-thirty in
the morning and he was feeling bilious from the flight between the
mountains – Parnassos's bulk to the north had been particularly
distracting – as well as apprehensive about what he was about
to see. Scene of crime technicians had marked out lines of footprints that he avoided. As he approached, his tame inspector at
his heels, a bulky figure in full dress uniform approached and
saluted. Although the local chief was technically in command,
there was no pretence about who was really calling the shots.

'Is the area completely sealed off?' Kriaras demanded, looking
around. There were officers along both stepped sides of the
stadium, and he saw men further up the mountainside.

'Yes. Fortunately another of the *phylakes* came up early in the
morning because the victim owed him money from a card game.'

'Have you made clear to your personnel and to the site staff
that this is a matter of national security and that anyone speaking
to the press will lose both their job and pension?'

The chief nodded. 'Everything you told me on the phone has
been carried out. But I don't understand—'

'Correct,' the brigadier said. 'You don't understand and that
situation is not going to change.'

The uniformed officer accepted the rebuke without comment.
He was two years from retirement and he wasn't going to mess
with a big gun from Athens. Though what the murder of a *phylax*,
gruesome though it was, had to do with Greece's national interests
was beyond him.

'Where's the victim?'

'The medical examiner has had him removed, as you requested.

They'll be in the hospital in Amfissa by now. My men have taken numerous photographs.'

'Let me see.'

Kriaras followed the chief into the shade and watched the stream of images on the technicians' cameras. The victim, Vangelis Gilas, was in his late fifties, a former merchant seaman from Itea who had sustained an arm injury in his twenties and been taken on as a *phylax*, no doubt because he'd promised to vote for someone. His service record was clean and he was popular with his workmates, though some of them found him rather dour. This much the brigadier knew from conversations when he was in the air. There was nothing to explain why he had been found sitting naked behind the start lines, his clothes in a pile beside him, stabbed in the heart. His head was five metres away at the top of the path that led to the main site, eyes wide open and reflecting the sun.

'Very well. Hand over the memory cards to the inspector here.' The brigadier frowned at the commissioner. 'All of them!' He turned to his subordinate. 'Talk to the scene of crime people and call me when you've finished. I'm going to check the victim's house.'

The chief caught up with him as he walked down the stadium. 'The ME just called. Do you want to talk to him?'

Kriaras took the phone and ordered the man to report.

'These are initial findings, you understand?'

'Of course. A team from Athens is on its way to pick up the body. This is a code red case, so keep everything about it to yourself.'

'I've already been told that by the Public Order Ministry,' the ME said, with a hint of resentment.

'All right. What have you found?'

'First, there's a puncture mark in the victim's upper back. Without doing a toxicology analysis I can only speculate, but I think the man was drugged with a needle, I estimate gauge twelve. The effect was probably not prolonged, as I understand there are two sets of footprints leading from his house to the stadium. The head was removed with a single blade, extremely sharp – the same weapon that was plunged into the dead man's heart. I'd say the killer is experienced. He waited till his victim bled out – there's a large patch of blood on the seats behind the starting lines – then cut off the head cleanly.'

'Time of death?'

'The ambient temperature was twenty degrees at midnight and the body is still in rigor. I'd say your man was killed between then and three a.m. The post-mortem should narrow that down.'

'Very well. Thank you.'

'There's something else, Brigadier.'

There always is, Kriaras thought gloomily.

'Inside the victim's mouth are five pomegranate seeds, bright red and apparently fresh.'

'Five? You're sure of that?'

'In the oral cavity, yes. Obviously there could be more in the oesophagus, stomach and so on.'

Kriaras handed the phone back. There had been seven of those objects in the burned man's gut. Now five. Did that mean there was an unknown victim somewhere with six seeds? He turned to the chief.

'I take it no witnesses have come forward since we first spoke.'

'None. Nothing much goes on in the upper town at night, according to the resident officers. There are no bars or tourist attractions, just houses. As you'll see, the victim's isn't overlooked.' They stopped at the open gate. 'The *phylax* would have had a set of keys for all the site entrances. We haven't found them.'

'So the killer retraced his – or her – steps to this gate, having led the victim up here.'

'It looks that way.'

The chief stopped outside a single storey house, the red roof tiles faded.

'I see what you mean about it not being overlooked,' the brigadier said. 'The dead man can't have touched these bushes in decades.'

'Maybe that was deliberate.'

Kriaras frowned. 'Don't speculate. That's my job. Have the technicians finished here?'

'They're still going through the rear rooms. So far, there are no prints except the victim's. Obviously the killer was wearing . . .' The chief broke off as his interlocutor walked away.

Kriaras went in the open door. He was glad to see there was no obvious police presence to get the neighbours talking, though the chief and his uniform weren't helping. They would soon come up with a story about the dead man being involved in antiquities theft, but the manner of his death would not be made public. He went back to the door. Could the victim have opened it to his killer? He kneeled down outside and saw fresh scratches around the wide keyhole. The lock had been jemmied. The murderer must have immobilised Vangelis Gilas, perhaps before gaining access. Could he have used a tranquilliser gun? That wasn't beyond his capabilities.

The brigadier got up and glanced around the kitchen, then went into the *saloni*. The small statue in the wall niche caught his attention – an austere ancient god with signs of worship beneath him. He would tell his inspector to pack it up and take it to the helicopter. There was a professor at the university in Athens who knew about the deities of pre-Christian Greece.

'I'm leaving,' he told the chief, leading him outside. 'You'll be provided with a story by the end of the day. I want the only copies of all relevant reports driven to me by eight p.m. You are personally responsible for deleting them from your officers' computers. Make sure the crime scene is cleaned up and the tourists allowed into the stadium as soon as possible. And think about this: if any of your people talk, you'll be sharing a shit-bucket with a cell full of illegal immigrants till your dying day.'

The chief cursed under his breath as the helicopter lifted off shortly afterwards. The arrogant fuckers from Athens. They ignored you for years, then they trampled all over you like elephants on heat. He hoped Kriaras and his bum boy crashed into the gorge in a ball of flames.

After Angie Poulou's call, Mavros considered his options, such as they were. Then he went downstairs, where the Fat Man was snoring on the sofa. He turned off the TV and gently shook his shoulder.

'No, Marilyn, don't go aw . . .' Yiorgos looked up at Mavros. 'You bastard. I was in the middle of—'

'I seriously don't want to know. Listen, we've got work first thing in the morning. Are you up for it?'

'Yes!' his friend said. 'What do you want me to do? Put the squeeze on that shit sucker Poulos?'

'Not quite yet. But what you can do is this . . .'

\*    \*    \*

He was woken by the Fat Man's heavy paw at six a.m. They drank a quick coffee and wolfed down some *galaktoboureko*, then took the trolley up Alexandhras Avenue to the hire car depot. His friend had a clapped-out Lada, but that would be about as useful for tailing as a double-decker bus.

'Remember,' Mavros said, 'the trick is to keep close enough to your target so she doesn't do a disappearing act on you and far enough away so she doesn't spot you.'

'Yes, yes, I can handle it.' Yiorgos was like a child let loose in a department store on Christmas Eve. He put his hand in the pocket of a remarkably uncrumpled white shirt. 'Look, I've written down the registration number of her Mercedes.'

'Very good. Keep in touch by mobile.'

'Yes, who knows? We might end up a long way apart.'

'Or the Bekakos couple might park in that multi-storey near his office and stay there all day.' Mavros immediately felt guilty about urinating on the Fat Man's parade. 'No, I'm sure we'll find something useful out. If you end up tailing Maria on foot, try to hear what she says but don't blow your cover.'

'What cover?' his friend asked, looking at his swollen midriff and grinning.

Mavros had a feeling this was going to end in an ocean of salty tears, but he smiled. The fact was, the lawyer and his sour wife were the only leads he had. He was hoping the former would take him to the mother-lode.

He hired the same small Citroen, this time for three days. His friend took one look at the Fat Man and found a Peugeot saloon that had seen better days but would bear his weight. They drove up Kifissias Avenue, Yiorgos practising his tailing on Mavros. He didn't do badly, considering the large numbers of official Olympics vehicles on their way to the athletes' village and various venues. The great arch of the main stadium was absorbing the sun like an ancient archer's bow at rest.

They parked at opposite ends of the street from the Bekakos house and waited. Mavros hoped the couple weren't early risers. As it turned out, they kept normal hours. The lawyer's Porsche appeared first. Mavros went after it, nodding to Yiorgos as he passed. He was apprehensive about how the Fat Man would do, but there was no time to worry about that. Rovertos Bekakos had his phone to his ear almost all the time. At first Mavros thought he was going into the centre, but he turned right and headed for the national road. He went north and accelerated hard. The Citroen struggled to keep up, managing to do so only because of the large amount of traffic. That thinned as they went over the ridge at the last of the suburbs. Mavros wasn't the world's greatest driver and he had to floor the accelerator to keep Bekakos in view. After a time, the lawyer indicated and took the exit for Thiva. The road from then on was slower and Mavros managed to get to within three vehicles. They bypassed the ancient city of Oedipus and continued to the junction north of Livadheia. It was then that it occurred to Mavros to turn on the radio.

The local station was broadcasting about only one topic: the demonstration that was blocking the road between Paradheisos and the Hellenic Mining Corporation's bauxite works. Now he knew where Rovertos Bekakos was heading.

Akis Exarchos had borrowed the tractor from a friend who supported the action, but didn't want to take part. He arrived outside the Ecologists for a Better Viotia office in Kypseli at six-thirty in the morning, the trailer loaded with rocks from a nearby quarry.

'Ah, here he is,' said the young bearded man known as Lykos, the Wolf. Like the other one, he was an Athenian, but at least his family had a small farm in the prefecture.

Angeliki, Lykos's wife, girlfriend, no one knew exactly what, smiled at him too. She was of medium height with long black hair, wearing combat trousers and a camouflaged T-shirt that was too big even for her substantial breasts.

'Aki!' she said. 'You are our hero. What would we do without you?'

The fisherman's cheeks reddened. The young woman always made him feel awkward. She was clever and he had a hard time following the fervent speeches she made about the aluminium plant's despoiling of the earth and polluting of the sea. But she and her man inspired him, as they had done many of the locals. Even some of the workers in Paradheisos turned up to listen, though they never participated in the protests. Not that there had ever been a demonstration like the one planned for today. There weren't many protesters, but they were going to make a difference. And, in case things turned nasty, Akis had his shotgun and a selection of fishing spears under a tarpaulin. It was time the ecologists were taken seriously.

Lykos led the procession of five vehicles in his battered VW van, Angeliki hanging out of the window and broadcasting through a megaphone.

'Stop the polluters! No more mining! Close down the works!'

The few workers who were up and about in Paradheisos showed little enthusiasm for the slogans. They probably imagined the procession was headed for the main square, which is where they'd held sit-ins before. But those had been carefully calculated diversions. This morning they were headed elsewhere.

Akis thought about Yiorgia. Would his wife have approved of what he was doing? She had been the local, born and bred in Kypseli, while he had been a labourer on the roads from the north of the country before he met her. They had fallen for each other in seconds and her father had approved, despite Akis's limited prospects. He'd shown his son-in-law everything he knew about fishing before his belly was riddled with tumours and he went to the place where his daughter had now joined him. Yes, he thought, Yiorgia would be in favour. She hated the permanent cloud that came across the water from the plant, as well as the red scars in the mountains behind it.

He looked over his shoulder as they drove along the town's sea front. There were banners streaming from the windows of the cars: 'Down with the HMC!' 'Close the plant NOW!' At the junction with the road to Dhistomo, Lykos bore right and soon the line of vehicles was on the road that led to the bauxite works. They had almost made it. The ecologists had found out exactly where the Hellenic Mining Corporation's land started, half a kilometre from the plant – there, even the road became private. Lykos stopped the VW. Even at this early hour, the pollution cloud was heavy over the hill that lay between them and what the workers called Red Gold Valley.

'On you go, Aki!' Angeliki called, through the megaphone.

He manoeuvred past the van and started the series of turns that would get the tractor and trailer at right angles across the road. Then he drove as far forward as he could and pulled the lever.

The trailer rose and the rocks thundered over the asphalt. He jumped down to see how far back he needed to go to block the road completely and then reversed to close the gap. Turning off the engine, he took the keys and hid them in his sock. He looked back towards Paradheisos. Already a line of HMC workers' cars was forming behind them. They wouldn't be going any further unless they got out and walked. That was when the fun would really start.

'Well done!' Lykos said. He had run the VW as close as he could to the ditch, as had the drivers in the cars behind on both sides. Anyone trying to walk would face a slalom between stationary vehicles and angry protesters. That wasn't the end of it. The night shift would be clocking off soon and several hundred tired men would be unable to get to their beds without running the gauntlet. The ecologists weren't going to be popular, but Akis didn't care. The workers had sold their souls and, what was worse, had condemned their own families to the illnesses caused by the poison clouds and the bauxite residue that was piled in heaps around the plant and illegally dumped in the bay.

By the time the police arrived, there had already been several fights. Akis had blood on his knuckles and face, but he hadn't been knocked down. At first, only the few officers stationed in Paradheisos showed up. The protesters knew them and their foibles. The adulterer was hit by condoms filled with yoghurt, the drinker drenched in local ouzo, the gambler pelted with coins and the dope smoker had dried grass thrown over him. Even the boiler-suited workers laughed. Soon cops from Viotia headquarters in Livadheia turned up. The man in charge was taller than most basketball players and, unusually, had an air of reason about him.

'All right, you've had your fun,' Akis heard him say to Lykos. 'Let the workers past. They're not the enemy.'

Angeliki started chanting slogans through the bull horn again and the protesters joined in.

The policeman came over to Akis. 'Give me the keys, will you?'

'Who the hell are you?'

'Deputy Commissioner Telemachos Xanthakos. You?'

'Akis Exarchos. Fisherman and anti-HMC campaigner.'

The cop smiled. 'Is the latter a job? Does it pay well?'

Akis wasn't falling for friendly overtures. 'Does yours? Can you sleep at night?'

Xanthakos scowled. 'The keys, please.'

Akis bent down and took them out of his sock. 'Here you are.' Before the policeman could take them, he threw them as far as he could into the bay.

Then a full-scale riot broke out.

Mavros stayed a reasonable distance behind Bekakos as they drove westwards. The lawyer took the turn to Dhistomo, where 218 men, women and children had been massacred by the Waffen-SS in 1944, then followed the bends down to Paradheisos. By now, Mavros had heard on the radio that the road to the bauxite works had been blocked and that fighting had broken out between protesters, workers and police. According to one sententious announcer: 'It's a disgrace that Greeks cannot conduct themselves in a civilised fashion while our country is hosting the Olympic Games, that inspiring symbol of Panhellenic peace in the past.'

'Yeah, right,' Mavros muttered. 'A few days off at Olympia and then internecine war for the rest of the fighting season.' He knew Greek history and he was sick of uninformed patriots harking back to the days of Pericles and Alexander. It was funny how rarely the twenty-seven-year Peloponnesian War that ripped the heart from classical Athens and numerous other cities was mentioned. Or that in the *pankration* event at the ancient Olympics, only biting and eye-gouging were penalized and contestants could end up dead.

As he drove past the zones of houses in pink, yellow and white, he realised he had come to some kind of cloud cuckoo land. He was no longer in Greece, but in someone's idea of a perfect community. He knew well enough where ideas like that led – to slaughter in the streets of towns like Dhistomo. The bay ahead looked inviting, but the water had a strange hue, as if the sea bed itself was bleeding. Across the Corinthian Gulf, the mountains of the Peloponnese were only just visible through the dirty cloud that emanated from behind a high headland. A line of cars over a kilometre long could be seen on the road from the dormitory town to the works.

Rovertos Bekakos took the Porsche as far as he could, before getting out and pounding his hands on the bonnet. Mavros watched the lawyer make a call on his mobile. A few minutes later, a young man on a motorbike, helmet on his arm, pulled up. Bekakos hitched up the legs of his expensive suit trousers and wrapped his arms round the rider's abdomen, then they set off for the centre of conflict.

Mavros had no choice but to follow on foot.

# NINE

Yiorgos Pandazopoulos was in twentieth heaven. Not only did he have a car that was considerably less decrepit than his old Lada, but he was actually being a dick – a private eye, Philip Marlowe in Athens. He'd always been envious of Alex's profession and his greatest joy had been hearing about his friend's cases. Apart from the one he'd foolishly got himself involved in and nearly ended up dead; his mother had given him serious shit about that, may the Saints preserve her. Alex would have ripped the crap out of him for that Christian thought. He'd never been able to understand how Communists could remain attached to the faith they'd been baptised into, even though they knew it was ideologically compromised. It was a shame Alex had only known his father Spyros for a few years. The old man would have explained to him that even Communists needed a religious crutch, especially where death was concerned. Still, at least Alex had found out about Spyros's activities during the Second World War. That had given him a fuller picture of the man who was one of Yiorgos's enduring heroes. But Alex would never be at rest until he discovered what had happened to his brother Andonis. Even though he didn't talk about him much any more, Yiorgos knew he still felt the absence keenly.

The Mercedes appeared about an hour and a half after the Porsche. The Fat Man started his engine and waited until Maria Bekakou had reached the end of the leafy street before setting off after her. He had a few anxious moments in the back streets of Kifissia, but then settled two cars behind her on the toll road that led towards the airport. Maybe she was doing a runner. He picked up his phone to call Alex, then decided against it. He was capable of doing this job without bothering his partner.

The Peugeot was going at full speed and only just keeping in touch with the Merc. At least there wasn't much traffic and he could still see it in the distance. Sure enough, Maria Bekakou was heading for the airport. She went into the short term car park. Yiorgos did the same, stopping a couple of rows behind her, then set off after her on foot as quickly as he could. The sun was hammering down and he felt his clothes dampen. She was wearing a white blouse and a short pale green skirt, and shoes with heels that slowed her down effectively. By the time she'd reached the road separating the car park from the terminal buildings, the Fat Man was only five metres behind her. She never looked round, suggesting either that she had nothing to hide or was careless.

Maria Bekakou went into the departures hall. She was carrying only a small handbag. If she was going to fly, it would probably be to a Greek destination. But she walked past the check-in counters and turned left, walking down the mini-mall of shops and restaurants. She glanced at the overpriced goods on display, but didn't stop. The place was festooned with Games-related flags and hoardings, making the scruffy old men selling lottery tickets stick out like cockroaches on a wedding cake. No one was buying from them. The tourists were loading up with Olympic souvenirs, including the appalling Athena and Phevos dolls, and locals with any sense were running for flights to escape the mayhem of Athens.

Then the target – Alex had used that word when he'd instructed Yiorgos – went into one of the restaurants, bought a small bottle of water and headed for a table in the far corner. The Fat Man was tempted by the pizzas and convinced himself that a couple of slices – oh, all right, four – would make his presence more convincing. He paid, choking back indignation at the exorbitant price, and found a table only two away from Maria Bekakou. She was speaking on her phone and completely ignored him.

It occurred to Yiorgos as he was chewing his way through the cardboard pizza that his appearance was actually an advantage when it came to surveillance. Who would imagine that a sweaty slob stuffing his face would be a private eye? The target certainly didn't. He was invisible to her as she sipped from her bottle, then lit a long cigarette. She looked at her watch a couple of times, convincing the Fat Man she was meeting someone. And so she was.

The man was wearing dark glasses and a Panama hat, the jacket of his cream suit over his arm. It wasn't until he glanced at Yiorgos and then swept his gaze around the restaurant that the drachma dropped. He was Paschos Poulos. What was the missing girl's father doing meeting his lawyer's wife – someone he was supposedly avoiding, according to Alex's client – at the airport? He wasn't even carrying a briefcase and, besides, it was impossible he could be flying anywhere, given his commitments with the Games. The Fat Man licked tomato sauce from his lips. Could they be shagging? They'd exchanged kisses and he had touched her hand a couple of times, but they didn't give the impression of being lovebirds. For a start, they were arguing, their voices sometimes raised above the racket in the busy eating-hall.

Yiorgos tried to make out what they were saying. He heard the word 'paradheisos' several times, then a loud French family took the table in between and he couldn't pick up a thing. Besides, the couple was getting ready to leave. He stood up a few seconds after them and lowered his head, ears straining. That was when he heard the words that sent several shivers up his overheated spine.

'They'll kill her, you know,' Pachos Poulos said.

'That's the price you have to pay,' Maria Bekakou said.

'Yes,' Poulos said. 'But none of them will escape the son.'

They split up in the central corridor without kissing. The Fat Man considered following the businessman, but thought Alex wouldn't approve – his target for the day was the woman. She went back to the car park. He moved as fast as he could towards the Peugeot after she'd got in and started the Merc's engine. She was four cars ahead of him at the exit gate and had accelerated away down the highway by the time he was out. With difficulty, he kept her in view. She got off at the Kifissia Avenue exit and went back home without making any other stops.

Yiorgos parked at the other end of the street from the one he'd been at earlier and tried to get his thoughts in order. Paradheisos. That was probably the town in Viotia where the Hellenic Mining Corporation workers lived. As for the rich people's final conversation, he wasn't sure which part of it horrified him most – the dispassion with which Poulos had mentioned the likelihood

of a female's (his daughter's?) death, Maria Bekakou's similar
detachment, or the mention of 'the son'.

He called Alex, but couldn't make himself heard. His partner
seemed to be in the middle of a combat zone.


Mavros answered his phone when he saw the Fat Man's number
on the screen, but he couldn't hear anything above the shouting
and the banging of drums and cooking pots. Yiorgos would have
to sort out whatever he was calling about himself. Pushing on
through the increasingly angry mob, he managed to keep Rovertos
Bekakos in sight. The lawyer stopped from time to time, speaking
to men in boiler suits and shaking their hands.

'What's going on?' he asked one of the few calm people, a
moustachioed man in his thirties, sitting by a boulder on the
roadside.

'It's the ecologists, isn't it? They've finally got their act together
and blocked the road. The night shift can't get home and we
can't get to work.' He didn't seem unduly concerned. 'I'd have
a dip if I didn't know I'd come out in lumps.' He peered at
Mavros. 'Hey, you're not a journalist, are you?'

'Certainly not,' Mavros replied, laying on the outrage. 'I hate
those scumbags. I'm with Mr Bekakos.'

The worker raised an eyebrow. 'Tell him the new contract's a
piece of shit.'

'All right. You wouldn't give me your number?'

The man laughed. 'Do I look suicidal?'

Mavros smiled and pushed on. Labour relations were obviously
bad at the plant, but he already knew that from his research. He
wouldn't pass himself off as a management lickspittle again.
Eventually he reached the front line. A banner had been raised
above an old Fiat. 'Ecologists for a Better Viotia,' it proclaimed.
The young men holding it up used their boots to kick back the
workers.

'Where are you going?' a woman demanded. She was in her
fifties and in the traditional black mourning blouse and skirt.

'Ecologists for a Better Athens,' he said, hoping his lack of
boiler suit would back up his words. His long hair might help
too. 'What's your leader's name, again?'

The woman eyed him suspiciously.

'I'm sorry for your loss,' he said, grabbing her as a stone flew close by.

She thanked him, leading him to the front of the car. 'My husband,' she said. 'He worked at the plant for fifteen years. Now he's in hospital with his lungs in tatters and I've been told to leave Paradheisos by the end of the month.'

'That's terrible,' Mavros said, no longer feigning.

She nodded. 'I've got nothing to lose.' She caught his eye. 'Lykos is our leader, though Angeliki does most of the work.'

The Wolf, Mavros thought, as he pressed on. He remembered the Axis occupation when resistance leaders had used noms de guerre to strike fear into the hearts of the enemy. Was something similar going on here?

Finally he got to within five metres of the blockade – a tractor and trailer that had spilled large rocks across the road. In front of it an animated discussion was taking place between Bekakos, a very tall policeman in uniform but without his hat and jacket, and a pair of protesters. The woman, well-stacked, was shouting, fortunately not through the megaphone she had in one hand, while the man, thin, bearded and belligerent, was waving his finger as he lectured the lawyer. The cop had taken a pace back and was watching the debaters with a look of mild amusement.

'We will not be moved!' the woman he took to be Angeliki screamed, repeating the words through the bullhorn. 'Take your filthy pollution to Switzerland!'

Mavros smiled. He was sure Poulos A.E. had numerous Swiss bank accounts, like all Greek big businesses, and there were probably plenty in Paschos Poulos's own name. He heard the noise of heavy machinery and looked between the tractor and trailer. The workers on the other side had moved their vehicles to the side of the road to allow a large bulldozer to approach.

'No retreat!' Angeliki yelled. 'No surrender!'

At the same time, the workers to his rear came together and charged the demonstrators. The few police officers were overwhelmed and thrown to the side, one of them tumbling into the bay.

Mavros was in the dragon's jaws. He made his decision. Running forward, he grabbed the tall policeman with one hand and the young woman with the other.

'Get up on the trailer!' he shouted. 'They won't have the nerve to bulldoze it if there are people aboard.'

The cop stared at him and then nodded.

Angeliki yelled to Lykos to follow. He did so, leaving Bekakos on his own. The lawyer took fright and climbed up too.

'Who are you?' the policeman shouted, raising both hands to stop the bulldozer. Bekakos and the others did the same.

'The name's Mavros, Alex Mavros.'

'Deputy Commissioner Telemachos Xanthakos. What are you doing here?'

Mavros watched as the driver of the Caterpillar stopped a few centimetres from the trailer. Rovertos Bekakos jumped down and went to speak to him.

'I'm looking for someone,' he replied to the cop.

'Aren't we all?' Xanthakos spoke into his walkie-talkie, ordering his men to regroup and await orders.

Angeliki was still shouting through the megaphone, while Lykos was beckoning to his supporters.

'I've heard of you,' the cop said, a grin spreading across his lips. 'You're that private investigator.'

Mavros nodded, relieved that Bekakos couldn't hear the conversation above the uproar. 'You're looking for someone too.'

Xanthakos narrowed his eyes. 'Meaning?'

'The killer of the burned body up on Kithairon. Any leads?'

'That's a conversation for later – if it happens at all.' The deputy commissioner jumped down and went to the lawyer.

'Good thinking,' Angeliki said, her voice hoarse. 'Who are you?'

'Alex,' Mavros replied. 'A sympathiser. Are you all right?' He'd noticed a large bruise on her forearm.

'Ach, that's nothing. Come and see us. We're over in Kypseli.' She pointed to a blur of white buildings across the bay. Then she went to Lykos and kissed him on the mouth. 'We've made our point, my love. Let's break this up. Look, the TV cameras are here. We can give them a rant.'

Lykos laughed.

After a few minutes the tension went out of the situation as the protesters were told by their leaders to stand down. Mavros watched as a thin-faced man climbed into the tractor cab and started the engine with a key he took from under the seat. The policeman turned round, looking surprised. There was a tarpaulin above the tow-bar, the muzzle of a double-barrelled shotgun visible. Mavros shivered as he saw the points of several harpoons. He had bad memories about fishing gear.

'You'd better cover those up,' he said to the driver.

The look he got would have melted rocks, then the man smiled.

'Thanks, my friend. Wouldn't want the cops seeing those.'

'Wouldn't want any of them to be used against your fellow human beings.'

The humour went out of the man's expression. 'There are worse weapons than these and the accursed plant produces many of them.'

'Steady,' Mavros said, giving his name.

'Akis Exarchos,' the driver replied. 'Are you one of the good or the bad? Maybe we'll find out.' He revved the engine and started to manoeuvre the tractor towards Paradheisos.

Mavros was pleased with the contacts he'd made in the course of only a few minutes. Then he saw Rovertos Bekakos staring at him from beside the bulldozer. He had been well and truly spotted by his target. All he could do was hope that the lawyer didn't know or find out who he was.

His phone rang. It was Yiorgos again. The news couldn't have been worse.

Telemachos Xanthakos stayed on the works road until the lines of traffic cleared in both directions. He'd posted officers at intervals towards Paradheisos to ensure that the protesters weren't attacked on their way back to Kypseli. The young man who called himself Lykos – real name Periklis Roubanis – and the tractor driver Akis Exarchos, had been booked for deliberate obstruction of a public highway, but not taken in. He had judged that would be unnecessarily provocative, even though the HMC lawyer Bekakos had exerted a lot of pressure to have all the demonstrators jailed in advance of trial. The deputy commissioner didn't react well to being pressurised, and he was relieved when his boss – somewhat reluctantly – backed him up. Bekakos glowered at him as he was driven back to pick up his flash German car.

Xanthakos turned to the private investigator Alex Mavros, who was looking across the bay. It wasn't often that a law and order celebrity turned up in Viotia. The deputy commissioner was curious.

'They have a point, you know,' Mavros said. 'That smoke cloud can't be healthy.'

'Is that why you're here? I thought you were a missing persons specialist.'

Mavros laughed. 'Have you been stalking me?'

Xanthakos wondered if the PI had clocked his sexuality. Surely he couldn't be that sharp. 'No, but you will insist on getting your photo in the papers.'

'True. I'd rather that didn't happen, but you know how it is. Journalists can sometimes be helpful.' Which reminded him – he should call Lambis Bitsos. If the ever-hungry hack had discovered anything, he wouldn't necessarily call Mavros until he'd followed it up.

The policeman smoothed back his hair. 'I can't say I've ever found those sewer-rats helpful.' That was one good thing about Brigadier Kriaras's involvement in the burned body case. Xanthakos had been able to refer all press calls to the Athenian's office. 'So, why are you here, Mr Mavro? Has someone gone missing from the HMC plant? Their security people normally have everything tied tighter than an anarchist's pony tail.'

'Alex,' the PI said, smiling. 'They didn't do too well today, did they?'

'No, they didn't. People have the right to protest, though obviously not to block a public highway.'

Mavros looked surprised. It was true that not many cops were as liberal as Telemachos. But he still hadn't heard why the investigator was there.

'Alex, I can help you. On the other hand, I'm not aware of any missing persons in Viotia apart from the usual school drop-outs and abused wives.'

'Deputy Commissioner—'

'Telemachos.'

'All right, Telemache. Who burned your man on Kithairon?'

'Why are you so interested in that?'

'I'm betting you don't get many torture-homicides in Viotia. On the other hand, we do see them from time to time in Athens.' The PI's gaze dropped, as if he was suddenly reluctant to continue.

'In fact . . . I had dealings back in 2002 with a couple of scumbags who could well have carried out your killing.'

Xanthakos tried not to look over-interested. Was the long-haired celebrity dick going to hand him the murderer on a plate? He had a vague recollection of the case. 'Russian gangsters, weren't they?'

Mavros wiped his forearm across his forehead. 'Can we get out of the sun? My car's back there.' He pointed towards Paradheisos.

'I'll give you a lift.' The policeman got into the unmarked Nissan that he had driven with great difficulty to the front of the tailback. He put the air conditioning on full blast.

'There was a Russian gang involved, yes,' the PI said, 'but a Greek crime family was behind the worst killings.'

Xanthakos nodded. 'I remember now. The Chiotes.'

'That's right. They employed some very nasty people.'

'Don't leave me hanging.'

'Hm. I think I'd better talk to one of your counterparts in Athens first.'

Xanthakos raised a hand at the last of his officers. 'Don't worry, they're fully aware of my investigation.'

Mavros stared at him. 'Really? I'd have thought they had their hands overflowing with the Olympics.' He pointed. 'It's that Citroen.'

The policeman stopped the car.

'Who are you talking to?' the PI asked.

'I shouldn't be telling you, but I need all the help I can get.' Xanthakos smiled. 'Plus you seem to be trustworthy.'

Mavros laughed. 'Thanks.'

'Brigadier Nikos Kriaras.' The deputy commissioner turned to watch his passenger, who had already opened the door. 'What? Don't tell me he puts the shits up you too?'

Mavros looked back at him. 'No, but he knows everyone who matters. Listen, give me your private number. I'll talk to you later.'

'All right, Alex,' Xanthakos said, handing him his card. 'Don't be a stranger.'

The PI smiled. 'No problem. Some of my best friends are cops.' He closed the door and walked away. 'Not.'

# TEN

Mavros drove into Paradheisos and stopped at a café on the seafront. He ordered a beer and a sandwich, then called the Fat Man.

'It could just be a coincidence,' he said, after listening for several minutes.

His friend sighed. 'How likely is that, with a naked corpse wired to a chair and set on fire? Who else's son would do something like that?'

'Come off it, Yiorgo, there's no shortage of thugs – Albanian, Serbian, Russian as well as Greek – at work in Athens these days. Besides, why didn't Poulos mention the Father? He was the lead operator.'

'He's probably dead by now, having his flesh picked apart by demons in the underworld like all the Junta's torturers.'

That was probable enough. The Father had been vicious when Mavros met him two years back, but he was getting on. The fast-learning Son could well have developed into a solo act.

'Hello?' the Fat Man said. 'Is there life in Viotia?'

'All right, smart arse. I've made friends with a senior cop here. Maybe I'll do some information-sharing.'

'Oh, you're friends with the beaters of the people now. Shame on you.'

Mavros groaned. 'Give it a break, Yiorgo. Have you got any better ideas?' He looked around – there was no one in the vicinity, Paradheisos being to tourists what cigar smoke was to mosquitoes. 'Besides, my contact told me that your friend and mine Nikos Kriaras is following the burned man case with extreme interest.'

'That would be the Nikos Kriaras who met Maria Bekakou yesterday – by the way, she's still at home.'

'Exactly. There are things going on here that I can't get my head around.'

'Well, you'd better get a move on.'

'Why?'

'If the Son really is at work, he's going to go after you as soon as he gets a sniff that you're involved.'

That was true. Mavros had put a stop to the torturers' activities, neither of them having been heard of since – until now. They, or the surviving family member, would be burning for revenge.

'What next?' Yiorgos asked. 'Shall I stay here all day?'

'If you can. I'm going to talk to the people who blocked the road to the HMC works. The fact that Bekakos came down here personally is interesting, especially since he and his wife have been before. If anyone knows what's going on, Ecologists for a Better Viotia will.'

The Fat Man repeated the group's name scornfully. 'What are they, a bunch of hairy males and hairier females? How are they going to help you find Lia Poulou?'

It was a good point, but Mavros wasn't going to argue it. Sometimes you had to follow your nose and his, stinging from the dirty air, was directing him round the bay to the village of Kypseli.

Lady, in your grief we make these offerings to you. The road ahead is long and rough, but we believe your quest will be successful with the passing of the seasons. Although the earth is barren now, the plants and crops withering in the blasts of hot wind, there will come a time when it is fertile and green again.

Accept this libation on behalf of your daughter, taken before her time and hidden in the dark halls of the death god. By his trickery she is confined and undergoing the worst of separations. She does not know what you are doing for her, the efforts you and your followers are making to bring her back. But this period of testing will not last forever, she is not one of the betrayers who will pay for all eternity for their blasphemy – Tantalus starving and maddened by thirst but unable to reach food and drink; Sisyphus rolling the great boulder up the hill and watching it career downwards for him to start over again; and wretched Tityus, whose liver is pecked away by eagles and snakes every day. Not even Hades would dare subject the Maiden to serious harm. Be comforted by that.

Green Lady, we share your pain as we plait these reeds and stems before you. They are meagre gifts, but we supplement them with the last of the honey made in this place before the bees fled. We also wash your feet with pure water, brought from mountain springs far from this cursed place. We crave indulgence as we send our prayers to you, then direct the Maiden to her temporary home beneath the earth. She is the world's great wealth, worth more than the gold and silver heaped in the treasuries at Delphi. She will return and you will dispense fertility, we know this.

Mavros took in the town of Paradheisos. Despite the heat, he had to suppress a shiver. The place was inhuman, a façade of colours that hid exploitation and unhappiness. He had seen the workers on the way to the bauxite processing plant. The people, mostly men but a few women, initially looked normal, but their eyes were empty – black holes leading to abysses he couldn't fathom. He got into the Citroen and drove towards Kypseli. He was halfway there when he remembered what he had to do.

'Speak!' Lambis Bitsos wasn't paid by the word, so he restricted use of them when he was working.

'Mavros.'

'Black by name, black by reputation.'

'Very amusing.'

'Yes, like that demonstration you got yourself caught up in.'

'Shit, I was on TV?'

'Only for a minute or so. Why? Worried your mystery client will fire you for not keeping a low enough profile?'

'No comment.' In truth, Mavros didn't think Angie Poulou would care about him being in Viotia – unless she thought he'd given up the search for Lia. In any case, Rovertos Bekakos had got a good look at him.

'So, is it true what they say?' Bitsos liked being cryptic.

'About what?' Mavros said, humouring him.

'About the pollution from the HMC works?'

'Well, put it this way – you wouldn't want to run a marathon around here.'

'Like I'm going to. Then again, female athletes don't wear much, do they?'

'Jesus, Lambi. Are you on your own?'

'Working from home. Have you got something juicy for me?'

'Not sure. First of all, have you heard anything more about the burned man on Mount Kithairon?'

'Not really. Except the Ministry of Public Order's been sending out the press releases, not that they say much apart from it being unattributable gang violence and asking us to give it only minor coverage. I asked why Viotia Police weren't doing that and was told they aren't up to homicide cases of this sort. It's obvious the ministry's trying to keep a lid on the case during the Olympics.'

Mavros wondered what Telemachos Xanthakos would think about that negative characterisation of his force. 'Wouldn't want the visitors being brought face to face with the real Greece,' he said, deciding against putting the journalist on to the deputy commissioner. 'What with the interest groups making such huge profits.'

'Been listening to that fat friend of yours?'

'Not more than usual. What would you say if I told you it was Nikos Kriaras who personally laid down the law to the Viotia Police?'

There was a brief silence. 'Interesting. Given his role with the Games, I'd have thought he'd delegate that to a minion. Then again, he is responsible for organised crime.'

'In Athens and Attica.' Mavros thought of Kriaras's meeting with Maria Bekakou. 'But Athens is the centre of the world right now.'

'What would *you* say if I told you the blessed Kriaras was in Delphi this morning?'

'Don't know. The Pythian Games were held there in ancient times. Did some party of Olympic VIPs go to pay homage?'

'Always the smartarse. No, it's much more succulent than that.' The journalist coughed. 'I'm afraid I can't talk about it.'

'What?'

'My source swore me to secrecy and the ministry hasn't released anything.'

'For fuck's sake, Lambi, Delphi's only an hour from here. Information share?'

There was a longer pause. 'OK, deal. Apparently a *phylax* was found in the stadium with his head several metres away from his body.'

Mavros immediately thought of the Son, his stomach doing several somersaults. Should he tell Bitsos about the torturer? He decided to hold back what the Fat Man had heard Paschos Poulos say for the time being.

'Are you receiving me?'

'How come it hasn't been on the radio?'

The journalist laughed harshly. 'Because that dickhead Kriaras got over there fast enough to close the rumour mill down – well, almost. Not that I can print anything. They were lucky. Another guard found the body – I mean body *parts* – before the site opened. They've cleaned it up and no one knows any different. Apart from the staff and they've been threatened with firing and pension removal if they talk.'

'No heavy-handedness there, then. Hm. Got to go.'

Bitsos wasn't letting him off so easily. 'Your rich man and his missing daughter. Is that what you're in HMC land for? HMC being part of Poulos A.E.'

Mavros knew he couldn't get away with, 'No comment', again. 'You got me, Lambi. I don't suppose you've come across—'

'Come across? Is that how you think I do my job – sit around waiting for hot information to appear in front of me?'

'No, that would be terrible for your weight.'

'Wanker. Do you want me to do some serious digging?'

Mavros thought of Angie Poulou's privacy. With the murder in Delphi and the potential involvement of the Son, she was no longer his sole priority, client or not. He would keep looking for Lia, but not at the cost of his life.

'Yes, Poulos is the one, Lambi. But make sure none of his family or sidekicks finds out I told you, OK?'

'Better than OK, Alex,' Bitsos said. 'You just made my day.'

Mavros got out of the car near Kypseli and looked across the bay. There were spots of oil on the narrow beach, a seagull studiously ignoring a dead fish. The whole area was soiled by the plant across the water. Delphi could wait. He hoped he could get Bitsos to give him the name of his contact. Deputy Commissioner Xanthakos would be no use as the town was in the neighbouring prefecture of Fokidha, though maybe he could smooth Mavros's way with the local cops. But first he needed to talk to the ecologists. They were the sworn enemies of the HMC and Paschos Poulos, and he'd seen how effective they were.

Might they know something about Lia Poulou?

Brigadier Nikos Kriaras ushered out the Olympic Games security committee, including officers from the FBI and Scotland Yard, then went over to the window of the conference room. From the fifth floor of the Attica General Police Directorate, he looked down at the old Panathinaikos football stadium. It was swathed in Games hoardings, one of the many examples of stringy mutton dressed as frolicking lamb in Athens. In under two weeks it would all be over and he could get back to his normal working life.

Or could he? The Poulos affair was expanding in directions he couldn't control and that made him nervous. The worst development concerned Alex Mavros. What had the long-haired private eye been doing at the protest outside the HMC plant in Viotia? Kriaras had seen him on the TV coverage, standing on the blockade like a revolutionary in 1848, even though he knew the dick wasn't political – or at least, he didn't use to be. Had he suddenly become a save-the-planet type? The brigadier dismissed that immediately. Mavros was investigating something. The question was, what? Could he have dropped a hint to Deputy Commissioner Xanthakos? He'd seen the pair of them talking behind the breathless broadcaster. Then he'd had Rovertos Bekakos on the line, demanding that the PI be arrested immediately for his part in disrupting the movement of workers to the plant – as well as asking why there was still no word on the missing girl.

The truth was, Kriaras was sick of Paschos Poulos and everyone connected with him. Considering that included all of the Greek Olympic Committee, he shouldn't have been surprised. Working with the grasping, self-obsessed thieves who had only got involved because they smelled profit had been the most frustrating time in his career – apart from the occasions when Alex Mavros had played him for a fool. Maybe he should ring Xanthakos and tell him to arrest the tosser after all. No, that would be counter-productive. On balance, Mavros had done more good than harm in the past. What Xanthakos could do was find out why he was in Viotia.

Kriaras went along the corridor to his office, nodding at the uniformed secretary in the outer room. His private domain was always kept locked. Although there was a master key held in case of fire, he had made sure that all the others had been delivered to him. That meant he could spread files out across the long table. Although they all had service blue cardboard covers, some were more personal. The Lia Poulou case was officially on the books, but aspects of it were known only to the brigadier. He sat down behind his desk and opened the reports that had been sent from both Viotia and Fokidha. There was nothing further on the burned man.

The victim was still unidentified, despite his teeth having been compared with dentists throughout the prefecture. Perhaps he wasn't a local, in which case pulling the records of thousands of tooth-pullers across the country would be necessary – but in no way justifiable in terms of man hours. DC Xanthakos reported that no vehicles had attempted to approach the scene. His officers were checking blue pickups for scrapes but had found none so far.

As for the beheaded man at Delphi, the forensics team he'd sent from Athens confirmed what he had already been told by the medical examiner in Fokidha – there were five pomegranate seeds in the man's mouth and nowhere else. On that subject at least, he hoped he was about to make some progress. The box containing the sculpture of the ancient figure taken from the victim's house was at the far end of the table and the expert was late.

Five minutes later, the secretary showed in an elderly, stooped man with thick white hair that almost reached his shoulders. Another superannuated hippy, the brigadier said to himself.

'Professor Epameinondhas Phis,' the old man said, blinking at Kriaras. 'You have something for me?'

The policeman went over to the box and opened it. 'What can you tell me about this?'

The professor pulled on a pair of white gloves and carefully lifted the figure from the strips of newspaper it had been packed in. He examined it front and rear, muttering to himself.

'Well?' Kriaras said, losing patience.

Phis looked up. 'You mentioned there were offerings.'

'In the box.'

The old man tossed pieces of newsprint on to the floor and removed two bowls that had been covered with transparent film, one containing meat and the other fruit. 'Pork,' he said. 'And apple and pear.'

'Are they significant?'

'Oh, yes, Brigadier.'

Kriaras managed not to bark another question, assuming that the professor would talk when he was ready.

'You said you have photographs.'

The policeman handed over a file.

'Mm, libations of wine, as would be expected. Niche in the wall, yes.' And more that was barely audible. Phis turned his attention back to the small statue, turning it up and examining the bottom with a lens in his left eye. Eventually, after putting the figure down and measuring it with a tape from top to toe, the old man smiled broadly.

'I must congratulate you, Brigadier. You've found something very rare indeed. This is only the third specimen of this size that I've ever seen, and the other two were from Sicily. Mid-to-late fifth century BC.'

'It's an original?'

'Oh yes. And it's in remarkably good condition, especially as it has been in recent use.'

Kriaras clenched his fists and took several deep breaths. 'Just tell me, Professor, which god is it?'

'Excuse me, in my excitement I omitted the most important fact. This is Hades – the Unseen, the Invisible, Aidoneus, son of Cronos and Rea, brother of Zeus and Poseidon, He Who Receives Many – usually referred to by mortals as Plouton the Wealth-Giver, lest his anger be aroused.'

'Hades, the King of the Dead?'

'Ruler of the underworld, yes.' Professor Phis raised a finger. 'Where did you say this was found? In Delphi?'

Kriaras nodded.

'I rather doubt it would have been an offering there. Apollo, Lord of Light, had no dealings with Hades.'

The brigadier was thinking about the small group of paganists that had demonstrated against the modern Olympic Games being a travesty of the original sacred festival.

'Do you know anyone who would worship Hades?'

'Nowadays?' The academic's mouth twisted in disgust. 'If you're referring to those lunatic revivalists of Hellenic polytheism, I have no dealings with them.'

Kriaras believed him. The few representatives he had met were several laurel leaves short of a wreath and Phis, for all his wild hair, seemed pretty much the rationalist. 'You said the statue is very rare.'

'Of course. Unlike most of their modern counterparts, the ancient Greeks weren't fools. Not even the most blood-crazed warriors worshipped the Death God, probably because of Homer's depiction of Achilles in the realms of Hades.'

A vague recollection crystallized in the brigadier's mind. 'He said he'd rather be the humblest farm labourer on earth than a ruler of the dead.'

'Very good. Worshipping Hades was a perversion to the overwhelming majority, even of non-citizens and slaves. We know very little about the few cults that existed – for example, there was a temple to the god in Elis, but it was open only once a year and to the priest alone. Who would pray to the bringer of his own end?' Phis gave a crooked smile. 'Apart from this person in Delphi.'

Who's gone to meet Hades without his head, Kriaras thought.

'However, there is another approach to Hades worship.'

'Please enlighten me.'

The professor cackled. 'There is very little light in the realm of the unseen one.' When the brigadier didn't respond, he continued. 'Anyway, Hades as Plouton was worshipped jointly with his wife, Persephone. You remember that myth, I imagine.'

'Persephone daughter of Demeter, the earth goddess, abducted by Hades and forced to stay with him during the winter months?'

'Quite so.'

Nikos Kriaras was interested now. He had remembered something else. 'Weren't there pomegranate seeds in that story?'

Epameinondhas Phis nodded and opened his mouth to give another lecture.

# ELEVEN

Mavros was about half a kilometre away from Kypseli when his phone rang – an unknown Athens number. It was probably Angie Poulou. He stopped and answered. 'I saw you on the TV news. Is Lia in Viotia?'

There was something in her voice that Mavros couldn't put his finger on.

'Did you also see your friend Rovertos Bekakos?' he asked.

'He's not my friend.'

Again, her tone was interesting, though perhaps she meant only that Maria fulfilled that role. Then again, Maria was playing a strange game, meeting Kriaras and also Angie's husband – he was prepared to bet she didn't know about what the Fat Man had seen and heard at the airport.

'Anyway, he was down there because of the protesters at the HMC plant. Why were you there?'

When in doubt, tell the truth, Mavros thought. 'I followed him from his home.'

'You what?' There was no doubt about how Angie Poulou sounded now – scared. 'If he saw you, he'll tell Paschos.'

'He saw me all right. You needn't worry. There's nothing to connect me to you.'

'Maybe not, but he'll start digging. Rovertos is very good at that.'

'That'll explain why he comes to the bauxite works so often then.'

There was a short silence. 'Was that a joke?'

'Not entirely. Tell me, apart from the trip to Kithairon when she disappeared, did Lia often visit Viotia?'

'Occasionally. I keep bees on the slopes of Mount Helicon. She came with me. Sometimes she would go with Paschos to that weird multicoloured town.'

'The inaptly named Paradheisos? There are worse places on the western outskirts of Athens, but you probably haven't seen them. No, you're right. Paradheisos is weird.'

'Have you found anything out about my daughter?'

'To be honest, no. But the investigation's still a live one.'

Angie Poulou sighed. 'Tell me you think Lia's still alive too.'

'Given the amount of money she's worth, I'd have to say she is. Don't give up hope.'

'Thank you,' his client said in a small voice and hung up.

Mavros drove on. He *did* believe Lia was still breathing, even after three months, but what he hadn't told Angie was that the case was getting both complicated and nasty. If the Son was burning and beheading people, it was unlikely to end well. But why would Poulos have hired him? What was the significance of his victims? The trick would be minimising the body count – and he was sure that he'd soon be on the torturer's list. He considered calling Nikos Kriaras, but decided against it. For one thing, he was already involved. For another, it was likely that the brigadier would be calling him after his appearance on the TV.

He drove into Kypseli. It was a pretty village, built round a small curved bay. On the hill behind he could see the bee hives that would have given the place its name dotted over the flank of a low hill. The nearer ones looked in disrepair. There were a few fishing boats tied up beside a wooden pier, but they too were in less than pristine condition. This was a place in decay and it was obvious why – across the larger bay, the dark cloud was pumping from the plant's high chimneys. He could make out a couple of large ships berthed, presumably loading finished aluminium. He wondered how much those cargoes were worth.

Not that the inhabitants of Kypseli were taking it lying down. There had been signs by the roadside objecting to the pollution all the way from Paradheisos. From there, a high headland blocked out the HMC works and the wharf, so the workers could pretend that they lived in rural bliss – apart from the muck in the sky. In Kypseli, almost every building had a banner hanging from its eaves. 'Put your carcinogenic waste in your own garden, Poulo!' read one; another, 'We can't work, we can't even swim – shut down the HMC works!' As he parked in the three-sided square, Mavros realised that he hadn't seen a single person. It was siesta time, but even then there would usually be some sign of life. He got out and looked around. The Ecologists for a Better Viotia office was easy to spot. It was the only building with its door open and people visible inside.

Mavros thought about how to play this. He could either be the ecologist from Athens come to offer support – running the risk of his lack of technical knowledge soon being uncovered – or he could come clean about his profession, without specifying who he was working for. The latter had a pretty obvious downside. As soon as he asked if anyone knew Lia, they'd think he was working for the owner of the plant they hated so much – he couldn't disclose that his client was actually the wife. He would be Mephistopheles to them and they'd clam up tighter than a bent doctor's hand around a bribe. Or they themselves were Lia's kidnappers and the same would happen – or worse. He decided that tweaking the truth was the better part of valour.

He went into the building and was greeted warmly by both

Lykos and Angeliki. The man from the tractor gave him a more
restrained look and went back to painting a banner.

'So, Alex,' Lykos said, after giving him a bottle of water, 'what
brought you down to the Inferno? That's what we call the HMC
plant.'

'Can you keep a secret?'

'We're all friends here,' Angeliki said.

'I'm a private investigator.'

There was an immediate froideur in the room, despite the lack
of air-conditioning. Akis Exarchos went over to the single
computer and tapped at the keyboard.

'And I've been employed to check out Rovertos Bekakos.'

Normal warmth was resumed.

'That bastard,' Lykos said. 'We can give you a bucket-load of
shit on him.'

Mavros smiled. 'I was rather hoping so.'

'Who's your employer?' Angeliki asked, her boldness touching
in its naivety.

'I can't—'

'No, of course he can't, my love,' Lykos said, putting his arm
round her. 'If he *had* given a name, I wouldn't have believed him.'

Mavros nodded, relieved to be off the hook.

'From what I see on the Internet, you're a missing persons
specialist,' Exarchos said.

Mavros tried to trump that, taking a card from his wallet. 'As
you can see, it says "Private Investigations" here. Sure, I do a
lot of missing persons work, but not exclusively.' He went back
to what he had been about to say. It was speculation, but he had
a bad feeling about the lawyer, remembering the way his eyes
had followed the girl down the street outside his office. 'There
are other rumours about Bekakos.'

All three of them were staring at him now.

'For instance, that he has a penchant for underage girls.'

Angeliki turned to Lykos and gave him an unfathomable look.

Lykos shrugged. 'That's no good without proof. He'll have us
shut down in an eye-blink. It's only because my aunt's an MP
– one of the few good ones – that we're still operating.'

Mavros asked who that was and heard the name Tatiana
Roubani, the veteran Communist parliamentarian whom he'd

recently seen on TV. She had been in the student resistance against the dictatorship and had known his brother, Andonis.

'Do you think Bekakos has been preying on the workers' daughters in Paradheisos?' Lykos asked.

Mavros was intrigued by the activist's question. Could his guess be right?

'Have you heard anything of the sort?' he asked

'Actually, I have.'

Mavros disguised his unease. Could that be what had happened to Lia Poulou? A pederast kidnapping his employer and friend's daughter, then successfully dissembling during the search for her? Had he abused local girls too? That was vile enough to have the ring of possibility, considering the lawyer's visits to the area. But his wife had been with him on many of those. Was she in on it?

'Yes,' Lykos said. 'A girl of fourteen. We run a workshop in Paradheisos two evenings a week, even though the mayor – who works for the company, of course – has tried to stop it and we have to change venue all the time. But there are good people in the town. Some of the HMC workers, especially the wives who aren't employed at the plant, are worried about the pollution.' He turned to his partner. 'She spoke to Angeliki.'

The young woman's face reddened as she picked up the story. 'The bastard. He scared the poor girl out of her skin. She didn't have it in her to speak to her parents, but somehow we got through to her on the ecological side. She stayed behind and started crying when we asked if we could help. Then it all poured out.' She glanced at Lykos. 'It's one of the reasons we raised the profile of our activities. And that piece of shit was in the middle of things today.'

'I'd have killed him,' Akis Exarchos said, shaking his head. 'But you and that cop turned up and Angeliki told me to hold back.'

'That would have ruined us,' Lykos said. 'The media would have portrayed us as terrorists and the plant would have gone on spewing out its filth.'

'Yes, but did the girl identify Bekakos?'

'Not by name,' Angeliki said. 'But she described someone who resembles him and we know he was in Paradheisos that day.'

'Come on, my love,' Lykos said. 'You know it was him.'

'When was this?' Mavros asked.

'She was a bit vague about the date,' Angeliki replied. 'Around the beginning of June.'

Mavros dropped his gaze. 'What did he do to her?'

'He didn't actually rape her,' Angeliki said. 'But he got her clothes off. There was more, but she wouldn't say.'

'Definitely enough to get him arrested,' Mavros said. 'Where did it happen?'

'In her home, would you believe? The father, an HMC forklift driver, was on shift and the mother was in the corner shop she runs.'

'No siblings?'

Angeliki raised her head in the standard negative way.

'It was early evening,' Lykos said, 'still light. Maybe someone saw his expensive car.'

'But will they talk?' Angeliki said doubtfully.

'They might,' Mavros said. 'I might be able to offer an inducement.' He didn't give details. He needed time to think.

Silence fell. Akis went back to his painting.

'So,' Lykos said, 'have you got anything to give us on Bekakos, Alex?'

It was payback time. Mavros played the only card he had. 'I know he's been down here with his wife offering people deals if they agree not to sue the company. I was hoping you could help me out with that.'

'Fair enough,' Lykos said. 'The simple fact is that there's been an increasing number of deaths from cancer in Paradheisos and Kypseli over the last five years.' He glanced at the man with the banners. 'Akis's wife Yiorgia was a recent victim.'

'My commiserations,' Mavros said.

The thin-faced man raised his head and studied him, before murmuring thanks. He had a hungry look and Mavros didn't fancy his chances if he got on his wrong side.

'The thing is,' Lykos continued, 'bauxite mining and processing needn't be anything like as damaging to the environment as it has been here, especially in the last few years. If you look at the mountains in Viotia and Fokidha, you'll see access roads for the heavy equipment all over them, serious deforestation – with all the consequences that has for the general environment – and great heaps of waste from the mining. Until recent changes in the law, it was mostly strip mining on the surface, but now there's underground work going on too.'

Mavros frowned. 'None of that sounds like it would cause a spike in cancer rates.'

'No,' the young man said, 'but the plant across the water is another story. It was supposed to be cutting edge technology when it opened back in the Sixties, but people didn't care about damage to the land and air quality back then. The bauxite ore is heated in pressure vessels and combined with sodium hydroxide – a dangerous chemical that's also used as drain cleaner. There should be effective filters, but what do you think?' He pointed to the dirty cloud above the bay.

Akis Exarchos came over. 'The problems really started when the Greek Mining Corporation was taken over by Poulos A.E. ten years ago. They're only interested in cutting costs and increasing profits, not in looking after the workers and the rest of us who live in the area. You'll have noticed the different coloured houses in Paradheisos.'

Mavros nodded.

'We've been gathering information. Over eighty per cent of the cancers and other lethal medical conditions have been suffered by people who live in the white houses, those nearest the shore.'

'The ordinary workers,' Mavros said.

'And their families. You'll have seen the red tinge in the water too. The company claims that the residues it discharges into the bay are non-toxic.'

'And, of course,' Lykos said, 'it has the chemists to prove it, as well as the clout in Brussels to satisfy EU inspectors. But the whole story has never been allowed to get out. That's what we're going to broadcast to the world.'

Mavros admired the activists and was sorry for the local man who had lost his wife, but he didn't give much for their chances against a human bulldozer like Paschos Poulos. And he still had to find the missing Lia.

'Do you think the girl Rovertos Bekakos abused would talk to me?'

Angeliki looked at him gravely. 'I don't know. Wouldn't your time be better spent gathering material about the bastard's involvement in covering up the polluting of Viotia?'

Mavros saw he had to be careful. 'I'll take anything I can get on that count too, don't worry.'

Lykos drew his partner aside and they spoke in low voices.

'All right,' Angeliki said. 'I'll take you to see her this evening. But you must promise to be sensitive.'

Mavros nodded distractedly. He'd just noticed what looked like an ancient statue of a solemn woman or goddess in a niche at the rear of the room. Tendrils from a plant in a pot had wound themselves around her robed lower body and there were bowls of dried seeds and fresh fruit next to her.

The Fat Man, forced to sit with the Peugeot's engine turned off as he watched the Bekakos house, kept falling in and out of a sweat-drenched sleep. Although the wide street was lined by eucalyptus trees, they didn't give him enough cover. He considered calling Alex and telling him he was going home, but he was unwilling to do that. He was on the job and he had to be prepared for all it threw at him. That included thirst – he'd emptied the two large bottles of water he'd brought; the need to urinate – he'd refilled one of the bottles; and, inevitably, hunger. His stomach was rumbling like a landslide. And then, when the sun had at last gone behind the tallest of the trees, the gate opened and Maria Bekakou's silver Mercedes nosed out. Yiorgos started his engine and turned the air conditioning up to full. There was no discernible difference until they were well down Kifissias Avenue, on the way to the city centre.

The likelihood was that the target was going to her shop in Kolonaki. The Fat Man began to worry about where he would park in the narrow streets of the rich people's quarter, but then the Merc took a left without indicating and he just managed to follow before the traffic lights changed. They were in a residential area around a couple of hospitals, which would make parking even more difficult. Two cars ahead of him, the Mercedes suddenly braked. Its hazard warning lights started flashing and then the white reversing light came on as Mrs Bekakou skilfully manoeuvred into a space.

'Typical luck of the thieving class,' Yiorgos roared, slamming a hand on the steering wheel. He tried to drive past slowly to see where she would go, but a fool in a 4x4 blew his horn repeatedly and he had to go to the end of the street. It took him ten minutes to find a space and he had to walk as fast as he could for nearly ten more before he was back at the Mercedes coupé. Fortunately, it was still there. Unfortunately, he had no clue where the driver was.

The Fat Man hung around in a doorway opposite, drawing looks from two old ladies that suggested they thought he was a rogue elephant. As the light began to fail, the sounds from his stomach were almost as loud as the traffic from the nearby avenue. He considered dashing to find a shop, but was glad he hadn't as the door to a block of flats across the street opened and then closed. Maria Bekakou walked the few metres to her car, got in and drove away. Yiorgos was powerless to follow, but realised there was still something he could do. He crossed the road and went to the door to examine the names by the bell buttons. None of them meant anything to him. He took out the notebook and pencil he had provided himself with, then wrote down the address and all the names. There was a selection of common ones including a Papadhopoulos, a Savalas and an Athanasiadhou.

Then he saw one that made him stifle a laugh because of the juxtaposition of a lengthy first name with ancient heritage and a brief, unusual surname. Epameinondhas Phis. He wouldn't forget that in a hurry.

# TWELVE

Mavros was sitting in a rickety chair at a desk in the Ecologists for a Better Viotia office reading the group's pamphlets, when a car he immediately recognised drew up outside. It was Rovertos Bekakos's dark blue Porsche. He got out from the driver's side with a briefcase, while a man mountain with short dark hair struggled to extricate himself from the passenger seat. The lawyer waited impatiently, then led his companion in.

Mavros took the opportunity to examine the alleged paedophile at close range. Bekakos looked cool and composed in his light business suit, his features more relaxed than they had been at the blockade, but there was tension about him, as if springs were about to erupt from his flesh. He ran his eyes round the room, taking in Lykos, Angeliki and Akis, then he glanced at Mavros with barely suppressed amusement.

'So, you idealistic idiots,' he said, 'you've hired a whore from Athens.'

Mavros didn't react, his eyes on the heavy behind his master, bulky arms folded.

'You think we have the funds to pay people, Bekako?' Angeliki said, her eyes wide.

Lykos touched the back of her hand briefly. 'Is there something we can do for you?'

'I think so.' The lawyer opened his case and took out a sheaf of papers. 'This is for you. A court order, duly signed and stamped, requiring you and your organisation' – he spoke the word with heavy irony – 'to desist immediately from any activity that impedes work at the HMC plant. That specifically refers to blocking the road – I do hope you enjoyed your little stunt earlier today because it'll be the last one – as well as to harassing HMC workers in any way.' He narrowed his eyes. 'Such harassment includes importuning personnel and talking to them or their family members.'

'What?' Angeliki shouted. 'You can't do that!'

Bekakos turned pages and pointed to a paragraph. 'You'll see that the judge specifically stipulates those activities. You will also desist from holding meetings – what I believe you misleadingly refer to as workshops – in Paradheisos which, as you well know, is HMC property. You will immediately stop erecting signs, hoardings, banners or any other sort of propaganda in the town.' He turned to the last pages of the document. 'The penalties for disregarding the order are laid out here, here and here. Heavy fines and imprisonment.' He handed it to Lykos. 'You are now officially in receipt of the order, as my colleague Mr Kloutsis has witnessed.'

Mavros looked at the gorilla, who had taken several photos with a mobile phone. 'You moved quickly,' he observed to the lawyer.

'Never unprepared – that's my motto, Mr Mavro.' Bekakos peered at him as if he were a rare zoological specimen. 'What brings you to these parts?'

'What do you think?'

The lawyer gave him the eye for a few more seconds, then turned to the door. 'I have more important things to direct my mind towards,' he said, nodding at the big man.

'You won't get away with this!' Angeliki yelled after him.

Rovertos Bekakos stopped and looked over his shoulder. 'I already have, young woman.' He gave a dry laugh and left.

Lykos took Angeliki in his arms and comforted her as she started to sob. Akis Exarchos went up and patted them both on their shoulders.

'You can fight it,' Mavros said.

'Of course we *could*,' Lykos said. 'But we don't have the deep pockets of Poulos A.E. I'll talk to my aunt and see if she can raise it in Parliament, but big business and its stooges in government don't pay attention to the Communists much these days.'

'It's a success,' Akis said, smiling grimly. 'I mean, we finally got them to declare war. What was it Alexander the Great said? "There's nothing impossible to those who would try"? I learned that at primary school.'

Angeliki wiped her eyes with the palm of her hand. 'Bravo, Aki. If they want to fight dirty, we'll do the same.'

Lykos shook his head. 'It's essential we don't break the law. Our legitimacy – and that of the whole ecological movement – is founded on the observation of existing legal codes.'

'Then you will be beaten,' Akis said, clenching his fists. 'I'll do anything to make them pay for Yiorgia's death.' He gave the activists a baleful look as he walked to the door.

Mavros sat down and thought about how to proceed. Having heard about the alleged child abuse and seen Rovertos Bekakos close up again, he felt sure that Paschos Poulos's lawyer was the key to finding the missing daughter. It was unclear whether Poulos was being deceived by Bekakos and his wife, or whether he too was in some way involved in Lia's disappearance. For the time being, that was immaterial. What he had to do was probe Bekakos's weak point. At least the court order didn't stop him going to Paradheisos.

'You'll have to call the girl and talk her into seeing me on my own,' he said to Angeliki.

She looked at her watch. 'In an hour. It's still siesta time.'

'OK. In the meantime, can I see your website? I'm guessing you have a forum for debate.'

The ecologists looked at each other.

'What about it?' Lykos asked.

'I think Bekakos and his sidekicks will have been infiltrating your set-up.'

Angeliki stared at him. 'We're not complete idiots. You think we haven't considered that? Everyone has to submit their personal details and email address for vetting.'

Mavros hid his interest in the last statement. He had been wondering if Lia Poulou was a 'secret' ecologist. Maybe she was horrified by what her father's company was doing in Viotia. But Kriaras's officers had her computer. If they'd found she'd had dealings with Ecologists for a Better Viotia, surely they would have been all over the group.

'Have the police ever shown up in the last three or four months?' he asked Lykos.

'Until today at the blockade, no. Why?'

Mavros shrugged. 'It wouldn't be beyond Poulos A.E. to set tame cops on you.'

'That's why they employ Bekakos,' Angeliki said.

Lykos waved him over to the computer. 'Here, I've brought up our discussion group membership list.'

'Thanks.' Mavros ran down it, not sure what he was looking for. If Lia Poulou had got in touch, it could have been from someone else's computer and with a cover name and details. Would he be able to spot those? The alternative would be grinding his way through the debates to see if any text struck him as having been written by her. That wasn't an inviting prospect.

'Have you actually met any of these people?' he asked Lykos, who was handing round pieces of fruit.

'I don't know.'

Mavros raised an eyebrow. 'Don't you have volunteers coming down to help?'

'At weekends and on holidays, yes. But we don't encourage

online supporters to reveal their real identities.' The young man tapped the side of his nose. 'Basic security.'

'Really? Surely that makes it easier for your group to be penetrated.'

Angeliki stepped forward. 'Volunteers in person have to fill in forms when they arrive. We take photos of them as well.'

'Is that right? Could I see them?'

There was a muttered conference and then Lykos went to the back room, returning with a box file.

Mavros went through the enrollment sheets. Although the people were mainly young, none was anything close to fourteen and none resembled Lia.

'What age do people have to be to participate?'

'Eighteen,' Lykos replied. 'We used to allow kids but, though they're keen, there's too much trouble when the parents kick up shit.'

'When did you give up on them?'

'Over a year ago.'

He finished the list and went back to the top. There were more females than males, many of them from the Athens-Piraeus conurbation. He knew that Lia was a good student. Was she also a smartarse? Could she have changed sex online? If so, what masculine name might she have chosen?

At second glance, a user name and email address made him sit up: LaiosGoodNews and laios.goodnews@yoo.com. The server was one of the transglobal companies that provided addresses to anyone with Internet access. The first half was the interesting bit. Laios – Laïos in Greek – was the mythical King of Thebes, father of Oedipus. To avoid a curse that the child would kill his sire, Oedipus was sent for exposure on Mount Kithairon. Mavros felt a stirring in his gut. That was where the burned body had been found. The boy was rescued and later did indeed kill his father. Mavros's memory for myth was good – he'd been fascinated by the subject as a child. The place where Laios was murdered was at the junction of three roads, one that was still pointed out to tourists. It was about fifteen kilometres from where he now was – the road from Thebes met those that led to Delphi and, via Dhistomo, to Paradheisos and the HMC works. More to the point, the first three letters of Laios were in

Lia's name, which was a diminutive of Evangelia, meaning 'good news'. The missing girl *was* a smartarse.

Mavros looked at the data that had been provided. There was a postal address in Piraeus, which he ran through a search engine and found did not exist. The phone number rang unobtainable when he tried it. She had made things up. He went into the Ecologists for a Better Viotia forum and tried to access LaiosGoodNews. The site showed that the user had logged in several times in February, March and April, but had never made a contribution.

Sitting back, Mavros thought about what he'd discovered. Nothing very useful. Then again, it appeared that the missing girl had been interested enough in the activities of the ecologists in the area where her father controlled a large plant to fake an identity. Maybe she had been a secret ecologist after all. But would that have driven her father or his slimy lawyer to hide her away or worse? It seemed unlikely, especially since they had apparently employed the Son to find her. He had another thought. Could Lykos and Angeliki have worked out who Lia was, as he had done, and contacted her some other way?

His phone rang. As he answered it, he realised that night had almost fallen.

'How goes it?' he said to the Fat Man.

'Wonderful. I lost the cow.'

Mavros listened to his friend's tale of woe. He got a shock when Yiorgos ran through the names of the people in the apartment block Maria Bekakou had come out of. 'Phis?' he repeated.

'Yes, Epameinondhas Phis. Crazy name, eh?'

'Not only that. I heard Rovertos Bekakos mention the surname to his wife when I was watching them.'

'So she went to see him, obviously.'

'I'd guess so. See what you can find out about Phis. I wouldn't worry about Maria Bekakou,' he said. 'She probably went home after visiting him, or to her shop.'

'Or she could have driven to the hideout where she and her husband have stashed our missing girl.'

'Unlikely – though possible, I suppose. Listen, I can't talk. I'll probably stay down here tonight.'

'You've got leads? I'm on my way.'

'Whoah! I might still make it back, but it'll be late. If I don't, I'll talk to you first thing.'

'Huh. I'm making *imam bayildi*.' The Fat Man knew very well that 'the imam fainted', a dish of aubergines stuffed with onion, garlic and tomato, was one of Mavros's favourites.

'Don't eat it all.' Mavros commanded, then rang off.

Epameinondhas Phis, he thought. The name meant something, but there was no time to follow it up because Angeliki was calling the girl in Paradheisos. He couldn't keep his knowledge of ancient history down, though. The most famous Epameinondhas was the great Theban general who defeated the Spartans at Leuctra in the fourth century BC – and Leuctra, modern Lefktra, lay in the foothills of Mount Kithairon, near where the burned man had been found.

Another coincidence, Mavros told himself. Eternal Greece had a habit of screwing you that way.

The Son finished his routine of five times fifty press-ups and fifty stomach crunches. The floor of the cheap hotel in Thiva was tacky and he had laid a towel under his naked body. The Father used to laugh at his fitness regime, saying all a true torturer needed was his equipment and the ability to terrify his victim. But the truth was, the Son had never really been interested in causing pain. Of course, he did it if he had to, as in the cases of the burned man, the eyeless woman in Trikkala, and the *phylax* who'd lost his head in Delphi. The Son was actually relieved when they'd refused to disclose where the girl was. That meant he could deprive them of life, which was what he really enjoyed.

In the two years he'd been out of Greece, he had come to realise that the Father was hidebound and old-fashioned. The old fool even believed in the rubbish the dictators had peddled of a Greece for Christian Greeks, even though he'd been happy enough to work as the Chiotis family enforcer for years, doing things that were neither civilised nor Christian. What would the old fool think of the influx of foreigners, especially those who had worked on the venues for the Olympic Games? He'd been proud that the festivities were coming back to Athens and had hit the Son across the face when he'd expressed contempt. Anyone with a brain knew that the Games would provide vast profits for Greek business interests and their political marionettes, but would tie a vast weight round the country's never healthy economy. What was the city in Canada that had been paying off its Olympic debt decades later?

Not that he cared. From an early age, he had set himself in silent opposition to the tyrant. He had learned everything he could and then left the country to avoid arrest. In his time abroad, he'd expanded his skills and was now capable of anything a single operator could achieve. His reputation had grown in the circles where such work was prized and, given the intrinsic lawlessness of the wealthy in his home country, he'd been sure it would only be a matter of time till he was called back, with immunity from prosecution guaranteed.

The Son stood in the shower and let the cold water course over him for ten minutes. During that time he cleared his head – a trick the Bulgarian assassin had taught him – and thought only of the split-second when life ended: the final flicker of eyelids, the last shallow breath, the abbreviated cry or cough as bullet or blade penetrated vital organ. He looked down. As usual he was erect, but he did nothing about it. Do-it-yourself sex wasn't for him.

Flaccid by the time he had finished towelling himself down, the Son walked out of the bathroom and turned on the TV. The news bulletins were the usual dreary mixture of politicians shouting at each other, journalists trying without success to be witty and moderators whose plastic surgery had failed big time. He flicked from channel to channel, registering little, then felt a jab of surprise and went back to one of the state channels. There was no doubt about it. The long-haired piece of shit standing on top of a trailer in the middle of a demonstration was Alex Mavros. The Son grabbed a pen and took notes on the first page of the Gideon's Bible – how the Father would have cursed him.

Mavros, the HMC plant near Paradheisos, Ecologists for a Better Viotia, and the snake who had acted as go-between – Rovertos Bekakos looked unhappy. On the contrary, the Son was ecstatic. He'd been planning on catching up with the private investigator who had driven him from his home country after the last case with the Father. Maybe he wouldn't have to wait much longer.

The call from his employer came on time. Truly the God the Father had believed in moved in curious ways. They wanted him to deal with the young male ecologist he'd just seen on the screen, after ascertaining if he knew where the missing girl was. They also wanted to know what Alex Mavros had been doing at the demonstration. However, the PI was not to be harmed.

The Son would see about that.

Telemachos Xanthakos was unimpressed. He'd got back to his office in Livadheia to find a message from the chief summoning him along the corridor immediately. He was then given a tongue-lashing for failing to intervene effectively at the HMC protest. Why hadn't he called for backup? Why hadn't he arrested the ring leaders? Why were the Ecologists for a Better Viotia even operating in the prefecture? He'd been tempted to reply that it would have been pretty odd if Ecologists for a Better Viotia had been going about their business in, say, Fokidha, but he managed to restrain himself. The commissioner was known as Vesuvius – he rumbled and puffed, but very rarely erupted into full-blown action. Xanthakos made a reasoned case in his defence and managed to calm the old man down.

'They watch these things in Athens, you know,' his boss said.

That was what this was about. Xanthakos had seen the TV crews, who'd presumably been tipped off by the protesters. Some king pin in the Public Order Ministry must have pulled the commissioner's chain.

'What was it really like down there, Telemache? Sit down, for God's sake.'

'Well, the workers were unhappy, especially those trying to get home after their shift. The protesters were serious, though, and I thought it better to keep a low profile. Backup wouldn't have made much difference, considering the tailback and the lack of room for manoeuvre. As for arresting the ecologists, we can do that whenever you like. They blocked a public highway, for a start.'

'I think their activities have been successfully curtailed by Mr Bekakos.'

'The HMC lawyer? I saw him at the blockade. He signalled to the driver of a bulldozer to crash into the tractor and trailer. People could have been injured. Actually, I considered arresting him.'

The commissioner went into pre-eruption mode, his face redder than a prime Boeotian tomato. 'You did WHAT? Are you out of your mind? You know how important the bauxite plant is to the local economy. We treat its executives and their officials with the smoothest of kid gloves. Do you understand?'

Xanthakos stood up. 'Yes, sir. Is there anything else?'

'There is. I hear a private investigator by the name of Mavros was nosing around at the demonstration. Make sure you keep an eye on him.'

The deputy commissioner saluted, though it wasn't the usual form when they were on their own, and went back to his office. He had never actually met Rovertos Bekakos, but he'd seen the chief bowing and curtseying to him when the plant hosted open days and festivities. The lawyer always stuck close to Paschos Poulos and his English wife. That reminded him. He'd read that Bekakos and his wife had been going around the white houses in Paradheisos. A disaffected worker whose wife had died of cancer and who had subsequently lost his job – and his right to live in the town – had complained that they'd tried to buy his silence. Xanthakos hadn't paid much attention as Paradheisos was generally off limits.

That was going to change. He didn't like being smacked around by the chief and he definitely didn't like the Athenian lawyer. On the other hand, Alex Mavros had struck him as a reasonable human being. He would take a drive down to Paradheisos in the evening and sniff around – even though he knew that would make his nostrils burn. There was something about the place that struck him as beyond strange. Besides, he'd been given a direct order to check up on the private eye.

# THIRTEEN

Lykos and Angeliki offered to come with Mavros to Paradheisos, but he told them not to put themselves at risk so soon after the court order had been served. He had a feeling that the muscleman Kloutsis and others like him would be out in force. The question was, how was he going to get into the town without being spotted?

'Your best bet is to leave your car here,' Angeliki said, pointing to the map on the wall. 'A line of trees and bushes marks the town boundary and they're pretty thick. If you walk up the watercourse here, you'll be able to slip through at the end of Themistokleous. Ourania's house is halfway down. You've got till eleven, when her mother closes the shop.'

'I won't need that long,' Mavros said. 'I don't want to stress the poor girl out.'

Lykos nodded. 'She's still very vulnerable.'

Mavros looked at him. 'You did a great job convincing her to see me.'

The young man gave him an admonitory glare. 'Just make sure you don't make it worse for her, you hear?'

'I'll try not to. I've got a voice recorder in the car, so all she has to do is tell her story.' He raised a hand towards the statue in the niche. 'Who is that?'

'Demeter,' Lykos said. 'Goddess of the earth and fertility.'

'The second part I knew,' Mavros said, smiling. 'And I can see her relevance to ecology. But there's more to her, isn't there?' He had decided to press the pair of them. He was almost certain they had nothing to do with Lia Poulou's disappearance – they wore their hearts very much on the short sleeves of their T-shirts – but he wanted to be sure, though he also had to be careful not to give the game away.

'What do you mean?' Angeliki asked suspiciously. 'She is the greatest of powers on the surface of the earth, the provider of food and fuel. Without the Green Lady's munificence, humans would not survive.'

Mavros had an acute sense of religious faith, probably because he didn't possess any himself. The offerings around the statue suggested some form of worship. He wasn't sure what significance that might have, but he pressed on.

'Demeter,' he said, 'if memory serves, was only effective for between a third and half of the year because her daughter Persephone was stolen away by Hades and taken to the underworld.'

'She was *raped*,' Angeliki said, sudden tears dulling the brightness of her eyes. 'The myths still speak to us, they enshrine the eternal truths. Men abuse girls and women, they overwhelm them physically and treat them as little more than slaves.'

'Well, it's not exactly so—' Lykos broke off when he saw the set of his partner's jaw.

'It's exactly like that,' she said, her voice shrill. 'It was in earliest times and it continues to be so. What's Alex going to talk to Ourania about?'

Mavros and the young man exchanged glances.

'So, are you one of those ancient religion revivalists?'

'We both are,' Lykos said. 'Does that disturb you?'

'No, I don't have any issue with religions that bring comfort to their followers and do no harm to others.' Mavros smiled. 'The problem is, I've never come across one of those.'

Lykos took Angeliki's hand. 'We worship Demeter and we do what we can to protect the precious earth.'

'What about Persephone?'

'We worship the Maiden too,' Angeliki said fiercely. 'Her return from the underground realms stimulates Demeter's fertility.'

Mavros decided to go for broke. 'So, since Persephone was married to Hades by Zeus's command, you must also worship the death god.'

Lykos gave him a cold look. 'No one gives offerings to the lord beneath the earth, no one who is a true Olympian believer. We do not even speak his name.'

'Sorry,' Mavros said emolliently. 'I'm an amateur in these matters.' He looked out the open door and across the dark water to the lights of the bauxite plant. 'I seem to remember that Hades was also known as Plouton because the bounty of the earth – minerals and so on – belongs to him. That would have given you another reason to oppose the HMC. The company is despoiling not just Demeter's top soil but Hades's wealth deep down.'

'That's very clever,' Lykos said, 'but, as I said, we don't concern ourselves with that murky deity.'

'Persephone is the ultimate symbol of female suffering,' Angeliki added. 'In the winter I cry for her every night.'

Mavros nodded. The activists were pretty low on his list of suspects.

Lord of the desolate regions and the darkness, great Hades, Aidoneus, grant us your favour in this most testing of times. The forces of ruination are all around, killing our fellow worshippers as well as destroying the land for short-lived profit. You, too, kidnapped a maiden, blameless Persephone, who is now and for every winter your dread queen. We know you will not turn your face from us. We have broken the laws of men, but we feel no shame because the justice of our purpose is manifest. The Maiden herself accepted your suit, despite her longing for the lovely light of day and the green domains of her mother. She consumed seeds of the pomegranate and was condemned to a dual life, part with you in the echoing halls of the dead and part as an essential life force on the surface of the earth.

Great Plouton, richest of all gods, give us your leave to bring our plans to fruition. We know you will protect us, son of Cronos, brother of Zeus, because no other god can gainsay you in your realm. Receiver of All Shades, grant us more time on earth to achieve our ends, which we know are yours too. Then we will contentedly follow Hermes Psychopompos as he leads our souls to your dominion for eternity.

Accept now the black blood of this animal and the dark vintage as a libation, great Hades. We are your servants and we will die before revealing the secrets you have entrusted us with.

Hail, Aidoneus.


Mavros drove in the dark along the coastal road and parked the Citroen by the trees, as he'd been instructed. He took the voice recorder from the bag he'd placed under the passenger seat and closed the door quietly. The lights of Paradheisos shone through the foliage. He walked up the incline, counting the streets. When he got to the fourth, he pushed through the bushes under the eucalyptus trees and looked around. There was no one to be seen. He moved swiftly across the road that led to the higher parts of the town – the yellow and pink houses of the more senior workers – and checked the street sign. He was at Themistokleous. He walked down the pavement under bitter orange trees and found number 15. The detached houses had been built in island style – flat roofs, corniced windows and pergolas over terraces. This one seemed to be well cared for, the bougainvillea tendrils pruned and the lower fronds of a five-metre palm tree cut right back. Apart from the light on the terrace, Mavros could see no sign of illumination inside. Had the girl taken fright and left?

The doorbell had been taped over. He knocked quietly on the door, glancing over his shoulder to see if he was being observed. There were lights in the houses across the street, but no one was at the windows. Then he heard the sound of flip-flops on stone tiles.

'Who is it?' came a timid voice.

'Alex Mavros, Ourania. Angeliki told you I was coming.'

The door opened slightly and he saw a girl of medium height and build, her jet black hair tied back. She was wearing jeans and a long-sleeved blouse buttoned up to her neck, an outfit that must have been uncomfortable considering the ambient temperature. Her brown eyes were wide open and her hands trembled.

Mavros gave her a tentative smile. 'It's better if people don't see me,' he said.

Ourania came back to herself. 'Yes. Come in.'

He followed her into a sparsely decorated hall, the only furniture a small table with a mirror above it.

'We should sit in the kitchen,' the girl said. 'The trees at the back of the yard mean it isn't overlooked.'

'Fine.' He followed her to the rear of the house. There was a smell of food – stuffed tomatoes – but the feel of the place, tidy but characterless, was more that of a hotel than a home. He remembered that the workers were only temporary residents, the houses owned by the HMC.

Ourania turned on an air-conditioning unit and sat down at the bare wooden table. 'Would you like something to drink?' she asked, her eyes off him.

'No, that's all right.' Mavros angled his head to catch her gaze. 'I'm here to help,' he said. 'Don't be frightened.'

The girl looked away again. 'Lykos said . . . said you want to ask me about . . . about *him*.'

Mavros had intended approaching the reason for his visit more circumspectly, but he respected Ourania's desire to get it over.

'I'm going to record what you say. Is that all right?'

She looked uncertain, but nodded.

He took the recorder from his shirt pocket and turned it on. Then he opened his mobile phone and clicked to a photo of Rovertos Bekakos that he'd taken at the protest.

'Is this the man who abused you?' he asked gently.

Ourania took one look and then lowered her head. 'Yes,' she said, trying to hold back sobs.

'Do you know his name?'

The girl got up and took a roll of kitchen paper from beside the sink. She used a piece to soak up her tears. 'It's Mr . . . Bekakos.'

'Mr Rovertos Bekakos?'

'Yes,' she said, almost whispering.

'The lawyer who represents the HMC, where your father works?'

'Yes.'

'Ourania, I have to ask you to tell me exactly what happened. And, first of all, when?'

The girl kept her head down and started to speak in a level voice, as if the only way she could describe her experience was to remove all emotional affect.

'June – the first or second, I think. I went blank for some days afterwards. I was doing my homework in my room upstairs and there was a knock at the door. The bell broke months ago and the company electrician never came round to fix it. Dad eventually put tape over the button. I thought it might be my friend Yiota, so I ran down and opened the door.' She paused.

Mavros got up and poured her a glass of water from a bottle by the window. 'Take your time,' he said.

After drinking, Ourania lowered her head again and recommenced her narrative. '*He* was there.'

'Rovertos Bekakos?' he clarified.

'Yes. He smiled at me and asked if my parents were in. He said something about important company business. I told him Dad was on shift and Mum was in the shop. He smiled again and asked if he could wait. I said I would call Mum and he said there was no reason, he was quite happy to stay with a pretty girl like me . . .' She broke off. 'I don't why I didn't do something, but it was like I was under a spell. He asked me if he could see my bedroom, said something about helping me with my homework. I took him upstairs. It was when he closed the door behind him that I realised I was in trouble. He said, "Don't be shy, young lady. I'm not going to hurt you". But I could see the . . . the lump in his trousers. I'm not stupid. The boys at school are always messing about, but they never touch us. He did. He held me by the arm and unbuttoned my blouse. Then he put . . . put his hand inside my . . . my bra. He told me I was nearly a woman, not a girl any more. And women like to do things to men. Before I could react – I couldn't move – he'd taken all my clothes off.' She stopped and lowered her head to the table top. She started to weep.

Mavros knew there was nothing he could say to comfort her and that touching her was impossible. He waited and then said, 'Ourania, this is terrible. Rovertos Bekakos has committed a serious crime. We have to catch him before he does the same or worse to other girls.'

After wiping her face, the girl started talking again. 'He touched me . . . down there. Then he unzipped his trousers and took . . . it out.' Suddenly she raised her head and stared at Mavros. 'Men are pigs!' she said. 'Pigs!' Then she started crying again.

He sat there squirming, overwhelmed with disgust for his gender.

Eventually Ourania took up her story, talking quickly. 'He told me to kiss it. I couldn't move. He grabbed me by the back of the head and . . . and put my lips on it. Then he . . . he finished on me, all over my chest, my . . .'

Mavros swallowed back the bitter liquid that had risen to his mouth.

'He made me wipe it up and watched me have a shower. Then he told me to get dressed and he said, "If you tell anyone – anyone, you hear? – your father will lose his job, your mother will lose the shop and you will all have to leave Paradheisos". He put his hands round my neck, but he didn't press hard. He just laughed. He said, "And wherever you go, one of my associates," – that's what he called them, I didn't understand at first – "one of my associates will find you and snuff out your life like a candle. Pft!"'.'

Ourania stopped talking abruptly. She was panting and Mavros pushed the glass of water towards her. She drank thirstily and glanced at him.

'Was that . . . all right?'

'You did very well,' he said. 'I'm so sorry. I promise I'll make him pay.'

'But what about Dad's job and the shop – Mum only has a lease on it?'

Mavros put the recorder in his back pocket. 'Don't worry. I'll be very careful.' He stood up, then remembered the long shot he had thought of earlier. He opened his phone again and found the photo he had taken of an image supplied by Angie Poulou.

'Have you ever seen this girl?' he asked. He didn't have much hope, but it was worth a try.

Ourania squinted at it. 'Yes, I know her. I only met her once, though.'

Mavros took a deep breath. 'Where? When?'

'At one of the Ecologists for a Better Viotia workshops. It must have been in April, after the Easter holidays. They're usually on weekday evenings, but this one was on a Saturday – I remember because I missed basketball training. I think her name was Lia. She was nice. We sat next to each other and did a project about soil erosion.'

'Can you remember anything else about her?'

Ourania sat back, her brow furrowed. 'No . . . wait, yes. She was wearing a gold chain with a pomegranate on it. I know, because I didn't recognise it and I asked her what it was.'

Persephone's fatal fruit, Mavros thought. 'Did you see who she came and left with?'

'Oh, yes,' the girl said, as if the answer was obvious. 'She was with Angeliki and Lykos.'

Mavros thanked her and praised her courage, then left the house. He didn't know what to make of the missing girl being with the ecologists. Could that mean they had taken her a fortnight later, or talked her into absconding? Would confronting them with what he had learned put her in greater danger? He couldn't be sure.

It was only as he approached the road by the trees that he realised he was being followed – and by more than one person.

The Varousi quarter of Trikkala had been quiet as the evening darkened, the local children drifting back to their homes. It had been a hot day even by the standards of Thessaly, one of the hottest areas of Greece in part because it was far from the coast and its cooling winds. The mountains had been blurred by a heat haze all day and people had stayed indoors as much as possible. There were the Olympics to watch.

Malamo Christakou, eighty-nine but still spry, hadn't even been able to sit in her Ottoman-style enclosed wooden balcony. The stench had been building as the days passed and now it was beyond bearing. She'd called the town council. The woman there said most workers were on holiday and, anyway, if there wasn't rubbish on the street, she didn't know what she could do. Eventually Malamo, who had outlived her husband and sons and had no grandchildren, called the police. They had shown little interest, but said they'd send an officer round if they could find one. To Malamo's astonishment, a patrol car drove up the narrow street shortly after nine o'clock and stopped outside her house. She went downstairs as fast as she could and got the front door just after the bell was rung.

'Good evening, Madam,' said a fresh-faced young man in a pale blue short-sleeved shirt and dark blue trousers, putting on his peaked cap.

'Good evening, my boy,' Malamo said, unable to take her eyes off the huge pistol on his belt. 'Can you smell it?'

The officer raised his nose and inhaled. 'Em, yes, that certainly is unpleasant.'

'Look up there,' the old woman said, pointing to the partially open window on the second floor. 'I'm sure that's where it's coming from.'

'Do you know the occupant?'

'Not really. A lady from Athens, I think. She inherited it, but she's hardly ever here. I certainly haven't seen her recently.' She signalled to the policeman and he lowered his head towards her mouth. 'I heard she's a university professor.'

The young man received that information with less reverence than Malamo expected. She had only finished primary school and, to her, people who taught in universities were superhuman, especially if they were female.

'I don't suppose you have a key, Madam.'

'Me? Of course not, my child.'

'All right. Stand back, please.'

Malamo watched as the policeman went to the door and knocked. She had noticed the curious knocker and often wondered what it was – it looked like those weights that men raised to make their arms thicker, or perhaps a thunderbolt. Then she heard the sound of the handle turning.

'The door was open, Madam,' the young man said, as if that was significant.

'I'll have a quick look.'

Malamo waited impatiently. It must have been only a minute later that the policeman came crashing downstairs and staggered into the street, his hands at his mouth. Soon afterwards vehicles with lights flashing arrived, and out of them came more people in police uniforms and others wearing white bootees like overgrown babies. The street filled with local residents consumed by curiosity.

All that Malamo heard was that a woman dead for several days had been found, and that something bad had happened to her eyes. At least the window had been fully open. If she was lucky, the stench would have disappeared by morning.

# FOURTEEN

**M**avros made a run for it. The men came after him and caught him before he got to the bushes. He was floored by a heavy blow above his right kidney, then grabbed and hauled back to his feet.

'The snooper.' The big man Rovertos Bekakos had called Mr Kloutsis leaned in close. 'What are you doing here?'

'Snooping,' Mavros gasped. He took another blow, this time to his gut, from one of the pair holding him up. He knew that catching his breath wasn't going to be easy in the immediate future.

'I'll bet,' said Kloutsis. 'What I want to know is, where?'

In his agony, Mavros was relieved that the hard men seemed not to have seen him at Ourania's house.

'You want another pounding?' Bekakos's bodyguard demanded. 'No problem. This time Beetroot here'll be aiming at your balls.'

'Aaagh!'

Mavros's left arm fell free. The guy who had been clutching him was prone on the road, hands at the back of his head. Blood was coming between the fingers. There was another scream and the second man, whose red face presumably had led to his nickname, was also writhing on the asphalt.

Kloutsis took several steps backwards.

'What's the matter, you big fairy?' came a familiar voice from behind Mavros. 'Fancy the odds less now we're going one on one?'

Akis Exarchos stepped forward, holding a metre-long piece of wood that had been cut from an oar.

'You!' Kloutsis said. 'I could have flattened you and that tractor with the bulldozer.' He pulled out a combat knife and went into a defensive crouch. 'Come and get me then.'

Akis swung the oar back but, before he could complete the blow, the lights of a vehicle moving at high speed came down Themistokleous, temporarily blinding him. Mavros shaded his eyes with one hand and saw Kloutsis run off down the slope. Then the car was on them, screeching to a halt where the big man had been. His sidekicks had got to their feet and were stumbling away after him. Looking round, Mavros realised that Akis had slipped away into the bushes.

The driver's door opened and Deputy Commissioner Telemachos Xanthakos got out, service weapon in his hand. He watched the three men turn into one of the lower streets.

'So, Alex Mavro,' he said. 'Friends of yours?'

'Not exactly. Well, no.'

'How about the other one? The man with the club?'

'Never saw him before. I must have walked into a local feud of some sort.'

'Uh-huh.' The tall policeman ran an eye over him. 'Are you all right?'

'I'll live.' Mavros took the hand away from his back and stood up straight, suppressing a groan.

Xanthakos smiled. 'For a hotshot PI, you're not much of a liar. Do you mind telling me what you're doing in Paradheisos?'

'Yes, as a matter of fact I do. It's a free country.'

'True, but brawling in the street is frowned upon. How about I arrest you and put you in a cell until you feel more talkative?'

Mavros was tempted to tell the cop to go and bugger himself, but there was a hard look in his eye. Not only that, he had the distinct feeling he was gay and he didn't want to provoke him unnecessarily.

'Brawling with who?' he asked, opening his arms and wincing.

'All right, come with me,' the deputy commissioner said.

'How come you're on your own?' Mavros asked, after he'd

sat in the passenger seat. He was relieved to feel that the voice recorder was still in his trouser pocket. 'And in plain clothes. Are you even on duty?'

Xanthakos started the engine. 'At the risk of sounding like a B-movie Nazi, I ask the questions.' He turned down the slope and then on to the road Mavros's assailants had taken. There was no sign of them. 'Besides, a doctor should examine you. How many times were you hit?'

Mavros sighed. 'I don't need a doctor. Let me out, will you? I've got a car.'

'No chance. You're coming to headquarters with me.'

'What?' Mavros said, horrified. 'In Thiva?'

'You obviously don't know much about glorious Viotia. The administrative capital is Livadheia now. It's not much more than thirty kilometres away.'

'Are you serious about this, Deputy Commissioner?' Mavros said. They had joined the main road that led out of Paradheisos and were heading north.

'Telemachos. Yes, as a matter of fact, I am. I really do want to know what you're doing here.'

Mavros thought about that. Xanthakos seemed like that rare breed – a cop he could do business with, though he'd have to sound him out further. Given the HMC's economic significance to the area, he would be naïve to imagine that the police weren't close to the company.

'All right,' he said, deciding that part of the truth and certainly not the whole truth was the way to go. After all, Xanthakos had been cooperative on the blockade. 'I'm after a guy who likes underage girls.'

The policeman glanced at him as they drove up a narrow valley. 'That sounds like a job for my service.'

'Have you caught any paedophiles recently?'

'I have, actually.'

'In Paradheisos?'

Xanthakos paused. 'No, outside Thiva. So your man's in Paradheisos?'

'Em, yes.' It was only a partial lie.

'Are you going to tell me why you were on the blockade? And don't say it's because you support the ecologists.'

Mavros thought of Lykos and Angeliki, and their as yet unclear involvement with Lia Poulou. He couldn't help admiring their zeal, even if it was based on the worship of an ancient goddess – and her missing daughter.

'Not exactly.'

The policeman laughed. 'What does that mean?' Then he nudged Mavros with his elbow. 'Here's what I think. The pervert you're after was on the blockade too. That means he's either one of the ecologists, meaning Lykos, a.k.a. Periklis Roubanis, or Akis Exarchos – see, I know their names – or he's one of the HMC people who were in the vicinity.' He turned to Mavros. 'Oh Christ, tell me it's not Rovertos Bekakos.'

'Who?'

Xanthakos laughed. 'OK, have it your way. You won't be able to do much investigating from a cell.'

'Oh really? What are you going to arrest me for?'

'Take your pick. Blocking a public highway, brawling, resisting arrest . . .'

'Uh-huh. How much does the HMC pay you every month?'

The policeman stiffened. 'Careful. I don't have any ties to the company.'

'Is that right?' Mavros thought about what had happened in Paradheisos. If Xanthakos had been in Bekakos's pocket, he would hardly have arrived to break up the fight. Unless he'd been watching and seen Akis Exarchos's intervention. He wondered what the fisherman was doing there. Had Lykos sent him to ride shotgun?

They drove through Dhistomo, passing the signs that pointed to the memorial for the victims of the Nazis.

'My chief's father was killed here,' Xanthakos said. 'His mother was pregnant with him and she was the only one of her family to survive.'

Mavros thought back to his experiences in Crete the previous year. 'Yes, the Germans did terrible things all right. But now it's Greeks who ruin other Greeks' lives.'

'Thinking of anyone in particular?'

'Plenty of people. Everyone knows who they are – the bent businessmen, the politicians who swallow their money and the EU's, the tax-evading rich, the tax inspectors on the take. And they're only the ones who show themselves in public. The worst exploiters keep their heads down and their money in Switzerland.'

The deputy commissioner shook his head. 'It's not that bad. Your job's turned you into a conspiracy theorist.'

Mavros gave that some thought. Maybe the cop was right. Then again, he didn't live in the big city. He felt his phone vibrate against his thigh; he'd turned it to that mode before going to Paradheisos. He took it out and answered.

The Fat Man's voice was breaking up, the signal obviously affected by the mountains between Viotia and Athens. '. . . Phis . . . professor . . . ancient . . . university . . .' There was a pause. '. . . hear . . . Alex?'

'No, I can't. I'll call you later.' He cut the connection.

'Not if I arrest you, you won't.'

'Are you still playing that game?'

'Why else do you think I'm driving you to HQ?'

Mavros didn't answer. Long experience of dealing with the police had taught him that letting them think they'd cowed you was effective.

'Look, Alex,' Xanthakos said, 'I'm not going to book you, but I am going to interview you. I have to.' He sounded reluctant.

Suddenly Mavros understood what was going on. The deputy commissioner had a Thessaloniki accent. His boss – the one who had been born in Viotia – was no doubt in cahoots with the HMC. Bekakos would have pulled his chain after recognising Mavros on the blockade and told him to find out what he was doing. Kloutsis and his sidekicks had similar instructions and the wires had got crossed.

'You're wasting your time, Telemache,' he said. 'I'm not a talker.'

Xanthakos glanced at him. 'You say that. I have unconventional methods. I know a particularly good taverna in Livadheia.'

Mavros began to wonder exactly what sort of pick up was going on.

Akis Exarchos had watched from the undergrowth as the private investigator was driven away by the cop he'd seen during the protest. He didn't trust Mavros, but Lykos had called and asked him to keep an eye on the Athenian. It was just as well he had. The slob and his steroid-addicted friends would have done him

serious damage. He felt good, having laid into them. They were
only the rich men's slaves, but it was a start, a small down
payment on the revenge he was going to exact for Yiorgia. He
considered following the lanky policeman, but it was obvious he
was going to Livadheia, no doubt to question Mavros. He went
back down the slope and found his Honda 50 where he'd left it
– his night vision was excellent after years on the boat.

Heading back to Kypseli, he intended to check in with Lykos
and Angeliki before going home to sleep. But on the way into the
village his keen eyes saw something out of place. Even during
the holiday season, there were few visitors. Greeks knew about the
HMC plant across the bay and the foreigners who hadn't gone to
the islands bypassed southern Viotia on their way to Delphi. Besides,
not many tourists would drive the battered blue pickup that had
been parked at the side of the church. The cargo space was empty,
so it didn't belong to an itinerant fruit seller or the like.

Akis cut the engine and coasted to a halt twenty metres from
the square. He could see the lights in the Ecologists for a Better
Viotia office. Glancing around, he also made out a shadowy figure
behind the tall eucalyptus near the harbour. He slipped into the
narrow passageway between two houses, one of them abandoned
and the other inhabited by an old lady who went to bed early.
Taking care not to reveal himself, he watched the man – the
gender wasn't hard to establish because of his height and bulk.
He was definitely watching the office and he was very still,
suggesting someone who knew what he was doing. Who could
he be? An undercover anti-terrorist officer? It wasn't impossible,
considering the protest had been on national TV. The authorities
were twitchy because of the Games.

Then the watcher moved and Akis saw something that made
his spine tingle. He had done his military service on the border
with Turkey in Thrace and he'd seen the sophisticated weaponry
used by Special Forces. The short rifle that the man was raising
to his shoulder was unusual, that much he knew. He called Lykos's
mobile number.

'Hit the floor!' he whispered urgently. 'There's a gunman
taking aim at you.' Then he did the only thing he could – came
out of the alley and sprinted straight towards the shooter.

*     *     *

The taverna was in a side street off the main square in Livadheia and it was obvious that Xanthakos was a regular. The obsequious owner came to their table and greeted 'Mr Telemachos', asking him how he was and recommending the lamb fricassee. The policeman nodded and also ordered half a litre of white wine. Mavros went for the lamb too, suddenly realising that he was starving. The bread took a major hit.

'This is a pretty unusual place for an interrogation,' he said, after he'd taken the edge off his hunger.

'Interrogation, no – friendly conversation.' Xanthakos smiled. 'I told you I was unconventional.'

'What do you want to know?'

'You won't tell me your client's name or who you're looking for, and you won't tell me who you suspect of being a paedophile. So why don't you help me out with the burned man?'

Mavros looked at the plate of lamb with wild herbs and lettuce that had arrived in front of him, his appetite wavering at the thought of the possible murderer.

'You look like you've seen the ghost of a meal past.'

Mavros took a mouthful. The food was good and rekindled his hunger. While he was eating, he thought about how to proceed. The deputy commissioner could be useful to him, especially if he wasn't in thrall to the HMC. In order to gain his trust, he had to give him something. The Son was the easy option, not least because he was sure the torturer would be out for revenge and Mavros needed all the friends he could get.

'The Chiotis family used a pair of enforcers called the Father and Son. The old man worked in the Security Police HQ in Bouboulinas Street during the dictatorship. I know several people he mutilated, though he told me he never touched my brother Andonis.'

Xanthakos nodded. 'I read the articles in the press.'

Mavros nodded, eyes down. 'You mentioned that Brigadier Kriaras has taken charge of the burned man case.'

'That's right.'

'He was in charge of the Chiotis killings too.' Mavros hesitated, then went on. 'At the end of the investigation – I got involved with an undercover cop with his heart in the right place – we asked Kriaras for the Father's name so we could bring him and the Son in. The brigadier didn't exactly say he had access to it – after all, a lot of the Junta-period records were destroyed. Still, I got the strong feeling he either knew it or could obtain it. But he refused to pass it on. We gave the story to the press, although they were forced not to mention the Father and Son by name. Which is interesting in itself.'

Xanthakos finished chewing, then set down his cutlery. 'Let me get this straight. You're suggesting that one of the most senior police officers in Greece, a man who's on the Olympic Games security committee, is protecting the wanted son of a notorious torturer?'

'I didn't say that.'

'But that's your implication. And it doesn't end there. You think the police officer in question connived in the Son's return to work.'

Mavros drained his glass and signalled for more wine. 'It's got to be a strong possibility. The Chiotis family is no longer active and everyone who had contact with the Father and Son is dead. The Father himself may be beneath the earth. There was no evidence of fish hooks, was there? He used to hang people from the ceiling with them.'

'Jesus. No, but something narrow and sharp was used on the burned man.'

'These are not men to be messed with.'

Xanthakos refilled their glasses. 'Why would Brigadier K give the green light to a violent enforcer or enforcers during the Olympic Games? It doesn't make sense.'

Mavros took a long pull of the excellent local wine. 'Maybe not to a bureaucrat like you.'

'Here we go,' Telemachos said, with a wide smile. 'Conspiracy central.'

'Look, you must know that senior cops in the cities have to do favours for the big beasts who approve their positions. Not just politicians, but the establishment groupings behind them.'

'So you're saying the brigadier's helping a faceless one, no doubt some extremely wealthy individual.'

'Or family, yes.'

'And how would he or they be tied to the man who was set on fire?'

Mavros gave a crooked smile. 'You tell me.'

The policeman pushed back his chair and stretched out his long legs. 'Tell you what, exactly? We've nothing on the killer except that he drove a blue pickup.'

'The victim's still unidentified?'

'Correct – and likely to remain that way.' The deputy commissioner narrowed his eyes. 'I'm going out on a limb here. I expect you to respect that, as well as respond in kind.'

Mavros nodded.

'There was one weird thing. The dead man had seven shrivelled pomegranate seeds in his stomach.'

Persephone, Mavros thought immediately.

'What?' Telemachos said. 'That means something to you?'

Mavros remembered what Lambis Bitsos had told him about Kriaras's visit to Delphi and the beheaded body there. 'It does, but let me ask you something first. Have you heard anything on the grapevine about a murder in the stadium at Delphi?'

The policeman stared at him. 'How the—'

'Were there any pomegranate seeds in that body? You know, don't you?'

Xanthakos nodded slowly. 'If this gets out . . .'

'It won't.'

'I'm a good friend of the Fokidha medical examiner. He told me there were five seeds in the severed head's mouth.'

'Five?'

'Yes, why?'

'Think about it. Seven in your burned man and five in the Delphi victim. Where's the—'

'Body with six seeds.' Telemachos's eyes were wide.

'Exactly.'

'But what's the significance of the pomegranate seeds?'

Mavros breathed a sigh of relief. A detour into mythology would mean he could keep Lia Poulou's disappearance and Rovertos Bekakos's child abuse to himself, at least for the time being.

'Do you remember the story of Hades and how he abducted – and raped, according to some versions – Persephone, daughter of Demeter?'

Telemachos Xanthakos, former classicist, was on familiar ground. As Mavros started to talk, he raised a hand for yet more wine.

# FIFTEEN

Lambis Bitsos got a call from a stringer on a Trikkala news-paper not long after midnight. The guy, a boozer with skin yellower than mimosa blossom, had heard about the dead woman from a tame cop before the Ministry of Public Order imposed a media blackout. Bitsos had jumped straight into his car and driven north. The traffic was light overnight and he reached the Thessalian city before 4 a.m. He met the local jour-nalist in a bar near the statue of Asklepios, god of medicine, whose earliest temple had reputedly been in the vicinity.

The stringer, Yiannis Manos, short and pot-bellied, inclined his head towards the statue. 'Didn't do the victim much good, did he?'

'Apparently not,' Bitsos said, signalling for drinks. 'What's that?'

'Whisky and lemon.'

'Christ and the Holy Mother, no wonder you're that colour. Ouzo for me,' he said to the waiter. 'Lethe, if you've got it.' He gave Manos a warning look. 'Not that I want you forgetting anything.'

'Small chance of that. Do you know what they found?'

'I've just driven over two hundred and fifty kilometres to hear that, fool.'

Manos gulped at his drink. 'Yes, of course. It's all embargoed, of course, so you can't use anything.'

'I'll handle that. Speak.'

'I'll need a thousand for this one.'

Bitsos rolled his eyes, but he knew he was over a barrel – the piss-head was quite capable of going to the competition. 'A thousand if it's as juicy as you said.'

'It's juicy, all right.' The stringer drank again. 'How's this for starters? Tongue removed and nailed to the wall above the bed? The victim, Amanda Velouchioti, professor of modern history at Athens University, aged sixty-two, divorced, no children, was lying on the said bed. She was naked, wrists and ankles tied to the bedstead.' He drank again. 'Get this. Her hair – silver-grey, apparently – had been cut off and spread around her head. Like the glow around the saint's face on an icon, according to my cop. Oh, and then there were her eyes.'

Bitsos looked up from his notebook. Though he had seen it all in his career, there was something sickening about the way Manos was recounting the tale. 'What about her eyes?' he asked, his voice even.

'They were on the pillow, one beside each ear.'

'Fuck.'

'There's more.'

'What a surprise.'

'In her eye sockets, the bastard had put pomegranate seeds, three in each.'

Bitsos gulped ouzo. Six seeds, he thought. Five in the head at Delphi. What was the betting that there were seven somewhere in the burned man on Kithairon?

'Hang on,' he said, looking at his notes. 'You haven't told me the cause of death.'

'Do I look like a medical examiner?'

'You look like shit. How did she die? And when?'

'At least three days ago, was the estimate. The cops went round because an old neighbour complained about the stink.'

'So she'd have been all swollen up.'

'Yes, but it was clear enough what did for her?'

'Oh yes?'

Manos emptied his glass. 'There was an ancient dagger – possibly a replica – in her heart.'

Lambis Bitsos sat back. The drive had been worth it, media blackout or not. Now, before he squeezed Manos completely dry, he needed something greasy and substantial to eat.

'You can stay at my place,' Telemachos Xanthakos said.

Mavros looked at him as they walked down a quiet street. 'Aren't there any hotels here?'

'Of course, but why waste your money? Then again, your client will pay.'

Mavros was interested by the policeman – he was more like a normal human being than any cop he'd ever met, but he'd admitted to being on Mavros's case, which made him, if not the enemy, at least not exactly a friend. Then there was the issue of his sexuality. Mavros had gay friends and had no problem with them. On the other hand, they knew he was hetero.

Xanthakos smiled. 'Don't worry, I won't come on to you. I know you have a long-term female partner.'

'Is that right?' Mavros demanded, irritated by the extent of the research that the deputy commissioner had carried out. 'Unfortunately your information's out of date. Niki and I are no longer together.'

'I'm sorry about that.' Xanthakos smiled. 'Maybe you'd like to try a walk on the wild side?'

Before Mavros could answer, his phone rang. It was Lykos.

'Where are you, Alex?' the young man said anxiously. 'Something bad's gone down.'

'What is it?'

'Akis saw a guy aiming a gun at us. He ran at him and got himself knocked out. I've called an ambulance. His attacker drove off before I could get to him.'

'What did the man look like?'

'Tall and well built. There was a cap on his head and I didn't see his face. He was wearing a black handkerchief over his face like a cowboy.'

'And the gun?'

'It was weird looking thing, like an air rifle, but with a bigger barrel. He took it with him. He drove off in a blue pickup. I didn't get the registration number.'

'But you and Angeliki are OK?'

'Yes. A bit shaken, but . . .'

'Right. Lock up the office and go home.'

'We don't have a home, just the VW van.'

'All right, stay inside the office. Close all the shutters. I'll be back in under an hour.'

'Alex, should we call the police?'

'I'll handle that.' He cut the connection and turned to Xanthakos. 'Come on, we've got to get back to Kypseli. I think the Son just tried to shoot the ecologists.'

'What?'

As they jogged to the policeman's car, Mavros filled him in.

'A blue pickup?' Xanthakos said. 'The killer of the burned man drove one of those.'

'What a surprise.' Mavros was thrust back in his seat before he'd got the belt on. 'Steady, Telemache. Let's get there in one piece.'

They drove out of Livadheia, siren wailing. The deputy commissioner cut it as he got on the radio to his officers in Paradheisos, telling them to set up blocks on the roads out of the town and to be careful – the suspect was armed.

'The Son, if that's who it is, might have got out of the immediate vicinity already. You should block the road in and out of Dhistomo too.'

Xanthakos nodded and gave the order.

'Are there any other routes he could have used?'

'He could have gone the other way from Kypseli, heading towards Itea. And then there's the HMC works. There's a road heading east on the other side of it, but he'd have to pass through the plant's security people to get to it.' He made more calls. 'I presume this Son is capable of looking after himself.'

Mavros nodded. 'You saw what he did with the burned man and it sounds like he was in complete control in Delphi.'

'Shit!' The deputy commissioner slowed as they approached Dhistomo, but not much. 'That was something else the Fokidha medical examiner told me. The victim had a puncture mark in his back. The body was taken away by Kriaras's people before he could do toxicology, but he thinks the *phylax* was felled by a dart or the like.'

'Maybe that's what the strange gun fires,' Mavros said, watching as a white pickup passed through the road block ahead. As Xanthakos spoke to the officers, he considered what that meant. Why would the Son be knocking people out with a tranquilliser gun? Answer – to get them into a state in which he could question them. If they didn't answer, they were either burned or decapitated. But what was he asking them? Where Lia Poulou was? Why would the unidentified man on the mountain and an ancient site guard be suspected of knowing the missing girl's whereabouts? Were they members of a group that had kidnapped her? If so, Lia would be in danger following those savage deaths.

They passed through the narrow defile towards the coast, the bulk of the hills on either side lowering in the moonlight. No blue pickup passed and the officers at the checkpoint at Paradheisos confirmed they hadn't seen one. Xanthakos called the other road blocks and the HMC people. None of them had seen the vehicle either. He gave orders that the blockades stay in place till dawn.

'I can't justify impeding the traffic to and from the HMC plant for a second day on what is nothing more than mild suspicion,' he said, avoiding Mavros's eyes.

'Mild suspicion?' Mavros said, in disgust. 'Lykos and Angeliki nearly got shot. Who knows what he would have done to them subsequently?'

The policeman nodded. 'I know, but I haven't got enough to go on. Let's hear what the ecologists have to say.'

'I'll do that on my own. You seem like a levelheaded guy to me, but they won't necessarily see it that way.'

Xanthakos's gaze hardened. 'You're telling me how to do my job.'

'No, Telemache. I'll pass on anything important, though I think Lykos already gave me all that counts. You need to find the Son. That fucker's capable of anything.'

'If it's him.'

Mavros chewed his lip. 'Trust me, it's him.'

Xanthakos dropped him off at the Citroen and went to check on his officers. Mavros looked around and sniffed the hot night air. The bastard was close, he was sure of it. Had he found somewhere to hide out on his own, or was he being looked after?

Lykos and Angeliki were huddled in the back room of the office, arms round each other.

'Are you sure Akis is all right?' the young woman asked.

'I'm not a doctor. You heard the paramedic. He should have gone for a scan, but he swore he was all right. They couldn't force him.'

'He did wake up quite quickly.'

Lykos hugged her closer. 'He's a tough one, there's no doubting that. He would have stayed on the trailer if the bulldozer had driven into it.'

'A martyr for the cause. A month ago, we didn't even know him.'

'He has his reasons, my love, you know that.'

Angeliki nodded. 'I'm just worried that he'll harm one of the enemy and we'll get shut down.'

'It's up to us to make sure that doesn't happen.'

'Easier said than done. He's on the roof with his shotgun and harpoons. What if that man comes back?'

Lykos turned towards the statue of Demeter. 'The Green Lady will protect us. You know that.'

'Yes, she will.' Angeliki paused. 'Are you sure we can trust Alex Mavros?'

Lykos kissed her on the cheek. 'Not more than we have to, no. From what we saw on the Internet, his heart is in the right place. He's certainly more reliable than the cops.'

'Except he's got an agenda and we don't know what it is.'

'Who cares, if it's to our benefit? Putting him on that bastard Bekakos's tail was one of my better thoughts, even if he was heading there under his own steam.'

Angeliki lowered her head. 'I hope he didn't disturb poor Ourania with his questions.'

'It'll be even worse if Bekakos's thugs saw him come out of the house. Akis said he thought they arrived afterwards, but he wasn't sure.'

'My wolf,' the young woman said in a low voice. 'Do you really think we have a chance against the HMC?'

'Of course. They can't pollute land, sea and sky, and destroy the health of people including their own workers without retribution. The HMC will be brought under control. My aunt will help us even if her party doesn't.'

His phone rang.

'Mavros has pulled up outside,' Akis said. 'There's no one else around.'

'OK. Come down and get some sleep.'

'I'll sleep when this is over.' The connection was cut.

Lykos went to the front room and looked through a gap in the shutter. Then he unbolted the door.

'Welcome, Alex.' He admitted the investigator and closed up after him.

'Are you all right?' Mavros asked, peering around in the gloom. There was a glow from a candle beneath the statue of Demeter.

'Yes, thanks to Akis.' Lykos told him where the fisherman was.

'Idiot. If he's got a concussion, he'll collapse at some point.' He caught sight of Angeliki. 'Hello. Relax, both of you.'

'Has the man with the gun been caught?'

'Not yet. But I doubt he'll try again, at least immediately.'

'Really?' the young woman said. 'Our experience is that the enemy doesn't give up.'

Mavros gave her a blank look. He asked them about the incident in more detail, taking notes under a desk lamp. Then he said he needed to sleep, leaned back in the battered office chair and was out in seconds.

Lykos and Angeliki went to the Lady to make their devotions.

Mavros was woken by his phone at six a.m.

'Rise and shine, long-haired freak,' said the Fat Man. 'I've just put a tray of *kataïfi* in the oven.'

'Congratulations,' Mavros grunted, not even vaguely tempted by the idea of shredded wheat in honey. 'And goodbye.'

'Wait a moment. We've got important things to talk about.'

Mavros looked at the young couple. They were leaning against the wall beneath the statue of the ancient goddess, heads touching as they slept.

'Shit and piss, Yiorgo, couldn't you have waited an hour. I've spent the night in a chair Procrustes would have been proud of.'

'All the more reason to get up, lazy bones.'

Mavros rubbed his eyes and opened his notebook. 'All right, spill your guts.'

'Be careful what you wish for,' the Fat Man said, with a guffaw. 'So, Professor Epameinondhas Phis.'

'Who?'

'I told you yesterday – the guy Maria Bekakou went to visit.'

'Oh yes. Sorry, I had a hard night even before I hit the chair.'

'Did you now? Anyone I know?'

Mavros considered telling him about the gay deputy commissioner he'd passed the evening with, but decided against it. Yiorgos had the old communists' distaste for homosexuals, as well as their hatred of the police.

'Actually, I got beaten up.' His back and belly were still aching.

'Shit, who was it?' his friend asked. 'Do you want me to come down and sort the fucker out?'

'It's a nice thought, but no. I seem to have got my back pretty well covered.'

'Really?' Yiorgos sounded disappointed. 'Anyway, do you want to know about Phis or not?'

'Get on with it, then.'

'He's been professor of ancient religion at Athens University since 1973—'

'So his appointment would have been ratified by Junta-supporting academics.'

The Fat Man was silent for a few seconds. 'I suppose so. What, you think he might be a fascist?'

'Tell me more first.'

'Actually, his title is emeritus now as he's seventy-seven, but apparently he still has an office in the faculty building. He's an international authority on the Olympian gods and he still attends conferences around the world – last year he was in Minnesota and Cape Town.'

'The Olympian gods,' Mavros repeated, glancing at the image of Demeter.

'Those very ones. Among his publications are *The Twelve: Heirs of Cronos*, *Olympians and Mortals*, *Zeus, Poseidon and Hera*, *Half-Gods and Their*—'

'Anything about Demeter or Hades?' Mavros felt the ecologists' eyes on him.

'Em, no. Unless *The Olympian Goddesses: Powers Beneath the Throne* fits the bill.'

'It might.'

'But if you're thinking that Professor Phis is one of those nutters who worship the old gods and demonstrated against the Olympic Games, tough luck. I've got an article here from *The Free News* this May where he rips into believers in ancient religion, accusing them of being – I quote – "nothing more than children with no conception of ancient religion's complexities". There's a picture of him too. He's a crooked old specimen with his hair all over the place and skin like poorly tanned leather.'

'Hang on, will you?' Mavros turned to the young couple. 'Hey, do you know a guy called Phis – Epameinondhas Phis?'

Lykos was immediately on the ball, making Mavros wonder how much he'd heard.

'Professor Phis? Yes, of course. His book on the goddesses is a classic.' He disentangled himself from Angeliki and went to a shelf. 'We've got a copy here.'

Mavros nodded. 'Anything else?' he asked the Fat Man.

'Just a hoard of inestimable value.'

'Just the facts, please.'

'The gratitude. He's unmarried – and never has been – but he's well-connected, sitting on the boards of numerous charitable foundations and museums, both here and abroad. Oh, and he has a personal collection of ancient relics concerning the Olympian gods – figurines, pots and so on – that's worth over two million euros.'

'I thought you said he lived in a back street off Kifissias.'

'His block certainly doesn't look like anything special from the outside. Maybe he has a gallery somewhere else.'

'Check that, will you? I still don't understand what he and Maria Bekakou could have in common.'

'Me neither. Maybe she likes a bit of geriatric.'

'Please.'

'No, seriously. You know that magazine *Theophrastus*? They ran a piece accusing him of being a randy old goat. Apparently he got into naked sunbathing in a big way when he was staying at some shipowner's villa on Naxos last summer. The daughter and her friends complained and he was packed off back to his hole.'

Mavros was about to dismiss that when he thought of Ourania and what Rovertos Bekakos had done to her. 'What age were these girls?' he asked.

'Hang on. Here it is. Fourteen.' Yiorgos paused. 'Ah, shit. Same as the missing girl.'

And Ourania, Mavros thought, his stomach churning.

'So what are your orders for today, partner?' the Fat Man asked.

'For a start, lose the lip. Let me think. It's either Maria Bekakou again or the professor. At his age, he probably doesn't go out much. Do you fancy going back to Kifissia?'

'Your wish is my etc.' Yiorgos sounded very upbeat.

'Be careful. Park in a different place. This'll be the third time you've been up there. You mustn't get spotted. If you are, pedal to metal, OK?'

'I can hardly wait.'

Mavros closed his phone and sat back in the chair. Could Lia Poulou's disappearance have to do with child abuse? Was she being kept as a sex slave? If so, who by?

His thoughts were interrupted by another call.

'This is Bitsos. Are you alone?'

Mavros moved to the front of the room. 'Yes,' he said, in a low voice. 'You sound like *Nipples of the Week* has handed out free samples.'

'No, but you'll be providing me with a life subscription when you hear this.

I'm on my way back from Trikkala, where . . .'

Mavros listened as the journo went through what he'd heard about the murdered woman, a professor at Athens University like Phis. The pomegranate seeds and the savagery were definite links to the other killings – and, he was sure, to the Son.

'Not a word to anyone,' Lambis Bitsos said, when he'd finished. 'Especially not your obese friend. There's a heavy-duty blackout on this story – supposedly because of the Olympics, but I'm not buying that.'

'Neither am I. Some rich and influential people's posteriors are on fire.'

'You should be a hack, Alex. But, yes, I agree. What I don't understand is the ritualistic traits of the murders. Any thoughts?'

'Actually, yes, but I'm not sharing them on the phone. I suggest you get down here as soon as you can.'

'What, to Neapolis?'

Mavros realised he hadn't said where he was. 'I'm still near Paradheisos in Viotia?'

'Why?'

'I'll tell you when you get here. If you look on the map, you'll see there's a village called Kypseli on the coast five kilometres further west. The stone killer we've been talking about was very likely here last night. I think he's still in the vicinity.'

'Viotia, land of cows, Muses and bumpkins, here I come.' Bitsos rang off.

Mavros put his phone in his pocket. He was taking a chance involving the hack so directly in the case. Then again, Lambis didn't know what his case was – and he was very good at digging the dirt. Opening the shutter slowly and seeing no sign of the Son, Mavros looked out across the polluted bay. In this neck of the deforested mountainsides, there was no shortage of muck at all.

# SIXTEEN

Angie Poulou slept fitfully, as she'd done since Lia had gone, and finally got out of bed at six thirty. Paschos's bed was already empty. She heard the shower in the ensuite bathroom and remembered the first time she'd seen the house in Ekali, only a street away from the then prime minister's private residence. She had been married for a few months and they'd spent the previous weeks in the Grand Bretagne in Syndagma Square, waiting for the final touches to be applied. She had never seen so much luxury, even after the hotel. Their room contained two double beds, but there was still enough space to house several families.

'We'll need it when we have five kids charging around,' Paschos had said.

But Angie had never wanted more than one and when Lia arrived that feeling grew stronger. Her daughter was perfect, there could never be another one like her, and Angie didn't want her deprived of anything. She didn't want to spread her love thinly. Paschos never knew, but she went on the pill after she stopped breastfeeding Lia. After years of sex that decreased in frequency and quality – her fault, she knew – her husband gave up trying. He wasn't angry. Paschos never displayed anger. He was happy enough with one child, though she knew he was disappointed there was no son. She satisfied her own desires without resorting to the lovers that many of her fellow wives took. The fact was, sex had become insignificant to her after Lia. She had been fertile and had given birth to the most beautiful child. She wanted nothing more.

Paschos came out of the bathroom, a towel round his thick waist. He looked at her quizzically. 'We're attending the athletics this evening, you remember?'

Angie nodded without enthusiasm. She would be overjoyed when the Games were over. The sight of muscular young limbs did nothing but make her think of Lia. How was it possible for the child of one of the country's richest men to disappear without trace? She had addressed the question to Paschos so often that he had banned it, saying the authorities were doing all they could and she should be patient. She wasn't the only one hurting, didn't she realise that? When Angie had hired Alex Mavros, she had been careful not to change her demeanour or patterns of behaviour. In truth, she no longer trusted Paschos, let alone his oleaginous lawyer. She didn't even trust Maria Bekakou, though at least she still expressed concern about Lia.

She watched as her husband came out of his walk-in wardrobe with a pale blue suit and white shirt. He was fastidious about his clothes, a characteristic she had once found endearing but which now irritated her. How could he care about what he wore when his wonderful daughter was missing?

Suddenly Angie was seized by a burning desire to call Alex Mavros. She managed to conceal it by wishing Paschos a successful day and walking into the bathroom, closing the door behind her. Something was very wrong and she had begun to suspect both Rovertos Bekakos and her husband. She had been thinking about it for days, trying to conjure up images that would provide clues, looks that had been directed towards Lia, terms of endearment spoken – not by Paschos, of course, he never used anything but the most conventional language with both his wife and his daughter. Could the unthinkable have happened? After refusing to consider such an obscenity and then gradually allowing the thought to rise from her subconscious, she was now convinced that Lia had been the victim of an awful act. She couldn't prove anything, she didn't have the slightest evidence, but she was sure.

Angie Poulou came back out of the bathroom, checked that Paschos had left in his chauffeur-driven Mercedes and quickly got dressed. There was a public phone less than five minutes' drive away.

\*    \*    \*

Mavros was flicking through Professor Phis's book on the Olympian goddesses, the chapter on Demeter being particularly well thumbed, when he got the call. He went outside and walked towards the small harbour. His client was struggling to express herself.

'Take deep breaths,' he said.

Angie Poulou did so and managed to calm herself. 'I'm sorry, I must have been having a panic attack. Listen, Alex—'

'No names on the phone, remember?'

'Yes, of course. Listen, there's something I have to tell you.'

'It normally works the other way.'

'Well, have you found anything?'

'Some leads that I'm checking, but don't get your hopes up yet.'

'Are you still down in—'

'Yes. Now tell me what you were going to say.'

There was a pause. 'All right. The thing is, it's nothing I can put my finger on.'

It rarely is, Mavros thought. 'Anything might be useful.'

'Yes,' his client said distractedly. 'Anyway, Rovertos Bekakos, my husband's lawyer?'

Mavros was listening carefully.

'He and his wife Maria don't have kids. I don't know if it was a conscious decision or if one of them's infertile. And they never showed the slightest interest in Lia and the other children in our circle when they were small.'

'But recently that began to change.'

'Is this one of your leads?'

'Possibly. What happened, exactly?'

'Nothing,' she said, almost wailing. 'That's the worst of it. I certainly wouldn't have allowed Lia to go with Maria the day she disappeared if I'd had any suspicions at the time.'

'Suspicions of what?' Mavros asked gently.

'I . . .' There was the sound of choking. 'Excuse me. I find it disgusting even to think about. Rovertos doesn't have a reputation for chasing women – he and Maria have always seemed devoted to each other. But I began to notice him looking at Lia in a different way last summer when we were on Mykonos. He never touched her or anything, but he would often be where she was – at the pool or on the yacht. And there was something in his eyes that I couldn't fathom. Then the old man came and they started hanging around together where Lia and the other girls were.'

'The old man?'

'Oh, he's a professor who helps Paschos and other friends of ours with their collections of antiquities. Phis is his name, Epameinondhas Phis. I took against him from the start – he's bent and has leathery skin, and he cackles like a madman.'

Mavros decided to show part of his hand. 'What would you say if I told you that Maria Bekakou visited Professor Phis at his home yesterday?'

'What?' There was a protracted silence. 'Well, I suppose he would be helping her with their collection. They started one last year.'

'OK. Do you by chance know another professor, Amanda Velouchioti?'

'Yes. She's a colleague of Phis. I've seen them together at art shows and the opera. I met her a few times. She seemed nice enough, but very intense. She never laughed like the old goat.'

'Why do you call him that?'

'After he'd been with us, I heard he was asked to leave by another family because he was getting too close to their girls.'

So the journalists at *Theophrastus* got it right, Mavros thought.

'You realise I can't do my job unless you're completely honest with me,' he said firmly. 'What else is there?'

'I don't know how to say this.' His client's voice was almost inaudible.

'Take your time. Remember, it may help me find your daughter.'

'It's . . . it's Paschos. I didn't think of it before Lia disappeared, but recently I've been tormented. He . . . I found him in her room last March. It was after she'd been playing basketball and she was in the shower. He . . . he was watching her through the glass door. I'd never seem him like that. He was stock still, his eyes locked on Lia like a hunting dog's, and he . . . he was holding the . . . the knickers she'd been wearing.'

Jesus, Mavros thought, was Poulos like Bekakos? 'What did he say? I assume you asked what he was doing.'

'Of course. He just brushed the question away, saying something about how untidy Lia was. He handed me the underwear as he went out. I . . . I don't know what to make of it.'

'Have you mentioned the episode to him since your daughter disappeared?'

'No.'

'Please don't.'

'Why?'

'I can't say at this stage. Is there anything else?'

'No, I don't think so. Bring her back to me. I don't care what's happened, I just want Lia back.'

Mavros tried to comfort her, then ended the call. He sat down on a rock and stared out across the glistening water. Bekakos was definitely in the frame for child molesting, maybe Phis too, but could Paschos Poulos be too? That was conceivable since Nikos Kriaras was on the case; he was so senior that he could manipulate the investigation. But it seemed Poulos had also turned the Son loose, resulting in three killings that were linked by the pomegranate seeds, but in no other obvious way. Had Rovertos Bekakos stashed Lia Poulou somewhere, without knowing that his employer had hired the Son? If so, was he running scared? That might explain Kloutsis and the musclemen who had attacked him.

'My catches have halved in the last two years.'

Mavros turned to see Akis Exarchos approaching, a couple of vicious harpoons in one hand. There was a large bruise on the left side of his face.

'Shouldn't you be lying down?'

The fisherman shrugged. 'The fucker knocked me out, then I woke up. End of story.'

Mavros asked him to run through his experience with the gunman.

'You were lucky,' he said, when Akis finished. 'I think I know who it was. People died the last time I had dealings with him.'

'People are going to die the next time I see the wanker. People meaning him.'

Mavros remembered the methods used by the Father and Son. Fishing equipment had been among them, but it seemed the younger torturer had gone more hi-tech.

'I've been round the village,' Akis said. 'There's no sign of the blue pickup.'

'I don't think he's gone far. For a start, he wasn't seen at any of the police roadblocks.'

Akis lit a cigarette with a match, screwing up an eye as he blew out smoke. 'I thought you were a private operator. Why did you get the cops involved?' He had obviously spoken to Lykos and Angeliki.

'Because they can do things I can't. Plus, they're not all bad.'

'You mean Xanthakos? He kept his head yesterday, true enough. But I'm betting he's on the HMC payroll like the rest of them.'

'I'm not sure about that. Let me ask you – the lawyer Bekakos, did he offer you compensation for your wife's death?'

The fisherman scowled. 'One of his female sidekicks did. Clever, using an attractive young woman on a widower. I wasn't interested. I'd heard about the contracts. You have to waive the right to sue the HMC. Fuck that.'

'It's a big company. What do you expect to do against it?'

Akis grinned, showing a newly missing canine. 'Kick the shit out of its hired help, for a start.'

'Yes, I meant to thank you for intervening last night in Paradheisos. Presumably Lykos sent you to keep an eye on me.'

'No, it was my idea. When he told me you were going in, I had a feeling you'd be targeted.' He dropped the cigarette butt and ground it under his bare heel.

'You know what Bekakos did to that girl, Aki. Have you heard of any other cases?'

The fisherman looked out across the bay. 'Only rumours. Bekakos has a bad reputation with teenage girls. They say that sometimes his wife watches and that other men participate. The workers are too scared to do anything.' He turned back to face Mavros. 'There's only one way to find out the truth.'

'Ask the man himself. Under pressure.'

'That's right. I have contacts in the plant. He's going to be there tonight for a union meeting. How about catching up with him afterwards?'

Mavros thought about it. The idea was high-risk and dangerous: exactly the kind of thing that would put the calculating lawyer on the back foot.

\*   \*   \*

The Fat Man had brought a book – *French Pastry Cooking* – to while away the hours on surveillance. The problem was that, even though he'd eaten a large portion of *kataïfi*, the illustrations were making his mouth water. Fortunately, he'd brought more of the sticky stuff with him. He was reaching for the plastic container when the gate opened and Maria Bekakou's Mercedes coupé nosed out. He started the Peugeot's engine and set off at a respectable distance. Although it was only nine in the morning, the sun was already pounding down and the hire car's air con wasn't up to much.

Again, the lawyer's wife turned south towards the centre. Were they heading back to Professor Phis's place? Yiorgos wondered. If so, he wasn't going to find out much from street level. The traffic heading into Athens was lighter than that going to the various Games venues in the outskirts. It wasn't long before they were approaching the turn to the old man's place. Maria Bekakou kept to the centre lane, eventually moving to the right when they came to the junction with Alexandhras Avenue. The Fat Man began to wonder if he was being led by the nose when the target turned left after the supreme court building and worked her way down the narrow streets, passing the one on which his house was located. Then she drove up the side of the low hill of Strefi and found a parking place. Yiorgos went past her and mounted the pavement. Alex's client could pay the parking fine.

The woman was dressed in loose white blouse and trousers and she'd taken a sunhat from the car. She set off up the path, looking neither left nor right. The Fat Man approached from the other side, using the trees to shelter him from her view. What the hell was she doing up here? No one in their right mind would come to this junkie-haunted, dog shit-encrusted lump of rock for a morning constitutional, especially when they lived in a leafy suburb. She must be meeting someone but, again, why here? He lowered his bulk behind a bush and watched as Maria Bekakou stood at the summit looking up at the higher hill of Lykavittos, one foot on the retaining wall. The doves churred and the crickets scraped, but no one else arrived. Even the dopeheads had gone elsewhere to shoot up.

Then he heard a rustle behind him. Before he could turn, he took a heavy blow on his back. He swung round, right arm raised, and took another hit, this one above the elbow. There were three of them, one with the length of wood that had made contact with his body and the others with wicked-looking knives, one curved like an old-fashioned yataghan. Their clothes were street-life chic – ill-fitting T-shirts, faded denims and incongruously new trainers. Yiorgos knew they were immigrants, probably illegal, but he couldn't tell where from. Besides, he had other priorities. Such as staying alive.

Mavros bought some bread from a run-down bakery and took it to the ecologists' office. The three of them ate it with honey from the last of the local hives, Akis having gone to his place to sleep. After they'd finished the tea from mountain herbs that Angeliki had brewed, Mavros looked across the table at the activists.

'You should consider getting out of here,' he said. 'At least until things calm down.'

'But this is what we've been working for,' Lykos said enthusiastically. 'The HMC is taking the group so seriously that it's hired a thug to shoot at us.'

'Look, if he's who I think he is, he'll be coming back. He's an animal.'

Angeliki gave him a sharp glance. 'He turned up not long after you did, Alex. Is there a connection?'

There might well be. Mavros decided to open up a bit – after all, the young couple's lives were at risk. 'All right. I think there's a paedophile ring operating down here. That slimeball Bekakos may be at the top of it, but Akis said there were others involved. Is there anything else you can tell me?' He remembered that Ourania had met Lia at a workshop. 'Are you aware of any other victims?'

The pair exchanged a look.

'You want us to give you information, but you don't give us anything in return?' Angeliki said, with open hostility.

'Like what?'

'Like telling us what you're really doing here.'

Gloves off, thought Mavros. 'Ourania told me you took Lia Poulou to one of your meetings in Paradheisos.'

'Lia Poulou?' Lykos said, puzzled. 'You mean Paschos Poulos's daughter?'

Mavros showed them the photograph he'd got from his client.

'No,' Angeliki said, 'that's a girl who turned up at one of our meetings a few months ago. I think her name was Lia. But she had a different surname, I'm sure of it.' She peered at the photograph. 'You're saying she's that bastard Poulos's kid?'

'A hundred per cent guaranteed.'

'What was she doing down here?' Lykos asked. 'I remember, she met us outside, saying she was new to our work and wanted us to introduce her to the others.'

'The bitch was spying,' Angeliki said, spittle flying.

'She's fourteen,' Mavros said. "Not even Poulos would put his daughter up to that.'

'I'm surprised you get by in your work with that level of naivety,' the young woman said scathingly.

Mavros looked at Lykos.

'I don't think she was spying, my love,' he said, touching Angeliki's hand. 'It's not as if we do anything except basic education at those sessions.'

'What happened at the end?' Mavros asked.

'She came outside with us,' the young man replied. 'We were in the nursery school near the centre. She walked down the street, turned on to the main square and that was the last we saw of her.'

Mavros held his gaze on him, then switched it to Angeliki. Neither of them had seemed disingenuous in what they said. He was about to tell them what had happened to Lia when his phone rang.

'This is Xanthakos. Are you in Kypseli?'

'Yes.'

'Meet me on the road to Paradheisos. I'll spare your blushes by not driving up to the ecologists' place.'

'Decent of you.' Mavros closed his phone and got up. 'I have to meet someone. Got any plans for the day?'

Lykos looked down. 'We might have.'

'Well, good luck with them. I'll be back in the evening, if not before. Akis has invited me out on his boat.'

From the looks on their faces, it was clear they didn't know about the idea to catch up with Rovertos Bekakos in the HMC plant. It would be better if Akis and he were on their own.

The deputy commissioner's car was parked behind a stand of bamboo.

'Morning,' Mavros said, as he got out of the Citroen. 'Any sign of the pickup?'

'Nothing. And the mystery gunman?'

'Ditto. I think he'll be holed up somewhere in the vicinity. Or maybe he waited until you raised the checkpoints this morning.'

'He could have taken the road to the west last night. The Fokidha officers didn't get there as quickly as they might have.'

'Believe that if you want. Listen, there's something you need to know.' Mavros ran through Ourania's story about Bekakos, without mentioning her name – he realised that he didn't even know her surname.

Xanthakos was shocked. 'And you've got this on disk?'

'I have. But you can't use it to arrest Bekakos. The girl's terrified her father will be fired and her mother will lose her shop – and that they'll be homeless.'

'I can find the guys who were beating you up and interrogate them.'

'If you want to waste your time. Even if they give you Bekakos's name, it doesn't link him to the girl.'

'I thought you'd want to see them behind bars.'

Mavros shrugged. 'There'll be plenty more where they came from. No, Telemache, we need more if we're going to nail the fucker. I'm working on that.'

'Make sure you don't break the law.'

'Wouldn't think of it. In the meantime, there's something else you should know.' He told him about the murdered woman in Trikkala.

Xanthakos closed his mouth when Mavros finished. 'Where do you get this information?'

'Contacts,' Mavros said, tapping his nose.

'There's obviously been a media blackout. Those fucking Games.' The deputy commissioner leaned against his car and wiped the sweat from his forehead. 'Presumably you think it's the same killer – this Son, who's somewhere around here. Your ecologists seem unlikely targets for him.'

'Not really. They've got up the noses of the HMC.'

'But Bekakos hit them with a court order.'

'Bekakos might not know everything that's going on.'

Xanthakos raised his sunglasses and glared at Mavros. 'Any idea who might be behind the killings, then? I mean, who employed the Son and why?'

Mavros gave that some thought. Paschos Poulos had mentioned the torturer to Maria Bekakou at the airport. Could it be that she knew things her husband didn't? Or was there some shadowy presence behind Poulos himself?

'Not really,' he replied.

'Thanks,' said the deputy commissioner. 'A lot.'

# SEVENTEEN

At first the young men were keen, but they didn't like it when the Fat Man fought back. They'd been told he was a lump of lard well past his prime. What they hadn't heard was that, despite never having been a frontline fighter for the Communists, he'd been on enough demonstrations to know how to look after himself. As soon as he was vertical, he concentrated on the man with the piece of wood. He gained possession of that by grabbing the hand that held it and crushing the fingers. That brought his assailant to his knees, with a lot of squealing. Once he had the thick club, the odds rapidly turned in his favour. He belted the man with the curved knife on the side of the head and watched him collapse like an undercooked meringue. The other man turned and ran.

'Right,' Yiorgos said, panting as he held the club under the conscious young man's chin. 'Tell me . . . who paid you . . . to attack me.'

There was an outbreak of babbling in a language the Fat Man couldn't understand. He didn't like bullying people, but his blood was up. He jabbed the club into the young man's belly, sending him flying backwards. Then he put one foot on his victim's chest and exerted pressure.

'Last chance.' He grinned. 'Think how easily . . . I can crush your ribs . . . puncture your lungs . . . flatten your heart.'

Suddenly the young man could speak Greek. There was a lot of, 'No, I can't tell', and, 'He'll kill me if I talk', but that died away when he saw the glint in the Yiorgos's eyes.

'OK, OK, I speak name. Please,' he begged, 'not to tell anyone. Not to tell man.'

'I'm listening,' the Fat Man said, shifting his weight to the immigrant's disadvantage.

'Man's name Roufos. Tryfon Roufos.'

Yiorgos immediately recognised the name despite the way it had been mangled. He'd heard it often in the past.

'And where did you meet this Roufos?'

The immigrant hesitated, but not for long. 'Not tell. Please not tell. He call my friend who ran away. We go to restaurant called The Tree in Menandrou. He give us your photo and say us to wait here for you.'

'What were you to do to me?' The Fat Man pressed a little harder.

'I . . . we not do it . . . kill you . . . we to kill you.'

An icy finger ran up Yiorgos's spine. 'And how much did he pay you?'

The young man turned his head as far to the side as he could. 'Five hundred euros.'

'Each?'

'No, for we all.'

The Fat Man moved the club back, picked up the curved blade and signalled to the immigrant to look after his friend. He went back to the bush, not expecting to see Maria Bekakou standing at the summit any longer. She wasn't.

Back at the car, he rang Alex to pass on what was definitely a break in the case.

'Roufos?' Mavros exclaimed. 'Fuck.'

'I thought you'd be pleased.'

'I'm over the moon and halfway to Venus.' There was a pause. 'Where are you?'

'Rescuing my *kataïfi* from the furnace that's the Peugeot. By the way, I was hugely flattered that my life is worth as much as five hundred of the European capitalists' currency.'

'Don't take it personally.'

'How much more—'

'I'm trying to concentrate, Yiorgo. Tryfon Roufos. I might have known that kiddie-fiddler would be involved in this, considering the antiquities angle.' Mavros had first come across the tall, balding and ultra-sleazy proprietor of Hellas History S.A. during a case on the small island of Trigono. More recently the man who was widely believed to be the country's most ruthless smuggler and dealer of illicit antiquities had turned up in Crete during the big case there. He'd managed to slip away from the police, no doubt using contacts in high places, but it was no surprise that he was still in Greece, despite the outstanding warrant for his arrest.

'I'm going back to Kifissia to kick down that gate and put the fear of Marx into Maria bitchy Bekakou,' the Fat Man said. 'She and her tosser husband are obviously in this with Phis and Roufos. Ancient artifacts and modern underage girls.'

'Hold on, Yiorgo,' Mavros said. 'You may be right, but getting yourself sued for criminal damage isn't going to help.'

'I should have taken the money off the little bastards too . . .'

'There's no point in you going to The Tree either. You know what a hellhole it is down there and Roufos will have made himself scarce. Obviously La Bekakou spotted you. The question is, do they know of your connection to me?'

'Oh, I see, it's all about you. I should have realised. The great Alex Mavros is the target, not his unimportant friend and dogsbody.'

'Finished?'

'For now.'

'Good. Your instinct is right, as it happens.'

'Which one? To piss on the Bekakos' rugs?'

'No, to strike back immediately. The best way to do that is to target their weakest link.'

'Which is . . . oh, I get it. Professor Phis.'

'Correct. Fancy trying to get into his place and seeing what you can find?'

'Why not? Except he'll likely have a serious security system and armoured doors if he's got antiquities in there.'

'I'm sure you can think of a way round and through those.'

'I'll see. Any sign of you know who?'

'Not yet.'

'I'm sure he won't be long.'

'Thanks for that thought. How are your wounds?'

'I'll survive.'

'So brave.' Mavros rang off.

Telemachos Xanthakos looked at him quizzically. 'What was all that about?'

'You're a smart cop, you'll have read the wanted bulletins. Remember a specimen called Tryfon Roufos?'

'The antiquities dealer?'

'I don't suppose you took any steps.'

The deputy commissioner shrugged. 'Nothing much I could do. Athens and Thessaloniki are the centres for that trade. I spoke to the antiquities ephors. They knew about him, but said he doesn't operate in Viotia.'

'He operates everywhere. Now he has to do it underground, he'll be even more slippery. Any significant robberies recently?'

'The usual kind of thing – icons and other ecclesiastical valuables disappearing from rural churches, but nothing from ancient times that I'm aware of.'

'The piece of shit deals in icons too – anything that'll give him a hefty profit.' Mavros took a deep breath and decided to open up further. 'He ordered a hit on a colleague of mine in the big city. Three immigrants, probably illegal – 500 euros was the fee. Not only is he a murderous bastard, he's cheap.'

Xanthakos looked at him. 'Presumably the hit was ordered as a way of getting at you.'

'I think so. The Fat Man – that's my friend – has been putting me up recently and he's not hard to spot.'

'You call your friend "Fat Man"?'

Mavros caught his eye. 'Why not? If you're really lucky, I'll start calling you "Tall Man".'

The policeman laughed. 'So we're friends, are we? Why do I get the feeling you're not telling me anything close to the whole story?'

Because, thought Mavros, you'll cramp my style. And I can't be sure how far I can trust you. Even if you're clean, your boss will have been kowtowing to the HMC for years.

'The suspect declines to answer.'

'What?' Mavros smiled. 'I'm not a suspect. I didn't take aim at the ecologists or knock out Akis Exarchos.'

'I heard the tough guy fisherman refused to go to hospital. You should steer clear of him. Since his wife died, he hasn't been in his right mind.'

'Anyone who takes a run at the Son is OK in my book. Speaking of whom, why don't you get after him?'

Xanthakos stiffened. 'I'm doing my job, difficult though it is. The question is, whose job are you doing?'

'Client confidentiality,' Mavros said. 'Look, could you send a patrol car to Kypseli and have it park near the ecologists' office? They're just kids and they don't stand a chance against the Son.'

'I've been warned off by my chief,' Xanthakos said, shaking his head. 'They've annoyed some major players.'

'So you're going to leave them to be burned or decapitated?'

The policeman's cheeks reddened. 'I'm working on it,' he mumbled.

'Did you know that Lykos's aunt is an MP?'

'I've read his file.'

Mavros glared at him. 'I bet you have. I suppose you think that since she's a Communist, no one will pay any attention to her.'

Telemachos Xanthakos turned away. 'Don't push your luck, Alex.'

Yeah, right, Mavros thought. He wasn't looking forward to babysitting Lykos and Angeliki. On the other hand, he was pretty sure they hadn't told him everything they knew about the HMC's activities or about life in the town by numbers that was Paradheisos.

Ourania had spent most days of the summer holidays in her room. From the day after the pig had pumped his mess on her, she'd started to withdraw from her friends. Her teachers noticed the change in her too – she'd been one of the better students, but had drifted towards the bottom of the class, showing little interest in any subject. They spoke to her parents, who were mystified but too overworked to do anything other than try unsuccessfully to find out why she had 'withered on the vine', as the director of the middle school put it. She ate irregularly and sported bruises she wouldn't explain. Her mother heard banging one evening after she'd closed the shop early and discovered Ourania pounding her arm against her desk. She gave no explanation for her behaviour and refused to see a doctor, muttering, 'The company controls everything'.

Today she felt better. Perhaps telling the long-haired, unshaven Alex Mavros had helped, though the shame of revealing her disgrace still burned in the depths of her being. Could he really do anything to punish her abuser? The man was rich and people like him didn't go to prison. Suddenly she was overwhelmed by a tide of resentment. Why should she cage herself in her room while the pig was out in the sunshine? Why should she be a victim? She wasn't guilty of anything, she'd never even broken a school rule until he ruined her life.

Ourania got up and pulled on a hoodie. She would be far too hot, but she wasn't sure if she'd be able to face people. In the month since the schools had closed, she'd got out of the way of being with others, even on the pavement. Taking her keys but leaving her mobile behind – it needed charging and who was going to call her? – she went downstairs and opened the front door. The sun blinded her, but she had no glasses or cap. Anyway, she preferred to walk with her head down.

There weren't many people around, even as she turned off Themistokleous and headed up the hill towards the main square. She'd have liked to go for a swim at the far end of the town beach, but none of the locals went into the water any more. There had been too many people dying before their time. The HMC said the rumours were rubbish and brought in doctors to prove it, but everyone knew the families of sufferers had been offered compensation – as long as they kept their mouths shut. It was all right for the people in the pink section of Paradheisos. The managers had swimming-pools provided by the company in each street. Ourania didn't have any friends up there. The bosses' kids ignored everyone else.

She was hoping that the girls she'd been friendly with – Fofo, Yiota, Maro – might be at the benches under the plane trees. In past summers the girls had congregated there, while the boys circled them on their bikes like vultures. Ourania would never touch a boy, never allow one near her – that was the legacy of Rovertos Bekakos. She stopped as a bitter liquid rushed up her throat, spitting it on to the road. Then she went over to the *periptero* and bought a small bottle of water. The old man inside the kiosk smiled at her, but she scowled. Men. They were animals. Even Alex Mavros would have the instinctive urges she'd read about in her biology book. Was there no one she could trust? She had a thought. Why had Mavros shown her that photograph of the girl called Lia? She'd only met her once and he hadn't been clear. Had she suffered in the same way?

There was no one at the benches. Ourania sat down and glanced around the place she had spent much of her childhood in. When she'd been at kindergarten, she ran around the dusty playground outside the multicoloured building to her right. Ahead was the town hall, a concrete monstrosity, and next to it the church, its high dome glinting in the sunlight. She'd been there every Easter, but she wouldn't be attending the ceremony of the resurrection again. Christianity was a lie. There was no goodness in the world. She turned to her left and took in the shops and restaurants. There were some well-known franchises as people in Paradheisos – especially the pink section residents – were better off than most Greeks. Where was everyone, she asked herself. Surely they couldn't all have gone off to attend those stupid Games.

Then a dark blue sports car drove past, Ourania didn't know the make. But she did know the driver, his arm hanging out of the open window. It was him, her abuser. She watched as the car slowed to a halt outside the most expensive of the restaurants. Rovertos Bekakos got out and stretched his arms. He was wearing a white short-sleeved shirt and his hair was in the back-brushed wave that she remembered so clearly. Then he took off his sunglasses and looked straight at her.

For Ourania, that was bad enough. Then a smile spread across his fleshy lips and he beckoned to her. Before she sprang up and ran as fast as she could in the opposite direction, she saw another car pull up beside his. It was large and gold-coloured. Men with muscular arms got out, one opening the rear door. The shorter man who emerged reminded her of someone. It was only as she was halfway to the sea front that she realised who that someone was – the girl called Lia.

\*     \*     \*

Lambis Bitsos arrived in Kypseli not long after Mavros had returned.

'Good day,' the journalist said, as he walked into the Ecologists for a Better Viotia office and ran an approving eye over Angeliki. 'Has the bastard come back?'

Mavros got up and steered Bitsos to the door. 'You don't have to go into detail about the Son in front of them. They claim the only reason he would be targeting them is their opposition to the HMC.'

'Oh, right. So they're civilians.' He stared at Mavros. 'No "Great to see you, Lambi", no "There's a superb *taverna* I'm taking you to", not even a 'How do you feel after such a long and exhausting drive?"?'

Mavros laughed. 'Tosser. I'll tell you one thing – don't eat any local produce, especially not sea food.'

The journalist peered at the HMC installation across the bay. 'There does seem to be a lot of muck emanating from that place.'

The wind had dropped, sending the temperature towards forty degrees and leaving the pollution cloud in place above the plant.

'Look, Alex, I need to justify being here. I'm already getting both ears bent by my editor for wasting time in Trikkala.'

'It's not your fault the government embargoed the story.'

'Ah, but was it the government? I reckon the Olympic security committee's running the country these days.'

The committee on which both Paschos Poulos and Brigadier Nikos Kriaras served, Mavros thought.

'So,' Bitsos continued, 'the Son – assuming it's him and, frankly, I don't doubt it – has done away with three people: one burned, one eye- and hairless, and the other headless.'

'And the number of pomegranate seeds in the bodies is going down.'

'Hm. Two points. Why did he kill those particular individuals?'

'And what's with the seeds?' Mavros sat on a bench under the bamboo shelter that served as the village bus stop.

'Not many people around,' Bitsos said, joining him.

Mavros told him about the cancer victims. 'This is all linked to the HMC works, I'm sure of it. Paschos Poulos's lawyer Rovertos Bekakos has been down here frequently in recent months.'

'And he was at the blockade yesterday – I saw the snake on TV. Why do you think he's doing anything other than his job?'

Before Mavros could open his mouth, Lykos ran out of the office.

'It's Ourania,' he said, when he reached them. 'She sounds terrified. Can you pick her up on the coast road in Paradheisos?' The young man shrugged. 'I would go, but the court order . . .'

Mavros got up. 'Stay here, Lambi, I'll be back soon. No doubt Lykos can tell you where to get something to eat.' As he left, he heard the activist telling Bitsos that he'd seen his reports on TV. That would keep them occupied – there was nothing the reporter liked better than boasting about his appearances as a crime expert, especially when there was a young woman in the vicinity. Christ, he thought. How will Ourania react to him?

He raced along the shore road, wondering where Xanthakos was. He wasn't at all sure that the cop would share information with him any more – and if he found out about the presence of the country's best-known crime hack, he'd stop cooperating immediately. Then again, it sounded like the Viotia police had been effectively sidelined by Athens. It suddenly struck him that Nikos Kriaras hadn't called him. He would know that Mavros was down here, if not from the TV then from Bekakos. If he was involved in some conspiracy with Poulos and his lawyer, why hadn't he told Mavros to get back to Athens? Then again, Kriaras was a consummate operator and he'd be keeping as many options open as he could.

As he came into Paradheisos, he passed a large gold Mercedes that had stopped on the waterfront. The rear windows were dark and he couldn't see the occupants, just a couple of steroid-crunchers in the front. Greek plates, so not tourists who'd missed the Delphi turn. He glanced in the mirror. The car had turned up the slope and disappeared.

Mavros looked ahead again. He was almost at the end of the white houses. There was a dumpster at the junction with the road that led to the HMC plant. A figure in a hoodie stepped out as he approached and he stood on the brake.

'Ourania?' he said, staring into the sun. He heard the passenger door open.

'Drive!' the girl sobbed. 'Quick!' She ducked down so she wasn't visible from outside.

Mavros did a three-point turn, then headed back along the

front. 'Are you all right?' he asked, moving a hand towards her back and then stopping himself. 'Ourania?'

The girl was weeping and gasping for breath.

Mavros approached the other end of Paradheisos, catching a glimpse of a dark blue Porsche in his mirror. It followed him and then turned up into the town.

'It's OK,' he said. 'We're out of Paradheisos and on our way to Kypseli.'

The crying gradually stopped, but Ourania kept her head down.

'Did someone hurt you?' Mavros asked.

'No. But . . . but I saw *him*.' It was obvious who she meant.

'At your house?'

'No, in the square. He . . . he beckoned to me . . . as if . . . as if he expected me to go to him willingly. I . . . I ran for it.'

'Good for you.'

'There . . . there was someone else. In a big gold car.'

Mavros reckoned that Bekakos and the other vehicle had been searching for the girl.

'I saw a man get out.' Ourania paused. 'He's her father, isn't he? I mean, Lia's.'

Mavros felt his heart rate increase. Paschos Poulos was in Paradheisos? In the middle of the Olympic Games? Something big was going down, but he had no idea what.

# EIGHTEEN

T he Fat Man went prepared. His late mother had made sure his tool kit was fully stocked, because she insisted that all the house's plumbing, electrical and other maintenance be carried out by Yiorgos. He had moaned about that for decades, especially when the drains blocked and the ancient wiring needed fixing. He'd lost count of the number of times his shoes had been soaked in shit and his hair raised by electrical shocks. But the end result was that he was a skilled handyman and even had the boiler suit to prove it – Kyra Fedhra had found it in a rubbish bin and resewn the seams, after adding extra material to encompass her son's girth. It had the name of a long-defunct plumber's business on it and was as good a disguise as he possessed.

Parking the Peugeot three streets away from Professor Phis's apartment block, the Fat Man set off with his tool box. One street would have done for the sake of cover, but the area was packed with cars even during what was now the summer holiday. It seemed that people really had been taken in by the hype and stayed in the city to attend the Games. After he'd watched the block from across the street for a few minutes, Yiorgos went over and examined the names by the entry buttons. One was handwritten, the spidery letters those of an old woman. He pressed her bell.

'Yes?' came a weak voice.

'Plumber.'

'I don't need a plumber.'

'Yes, but there's a leak in the basement and no one else is answering.'

'I hope you're not a burglar.'

'Certainly not, Madam.'

The Fat Man was buzzed in. Exaggerated politeness usually won the day, not that he used it much. All he had to hope was that the old bag wasn't on the ground floor. It seemed not. There was another list of the occupiers inside, this one showing which floor they were on. Epameinondhas Phis appeared to have the whole fourth floor. Getting into the lift, which claimed it was designed for six people but barely took him, Yiorgos pressed five. When he got to the top floor, he walked down as quietly as he could, looking round the corner as he approached the professor's domain. There was a marble-tiled corridor and, at the end, a black door and frame that could have come from Fort Knox.

'Shit,' the Fat Man said, under his breath. It was then that the fundamental flaw in Mavros's idea revealed itself to him. Phis knew Maria Bekakou. What if she had told him about the man who had been tailing her? What if Tryfon Roufos had told him about the hit he'd arranged? Then again, maybe the immigrants had gone into hiding and kept their cock-up to themselves. But still, how was he to talk his way into the apparently hyper-secure flat? Maybe that wouldn't be necessary – maybe the old man was out. In which case, all he had to do was call one of the comrades and get him to bring round a bucket of TNT.

'Thanks a lot, Alex,' he muttered. 'Oh well . . .' He slid a screwdriver into one pocket and a chisel into the other, then set off down the hallway. He put his ear to the door, but it was so thick that he couldn't hear a thing. There was nothing for it. He had to ring the bell.

'Who is it?' The high-pitched voice made him jump. It came from a small speaker he hadn't noticed.

'Any jobs to be done?' he said, in his most ingratiating voice. 'I tighten taps, I clean out drains, I fix plugs—'

'How did you get in?'

The Fat Man went into full mendacious mode. 'I was in Mrs Manelli's replacing a U-bend so I took the opportunity of trying the other doors. I hope you don't mind, sir.'

'Mrs Manelli, eh? She needs more than her U-bend replaced.' There was a harsh cackle. 'As a matter of fact, there is something I need done.'

There was a series of loud clicks and the door swung open like the entrance to a tomb. There was very little lighting inside and the floor was of black slabs.

'My, you're a big one.'

Yiorgos looked down. More than can be said for you, he thought, nodding at the wizened hunchback with the Einstein hair in front of him. He ran his eye around the place. Several doors were closed. He was led into a large sitting cum dining room. Almost every part of the wall space was covered by glass-fronted display cases.

'Christ and the Holy Mother,' the Fat Man said, under his breath.

There was nothing wrong with Professor Phis's hearing. 'On the contrary, my dear man. They are unrepresented in my collection, but every Olympian god is. Look.' He pointed to a red-figure vase with a bent finger. 'Zeus in his splendour, thunderbolts in each hand.' The old man turned to a small bronze statue. 'Poseidon with his trident.' Then he moved towards the other side of the room. 'And Hades in his helmet of invisibility. Do you know how rare that is?'

'Er, no.'

'It's the only one that's ever been found.'

'Really?' The Fat Man decided playing dumb would be the best way of eliciting information – not that much playing was necessary regarding ancient pottery. 'Where did it come from?'

'Ah, that would be telling,' Phis said, with a crooked grin.

Yiorgos shrugged. 'Doesn't work anyway.'

'I beg your pardon?'

'The helmet of invisibility. I can still see him.'

The old man blinked. 'Anyway, what I need you to do is check the wiring behind that cabinet over there. The lights keep flickering.'

'These are all women,' the Fat Man said, peering at the statuettes and pots.

'Demeter and Persephone,' the professor said. He pointed at a black figure vase. 'Only on this piece can you see a male figure – Hades again, in his role as husband of Persephone.'

Yiorgos stared at the pieces in as bovine a fashion as he could manage. 'Who's Persephone, then? There was a song about her, how did it go?'

Epameinondhas Phis laughed harshly. 'The public education system really is a disgrace. Demeter is the goddess of crops and fertility. Her daughter Persephone was abducted by Hades. You do know who he is?'

'Em, Death?' Yiorgos hazarded.

The professor sighed. 'Lord of the underworld. Because Persephone ate pomegranate seeds – three, four, five, six or seven, depending on which source you believe – she was condemned to spending every winter beneath the earth, but her return in spring signals the beginning of the earth's annual flowering.'

The Fat Man knew most of that, but he was interested in the reference to pomegranate seeds. Did that mean there would be more murders, the future victims containing three and four seeds? As he unscrewed the case from the wall, he pressed the old man casually.

'Why pomegranate seeds, then?'

'Well, they're among the few seeds with liquid as well as solid content, so they can be construed as life-giving. The ancient Egyptians believed they symbolized fertility and prosperity. Conversely, our ancestors saw them as the fruit of the dead because of the Persephone myth. In more recent times we have deviated from ancient knowledge and use the fruit at weddings as well as funerals, on religious feast days, and to bring luck to new houses.' Phis stepped back as the cabinet came away from the wall. 'Be careful, these pieces are worth a fortune.'

Which begs the question, how did you come by them on a professor's salary, Yiorgos asked himself.

'Ah, I see the problem,' he said aloud. 'Some of the wires have come unspliced. Tut, tut, this is very shoddy workmanship.'

'But you can fix it?'

'Oh, yes. Fifty euros should cover it.'

'Thirty.'

The Fat Man moved away and put his screwdriver into the tool box. It was always the rich who argued over money. 'Nice meeting you,' he said, heading for the door.

'Wait,' Phis said, coming after him. 'All right, we'll say forty.'

'Forty-five.' Yiorgos didn't care about the money, he was enjoying winding the old skinflint up.

'Oh, very well. I have people coming this afternoon and I need everything to be in perfect order. But for that price you'll tighten the screws on all the other cabinets.'

'All right.' Yiorgos had to be acquiescent. There were some framed photos on a table by the French windows that he wanted to check out.

The professor was the kind of employer who wanted to oversee everything.

That was good because it meant he could be questioned.

'Did you dig these things up yourself?' Yiorgos asked, as he respliced the junction wires.

'Some of them,' the professor said guardedly. Then he seemed to remember he was talking to a nobody. 'But most I bought.'

'You must be loaded.'

All but the most wealthy liked to be complimented on their prosperity. 'I inherited some money and –' the old man grinned lopsidedly – 'I made a killing on the stock market.'

That would be the same stock market that ate up the savings of many misguided Greeks, the Fat Man thought.

'Right, let's try these lights,' he said. 'There you are. Perfect.' He moved the cabinet carefully back to the wall and reinserted the screws. Phis then followed him around the room as he checked the other display cases' fixings. They were fine – the old man was paranoid. Then he got to the last cabinet and casually cast glances at the photos. He got several shocks. One showed the professor with the ex-king, another with Aristotle Onassis, another with

Melina Mercouri and yet another with the bastard antiquities dealer Tryfon Roufos. Alex would be happy to know about that connection, while he himself had to hold back from belting the old fool.

Phis saw the direction of his gaze. 'Yes, I knew the king,' he said. 'Are you a monarchist?'

Mouth filling with bile, Yiorgos said he was – the sacrifices he made for Mavros.

'I'm glad to hear it. What this country needs is the ancient model – gods who inspire fear and kings who apply order. Parliament is full of swine.'

He was right on the last count, Yiorgos thought – apart from a few honourable Communists. Then it struck him that the old lunatic had used the present tense when he talked about gods and kings. He discounted the latter as there was no chance of the monarchy being restored, but there were people openly believing in the Olympian gods. Was Phis one of them after all?

He hung around as long as he could, even checking the professor's kitchen and bathroom drains, but he wasn't allowed into the majority of the rooms and eventually he took his leave. Phis tried to stiff him on his fee, handing over forty euros, so he put his large foot down.

Back on the street, he knew he had to wait – who were the people the old man was expecting? He was lucky. He found a parking space near the apartment block and sat back to await the arrival of Phis's guests. At least the old fool hadn't known who he was.

Angeliki took Ourania into the back room and closed the door behind them. Mavros sat down with Lykos and Bitsos. The former had a curious smile on his face, while the latter was shovelling the contents of tins of *mousakas* and *dolmadhes* into his mouth, having decided against the sole café-restaurant in Kypseli.

'Stuffed vine leaves are good for your sex drive, my old man always said.'

Mavros glared at him. 'Lambi, that girl's been abused. Cut it out.'

'What, my sex drive? I'll need a bigger knife. Anyway, when am I going to get to talk to her? You told me her story's hot.'

'I think I'd better tell you,' Mavros said, getting the nod from Lykos. 'She won't be able to cope with you.'

'I'm not a paedophile,' Bitsos said indignantly.

'Are you sure all the girls in the magazines you salivate on are over fifteen?' Mavros give him a bitter smile. 'Thought not.' Then he told him what had happened to Ourania.

'I always thought Bekakos was a slimy specimen,' the journo said, when Mavros finished.

'Takes one to know one.'

Lykos laughed.

Bitsos turned to him. 'Quiet, sonny. This is an adult conversation.'

The young man smiled knowingly and went on tapping at his keyboard.

'You know I can't use it.'

Mavros nodded. 'Bekakos has friends everywhere.'

'Including in my management. But it might lead to something that even they can't shut up.'

'That's what I'm hoping. Ourania may have seen Paschos Poulos in Paradheisos earlier today. She thinks Bekakos and his boss were chasing her.'

'Why would they do that?'

'The lawyer smiled at her.'

'Ah. He wanted another go.'

'Maybe.' Mavros turned to Lykos. 'You said you'd heard of other girls being abused.'

'Not exactly.'

'What the fuck does that mean?' Bitsos exploded.

'Keep it down, Lambi,' Mavros said, frowning.

'Not exactly as in girls aged fourteen, i.e. under the age of consent. I have heard rumours of sex parties involving girls over fifteen – not illegal, but morally reprehensible, considering the people who supposedly take part.'

Mavros and Bitsos exchanged glances.

'Who might they be?' the journalist asked.

'Who do you think?'

'HMC management?' Mavros guessed.

Lykos nodded slowly and then looked outside – a van had drawn up in a cloud of dust.

'Oh-oh,' Bitsos said, taking in the well-built young men in T-shirts and jeans who were getting out.

'Don't worry,' Lykos said. 'My aunt sent them down from Athens. Party cadres.'

'His aunt's Tatiana Roubani,' Mavros explained.

'Oh.' The tension left the journo's skinny frame. 'Good.'

The four men came in and nodded to Lykos, then turned to Mavros and Bitsos.

'It's OK,' Lykos said to the cadres. 'They're on our side. I think.'

One of the men stepped forward. 'We are to act as your personal bodyguards. Where you go, we go.'

The door to the rear opened and Angeliki came out.

'Hello, boys,' she said, smiling widely.

'They've obviously worked together before,' Mavros said to Bitsos.

'Yes, we have,' Lykos said. 'The Communist Party has ecological aims too – especially when those are being compromised by a plant that has expelled the union.'

Mavros introduced himself.

The young men looked at him and then at each other.

'Spyros Mavros's son? Andonis Mavros's brother?' asked one. There was admiration in his voice.

'The same. Not that I'm like them. I'm not in the Party, for a start. What do I call you guys?'

'Em, I'm Cadre One, he's Cadre Two, he's—'

'I get it. Anonymity in case of problems. Don't worry, my old man had a code name during the war – Kanellos. Slightly more imaginative than yours.'

Akis Exarchos came in, fish spears in both hands. He shook hands with the cadres, obviously having met them before.

'So you think you're safe now,' Mavros said. 'But unless your friends have had Special Forces training and are armed to the teeth, the Son is still a big danger.'

'We can look after ourselves,' said Cadre Two.

'Using what?' Bitsos asked.

'Our fists. And we have clubs in the van.'

Mavros scratched his stubble. 'Well, they're better than nothing. I still think you'd all be better off in Athens.'

'What, even me?' Akis asked.

'Er, no. We have plans for later, don't we?'

Bitsos missed nothing. 'Count me in.'

Mavros looked at the journalist. He was well into his fifties, out of condition and an inveterate moaner. Then again, he had a camera and the experience to sniff out criminal activity at long range.

'All right, Lambi.' He ran his eyes over the others. 'The rest of you hold the fort. Now, is there somewhere Bitsos and I can get some sleep?'

'I'll take you to my place,' the fisherman said. 'It's still reasonably clean.'

'Not for long,' Mavros said, glancing at the journalist.

The Son was puzzled by the latest order he'd received. He wasn't to target the ecologists any more, at least for the time being. That irritated him, as he had unfinished business with the skinny guy who'd erupted out of nowhere and run into him. Belting him in quick succession on the mouth and the side of the head had been no problem – his reactions were lightning-fast – but being forced to leave the scene with the job unfinished counted as failure in the mental ledger he kept of his performance. Plus, the young woman inside the office had attracted his attention. He'd have killed her partner after interrogating him, but he had seriously considered keeping her alive, at least until he tired of her. Then she'd have gone the same way as the others.

Now he was to go back to Athens and deal with another woman, this one not as young though, if the photos were accurate, still striking. Perhaps he'd have the chance to get to know her intimately, though the timetable he'd been given was tight and her death was to appear an accident. He'd already left the pickup in the garage of the safe house in Paradheisos and was driving an unremarkable Fiat towards Dhistomo. He'd been told to stay overnight as an over-enthusiastic police commander had set up roadblocks following the failed mission in Kypseli. He didn't care. The detached pink house at the end of a road was out of the way and there was no one else in it. That was the good thing about a company town. The HMC could more or less do what it liked, although someone had screwed up with the over-enthusiastic policeman.

Driving into Dhistomo, the Son saw the signs to the museum and massacre memorial. The Father would have insisted on stopping and paying his respects, even though some of the victims would have been commies or similar scum. The old man had been strange like that. He hated the war-time resistance because of its left-wing bias but, as soon as they were dead, they became heroes. That didn't apply to the bedraggled remnants who had fought the Civil War against the British- and then American-backed national army. They were traitors in life and in death. The Son couldn't give a shit. People who threw away their lives for shadowy ideals like fatherland or resistance were fools. Even the Father had been seduced by the Junta's semi-literate ideology of Greece rising phoenix-like from the flames, its contradictory ancient and Christian elements somehow expected to co-exist. Money was all that mattered, as Greece's population had showed in recent years. Everyone was on the yellow brick road to affluence – two or more cars in every family, a house by the sea and another in the mountains, credit cards, Italian fashions.

He drove quickly towards the main highway, though he was tempted to take the turn into Livadheia and deal with the troublesome policeman. No, he needed to control himself. His employer had things in hand. All he had to do was get to the address in the Athens suburb, deal with the woman and get back to Paradheisos. If ever there was a place less deserving of that name. Then again, the road from paradise to the halls of Hades wasn't long. The Elysian Fields themselves were in the underworld. Whether his next victim ended up there or in the punishment park of Tartarus was of no concern to him.

# NINETEEN

**M**avros had fallen into a deep sleep on the sofa in Akis's *saloni*. It had taken some time, as Bitsos had insisted on loudly making himself a toasted sandwich in the adjoining kitchen, before crashing out upstairs.

In his dream he was walking across a dusty plain, a hot wind whipping his hair and distant screams all around. Then he heard a familiar voice say his first name. It was Niki, his former lover. She sounded close, but he couldn't see her through dirty clouds that suddenly rose up all around. He heard himself call her name several times. His arms were extended and his hands touched something soft: flesh, bare and drenched in sweat. He embraced the body, feeling her breasts against his inner forearms. Then the dust storm cleared and she turned into a picture of horror. He jerked awake, the worm-ridden face still in front of him.

'Welcome back to the land of the living,' Akis Exarchos said, from the table at the other side of the room.

'What . . . where am I?'

The fisherman told him.

Mavros got up, limbs stiff, and went over.

'What the hell is that?'

'A Webley .38 Mark 4 British officer's service revolver. My father got his hands on it in the war. He never told me how.'

Mavros watched as Akis wiped oil from the hammer and cylinder. 'You're seriously taking that with you across the water tonight?'

'Seriously is the word, my friend. The HMC security men are armed with Glocks. I had big trouble finding rounds. Eventually a guy in Crete sold me twenty.'

Mavros remembered his time on the Great Island. There were probably more antique weapons there than in the rest of Europe put together.

'Maybe this isn't such a good idea,' he said, sitting down opposite the fisherman.

'Listen, we know Bekakos is going to be there.'

'I saw him in Paradheisos earlier. Why go into the lion's den?'

Akis gave him a tight smile. 'I was wondering when you were going to ask that. All right, I'll tell you why. One of my contacts over there told me they've found an ancient temple on the hill above the plant.'

'What?'

'You heard me. It's in very good condition. And it's not just any temple. Apparently our ancestors worshipped Hades and Persephone there.'

Mavros immediately thought of Lia Poulou. Could this be where she'd been taken? There was some link between her and Persephone, also known as the Maiden – he suspected the pomegranate seeds in the victims indicated that. But what would the daughter of the HMC's owner be doing on the site? Unless Paschos Poulos knew she was there. Could that be why he was in the vicinity?

'Why are you so interested?' he asked Akis.

'Because they only uncovered it when they were testing for ore in old workings on the hillside a few months ago. The temple's going to be taken to pieces and removed from the site. I want the world to know and your friend Bitsos can tell them. I've got a camera myself, but I'm sure he's more skilled than I am.'

'What about Bekakos?'

'If I see him, I'll shoot him.'

Mavros thought he was joking – for a split second. 'Why?'

'Because he's the worst of them. Not only did he abuse that poor girl, but he tried to buy my dead wife.'

Mavros opened his mouth to speak, but was interrupted by another sight of Niki's worm-ravaged face. Jesus, what if the Son goes after her, he thought. He scrabbled in his pocket and pressed out the sequence of numbers that he hadn't forgotten. It rang until her voicemail kicked in.

'Niki, it's me. Listen, this isn't a joke. You may be in serious danger. Get out of your flat and stay away from it and from work. Call me when you get this.'

'Who's Niki? Girlfriend?'

'Ex.'

'Ah. Still in love with her?'

'What kind of a question is that? You hardly know me.'

Akis shrugged. 'Since Yiorgia died, I can't be bothered with niceties. There's life, there's love and there's death. Nothing else matters.'

Mavros examined the wiry fisherman. 'That's pretty profound. Do you read philosophy in your boat?'

'No. It's what my grandfather used to say. He lost a leg fighting the Italians. My family's from Epirus, so he was among the first troops who pushed them back in Albania.'

'I wondered about your accent. So how come you ended up in Kypseli?'

'My wife. We met when I was working on a road gang here. I stayed when they moved on.'

'You haven't got kids,' Mavros said, having seen no toys or drawings in the house.

The fisherman slipped the gun and ammunition into a shoulder bag. 'No. The plant's probably to blame for that too.'

Mavros had a flash of Niki's anguished face when she talked about having children. 'Listen, what good will killing Bekakos do? He's only one of hundreds, more like thousands, who work for the HMC.'

Akis's eyes flared. 'What good will it do? The bastard's a child-molester, as well as an apologist for the death-dealing plant. Do you seriously imagine anyone will ever bring him to justice?'

'I will,' Mavros said firmly.

The fisherman looked at him sadly, then shook his head. 'You and whose imaginary army?'

Lambis Bitsos staggered into the room. 'Army?' he asked blearily. 'Count me out.'

Mavros and Akis exchanged glances and shook their heads.

The Fat Man dozed off in the sauna that was the Peugeot. He was lucky. Although he missed their arrival, he was awake when Professor Phis and his guests appeared on the pavement in the late afternoon. He tried unsuccessfully to shrink down in the seat, but they were paying him no attention. He recognised Maria Bekakou, dressed in an ankle-length white dress that one of the goddesses in the old man's collection could have carried off. Her hair was drawn back tightly and she looked severe in the extreme. Next to her was a tall man in a dark suit and a wide-brimmed hat. When he stepped towards the black BMW that pulled up, a chauffeur opening the doors, Yiorgos caught a glimpse of the thin face. It was Tryfon Roufos, the antiquities dealer who had tried to have him killed. He managed to restrain himself. He was about to call Alex when he realised his phone had fallen beneath the Peugeot's seat.

'Shit,' he muttered, eyes on the BMW. The passengers had got in and it was moving off. The Fat Man abandoned the search for his phone and set off after the black car. It was probably only going up Kifissias to the Bekakos house. He'd be able to call from there.

But that wasn't what happened. The BMW cut through the northern suburbs and joined the main highway north. Yiorgos struggled to keep up with it and was still without his phone – every time he stopped at traffic lights, he stuck his thick-fingered hands under the seat, but succeeded in doing nothing more than pushing the device further away. Loud was the swearing.

Then the chauffeur-driven vehicle took the exit towards Thiva, but didn't head for the town. It drove west, towards Livadheia and Delphi. The Fat Man began to realise that a phone call might not be necessary. He never wasted his money on betting, even though he'd been happy enough to run card syndicates in his café, but he was pretty sure he'd soon find himself in Paradheisos with Alex. He glanced around at the harvested fields and the dun-coloured mountains. He hated the countryside, but this was less harsh than his home village near Sparta. Then he remembered the burned man who had been found on Mount Kithairon. Ahead was the great bulk of Parnassos, while to his left was Helikon, home of the Muses. Screw ancient mythology, he told himself. He needed to make sure he wasn't spotted by the occupants of the target vehicle. He was looking forward to a meeting with Tryfon Roufos. It would be brief but painful.

Mother, where are you? It's been so long that I can't remember your face. If I could use my fingers, if they hadn't started tying my wrists together, I could feel your imaginary features, I could bring you closer. But it's so dark in here, the only light coming under the door that crashes open when they bring me food and take me to the toilet. I have no self-respect left. They wipe me after I've finished, they pull up my knickers. I'm so hot all the time, why have they made me wear the white robe that reaches to my ankles? Why has my hair been plaited? I don't even know if they're men or women, their robes black as night and their faces covered by masks. The features are bland, but the white paint makes them look like ghosts. Why are they haunting me?

Mother, I called you Mummy when I was small and Mum when I last saw you. My father disapproved, preferring the Greek equivalents – Mama, Babas. I stopped calling him 'Baba' when my periods started; 'Patera' seemed more natural. I didn't know why, it just happened. But now I understand. He put a distance between us, he . . . no, I won't think about it.

And what about Uncle Rovertos? I remember asking you why I had to call him that, since he and Aunt Maria are not blood relatives. You smiled like you always did and said they were as good as my real uncles and aunts, Father having no brothers or sisters and you not speaking to your family since you came to Greece. But they aren't as good. They are much worse. I don't know if they're the ones wearing the masks and robes, but I'm sure they have something to do with it.

I have to tell myself I'm still only fourteen. Why have they done this to me? Being locked up for weeks, months, I don't know how long, has been bad enough, but I'm tortured by the thought of what is going to happen to me. The end of this part of my life is close.

Mum, save me from what's going to happen. Save us.


Lambis Bitsos consumed a four-egg omelette and half a loaf of bread, hunger having overcome his worries about the food in Kypseli. He looked out across the water, the sun darkening it to imperial purple, and lit a cigarette.

'So how many security personnel does the HMC employ over there?' he asked.

Akis Exarchos took the plates to the sink. 'A hundred plus.'

'Christ and the Holy Mother.'

'But there are three shifts and fewer men work the night one. So maybe twenty, twenty-five at most.'

Mavros smiled at the journalist's discomfort. 'You've seen the plans of the plant, Lambi. It's massive. They'll be split up all over it.'

Akis nodded. 'I know their locations. It won't be the first time I've been across.'

'Really?' Mavros said. 'What did you do?'

'You'd better ask Lykos.'

'Well, I can't, can I? The four laughing cadres have taken him and the girls off to Itea so they aren't implicated in whatever we get up to.'

Akis shrugged. 'You either come with me or you don't. I'm going whatever.'

Mavros glanced at Bitsos. It seemed better if they went with Akis. They might be able to stop him doing anything foolish, as well as find out useful information – not to mention check out the temple to Hades and Persephone in case Lia Poulou was there. Which reminded him. He hadn't heard from his client since the morning. He wanted to ask Angie about Lia's trip to Paradheisos in March. Then he remembered Niki and the Son's possible interest in her. He called again, but got voicemail. He left a fourth message.

'We'll come,' Mavros said. 'When do you want to set off?'

'In half an hour.' The fisherman left the kitchen and went upstairs.

'Are you sure this guy's not playing us?' Bitsos asked.

'Pretty much. What's your problem? He told you there are dozens of health and safety violations. You'll get a scoop even if we don't find Bekakos. And the HMC is obviously way out of line with the ancient temple.'

The journalist stubbed out his cigarette and immediately lit another one. 'Yes, but what if we get caught?'

'He's armed,' Mavros said unhappily.

'What, with those harpoons?'

Mavros's phone rang, so he let Bitsos think that was the extent of Akis's arsenal.

'Alex, where are you?' The Fat Man was speaking above the noise of a straining car engine.

'Kypseli. Why? Where are you?'

'South of Dhistomo. They stopped at a *kafeneion* there – toilet break, I'd guess – and I managed to find my phone. Fucking thing had—'

'Woah, Yiorgo, slow down. You're heading in this direction?'

'That's what I just said, isn't it?'

'What a pleasant surprise. Who's "they"?'

'Maria Bekakou, Professor Phis, a chauffeur and guess who?'

Mavros looked at the ceiling. 'Guess who? All right, Kevin Spacey.'

'Not even close. Tryfon Roufos.'

'You're kidding.'

'Thought you'd like that. And there's more. I spent an hour with the professor in his place this afternoon—'

'You what? You were supposed to get in when he wasn't there. What if Roufos or Maria Bekakou told him about you?'

'Obviously they didn't. I don't think he knows his pet assassins screwed up yet.'

'Bloody hell, you took a risk. Find out anything interesting?'

'I think so,' the Fat Man said proudly. 'For a start, his flat is full of ancient stuff – vases, statuettes and the like. Get this. A lot of them have to do with Hades, Demeter and Persephone. He's even got a bowl full of dried up pomegranates.'

'Hm.'

'Is that all I get for risking my skin?'

'Hm. What else?'

'What else? Well, he's got a display case full of ancient pots covered in porn. Men rubbing themselves up against boys, men shafting women, men and goats—'

'I get the drift.'

'Oh, and La Bekakou is dressed like an ancient goddess.'

'What?'

'Long white dress like a robe, hair drawn back . . .'

'All right. Are you sure they haven't spotted you?'

'No, but they haven't done anything to lose me.'

'See where they're going and call me back. Oh, and Yiorgo, you've done well.'

'It'll cost you. I want a salary and pension contributions.'

'OK. Watch yourself.'

Akis came back in with yellow waterproof clothing. 'You might want to put these on. There'll be spray.'

'Haven't you got an enclosed cabin?' Bitsos asked.

'Yes, it's called the engine compartment. A minute down there will complete the damage your cigarettes have done to your lungs.'

Mavros picked up a jacket and trousers. 'Not exactly camouflage gear, this.'

The fisherman laughed. 'We'll take it off before we go on dry land.'

They kitted up. Akis had his fish spears wrapped in a piece of tarpaulin and the bag over one shoulder. At least there was no sign of the shotgun.

'Are you sure you need that?' Mavros asked, in a low voice.

'You'll see.' Akis led them to the front door.

The trio walked to the small harbour. There were only a few lights and the water beyond was now dark, the HMC plant shrouded in red.

'It's weird how the lights over there react with the smoke,' Akis said, pulling on the bowline of a small fishing boat.

'Weird?' Bitsos said, hoisting the bag with his camera and other gear on board. 'It looks like hell.'

Mavros smiled, then answered his phone. It was the Fat Man again.

'The BMW went to the HMC plant,' he said. 'I stopped about

a hundred metres from the gate. They didn't see me. There are plenty of other cars. The shift must be changing.'

'Fine. If you think you can conceal yourself somewhere in the rocks nearby, do so. Otherwise, call it a night and come over to Kypseli. My friend Akis's house is on the front. It's the only one with a bougainvillea surrounding the door. The key's under the second tile on the left.'

'Right. Where are you going to be?'

'Never mind. I'll see you later.'

'Never mind? I bust my ass getting down here and—'

'Lovely image. Go to the good.'

Mavros cut the connection and clambered aboard the boat.

The Son had turned off the national highway and driven into Ekali, one of the northernmost suburbs of Athens. It was like entering a billionaires' enclave in Switzerland or an ultra-exclusive area outside Washington DC. The houses were large and surrounded by gardens and trees. Private security guards were posted at some of the gates and police officers were patrolling outside the homes of politicians. Mount Pendeli to the east glowed in the sunset and planes glinted above the new airport at Spata. The air was clear and cool, far enough from the city centre and the crowded Olympic venues for the neighbourhood to seem completely disconnected. In any case, the Son was so tuned to the job that he was in a zone of his own. He drove the Fiat to a junction, turned right and approached the target's house. He parked on the street and went up to the heavy blue gate, broad-brimmed hat concealing his face from the numerous cameras. He was carrying the rake and spade that he'd put in the car's boot in gloved hands. For as long at it mattered, he was a gardener. There was a smaller door for pedestrians. He pressed the sequence of numbers he'd been given and it swung open. The sun had dropped behind the western mountains and he was well concealed by the heavy foliage at the edge of the asphalt drive. The door closed quietly behind him and he headed for the house.

He had memorised the layout and knew that at this time of day the target was usually to be found in the tinted glass extension by the swimming pool. The only other person in the house at this time would be a Filipina cook. If she kept out of the way, she would live. The Son slipped round the corner of the pristine wall, brushing past hibiscus and oleanders. When he approached the next corner, he leaned the spade and rake against the warm stone and took the silenced Glock from the waist of his jeans. Slowly moving his head round, he saw the woman. Angela Poulou was lying on a recliner, one foot dipping in the water. She was a fine looking woman, her legs long and smooth and her upper body generously proportioned beneath the zebra-striped swimming costume. The Son felt a pang of sadness. He would have liked to sample this one either before or after killing her, but his orders were clear. It had to look like an accident – or, even better, suicide. He could easily have drowned her, but that would have left marks on her body from the struggle. Instead, he had to get the woman upstairs.

He walked slowly towards her, the soles of his worn yachting shoes silent on the marble. Two cats sprang up from beneath the recliner and ran away. He had the muzzle of the silencer against the side of Mrs Poulou's head before her eyes opened and his hand over her mouth before she could make a sound.

# TWENTY

**M**avros sat next to Akis at the stern, while Bitsos tried to hold on to his last meal nearer the bow. There was a swell out in the bay and their protective clothing was soon drenched. As they got closer to the plant, the air became more acrid and Mavros felt his lungs burn.

'How come the workers survive more than a few months?' he yelled.

The fisherman pursed his lips. 'Most of them wear masks. Not all *do* survive.'

Anger coursed through Mavros. How was such a lethal plant allowed to operate? If what he'd read was correct, the HMC had observed safety regulations sufficiently in the decades before Paschos Poulos bought the company, but in recent years standards had been flouted.

Akis pointed past a large ship moored alongside a pier. 'There's a quiet cove round there beyond the lights. That's where we're heading.'

It took another twenty minutes. Then they were in the dark on the other side of a steep promontory and the fisherman cut the engine revs. Mavros went forward and took the coiled rope. Akis had told him there was a securing ring hidden beneath an outcrop of rock. Akis manoeuvred the boat expertly and Mavros found it, slipping the rope through. A few minutes later they were ashore, having discarded the yellow gear.

'We have to climb a bit,' the fisherman said.

'Oh, great,' said Bitsos.

'It isn't far. The temple's on this side of the plant. It shouldn't take us more than a quarter of an hour.' Akis selected a spear from the tarpaulin shoulder-bag across his chest. 'Help yourselves,' he said to the others.

Mavros declined. The journalist was tempted, but decided his camera was enough to worry about. They set off up a scree-ridden slope, the lights from the plant shining beyond a ridge. That meant they could see where to put their feet, but were unable to make out anything in the distance. Mavros struggled for breath, the air even fouler here, and he could hear Bitsos wheezing like an aged steam engine to the rear. Akis was quick on his feet and kept having to wait for them. Finally, they reached a large boulder rooted in the hill's stony flank.

Akis beckoned them forward and they looked over the ridge. The sight was breathtaking, and not only because of the tinted pollution cloud. It reminded Mavros of Hieronymus Bosch and of the nocturnal cityscape at the beginning of Ridley Scott's *Blade Runner*. Hadn't that been called Hades? If so, this was Hades in spades – and they hadn't even reached the death god's temple. The front part of the space in the triangular plain between two mountainsides and the sea – measuring perhaps three by two by three kilometres – was filled by furnaces and chimneys, long rolling plants and loading yards. Tall cranes stood over the ship on the waterfront, trucks constantly moving beneath them as they brought finished batches of aluminium for the deep holds. But it was the rear of the plant that had the real look of the infernal. The mountain had been scoured away, access roads circling it and great heaps of red ore dully reflecting the lights. Huge earthmovers ground up the roads, while the whole area was strung with electrical wires, as if a colony of gargantuan spiders had spun their webs over the factories and machines.

'Jesus Christ,' Bitsos said, coughing harshly. 'I've seen photos of this kind of place in Russia and China. I didn't know we had our own version.' He started clicking away.

Akis turned to Mavros. 'Look beyond the towers there,' he said, raising a hand. 'See the four-storey building? That's where Bekakos will be meeting the workers' representatives.'

Mavros saw it, cars parked in a space behind it. He thought he could make out the lawyer's Porsche.

'See the lights on the hill?' Akis said, moving his head to the rear of the plain.

Mavros looked towards a dimly lit area about five hundred metres away at about the same height they were. A narrow track led up to it.

'That's the temple.'

'It's more like a cave,' Mavros said, struggling to focus on the small number of columns and pitched roof.

'It was built into the mountainside.'

Mavros ran his eye over the plant again. 'Seems strange the ancients put a temple to Hades on a hill when there was a perfectly good plain below.'

'Maybe they found something valuable up there – you know, Hades as Plouton, the Rich One.'

Maybe they did, Mavros thought, only dimly registering the fisherman's knowledge of mythology. And maybe there's a rich man's daughter there too.

'Is there a guard on it?'

Akis grinned. 'Only one way to find out.' He moved off.

The other two followed, out in the open now although they were under the shadow of night. Suddenly a loud siren screamed and they froze. It stopped after what must have been half a minute. Then there was a boom from further up the valley.

'Blasting,' the fisherman said. 'It goes on all the time. Fortunately we only hear it when the wind's from the east, which is rare.'

It didn't take them long to get to the temple. There was a barbed wire fence around it, but it was only knee-high.

'The workers know not to come up here and who else would?' Akis said, lifting his leg.

Mavros went after him and then helped the less agile Bitsos over.

'This is all I need,' the journalist gasped. 'Kneecaps shredded for a story my editor will never print.'

Mavros left him and approached the ruins. They were in such good condition that the term was hardly appropriate. There were spades, wheelbarrows and other equipment around, showing that work was still underway, but little sign of imminent dismantling. The glow from the valley was sufficient for him to make out traces of dark marks on the columns. Had the temple to the underworld deities been painted black?

'How do we know this was dedicated to Hades and his bimbo?' Bitsos asked, as he took pictures.

'Come inside,' Akis said, taking a torch from his bag. He shone it towards the inner recesses of the building. They had been hewn from the rock. The floor was tiled with marble and there was a strange smell – damp combined with a ripe, fruity odour.

'The statues are in perfect condition,' Mavros said, approaching the larger than life-size figures. The male, stern and forbidding though his eyes were blank, stood in the centre, while the female, slightly smaller, was on his right side. Her head was shrouded and there was an expression of infinite sadness on her beautiful face.

She held a round object in her left hand.

'Grenade?' the journalist suggested.

'Not far off etymologically,' Mavros replied. 'A pomegranate.'

'Well, well.'

There were strands of vegetation and fruit on the floor beneath the statues. The plinths were stained red. Akis bent down and sniffed.

'Wine,' he said. 'Nothing worse.'

Mavros extended a hand. 'Give me the torch, will you?' He went round the back of Hades and shone the light. A tunnel had been cut into the rock, which was spotted with red bauxite ore. 'When do you think this was done?'

The fisherman went forward and ran his hand over the stone surfaces. 'Not recently. It's smooth.' He looked up. 'Water's been dripping over it for a long time.'

Mavros was seized by the idea that Lia Poulou was down there. 'I want to see how far it goes.'

Bitsos ran up, his eyes bulging. 'We've got company. We need to get out.' He followed the direction of the beam. 'Or in.'

Akis went to the temple entrance and peered out cautiously. 'Three plant pickups,' he said, on his return. 'Only 4x4s will get up that track. They'll be here in a few minutes.'

'I'm for going down the tunnel,' Mavros said. 'We'll get caught in the headlights if they're that close.'

Bitsos stared at him. 'Why do I think you haven't told me everything?'

'The Son could be in one of those pickups,' Mavros said. 'The last time Akis here saw him, he had a silenced rifle.'

'Let's go down the tunnel,' the journo said.

Mavros led them a few metres down and stopped. 'I want to see and hear what happens. If we're lucky, they won't come down here.'

'And if we're not, I've got this.' The fisherman took out the Webley.

'Jesus,' Bitsos gasped. 'No shooting!'

'Quiet,' Mavros said. He listened as the engines slowed and then stopped all together. There was a slamming of doors and the sound of footsteps approaching. Then lights were lit in the temple – brands burning in sockets on the walls. Pushing the others further down, Mavros edged forwards, trying to see who was in front of Hades and his bride. Then the voices started, low and chanting. He struggled to make out the words.

'. . . lord of darkness . . . ruler of all souls . . . and your queen, dark Persephone, bringer of beauty to those beyond all hope . . . accept, we beseech you, these humble offerings.'

There was the splash of libations on the floor and the rustle of flowers and dried grass.

Then a cracked and elderly male voice began to speak alone.

'Great Hades Aidoneus, wearer of the cap of invisibility, grant success to our endeavours. Do not turn away from us now, oh Powerful One, in our hour of need. Accept these live offerings as more evidence of our devotion.'

Mavros found Akis's hand in the dark and took the revolver from him. He wasn't going to let the Son or anyone else kill again. He looked between the statues and saw the thug named Kloutsis and another of the men who'd attacked him in Paradheisos carry a large sack towards the deities. Whoever was inside it was jerking about.

Whispering to the fisherman to back him up with the harpoon, he prepared to move into the light.

The target froze, her eyes wide. The Son smiled at her.

'Get up,' he said, his voice low. 'Slowly.' He put the hand that wasn't holding the Glock under her arm and helped her up. 'Now, Mrs Poulou, we're going for a walk. Inside and upstairs. If you cry out or make any sound whatsoever, I'll shoot you in the lower abdomen. Believe me, the pain will be appalling. I'll disable your cook in the same way if you manage to alert her.'

Angie Poulou shivered, her swimsuit damp.

'You don't need your robe,' the Son said, with a slack smile. 'You don't need anything at all.' He kicked away the wooden-soled sandals that would have made a noise on the stone floors. 'Lead the way.'

The target walked slowly into the glass-walled extension, her feet initially leaving wet prints. Her chest was rising and falling rapidly, and her arm twitching in the gunman's grip. The door to the wide hall was open, the staircase on the left.

'Up!' urged the Son.

She complied, pausing on the landing.

'Your bedroom,' her captor whispered.

She whimpered.

'Don't worry, I'm not going to rape you. Though it is tempting.' The Son poked a finger into her left breast. 'Move.'

Angie walked down the corridor to the master bedroom at the end. The Son looked around it, then closed the door behind them and locked it. He pointed her to the nearer bed and went into the en suite bathroom to check it was empty. Then he sat next to the target.

'Right, Mrs Poulou, here's the situation.' He smiled at her again, this time more reassuringly. 'You're going to die. What we have to decide is how.'

'Who sent you?' Angie asked, her voice faint but even. 'My husband?'

'Does it matter? Now, you can jump from the window, though there's a good chance that won't kill you unless you go headfirst. Can you do that?'

'This is about my daughter, isn't it? You piece of shit, what have you done to her?'

The Son raised his shoulders and ran the muzzle of the silencer over her right nipple. 'Another possibility is the stairs. You could fall down them – but again, it would have to be headfirst. Do you fancy that?'

Angie Poulou sat very still. 'It's because of Alex Mavros, isn't it? You're killing me because I hired him.'

The Son's eyes opened wide. 'Alex Mavros? What do you mean you hired him?'

'To find my daughter.'

'Alex Mavros with the long hair and the weird eye?'

'Yes.' Angie gave him a scathing look. 'You don't seem to know very much.'

'Watch it, bitch. Tell me about Mavros.'

'I just did. He's looking for my daughter, Lia.'

'Where is he?'

'I don't know exactly. The last time I saw him was on the TV, at a demonstration outside the HMC plant near Paradheisos in Viotia.'

'Ecologists for a Better Viotia,' the Son muttered. What was the fucker doing down there? He suddenly had the impression that he was being played for a very large fool. His beef with Mavros was well known to the person who'd hired him, but that individual had kept the PI's involvement in the pomegranate seeds case secret. He would pay for that.

'When did you last speak to him?'

'This morning.'

'Did he have any progress to report?'

'Not really. He seems convinced there's some connection between Lia and the HMC plant.'

Maybe there is, the Son thought. He would have to investigate that himself. He took a deep breath and got himself back into the zone.

'Another option,' he said, looking her in the eye, 'is cutting your wrists. You can do it in the bath. It doesn't hurt much if the water's very hot.'

'Please,' Angie said, her eyes damp. 'All I want is my Lia back.'

The Son shook his head. 'Some things are too expensive, even for a member of the hyper-rich.'

Mavros was about make his move when Akis put a hand on his arm.

'Wait,' he whispered.

Squeaking noises were coming from the sack. Kloutsis took out a knife and opened one end, grabbing the pink animal that appeared. Five more followed, each seized by one of the company.

Mavros had a vague memory that pigs were sacrificed during the Eleusinian Mysteries. Was this something similar? Then he saw the faces beneath the black veils worn by the men and the white ones worn by the women. Tryfon Roufos, struggling to keep hold of his porker; Maria Bekakou, a knife in her right hand and the piglet under her left arm; her husband, Rovertos, knife between his teeth and both hands on his sacrificial victim; a stooped old man, presumably Professor Phis, who was relying on one of the heavies to hold up his piglet; and, in front of Persephone, none other than Paschos Poulos. The tycoon had a tight grip on his sacrifice, knife blade already at its throat. A shorter woman Mavros couldn't make out was to the rear. The noise of the terrified animals increased in volume.

Bitsos was swearing under his breath, unable to take photographs because of the flash. Mavros held him back, the Webley still in his hand.

'Accept, oh chthonic gods, this humble sacrifice,' said the old man. 'May the blood of these healthy creatures nourish you and persuade you of our devotion.'

The squealing of the pigs suddenly stopped. Mavros saw jets of blood spurt over the statues' robes and plinths. He frequently ate pork, but he felt sickened. These people were savages. Then he felt a throbbing in his pocket – he had turned his phone to vibrate. He took it out and saw Niki's name on the screen. He cut the call and turned off his phone. His ex-lover always did have an exquisite sense of timing. Turning his attention back to the scene in the temple, his heart took a hit. The celebrants had gathered close around the deities and were placing the dead animals beneath them. If Lia really was down the tunnel, would they go to visit her? Or was it Lia in the robes behind Paschos Poulos. He clutched the revolver even more tightly.

Then the people in black and white stepped back from the statues, bowing low. Phis was mumbling a prayer, this one in ancient Greek. A few seconds later, they were at the temple entrance. It was then that Mavros saw the face of the second woman. It was Angeliki, the ecologist.

Then the tip of a fish spear pierced the skin of his lower back and the Webley was swiftly removed from his hand.

'Time you two intruders met the VIPs,' Akis Exarchos said, pointing the revolver at Bitsos and keeping the harpoon in place.

They stumbled forwards and were surrounded by security men, as well as the celebrants.

'You sold us out,' Mavros said, glaring at the fisherman.

'The company's offer was generously increased earlier today,' Akis said, shrugging his shoulders. 'We decided that bringing you over was a plan worth sticking to.'

'So, no shooting Rovertos Bekakos?' Mavros said, with heavy irony.

The lawyer stepped forward. 'That would be somewhat counter-productive on Mr Exarchos's part.' He looked over his shoulder at Paschos Poulos, who was keeping his distance. 'You've been poking your nose into things that don't concern you, gentlemen,' he continued, glancing at Bitsos and then Mavros.

'And *you've* had a spy in Ecologists for a Better Viotia all along,' Mavros said, giving Angeliki a filthy look.

'My loyalties are to the great gods,' the young woman said, her head high.

'Not much sign of Demeter here.'

'Her daughter is present,' Angeliki said. 'Can't you feel her aura all around?'

'Kiss my aura,' said Bitsos. 'Will you crazies just fuck off?'

Mavros grimaced. Diplomacy had never been in the journalist's armoury.

'Crazies?' the old man shrieked. 'How dare you? The Olympian gods are omniscient and all-powerful. You will regret those words.'

'I rest my case,' Bitsos said.

'And what are you doing here, you slimebag?' Mavros demanded of Tryfon Roufos. 'Going to sell the statues?'

The antiquities dealer gave a tight smile. 'Of course not. They are holy objects. But there have been other finds of interest.'

'Enough,' Paschos Poulos ordered. 'Mr Mavro, I know that my wife employed you to find Lia. She has paid the price for that.'

Mavros's gut clenched.

'As will you,' Poulos continued.

'You know where Lia is, don't you?'

Poulos's gaze wavered. 'As a matter of fact, we don't. But Angeliki will soon find out from Lykos.'

'He has her?'

'So it would seem. He's been very secretive about it.'

'You know his aunt is involved?'

Poulos waved his hand loosely. 'That Communist hag is of no significance. The same goes for the strongmen she sent.'

'What about the Son?' Mavros demanded. He was fast running out of ammunition. 'He's been picking off members of your lunatic cult.'

Professor Phis let out a chilling cackle. 'No, he's been killing off members of a rival group, one which, unlike ours, could indeed be described as a cult – a minor and misguided group of Olympian enthusiasts. Lykos is also one of them. The young man is strong-willed. He has been sent photographs of their terrible deaths, but has not deviated from his course. And he has kept Angeliki out of the – how does the expression go? – loop.'

Mavros looked at Paschos Poulos, deciding that it was time to shake the tycoon up. He had nothing to lose. 'So, do you ejaculate over fourteen year olds like your lawyer?'

Kloutsis came forward in a rush and put his arm round Mavros's neck. Poulos followed him.

'Girls became sexually available as soon as they started their periods in ancient times,' he said, sour breath snaking into Mavros's nostrils. 'We follow the traditions.' He signalled to Kloutsis to relax his grip.

Mavros gasped for breath, then remembered what his client had said. 'I don't remember incest being a feature of ancient Greek life, except in myths where the people who practiced it met bad ends. How many times did you rape Lia?'

This time Kloutsis felled Mavros with a punch to the side of the head. Stunned, he heard the professor's high voice.

'In this, as in so many things, you are wrong. Demeter was impregnated by her brother Zeus and Persephone was the product of that union. In turn, Persephone was given to Hades, brother of Zeus and Demeter, and the Maiden's uncle.'

'Given?' Mavros panted. 'Hades raped Persephone.' He took a kick from Kloutsis in the belly and writhed on the stone floor.

'We are finished,' Poulos said. 'You and your snooping friend will not see the light of day again.' He nodded towards the tunnel. 'Down there lies Hades' kingdom. May you have joy of it.'

'Kiddie fiddlers!' Bitsos shouted. He hit the deck after a heavy blow to the ribs.

Kloutsis grabbed Mavros and one of his sidekicks the journalist.

'Oh, by the way,' Bekakos called. 'That fat slob you had following us. He'll shortly be feeding the fish in the bay.'

Bile rushed up Mavros's throat. Not only had he killed himself and Bitsos, he'd also condemned his best friend to death – as well as giving his mother another lost son to mourn and his sister another brother.

# TWENTY-ONE

The Fat Man understood why Mavros had told him to stay away from the parked Peugeot. Obviously he was safer hiding behind a boulder ten metres up the hillside, even though getting there almost killed him. He ruined a perfectly serviceable pair of shoes that he'd been wearing for a decade. Having got used to being a private eye, he'd taken tools from his box with him. Forearmed was forewarned, or something of the sort.

The problem was, it had got dark and he didn't know what to do. The BMW had disappeared beyond the gate to the HMC plant and was still in there – unless it had gone out the other side, which he could do nothing about. He considered calling

Mavros, but decided against it. He would be busy and wouldn't like being distracted for no good reason. Yiorgos lay back on the stony ground and looked up at the stars. They weren't as bright as they should have been out here in the sticks, the lights from the aluminium works polluting the night sky almost as much as the cloud of poison gas. How did people live down here? Even in Athens in the years of the *nefos*, before filters had been applied to vehicles and chimneys, his lungs hadn't burned like this. Maybe you got used to it. Yeah, right. Probably you died.

The other problem was, he was starving. There was a bag of food in the car, but going down to get it might blow his cover. Then again, hardly any cars had passed either way in the last half-hour. Yiorgos gave it another five minutes and then lumbered down the slope, ending up on his arse more than once. He slid the key into the lock and slipped his hand under the passenger seat. The bag had moved during the race to keep up with the BMW and he had difficulty reaching it. That was why he didn't hear the approaching car till it was too late. He stood up in the headlights, one hand in the pocket with the screwdriver.

A very tall man in white shirt and dark blue trousers got out of the other vehicle, holding up a plastic-covered ID card. The Fat Man swore under his breath.

'Good evening, sir. Need any assistance?'

'No.'

'Can I ask what you're doing here?'

'Yes.' Yiorgos grinned and kept silent.

'I see. Is this your car, sir?'

'No.'

'I'll need to see the insurance document, as well as your licence and ID card.'

The Fat Man put the bag of food on the roof and bent down, fumbling with the handle of the glove compartment. He found the certificate, which was stapled to the hire agreement, and handed it over, along with his personal documents.

'This car was hired by Alexander Mavros,' the policeman said, his brow furrowing.

'And my name's on the insurance cover.'

'So it is, Mr Pandazopoulo.' He came closer. 'My name's Telemachos Xanthakos.'

'Oh, yes. He mentioned you.'

'Am I right in assuming you're a colleague of his?'

'Yes.' Yiorgos smiled proudly. 'I'm assisting him with his inquiries.'

'Are you now? And that includes parking on the side of the road leading to the HMC plant? You're lucky the security section hasn't been out to ask what you're doing.'

'It's a public highway, isn't it?'

Xanthakos nodded. 'Here it is. That doesn't mean they won't get curious. Just out of interest, what are you doing here?'

'None of your business.'

The policeman sighed. 'You wouldn't happen to be a member of the Communist Party, would you?'

'Yes.'

Xanthakos smiled. 'Now I understand. Listen, I had dinner with Alex last night. We've been working together on the case.'

Yiorgos raised an eyebrow, his hand inching towards the food bag. 'What case would that be?'

The policeman looked around. 'The Son's murders. And Rovertos Bekakos's activities with an underage girl.'

So he doesn't know about Lia Poulou, the Fat Man thought. 'Disgusting what rich lawyers get up to. Have you arrested him?'

'Not yet. Look, do you know where Alex is? I've called him, but he doesn't answer.'

Yiorgos tried his friend's number and got the unobtainable signal. He felt a twinge of unease. It went against the grain to talk to a cop, but Alex seemed to trust this one. 'He told me he was coming across to the plant from Kypseli by boat. Some fisherman called Akis was bringing him.'

'That would be Akis Exarchos.'

'Is he dependable?'

'He's with the Ecologists for a Better Viotia. He lost his wife to cancer recently.' Xanthakos looked across the bay to the lights of the village. 'Why don't we go and see if they're back? Alex shouldn't have tried to enter the plant by stealth.'

'Em, I think there was someone else with them.' The Fat Man saw no reason not to include Lambis Bitsos in the equation – it would serve the nosy fucker right if he got charged with trespassing. Though that would mean Alex did too. He gave the cop the hack's name, all the same.

'Bitsos? The guy on TV? What's he doing down here?'

'You're asking me?'

Telemachos Xanthakos laughed. 'All right, I should know what's going on in my own backyard.'

'Especially since you're deputy commissioner. Why are you on your own? Doesn't your rank drive about with convoys of bully-boys?'

'Not in Viotia. Turn your heap round and follow me.'

The Fat Man did as he was told, but slowly. He grabbed bites from the large sandwich he'd made earlier in the day as they drove along the water's edge. The lights of Paradheisos rose up the slope ahead. It looked like a kid's drawing of a pyramid, in layers of white, yellow and pink. Christ and the Holy Mother, where have I ended up, he asked himself. And what am I doing taking orders from a cop? This isn't paradise, it's the other place.

Angie Poulou was in the bath, the water so hot she could hardly breathe. Her assailant's face came out of the cloud of steam, then a hand. In the latter was the cut-throat razor with the ivory handle that Paschos had inherited from his father, though he never used it. At least the man who was orchestrating her death had allowed her to keep on her swimming costume. That made her feel less vulnerable, which in turn made her more determined to fight for her life. She would see Lia again, she'd do anything to ensure that.

'Now,' the smooth-faced man said, still wearing his wide-brimmed hat. 'You take the razor. You cut these veins here, in this direction.' He demonstrated, then raised the pistol. 'Don't try to take a swipe at me.'

The threat was empty, Angie knew. Whoever was paying him – and she thought her husband was the most likely contender – wanted it to look like she'd been driven to suicide. She had no idea of his plans for Lia, should she still be alive. Whatever they were, he would find a way of attributing her death to their daughter's absence. Shooting her would make that harder to explain, though Paschos's contacts in the police would probably cover it up. But did the dead-eyed man with the pistol know all that?

'What's Alex Mavros to you?' she asked, keeping her eyes off the razor.

'Never mind. Take the blade.'

'I can arrange a meeting. He'll come running when I ask him.'

'Take the blade.' The voice had a harder edge, but it was still low, almost conversational.

'I know his mother as well.' Angie's eyes met her killer's. 'Would you like me to introduce you? I'm sure you'd enjoy that.'

'You're a cold one.'

Angie smiled. 'On the contrary, it's a sauna in here.'

'Take the fucking blade!'

She let out a scream, then his other hand was on her mouth. He must have dropped the pistol. She bit down hard, feeling her expensive crowns shear through skin and muscle. She locked her jaws. The razor dropped from his other hand into the water and he hit her hard on the cheek repeatedly. She felt for the blade, knocking it away with her fingers the first time. Then she grasped the handle and whipped it out of the bath, striking him on the side of the head. He pulled away quickly, gasping in pain. Blood fountained horizontally before he jammed his hand against the wound. She felt her teeth move as he tried to wrench away his other hand. She slashed at him again, this time opening a wound higher on his head.

'Fucking bitch!' he screamed, taking the hand off the wound and scrabbling for the pistol.

There was a dull crack as her crowns left her mouth, but by then she had located the pistol. She pulled herself out of the water and aimed the weapon at the bleeding man. He glared at her, then turned and left.

Angie Poulou looked down. Her shattered teeth were on the floor alongside her assailant's hat. There was a piece of his ear in the bloodied bathwater.

Kloutsis and one of his thugs pushed Mavros and Bitsos against the wall at the rear of the temple and searched them. Mobile phones, keys, watches and the journalist's camera and other equipment were taken. Mavros watched as the robed figures left, none of them casting a backward glance.

'This way to the underworld, snoopers,' Kloutsis said, taking one of the burning brands from the wall and pushing Mavros into the tunnel. His sidekick also took a light and drove Bitsos after them.

'You're making a mistake,' Mavros said. 'Both of us are well known. We'll be missed.'

'Not by us you won't,' the heavily built man said, swinging the brand at Mavros.

'I'm a television personality,' Bitsos said.

'Not down here you're not.'

'The police in Viotia know where we are,' Mavros said, the damp mineral air sticking in his throat.

Kloutsis laughed. 'The police in Viotia do what we tell them. Now fucking shut up.'

After five minutes of descent, the flames showed a frame with bars ahead.

'The miners used to keep their dynamite here,' the other thug said. 'Got anything explosive to say?'

Mavros and Bitsos watched as a rusty key was put in the lock and the door squealed open.

'Thought not.'

They were pushed inside and the door slammed after them. The key was turned and removed.

'Have a nice death,' Kloutsis said, as he and his colleague started the walk back up to the surface. It wasn't long before the lights disappeared completely.

'Fuck,' said Bitsos.

'I rather doubt it,' Mavros replied, crawling away from the bars. His head soon banged into a rough wall of rock. 'No, you're right,' he said. 'Fuck.'

'I'm scared of the dark,' the journalist moaned.

Mavros moved closer to him. 'I think that may be at least part of the point.'

The Fat Man followed the lanky cop's car round the seafront in Paradheisos and towards the faint lights of Kypseli. He was now officially worried, mainly because Alex wasn't answering his phone but also since he'd never trusted a policeman further than he could throw him – and he'd thrown plenty over the years on demonstrations. What option did he have, though? Xanthakos seemed concerned and, surprisingly, was prepared to do something. Whether it would get them any further was another story.

The vehicle ahead stopped in the village's small seaside square. Yiorgos drew up next to him and got out. He looked around anxiously, aware that the Son had been there. Where was the fucker now? Xanthakos had gone over to an unlit building and was knocking on the door.

'Ecologists for a Better Viotia,' the Fat Man read. 'This is the group Alex was with. Where are they?'

The deputy commissioner stepped back and scanned the upper storey. 'I don't know. Maybe they all went across the bay.' He turned to the harbour. 'There isn't much we can do except wait. We should move the cars out of sight.'

They did so and then sat on the bench by the pier.

'Why are you doing this?' Yiorgos asked. 'Shouldn't you be back at home with your giraffe-like wife and kids?'

Xanthakos laughed. 'I'm not married.' He glanced at his companion. 'Nor am I likely to be.'

The Fat Man's eyes opened wider. He edged away.

'Don't worry, it isn't catching.'

'Better not be. Next you'll be telling me you voted for the Party at the last elections.'

The deputy commissioner grunted. 'I did, actually. Not that it's done much good. I hoped they would mount more of an opposition to the Olympics.'

Yiorgos shook his head. 'You're too idealistic for a cop. Anyway, why should workers give up the chance of unlimited overtime with premium wages?'

'The way I heard it, most of the work at the venues was done by immigrants being paid well below the minimum.'

'And most of the profits went into the pockets of rich fuckers like the one who owns the HMC plant.'

Xanthakos nodded. 'It's the way of the world. What do you expect me to do about it?'

The Fat Man glared at him. 'Catch the thieving shitheads, for a start.' He took a deep breath and coughed. 'If this pollution isn't illegal, I don't know what is. Why isn't Paschos Poulos behind bars?'

'Do you want the official reason or the real one?'

'I know the official one – he hasn't done anything wrong and, besides, cops aren't responsible for factory inspections. The real one?'

'Is that the HMC, one of Greece's largest companies, provides a large number of jobs in Viotia.' He raised a finger towards Paradheisos. 'Over two thousand people live there. It would be deserted in weeks if the plant was shut down.'

'I'm not saying it should be shut down – neither is the Party. But the emissions should be controlled. People are dying.'

Telemachos Xanthakos hung his head. 'I know. Now maybe you understand why I'm here.'

'How noble.'

The deputy commissioner looked up at him. 'You're a hard person to like, you know that?'

'If Alex comes back safely, I might lighten up.'

Xanthakos flicked the button on his holster. 'Maybe this is him now.'

The lights of a small boat were approaching, the engine sounding above the rippling waves.

'Let's withdraw into the bushes,' the policeman said. 'I don't trust the man at the tiller.'

Yiorgos rubbed his eyes and made out a figure in yellow waterproofs. 'Is he on his own?'

'Let's see. Alex may be taking cover from the spray.'

They watched as the fishing boat came closer, the engine revs dropping as it passed the breakwater and drew alongside the pier. The man in yellow manoeuvred skilfully with one foot on the tiller, lassoing a rope over a bollard and then killing the engine.

'Now!' Xanthakos whispered. 'You cut round to the right.' He watched the big man go and then stepped out of the darkness.

'Catch anything worthwhile?' he called, walking quickly towards the boat, service weapon behind his back.

'Who's that?' called the sailor.

'Deputy Commissioner Xanthakos, Mr Exarcho. Tell me, what happened to your passengers?' He ducked as a large revolver appeared in the fisherman's hand and a shot rang out. He brought his pistol to bear and loosed off a pair of shots, but the bobbing of the boat didn't help his aim.

Akis Exarchos was on land now, a harpoon glinting in his

other hand. He saw where the policeman had gone and raised the gun again. That was when the Fat Man hit him, smothering him with a tackle a linebacker would have been proud of. The revolver skittered across the wooden pier and fell into the water. Two sharp thuds of Akis's other hand on the decking made him release the fish spear. He gasped as his chest began to collapse under the assailant's weight. The muzzle of the deputy commissioner's pistol appeared at the side of his head.

'OK, you'd better get off him,' Xanthakos said. 'We need him unflattened.'

Yiorgos rolled away. 'You all right?' he asked the policeman.

'Yes. Let's get this madman over to the bench.'

They took Akis under the arms and dragged him over, sitting him down with the pistol against his head.

'Where's Alex?' the Fat Man demanded, grabbing the fisherman's throat. 'Alex Mavros – what have you done with him?'

Akis Exarchos tried bravado. 'I don't know what you're talking about.'

Yiorgos grabbed him by the arms and shook him like a marionette.

'All right . . . all right . . . I took them . . . to the plant.'

'Them?' Xanthakos asked.

'That journalist . . . was with him . . .'

'What did you do with them over there?' the Fat Man demanded, continuing the shaking.

'Not . . . not me . . . the faithful . . .'

Yiorgos stopped. 'Who?'

The fisherman repeated the words, his head down.

'You mean Epameinondhas Phis, Maria Bekakou—'

Akis's head jerked up. 'How do you . . .?' The words trailed away.

'Have you got enough fuel to go back?' the deputy commissioner demanded.

The fisherman nodded. 'I need to fill the tank.'

'Right, here's what you're going to do,' Xanthakos continued. 'You take us to where you landed with the others and then you show us where they are.'

'I don't know where they were taken,' Akis said, avoiding their eyes.

'Then you'll find out from the so-called faithful,' the policeman said, pressing the muzzle hard against his captive's cheek. 'Or I'll put a bullet in your brain.'

The Fat Man glanced at him. 'Steady, Mr Cop,' he said, but he was impressed.

'Check the boat for anything this piece of shit could use against us, will you?'

Yiorgos went over and dumped poles, knives and hooks overboard.

'Thanks a lot,' the fisherman said, after he'd been marched to the boat, carrying fuel cans. 'I don't know if she'll take your weight.'

The Fat Man grinned. 'In that case, I'll take you down with me.'

The fuel was transferred and the engine started. In minutes they were out in the darkness of the bay, heading for the infernal lights of the HMC plant.


'Are they going to leave us here?' Bitsos asked, his voice rasping. 'I'm dying of thirst already.'

'I'd say the former is a distinct possibility,' Mavros replied. His throat felt like it was covered in thorns. 'We know too much.'

'Speak for yourself. I'm struggling to understand how this all hangs together.'

Mavros ran his hand over the rough rock, feeling the surface crumble. He moved on his knees, feeling for the bars. When he found them, he struggled against them with all his strength. They hardly moved.

'Shit!' he gasped. He tried in the opposite direction, as far as he could gauge in the complete darkness, hitting Bitsos's legs as he went. The tunnel continued for a few metres and then met a solid wall. 'Dead end.'

'Very witty. Conserve your energy, fool.'

'Why? So it takes me longer to die?'

There was a silence. 'Well, yes. Won't people be looking for us?'

'Not if the bastards pick up the Fat Man.'

'What about that tame cop of yours?'

'He's not that tame. Besides, what will he have to go on, Lambi? Akis will say he never took us across the bay. Nobody saw us get on the boat. He'll hide the cars and concoct some lie about us having left of our own accord.'

'Were those fuckers taking it seriously up there in the temple? It's 2004. Who worships the ancient gods?'

'Quite a lot of people, if your pals in the media are to be believed. Remember those protests about the Olympics being a travesty of their original form? They were by the Olympian gods' faithful.'

'Yes, but millionaires like Paschos Poulos, hard-nosed business types, what are they doing dressing up in robes and slaughtering piglets?'

'Shame you couldn't take any pictures.'

'They took my camera anyway, the thieving tossers. It cost me a fortune.'

Mavros laughed. 'You're worried about your camera at this juncture?'

'I managed to get the memory card out. It's in my pants.' Bitsos was quiet for a while. 'Anyway, it's time you came clean. What brought you down here in the first place? You haven't suddenly gone all ecological.'

'Er, no. Though the muck in the air and sea around here is pushing me rapidly in that direction.' Mavros thought about it. There was no point in keeping secrets any more. 'I was hired by Angie Poulou.'

'The tycoon's wife? What for?'

'They kept it quiet, but their fourteen-year-old daughter Lia disappeared on May 1st. They've been pretending she's at school in Switzerland while Kriaras coordinates the search for her.'

'Jesus. The fucker certainly nailed the news blackout. Have you picked up any trace of her?'

'She was down here in March at one of the ecologists' work-shops. She also met Ourania, the girl Rovertos Bekakos abused.'

'She's fourteen too, isn't she? Shit, there's something very nasty going on. A paedophile ring?'

Mavros tried to get comfortable, but the stone floor was jagged. 'Angie said she suspected Bekakos and maybe even her husband of that kind of thing.'

'Hang on, there's also the Son. I didn't see him tonight.'

'Just as well. He'd have hung us from the roof with fish hooks.'

'Thanks for reminding me of that modus operandi. At least the Father hasn't shown his face.'

'Mm. The question is, where is the Son? He's been killing off rival Olympian believers, but I think he's also looking for Lia. Christ, Niki.'

'What, you think he might have gone after her?'

'I left her numerous messages to clear out.' Mavros clenched his fists. 'But it's not only her. My whole family could be at risk.'

'Cool it, Alex. Deep breaths – though the air down here stinks worse than a whore's armpit.'

Mavros couldn't help laughing. 'Delicate as ever. Hang on, what about my client?'

'You mean she'll start asking where you are?' Bitsos said hopefully.

'No, I mean what if the Son's been turned loose on her?'

'Why?'

'She was petrified about her husband finding out she'd hired me.'

'But who hired the Son? Surely Poulos is behind that.' He paused. 'Fucking hell. You mean he might want his own wife dead?'

'He might want Lia dead too.'

'Because he abused her?'

Mavros didn't reply. He was suddenly overwhelmed by the horror of the case – people cut to pieces, pomegranate seeds stuffed in their bodies, underage girls used as sex objects, animals sacrificed; let alone the premature deaths from the pollution. He almost resigned himself to dying in the underworld, so vile was life on the surface.

Then he pulled himself together.

'Come on, Lambi, let's see if the two of us mightn't be able to shake the bars free.'

They gave it their best shot, but to no avail.

# TWENTY-TWO

Angie Poulou crept to the bathroom door, pistol in her right hand. She listened, but could hear no sound. That immediately made her wonder about the cook, Fidelia. Surely she would have heard the shot. She slipped down the corridor, noticing a trail of blood. That made her more confident, as she could see spatter all the way to the top of the stairs. She checked the hall from above and saw no sign of her assailant. What she did see stopped her heart for a couple of seconds. Fidelia was sprawled on the marble, blood emanating from the swathe of her dark hair.

Telling herself to keep her cool, Angie moved to the stairs and went down, looking around continuously. When she reached the ground floor, she checked the doors. They were all closed, except the French windows that led to the pool. Her killer had left the way he'd come, the blood leading round the corner beyond the recliners. She ran through the extension and pulled the doors to, engaging the lock. Then she rushed back to the cook. Her breathing was shallow and her pulse slow. There was nothing for it. Despite the fact that, from the time Paschos got involved with the Olympics he had told her to contact Brigadier Kriaras in any emergency, she'd had enough of her husband's rules. She dialled 166 and asked for an ambulance, giving details of Fidelia's condition. She was told to put a blanket over her, which she did. Sitting by the motionless servant, Angie realised she would have some explaining to do. She got up and looked at herself in the large gold-framed mirror, barely suppressing a scream. Instead of teeth, the fronts of both upper and lower jaws were lined with metal pegs, most of them bent outwards. She went to the nearest bathroom and wiped the blood away. She put on a towelling robe, then stuffed the pistol into the laundry basket and ran upstairs. The bathroom looked like a slaughterhouse. She pulled out the plug and let the water run out of the bath, using the hand shower to wash away the worst of the blood. The ear fragment she picked out with a facecloth and dumped in the rubbish. She had a vague idea that reattachment might be possible, but she was damned if the bastard was getting it back.

The bell from the gate rang. She went downstairs and checked the screen by the phone. The ambulance looked normal and there was no sign of the killer, even though he might have been waiting for the gate to open in order to make his escape. As she waited for the paramedics, Angie had a thought – how had he got in? The perimeter wall was supposed to be impassable. Had he been given the pass code? Was that more evidence of her husband's betrayal?

One of the green-overalled personnel was female, the other male. They headed straight for Fidelia and did what they'd been trained to do.

'What happened, Madam?' the woman asked, looking round.

'She must have slipped,' Angie said. 'I was upstairs.'

'And you?'

Angie realised the paramedic was looking at her face. 'Oh, I went headfirst myself when I heard her scream. I collided with the door frame.'

'And lost all those teeth? You should come with us too.'

'No, no, I'm fine.' She showed the family's private health insurance papers. 'Please do everything that's necessary for poor Fidelia.'

'If you're sure, Madam,' the woman said dubiously. 'But you really should get those contusions looked at – there may be bone damage.'

Angie nodded. 'I will. It's just, I have to meet my daughter at the airport. Don't worry, the chauffeur will drive.' She watched the paramedics remove the cook on a wheeled stretcher, one of them holding a drip high. When they were gone, she went back to the first-floor bathroom and got down on her knees to pick up the remains of her crowns. Suddenly the dam she'd erected to contain her emotions burst and she started weeping uncontrollably, the broken pieces of gold and porcelain scattering across the tiles as she lost control of her hands. How could he? How could Paschos send someone to kill her? Or was it someone else?

Then it occurred to her that the assassin might have advised his employer of his failure – or might be preparing a second attempt after patching up his wounds. Gathering the crowns into a plastic bag, she ran to the bedroom and changed into a pale blue linen trouser suit. Then she threw clothes and shoes into a suitcase. Until she'd found Lia and uncovered whatever Paschos was up to, she wouldn't be coming back to the house. Then she located her mobile phone and called Alex Mavros. It rang unobtainable. She tried again, with same result. Had he been got at by another assailant? That thought made her sob again. If he was gone, who could she turn to?

Angie Poulou put the pistol into her Hermès handbag and hauled the suitcase downstairs. Now she had to get to the garage and take a car without her driver/bodyguard getting in the way. Although he was off duty, he lived above the garages. It was strange that he hadn't come round to the main house with all the commotion caused by the ambulance arriving and then taking poor Fidelia off to the hospital. Angie went to the far end of the house and opened the door that led to the outbuildings. She expected to be accosted by the man – a muscular Ithacan whom she disliked intensely – but there was no sign of him. How could that be? One of the men was always on duty. She groaned, realising this was also part of Paschos's plan. She and the unfortunate Fidelia had been left on their own with the killer. Fine, she thought. If that's how he wants to play . . .

Her BMW saloon was in the middle garage, next to the Mitsubishi 4x4 they used on the estate on Evia. Angie decided she would take the latter. As she stowed her luggage, she made her mind up where she was going. Alex Mavros had last been heard from in the vicinity of the HMC plant by Paradheisos. Rovertos Bekakos was down there too.

Viotia here she came – and this time she would ignore her bees.


Mavros began to shiver. He had come into the cage covered in sweat, but the ambient temperature so far beneath the surface of the earth was low.

Alongside him, Lambis Bitsos clenched his arms to his body. 'Do you think it's possible to freeze to death in Greece in August?'

'I'm beginning to fear so. Then again, we're also up against dehydration, lack of food and whatever creepy-crawlies live down here.'

'Did you see any spiders before the lights left? I fucking hate spiders.'

Mavros laughed weakly. 'Before this is over, you'll be eating them, my friend.'

'I'll eat you first.'

Mavros edged away, aware of Bitsos's permanently raging hunger.

'Don't be stupid,' the other man scoffed. 'We'll be out of here before we get that desperate.'

'You reckon?'

'I do, and I'll tell you why. The Fat Man hasn't been brought to join us.'

'Jesus, Lambi, you're right. He must still be at large.'

'At large? Very good. But you take my point?'

'I do. The problem is, he has no idea where we are.' He thought of Telemachos Xanthakos. The policeman would help, but he didn't know their location either. Which left . . .

'That wanker of a fisherman,' Bitsos said. 'If he goes back to Kypseli, which logically he has to in order to keep in with the ecologists, he could be a weak link.'

'He could be.' Mavros found his mind moving away from their immediate plight to the females in the case. He wished he'd managed to get more out of Angie Poulou about her husband – it was clear she had suspicions about him, and she wasn't involved in the Hades and Persephone cult. He also regretted not managing to ask her about Lia's involvement with the ecologists and the abused girl, Ourania. Had she been to Paradheisos more than once, perhaps when Angie was tending her bees on Mount Elikonas? Could it be that Lykos had kidnapped her and kept that from Angeliki? And then there was Niki. Had the Son really gone after the woman Mavros had loved for years? If so, she was doomed – perhaps already dead. He felt his heart constrict as he realised how much he loved her. He should never have driven her to leave him. So she wanted children. What was wrong with that? He thought of his father, Spyros, who had died when Mavros was only five but who still influenced his life. Inevitably, his brother Andonis also flashed before him, his lips in their perpetual smile and his blue eyes wide open. If Mavros had kids with Niki, the ones he had lost would be kept alive, their genes passed on.

'What is it?' Bitsos demanded. 'Are you crying?'

'No,' Mavros mumbled, but his eyes and cheeks were damp. He was thinking of the children he would never have and the women he had failed – Niki, Angie Poulou and her daughter, the last only fourteen years old but, if Ourania's abuse by Rovertos Bekakos was anything to go by, already mature beyond her years in the worst of senses. The question was, had Paschos Poulos been involved? Had he really abused his own daughter?

Given he was deep in the underworld with little hope of rescue,

Mavros supposed he would never find out the answers to those and many other questions.

'Alex?' Bitsos said tentatively.

'What, Lambi?'

'Can you . . . can you hold my hand?'

He took the journalist's scrawny paw and sank into an inner darkness that was even more absolute than that in the former dynamite store.

The Son grabbed a towel after he sent the Filipina flying and ran to the gate. He held the fabric against the wounds to his head and ear until he got to the Fiat. He drove towards the national highway, but pulled in before he got there and looked at himself in the vanity mirror. His left ear had been halved and was still gushing, but the razor slashes to his face and scalp were less bloody. He managed to tie the towel in such a way as to cover all three cuts, but he knew he needed surgery urgently. He called the emergency number he'd been given and told the gruff man who answered what he needed. Five minutes late he received directions to a private clinic and was told to enter at the rear. When he was finished, he was to phone again to report.

The clinic was in Vrilissia, a suburb further to the east. The building was modern and multicoloured, its car park full apart from a space at the far corner. The Son drove to it, got out and kicked away the cone that had been placed there, then parked. He walked round the edge of the building and went in a door that had been left ajar. A young male orderly was waiting for him, his eyes lowered. He took him straight to a consulting room. The doctor was suave and grey-haired, his hands steady as he applied anaesthetic spray and got down to stitching. He didn't speak until he examined the ear.

'I take it you don't have the missing piece.'

'No.'

'Plastic surgery can make up for it later, but I was told to get you on your way as quickly as possible.'

'Were you?' the Son growled. He had clearly pissed his employer off. A needle ran through his tattered ear, the pain easily negating the anaesthetic, but he didn't flinch. It was mutual – he was pissed off with his employer, not to mention the woman who had resisted like a tigress. He would take her life, but it wasn't a priority. If Alex Mavros really was involved, he got top billing, even over the next Olympian worshippers on his list. Then he had another thought. Mavros had a family – a famous father and brother, dead and disappeared, and a mother who published books. There was also a lover – what was her name?

'Niki,' he said, a minute later.

'I'm sorry?' the doctor asked, pausing in mid-suture.

He could get her address, he could get the mother's too. He had the feeling there was a sister too – he'd assembled a detailed file on the bastard when he was in Bulgaria. To hell with Lia Poulou. It was time Alex Mavros's family paid for what he'd done during the Father's last commission.

The doctor stopped again. 'You're the only patient I've ever had who's laughed during this procedure.'

The Son caught his eye and the medic stepped quickly backwards, his hands raised.

Bitsos had actually managed to fall asleep, his hand curled within Mavros's.

'No sleep before you're dead, eh, Lambi?' Mavros murmured. He felt curiously calm, like a condemned prisoner who had come to terms with his fate. He thought about the statues of the deities in the temple at the top of the tunnel. The Hades and Persephone myth, coupled with that of the Maiden's mother Demeter, wasn't downbeat. Unlike the traditions of the waste land, brought together by T.S. Eliot and the Greek poet Seferis, it didn't signify the end of life on earth. Rather, it gave weight to the fertility that rejuvenated the natural world every spring. Even though many individual humans would not survive the harshness of winter, the species as a whole, along with many others, would flower.

Then he thought of the real waste land that was the HMC plant – the mountainsides scored by huge cutting machines; the ore hauled away in monster trucks; the clouds of fumes that shortened the lives of people in Paradheisos and Kypseli; the waters of the gulf reddened and poisoned. The worst thing was that the mineral wealth that belonged to Hades Plouton in ancient times went to a small number of people. The workers were little more than slaves, thrown out of their homes when they could no longer pull their weight – and their children were abused and ruined, treated worse than sinners in the paintings that terrified people in the Middle Ages. How could the responsible parties look themselves in the mirror? Was that why Paschos Poulos, the Bekakos couple and the arch-thief Tryfon Roufos comforted themselves by believing in the Olympian gods? Did they think they could escape the torture region of Tartarus by cutting the throats of a few piglets?

And then it struck him. Even though Lia Poulou may have been sexually abused like Ourania, that wasn't why she had been taken. The bastards – whether Lykos and his fellow believers or the other faithful who included Paschos Poulos in their number – were going to sacrifice her. Not only that, he was sure the act was connected to the Olympic Games which had made Paschos Poulos even wealthier; sacrificing his own daughter to the gods of death and fertility would guarantee his future prosperity. Then again, the great King Agamemnon had sacrificed his daughter Iphigenia to ensure a fair wind to Troy. That deed had revolted his wife Clytemnestra so much that she had executed him in his bath with an axe.

Mavros thought Angie Poulou would be capable of an act like that. One of his many sorrows was that he wouldn't be on the surface of the earth to hear about it.

Telemachos Xanthakos was at the bow of the fishing boat, watching as it swung away from the huge cargo ship and headed behind a ridge that dropped sharply into the sea. On the far side there was darkness. He held the unlit torch that Akis Exarchos had given him and looked over his shoulder. Alex Mavros's friend, the Fat Man, was a metre from the fisherman, the policeman's pistol trained on the man at the tiller. When they passed into the lee of the ridge, Akis raised an arm cautiously and Xanthakos turned on the torch. He gasped when he saw the jagged rocks straight ahead, then Exarchos cut the revs and manoeuvred the boat towards the land.

'Under the shelf!' the fisherman shouted. 'There's a mooring ring.'

The deputy commissioner knew he was taking a risk leaving

Akis with the Fat Man, but he had no choice – neither of them could handle the controls. He leaned forward and ran his hand under the line of rock. Nothing, nothing . . . yes, a cold steel circle. He looped a rope round it and pulled hard, as the fisherman finished steering and killed the engine.

'You know how to secure that?' Akis called.

Xanthakos shouted back in affirmation as he made the line fast – he had been fishing often enough with his father in the Gulf of Thessaloniki. He went sternwards, divesting himself of the yellow waterproofs. Then Exarchos made his move. Suddenly the detached tiller arm was in his hands. He swung it straight at the Fat Man's head.

'No!' Xanthakos screamed, slipping on the wet deck. Then he realised that Mavros's friend had ducked with surprising speed and jabbed the muzzle of the pistol hard into the fisherman's belly. By the time the policeman reached the stern, Yiorgos was standing over Akis, the muzzle against his head.

'Shit, that was close,' Xanthakos said.

'I can jive with best of them when I have to,' the Fat Man said, with a grin. 'Come on, bellyache. You've got places to show us.' He handed the pistol to the deputy commissioner and pulled off the ill-fitting wet weather gear. Then he picked the fisherman up by the scruff of his neck and staggered with him to the bow. He swayed alarmingly for a moment, then stood safely on a flat piece of rock with his prisoner.

Holding his pistol, Xanthakos followed them off the boat and up a steep outcrop. The lights of the plant glowed on the other side of the ridge. The wall of rock dropped at one point and he saw the extent of the installation. He had visited it on official business several times, but the view from above confirmed how huge the place was. And how ugly. A dense pall of dusty fumes hung over the valley floor and, to the rear, the ravaged mountain was like a half-eaten corpse with insect-like machines crawling over it. No matter how valuable the minerals extracted were, they couldn't be worth this picture of desolation.

They struggled on, keeping out of the lights from the buildings and towers. The Fat Man was wheezing for breath but he moved upwards doggedly, his heavy hand tight on Exarchos's neck. Xanthakos heard him speaking to the fisherman in a low voice, but he couldn't make out the words. Whatever they were, their effect was to make the thin man's body loose, as if the fight had been knocked out of him.

Eventually a pale stone building began to show in the distance.

'What is that?' the policeman asked.

'It's where the faithful worship,' Akis said. 'We shouldn't go there. You aren't allowed. You have to be ritually cleansed.'

'Dirty, are we?' the Fat Man said, raising his free hand. 'I told you, you'll be shitting through twin arseholes if you waste our time. Are you sure that's the last place you saw Alex?'

The fisherman's head dropped again. 'Yes, I swear it.'

'What, by Demeter?'

'This temple isn't dedicated to the Green Lady,' Akis said. 'It's Hades' and Persephone's.'

Xanthakos felt a tremor. He knew the myths and he knew about the pomegranate seeds. Was the man who had planted them in his victims nearby? He looked around anxiously, but saw no one near the fenced-off structure.

Ten minutes later, they were over the fence and at the entrance. There was a smell of burned pitch cut with the metallic tang of blood.

'I can't go in with the profane,' the fisherman said, in a low voice.

'You're coming voluntarily or I'll wrap you in some of the barbed wire we just clambered over,' the Fat Man said. 'This is my best friend we're looking for.'

Exarchos started to move forward slowly, the hand still on his nape. The policeman checked that the winding track to the temple was empty of vehicles and followed the others in.

'Marx and Engels,' Yiorgos said, taking in the heaps of entrails that had been plucked from the piglets' mutilated bodies.

'Please don't blaspheme,' Akis said. 'Hades and Persephone are vengeful gods.'

'Where's Alex?' the Fat Man demanded. 'Tell me or I'll pull these statues down on top of you.'

The fisherman glanced at Xanthakos for help, but none was forthcoming.

'I don't know exactly,' he said, flinching as the grip on his neck tightened. 'I left before he and the journalist were disposed of.'

'DISPOSED OF?' Yiorgos roared. 'You better hope Alex is alive or I'll dispose of *you* like these little pigs.'

Akis Exarchos pointed to the brands on the walls. 'Light a couple of those. Behind the deities there's a tunnel.'

The Fat Man watched as the policeman got two of the torches burning and handed one to him. 'Right,' he said, pushing the fisherman between the blood and soot marked statues. 'It looks like this leads downwards.' He grinned. 'It's a full-blown highway to hell.'

Telemachos Xanthakos walked after the asymmetrical pair. One thing he'd never have imagined was that the corpulent Communist would be an AC/DC fan.

# TWENTY-THREE

L ykos and Cadres One to Four had returned to Kypseli in the early morning. Angeliki's earlier insistence that she had to see the doctor in Dhistomo urgently had taken him by surprise, not least because she'd refused to say what the matter was. She had borrowed Akis's motorbike. Despite his easy success with women, he understood very little about them. She was waiting for them at the Ecologists for a Better Viotia office.

'Where's Ourania?' Angeliki asked.

'She . . . she wanted to go home,' Lykos replied, keeping his eyes off his partner's.

The young woman looked at him gravely. 'She might talk.'

'Who to? Her parents? They're company stooges. Her friends? She said herself that she hasn't got any.'

'Yes, but she should have stayed with us. We need her.'

Lykos smiled. 'We know where she lives. Can you help the cadres with the cooking? We haven't eaten since yesterday afternoon.'

It seemed Angeliki was going to object, but in the end she went into the back room and helped the young Communists cut up vegetables and herbs. When the soup-stew hybrid was on the gas, she came back out.

'What is it?' Lykos asked. 'You look worried.'

'Where's Akis? His boat's not in the harbour.'

'He went off on that expedition with Mavros and the journalist, remember?'

'They should have been back hours ago. I'm worried something's happened to them. That's not all.' She went to the front window. 'Did you notice those cars down the road?'

Lykos got up and joined her, putting his hand on the back of her neck. Despite the heat of the night, the skin was very warm. 'Are you all right?'

'Yes.' She pointed through the open window. 'The further one looks like an unmarked police car. The Peugeot, I don't know, but I'm worried. I'm going round to Akis's house to see if he's there. His boat could have been stolen.'

'Why not call him?'

Angeliki stopped at the door. 'If he's in trouble, the last thing he needs is his phone ringing. And we should close the shutters. The guy with the funny rifle is still at large.'

Lykos did as she said, then made a call. He recounted his overnight activities to his aunt and was praised. All he needed to do now was wait for things to come to the boil.

Mavros heard it first. He let go of Bitsos's hand and stood up, head turned and one ear in the gap between the bars. Nothing. It had sounded like a voice, but he must have imagined it. Then he heard it again, followed by a deeper one. People were coming down the tunnel. His heart started to beat fast, then it struck him that the visitors would probably be Kloutsis and his sidekick, coming to gloat.

Lights began to flicker higher up, gradually becoming brighter. Then an unmistakable voice called out.

'Alex? Are you down this shit-hole, Alex?'

Never had Mavros been happier to hear the Fat Man's less than dulcet tones.

'Yes, Yiorgo, keep on walking down. We're in a cage.'

Bitsos woke up with a grunt. 'What is it? Are those fuckers coming back?'

'No,' Mavros said, grabbing him round his thin shoulders. 'These are *our* fuckers.'

Bitsos strained to hear. 'The Fat Man,' he said. 'I never thought I'd be pleased to hear his elephantine tread.'

The lights came closer and they realised they were flaming brands from the temple. Mavros made out the tall figure of Telemachos Xanthakos and the Fat Man. A shorter thin man was in front of them. Akis Exarchos did not look happy.

'Christ, Alex, what is this place?' Yiorgos asked, when they reached the bars.

'Former dynamite store. Good to see you too.'

'Piss off. We're rescuing you, aren't we?' He glared at Bitsos. 'No thanks from you, eh, hack?'

'I think I love you,' Lambis said fulsomely. 'Now get us out of here.'

'Deputy Commissioner,' Mavros said. 'Any thoughts on that?'

Xanthakos held his brand as close as he could. 'I can't see any sign of explosives.' He handed the torch to Yiorgos, who pushed Akis close to the bars. 'We've already established that the fisherman doesn't have a key, so stand back and cover your faces.' He pulled out his service pistol and aimed it at the lock. 'Yiorgo, you might want to pull your prisoner back a few steps.'

'Screw that. He can take whatever's coming to him.'

The policeman shook his head, then fired three shots. The bullets ricocheted away with loud zings.

'That did it,' Mavros said, pushing open the gate.

'Stick that Hades-worshipping piece of shit in there,' Bitsos said, glaring at Akis. 'Have you got any water?'

The Fat Man handed a small bottle to him. 'Half of that's for Alex,' he said, with a growl.

'This is a police operation, Mr Bitso,' Xanthakos said. 'Kindly follow instructions.'

As they walked back up from the depths, Akis Exarchos in tow, Mavros told the others what he and the journalist had witnessed in the temple.

'Paschos Poulos?' the deputy commissioner said in amazement. 'And the fugitive Tryfon Roufos? What kind of conspiracy is this?'

'One involving underage girls.' Mavros turned to the fisherman. 'What do you know about that?'

Akis hung his head. 'Nothing.'

'Oh, yes?' Mavros shouted. 'Where's Ourania?'

'I don't know. Honestly. You'll have to ask Lykos.'

Mavros explained to Xanthakos about Lia Poulou and her link to the abused girl from Paradheisos as they came up into the temple.

'Hold on,' the policeman said, glancing at the Fat Man and Akis. 'Make sure he doesn't make a sound.' Yiorgos duly covered the fisherman's mouth with his fleshy hand.

Xanthakos crept forward, gun in two hands, swivelling from side to side. He reached the front of the ancient building and looked down the track, then returned to the others.

'All clear. What now?'

'Give me your phone, please,' Mavros said. He pressed out Niki's mobile number. It was answered immediately.

'Alex!' his ex-lover exclaimed. 'What's going on? I'm at your sister's. We've got your mother here too.'

Mavros sighed in relief. Niki had done more than he'd imagined she would – then again, she had been through alarms in the past.

'Thank you . . . thank you for doing that. I really appreciate it. Can you get Anna and Nondas – not my mother – around a speaker phone and call me back in a couple of minutes?' Niki agreed and he cut the connection.

Mavros took Xanthakos by the arm and steered him away from the others. 'I think my family's under threat from the Son. You haven't seen anyone like him down here tonight?'

The policeman shook his head.

'I think he's in Athens.'

'Should we call Brigadier Kriaras?'

'Bad idea, Telemache. For a start, he hasn't been in touch with me since I was filmed on the blockade. We have mutual history with the Son, but he isn't curious to find out what I'm doing? That's suspicious in itself. He's in with Poulos, I'm sure of that – maybe not as a Hades worshipper, but as Public Order Ministry official or even Olympic security committee facilitator.'

'These are deep waters, Alex. I should tell my chief.'

'Another bad idea.'

The phone rang and Mavros heard the voices of his sister and brother-in-law asking if he was OK. He confirmed that he was.

'Listen,' he continued, 'a particularly nasty killer known as the Son may be after one or all of you. The problem is, we can't bring the police in. What do you want to do?'

'Stay here,' Nondas said. He was a solid Cretan businessman. 'I've already secured the house – you know how thick the shutters are.' He laughed. 'Plus, I've got several things that go bang.'

Mavros raised his eyes to the sooty ceiling. 'Anna, what do you think?'

'Better here than risk an ambush outside. What's happening, Alex?'

'I'm not exactly clear yet, but the main shit's going down in Viotia, not in the big city, so you may be out of it anyway. If the worst happens, call the ordinary cops. Whatever you do, don't get in touch with Brigadier Kriaras. He's involved in some way. Look, I have to go. Use this number, not mine – it's been taken. Talk to you all later. Oh, and Niki? Kill the speaker phone.'

'What is it, Alex? she asked, after a click.

'I . . . when this is all finished, I need to talk to you. Face to face.'

'All right,' his former lover said, her voice wistful. 'I'd like that.' Then her voice hardened. 'I can't believe you've got us into another shooting match, Alex. Now do you understand why I left you?'

'That's not why you left,' he said, turning away from Xanthakos. 'Listen, I'm standing under a statue of Persephone. She was all her mother Demeter cared about. I understand that now. Do you get my drift?'

'I . . . yes, I do. All right, we'll talk. Just make sure you come back without any extra holes in your sorry carcass.' Niki terminated the call.

'Shit,' the policeman said, from the temple entrance. 'We're about to have company.'

The Fat Man stepped forward, hand on Akis's nape. 'Oh, good,' he said, with a wide grin.

The Son was sitting in the Fiat outside Niki Glezou's apartment block in Palaio Faliro in southern Athens. There were no lights on and he couldn't be sure whether she was in and asleep, or out. It didn't matter. He would wait for as long as it took. He could survive for days without sleep, having trained himself with the help of the Bulgarian – the latter recommended amphetamines, but the Son avoided drugs. Instead, he swallowed a laugh. His body was a temple, but not one to Demeter, Persephone or Hades. The idiocies of his fellow Greeks no longer surprised him, but worshipping the Olympian gods was seriously ridiculous. Even the Father's ancestor worship hadn't gone that far.

Then his phone rang. He straightened his back in the uncomfortable seat.

'Find a public phone and call me NOW!'

The Son would normally have walked in case he lost the parking space, but the bandages on his wounds would attract attention. He drove down the street and headed for the suburb's centre. There was a phone outside some shops, deserted at this time of night. He rang the number he had memorised.

'Where the fuck are you?' Brigadier Kriaras demanded. 'I told you to get in touch after you'd finished at the hospital.'

'You didn't tell me Alex Mavros was involved,' the Son said stonily.

'Mavros?'

'Don't play dumb. Why didn't you tell me?'

'I . . . thought it would distract you.'

The Son gave a hollow laugh. 'Did you? Thanks for the vote of confidence. You know what? You can stuff the second half of my payment up your haemorrhoidal arse. I'm otherwise engaged.'

'Wait!' There was panic in the brigadier's voice. 'For God's sake, wait. All right, I agree I should have told you about him. I only found out when I saw him on TV a couple of days ago.'

'So?'

'So, things are complicated. I would have told you later.'

'Later? That wouldn't have been much use if I'd come up against the fucker. He and his friends almost killed me and the Father the last time I saw him.'

'What if I offer an increased fee?'

'What if I find out your home address?'

There was a protracted silence.

'Ten per cent,' Kriaras said.

'Fifty.'

'Twenty-five. On the balance only.'

'I'll soon know where you live.'

'Very well, thirty. On the whole fee'

'On condition that I do what I like with Mavros, anyone with him and anyone in his family.'

'I can't give you immunity from—'

'I'm coming to visit . . .'

'All right! Try not to turn it into a total slaughter. As for now – here's what you have to do.'

The Son listened carefully, concentrating on the salient points, and then hung up. Mavros's girlfriend was temporarily off the hook. He would deal with her when he came back from Viotia.

'Back down the tunnel!' Telemachos Xanthakos ordered.

'Bugger that,' the Fat Man and Lambis Bitsos said, in unison.

'How many vehicles?' Mavros asked.

'Just one.'

'We should be able to handle them, even if there are four or five heavies. Yiorgo, gag the fisherman. Then put out the torches and take cover. Telemache, you hide behind Hades, I'll get behind Persephone. Lambi, you and the Fat Man go to the beginning of the tunnel. We'll let them come towards you, then surround them.'

'They'll probably have guns,' Bitsos said, realising what he'd got himself into.

'Well, we'd better relieve the tossers of them,' Mavros said, taking one of the still hot torches. 'These should help.'

They waited in the darkness, aware that the smoke from the brands would make it obvious people had been present, at least until very recently. The vehicle revved hard as it came up the final slope. Then cautious footsteps sounded on the marble steps. A high-power electric torch was shone round the interior of the temple.

'Any of the worshippers been up here again?' Kloutsis asked.

'Dunno. D'you want me to call?'

'No, forget it.'

'You don't think those wankers in the cage could have got out?' said a third man.

'We'd better check,' Kloutsis said, shining his beam on the walls. 'Someone's taken the torches.'

'Maybe there are rescuers down the tunnel,' said the second

man. They seemed to be three in total – unless more were waiting outside.

'Rescuers?' Kloutsis scoffed, leading them forward. 'Who could have found them?'

'Hades himself,' said Mavros, in a deep voice, as he swung the brand at the lead villain.

Kloutsis screamed as the hot tar hit his face. Xanthakos rammed his pistol into the rear man's back, making him drop his own weapon. At the same time, Lambis Bitsos ran forward and drove his unlit torch into the second man's belly. There was a squeal when he grabbed the pitch with both hands. Mavros picked up his gun and electric torch, along with those Kloutsis had been carrying. Then he went to the entrance of the temple and looked out carefully. There was no one else by the Japanese 4x4.

'Right,' he said, 'we're in the clear, at least for now. Let's get these tossers down to the cage.'

'What about the lock I blew apart?' the policeman asked.

'Good point. All right, we'll shred their clothes and tie them up out of sight down the tunnel.'

'Gag them, too,' the Fat Man said, with relish.

The three men all wore belts, so securing their legs was easy. Their arms were lashed behind their backs with strips of their shirts, the remains of which were balled up and rammed into their mouths. Finally, they were tied together, making it almost impossible for them to crawl.

When they were back in the temple, Bitsos indicated the already silenced fisherman and asked, 'What about him?'

'You and Yiorgos go back with him to Kypseli on the boat,' Mavros said. 'Deputy Commissioner Xanthakos and I are going to find Poulos and the Bekaki.'

'Shouldn't we stick together?' the Fat Man asked.

'The boat isn't big enough for all of us. Besides, we need a reserve team. If Telemachos and I don't reappear, get Lykos to call his aunt. She'll mobilize the Party.'

Yiorgos raised an eyebrow but went along with that. Mavros gave him and Bitsos a pistol each, keeping one for himself. Now they were all armed.

'Good luck,' the Fat Man said, embracing Mavros, who almost fainted in shock.

Bitsos patted him on the shoulder. 'Stay alive, Alex. This is going to be the story of the decade.'

Mavros watched them head off around the hillside.

'What's the plan?' the deputy commissioner asked.

'We drive down to the plant and see if there are any flash cars in the vicinity. If so, we go in. You can wave your ID and arrest the bastards for abducting and imprisoning me and Bitsos. If the VIPs aren't here, which I think is likely – look at the state of this hellhole – they'll be in Paradheisos. Unless they've gone back to the big city, of course. We'll drive around till we find Bekakos's Porsche or any other rich man's car. I haven't noticed too many in the town.'

'OK.' Xanthakos took the radio from his belt.

'What are you doing?'

'Calling for backup.'

'Are you out of your mind? Your chief will hear of it and he'll be straight on to Brigadier Kriaras.'

The policeman shook his head. 'I can't believe a senior officer – let alone one on the Games security committee – is involved in this. You haven't seen him here, have you?'

'No, of course not. He keeps his hands clean.' Mavros took the radio and switched it off. 'If we find the VIPs, you can call for local help, all right?'

'What the devil am I doing, taking orders from a private dick?'

Mavros extended an arm and moved it over the reddened terrain and buildings below them. The lights cast eerie shadows from the chimney stacks and piles of ore.

'This is the devil's domain, my friend. If you clean it up, you'll be on the fast track – not even Kriaras will be able to stop you. The place is killing people.' Mavros dropped his arm. 'But that's not all. The shit heads who own and run it are doing something even worse.' That made him think of his client. Taking Xanthakos's phone again, he called her.

'Mr Mavros,' Angie Poulou lisped, the noise of a car engine in the background. 'Thank God. I was beginning to think you had disappeared into thin air like Lia.'

'Are you all right?' Mavros asked.

'A man attacked me.'

'What? Who? Where?'

'You're confusing me. It happened in my home. I think . . . I think Paschos put him up to it.'

'What happened?'

'I managed to see him off. I lost a lot of teeth, that's why I can't talk properly.'

'Describe your assailant.'

'A big man, not old, probably late twenties. Short blonde hair. Very self-assured. He tried to make it look as if I slashed my wrists in the bath. I . . . I cut off part of his ear.'

'Christ. Are you on the way to hospital?

'No, I'm coming to Paradheisos. I want to confront Paschos. I'm sure he knows where Lia is.'

'We need to do that together. Where are you?'

'Just past Thiva.'

'All right, I'm with a policeman I trust. Call this number when you've gone through Dhistomo. We'll arrange a meet.' Mavros had a thought. 'Where does your husband usually stay when he's down here?'

'There's a guest house in the pink sector for senior management – at the far end of Isiodhou Street.'

'I've been wanting to ask you something. Did Lia often come down to Paradheisos?'

'Several times in the winter and early spring.' Angie Poulou paused. 'With Paschos. She said she was doing a geography project. Oh, God.'

'What is it?'

'I have a terrible feeling about . . . about my husband and . . . and Lia.'

Mavros confirmed the arrangements, extracting a promise from his client that she wouldn't act alone. He turned to Xanthakos.

'I think I know where they are.' He gazed down at the infernal nightscape, and then glanced into the temple. 'Screw the devil. We're in Hades' kingdom and we have to get out.'

The policeman laughed harshly. 'You know how many people managed that in the myths? Persephone doesn't count as she was a goddess.'

'Em, Heracles.'

'Semi-divine.'

'Orpheus.'

'Ditto.'

'I know,' Mavros said, taking out the key he'd removed from Kloutsis and heading to the 4x4, 'Theseus.'

'True,' Xanthakos said. 'But he had to leave his friend Peirithoos behind for eternity.'

'Great,' Mavros said, as he started the engine. 'We'll toss for it.'

The policeman raised an eyebrow and laughed, but not for long.

# TWENTY-FOUR

The Fat Man was less than impressed. Not only had he scraped his knees several times on the way back to the boat, but a wind got up and he'd been drenched frequently by sea water on the voyage to Kypseli. Fortunately, the fight seemed to have gone out of Akis Exarchos and he sat glumly at the tiller. Then again, Bitsos was pointing a pistol at the fisherman's belly. When they passed the mole and Akis cut the engine revs, Yiorgos raised his own pistol, aware that the approach to the pier would be the fisherman's last opportunity to put one over them in his natural element. As it happened, Akis drew alongside smoothly and slipped a rope round a bollard compliantly enough.

Bitsos looked across the square to the lights in the ecologists' office. 'They're back,' he said, swallowing a laugh as the Fat Man made an unsteady landing. He poked the pistol into the fisherman's back. 'Come on, you. Time to tell your friends you're a rat.'

The trio walked to the office. The shutters were closed, although lines of light came through the gaps in the slats.

'They'll be on edge about the Son,' Bitsos said. 'You'd better make friendly noises to the Party cadres.'

Yiorgos nodded and knocked on the door, identifying himself with a line from *Das Capital*. 'Akis is with us, too,' he added.

There was a rattle of bolts and the door opened. Lykos stood back to allow them entry, a long knife in one hand. One of the black-clad Communists was with him, holding a length of wood.

'That smells good,' the journalist said, glancing at the Fat Man, who was also sniffing the air.

'Where's Alex?' Lykos asked, on his guard when he saw the gun in the fisherman's back. 'What's going on?'

'Your friend here sold us out,' Bitsos said. 'He took the HMC's money. As a result, Mavros and I were imprisoned underground and left to die.'

Another of the cadres appeared from the back room. He glanced at the new arrivals suspiciously. 'The food's ready,' he said.

Lykos went toe to toe with Akis. 'You took their stinking money? Get the fuck out of here.'

'No,' Yiorgos said. 'Not until Alex comes back safe and sound.'

Lambis Bitsos motioned to him to hold his gun on the fisherman and then headed towards the back room. 'Is that bitch friend of yours here? She's one of them too.'

'What?' Lykos said, his voice breaking.

The rear door was open.

'Where is she?' Bitsos asked the cadres.

'She went to get some oregano from the garden,' one of them said.

'Oregano, my bollocks.' The journalist went out into a dark yard. 'Is there a light?' he called, over his shoulder.

The area was suddenly illuminated by a single bulb on the back wall of the building. There was a low wall beyond the rock garden and plant pots, but no sign of Angeliki.

'Shit!' Bitsos yelled.

'Come inside,' Lykos said, from the back door. 'The man with the rifle might be out there.'

The journo beat a rapid retreat and the door was secured behind him. His eyes fell on the statue of Demeter in the recess on the wall.

'She's been playing games with you, my friend,' he said to the ecologist. 'Maybe she does worship the goddess of fertility as well, but I saw her in robes before Hades and Persephone. She sacrificed a piglet to them.'

Lykos took him by the arm and led him into the front room, where Akis was in a chair, the Fat Man behind him. 'Tell me what happened.'

Bitsos obliged, laying on his outrage over being left to rot. 'Anyway,' he said, 'what are we doing here? We should be chasing the cow.'

'There's no point. I know where she's gone.'

'Really?'

The young man looked down. 'I had my suspicions about Angeliki, but—'

'You let yourself be guided by your cock,' Bitsos interrupted, with a grin. 'Don't worry, it happens to us all.'

'Speak for yourself,' Yiorgos muttered.

Lykos looked at them one by one. 'Anyway, I kept things from her.'

'Like, for example, where the girl is.'

The ecologist stared at Bitsos. 'What do you mean?'

'The girl from Paradheisos – what was her name? Ourania.'

'Oh, yes. Of course.'

The journalist was watching him carefully. 'So where is she?'

'At . . . at a friend of my family's place.'

'A friend of Tatiana Roubani too?' the Fat Man asked. He didn't know the Communist MP personally, but admired her full-blooded performances in parliament.

The oldest of the cadres shook his head. 'No, the man wasn't a comrade. He seemed decent enough. Small farmer, salt of the earth.'

'And you took her there for her own safety?' Bitsos asked the ecologist.

'That's right. Even without the defections of Angeliki and Akis, I knew things were coming to a head. Your friend Alex made sure of that.'

'What now?' Yiorgos asked. 'Can we eat?'

'Why not?'

Bitsos glared at Akis. 'None for that tosser, though. They left us in a cage half way down the mountain without even a drop of water.'

The leading cadre came forward with a rope. 'I'll tie him to his chair. Then you can feed him as much or as little as you like.'

Bitsos and the Fat Man exchanged smiles for the first time.

\*     \*     \*

'Jesus, this really is an inferno,' Mavros said, as he drove the 4x4 along the dry red track between lines of dust-covered tanks. Trucks laden with ore lumbered from the heaps at the rear to the smelting units, and the air was laden with fumes. The long rolling sheds were windowless, their corrugated sides layered with multi-coloured residues. Chimneys spewed dirty smoke into the night air, blurring the lights that were strung from webs of cables.

'How many shades of red can you get?' Xanthakos asked.

'Don't know. However many, they're all here.' Mavros slowed as he approached what looked like an administration block. At least it had windows. There were several cars outside, but none was remotely up-market.

'Time to go,' the policeman said, as a security guard waved at them.

Mavros raised a hand and accelerated away. 'Do you think he saw our faces?'

'We'll find out at the exit. There are barriers.'

'Oh, great.'

Mavros drove on to an asphalt road and disengaged the four-wheel drive system. Nearby, rolls of aluminium were being lifted on to the large ship they had seen during the trip from Kypseli.

'Car parks over there,' he said, looking to the right. They were lit up. 'Nothing that Paschos Poulos would put his Merc in.'

'Same on this side. Let's get out of here.'

'Done.' Mavros slowed as he approached the checkpoint. He was prepared to floor it, but the guard nodded and raised the barrier before they got to it.

'That was exciting,' Xanthakos said.

Mavros glanced at him. 'You haven't even broken into a sweat.'

'Years of training.'

They laughed.

'You realise it won't be long till they start wondering where Kloutsis and his sidekicks are,' Mavros said. 'And then they'll remember this car leaving the plant.'

'Won't matter,' the deputy commissioner said. 'As long as I make some high profile arrests.'

'That's the next objective.'

'What are you planning on doing? Going straight to the pink house and barging in? There will be security there too.'

Mavros nodded. 'But we have two aces up our sleeves. Make a call, please.'

He dictated the Fat Man's number and took the phone. 'Hey, we're out. You?'

'Eating.'

'I can hear that. Control your gluttony for a few moments and listen. If Poulos and the others are still in Paradheisos, I know where they'll be. Telemachos and I are heading to the town. We'll meet you on the Kypseli side. There's a line of trees. Akis knows it.'

'What, we're bringing that traitor?'

'Bind and gag him. He might come in handy later. Lykos and a couple of the cadres should stay with Ourania. Did Angeliki show up?'

'Yes, but she ran before we could grab her. As for Ourania, Lykos took her to some family friend, so all the big boys are free.'

'OK, split up into as many vehicles as you can. We might have to block roads.' He looked at the clock on the dashboard. 'See you at 04.00 hours.'

Yiorgos laughed. 'Roger, control. Over and out.'

'We have more aces than I thought,' Mavros said, telling the policeman about the cadres.

''I'm not happy about Mrs Poulou's potential involvement,' Xanthakos said. 'She could be in danger. We don't know where the Son is.'

'True. On the other hand, she might be able to incriminate her husband. Listen, Telemache, she knows things she hasn't told me yet. If you really want to nail the VIPs, you'll need all the help you can get.'

'All right,' the deputy commissioner said, after a pause. 'But we keep her away from firearms.'

'Agreed.'

A few minutes later, as they approached the outskirts of Paradheisos, Xanthakos's phone rang.

It was Angie Poulou. She had left Dhistomo and was heading for Paradheisos at speed.

The Son floored the accelerator as soon as he joined the national highway. There wasn't much traffic in the early hours and he made good time to the Thiva exit. After that, he was forced to take some chances overtaking and used the horn more than he'd have liked, but he kept up a decent speed. There wasn't much of a moon, but he could make out the mountain masses on his left and ahead. They reminded him of the town he had grown up in. Kastoria was near the Albanian border and the mountains were covered in snow throughout the winter. There was a lake too, where he had spent much of his childhood fishing. Inevitably that made him think of the Father.

What would the old bastard have said about this case? Would he have even taken it in the first place? He had worked for a single major crime family for decades and more than once he'd said that loyalty engendered trust. There was more to that than most of his crazy ideas. The Son had been surprised when he'd been contacted by Kriaras, as well as shocked that his whereabouts had been made available to the brigadier. Then again, as his Bulgarian instructor had told him, never trust a Bulgarian. The individual who had divulged the Son's location was now beneath the earth. Although his instincts had told him not to meet the intermediary who crossed the border, he decided to hear him out, not least because he held a gun on the minion throughout their conversation. In the end, what had swayed him wasn't the money – he had already earned enough as a gun for hire in the Balkans to keep him for years. It was the Greek passport and other documents providing him with a new identity. Now he could take on jobs beyond the Balkans. He could become the new Carlos.

Swerving past a slow-moving pickup near Livadheia, the Son thought about his homeland. He had no illusions about it, unlike the Father. He knew the politicians were rotten – puppets dancing to the tune of the traditional vested interests – and the common people as thick as the fertile earth of Viotia. They had been conned into wasting their money on state-controlled gambling, throwing their savings away on the deregulated Stock Exchange, and taking on multiple credit cards and loans for houses and cars. Even worse, the overwhelming majority supported the vast white elephant that was the Olympic Games. In the years to come, they would come to regret all of that. There was a reason the rich were rich: because the poor were stupid.

As he headed towards Dhistomo turn, the Son considered his

instructions. As usual, the details had been left to him – he
wouldn't work any other way. Even the pomegranate seeds, a
bag of which he had in a cooler pack in the boot of the Fiat, had
cramped his style. But he was puzzled by the change in policy.
Until now, the murders he'd committed were given minimal
coverage because of the Games. The kind of carnage he'd been
authorised to carry out before the next break of day couldn't be
kept from the media. People were being hung out to dry – they
would be used as scapegoats after their deaths. It amused him
that Alex Mavros was on the list. He had his own plans for the
private dick. If his employer didn't like them, he could suck on
the barrel of his Glock.

Mother Demeter, protectress of earth and fields, come to us
now, we beseech you. Like your Persephone, I am a lost
daughter, though I am no longer a maiden. I lie here beneath
your images, hands and wrist bound, mouth taped, the life inside
me swelling. Surely you cannot leave us to die in this
underground place. Surely you will not let them sacrifice our
young lives. Green Lady, give us back the light of day and the
kiss of the wind. We are the embodiment of fertility. Save us.

And save the other girl who was placed beside us some time
ago, I cannot tell how long. In the seconds of light, I saw her
face. Despite the tape over her mouth, I think I know her. I met
her in Paradheisos, we worked together on something. I cannot
remember her name, but there was the same sadness in her eyes
that I saw in my own later. Include her in your act of salvation,
I beg you. We were maidens once.

Great Demeter, I too have a mother. Allow me to see her again.
I must tell her what is happening inside me – it was a mistake
to keep it hidden from her until it was too late. My poor mother.
Does she think I am dead or the victim of some vanished killer?
Maybe it would be better if she did.

Green Lady, save us. Bring us, all three, back from Hades'
realm.

Mavros and Xanthakos got to the rendezvous point to find
Angie Poulou standing by her car. She moved out of their
headlights.

'Good to see you,' Mavros said, shaking her hand.

In reply she opened her mouth.

'Jesus Christ! That bastard! Have you seen a doctor?'

'Dentist, more like,' she lisped. 'Not yet.'

'You've got some pretty nasty bruises too. Does your head hurt?'

'No.' She gripped his arm. 'My husband knows where Lia is, I'm sure of it. We have to get him to talk.'

Mavros looked over his shoulder and introduced the deputy commissioner. 'As you see, we must follow the law.'

'Vehicles approaching from the west,' Xanthakos said, hand on his pistol grip.

'Duck behind your car,' Mavros said, leading Angie out of sight. 'These should be our backup, but I'm not taking any chances.'

The cars slowed and then turned into the area behind the trees. There were four of them – Lykos's VW van, Bitsos's hire car, the Fat Man's Peugeot and the cadres' black van. The lights were doused and doors started opening.

More introductions were made. The young Communists were less than comfortable with the policeman's presence, but they stood their ground. Two were carrying fish spears, the others thick wooden clubs. Akis Exarchos stood to the side, his arms tied behind his back and a strip of masking tape over his mouth.

'So,' asked Cadre One, 'who's in charge of this joint operation?'

Xanthakos nodded to Mavros.

'All right,' the latter said. 'There are several priorities. One, we find out where Mrs Poulou's fourteen-year-old daughter Lia is. If she's in the target house, she must be protected.' He glanced at the leading cadre. 'You and another of your men can take that on.'

The Communist nodded.

'Two, the deputy commissioner gets the chance to arrest Tryfon Roufos, the fugitive antiquities dealer. Paschos Poulos, the Bekakos couple, Professor Epameinondhas Phis and Angeliki –' He turned to Lykos – 'if she's there, will also be arrested, initially for conspiracy to imprison Bitsos and me. They were all present at the Hades temple above the HMC plant.'

Lambis Bitsos stepped over to the fisherman. 'You can arrest this piece of shit on the same charge right now, Deputy Commissioner.'

'That doesn't matter for the time being,' Mavros said. 'Take the tape from his mouth. He may be able to help us.'

Cadre Three obliged.

'Well, Aki?' Mavros said. 'For a start, do you know where the people we want might be?'

The fisherman shook his head. 'I only made my deal with Bekakos yesterday, on the phone. I don't know where the fucker is.'

'Having second thoughts?' Bitsos said sardonically. 'Too late for that.'

'Be quiet, Lambi,' Mavros said. He caught Lykos's gaze in the light from the single street lamp on the roadside. 'How about you? Any idea where they might be?'

The young man raised his head in the negative gesture. 'Angeliki probably knows, but she never told me.'

'All right,' Mavros said, with a slack smile. 'Fortunately we have another source of information.' He beckoned Angie Poulou forward.

'There's a house my husband and Rovertos Bekakos often use.'

There were sharp intakes of breath around the group as she spoke, revealing the damage to her mouth.

'Who did that to you?' Lykos asked. 'Your husband?'

'No, the man he hired to kill me.'

There were more looks of amazement.

'I can understand you might think I'm the enemy,' Angie continued, in fluent Greek. 'But, believe me, I'm not. I want my daughter. To find her, I'll support you any way I can.'

Telemachos Xanthakos took out a map of Paradheisos and spread it over the bonnet of the HMC 4x4. 'Isiodhou Street is here.' He pointed to the highest road in the pink section of the town. 'As you can see, it's a dead end. The house we want is the last one. We need to block both the entrance to the street itself and this perpendicular side street, Omirou. I think it would also be a good idea if someone took the 4x4 up the line of trees here in case any of them make a run for it out the back.'

'What about security?' Bitsos asked. 'There are bound to be more scumbags like the ones we tied up above the HMC plant. And they'll be armed.'

Trust Lambis to bring up the biggest problem, Mavros thought. 'Well, I see clubs, I see fish spears and I see—'

'Pistols,' the Fat Man said.

Mavros noted who was in possession of a firearm – himself, Xanthakos, Yiorgos and Bitsos. None of the cadres were carrying.

'All right, whoever goes up the back should have a pistol,' he said, looking at the black-clad young men. 'Any of you done firearms training?'

Cadre Two nodded, giving no more away.

'OK,' Mavros said, 'you're in the vehicle at the far end of Isiodhou Street, armed. Yiorgo, you take another vehicle and block the side street.' If his friend was disappointed about not taking part in the assault on the house, he didn't show it. 'Cadre Three, armed, in the 4x4 up there.' He looked round the rest of the group: Cadres 1 and 4, both carrying harpoons and clubs, Xanthakos, Bitsos – in charge of Akis, Lykos with his long knife, Angie Poulou, unarmed, and himself. He assigned positions to each, keeping his client with him.

Then Mavros checked the time. 04.25. As they moved to the vehicles, he had a thought he didn't share. He had no idea where the Son was or what he was planning to do. Screw the Uncertainty Principle.

# TWENTY-FIVE

Tryfon Roufos lay back on the bed and let the girl crawl over him. She had been reluctant at first – they always were – but the trinkets, perfume and money had brought her round. He'd been doing this for decades and he knew exactly how to handle them, girls and boys. This one was pasty-faced and slightly overweight – a typical product of the workers in the white houses – but her breasts were minimally developed and that was the way he liked them.

'Use your tongue,' he said irritably, 'not your teeth.'

As she began to get some rhythm going, Roufos found himself thinking about the last year: the escape from Crete, facilitated by his contacts within the police and government; the suite in the house in Kifissia afforded him by Rovertos Bekakos and his wife – long-time comrades in both illicit antiquities trading and forbidden love; his ongoing trading activities, now enhanced by the finds from the Hades temple; and his participation in Hades and Persephone worship. He didn't really care about the last, but it had been worth killing a piglet and wasting good wine on the libation to see Alex Mavros confined to the underworld. The investigator had nearly been the finish of him in Crete, but he didn't have the instinct of the true transgressor – he should have killed Roufos when he could.

'Slower,' he ordered, slapping the girl's buttocks. In his sixties, he found the prolongation of a single act more pleasurable than the frequent but brief encounters of earlier years.

Of course, Paschos Poulos had been the architect of his escape from justice. Roufos had always suspected that the entrepreneur shared his taste for young flesh but, until recent months, he hadn't realised quite how deviant Paschos was. The entrepreneur's contacts in the Olympic movement had brought Roufos a huge increase in business, ancient Greek pieces having gained a higher profile because of the Games. Fortunately Professor Phis, one of his long-term suppliers, had managed to lay his hands on many more objects. The old man really did believe in Hades and his bride and, although he liked to leer at young female flesh, he could no longer perform. Right now he was in the study, updating his digital archive.

'All right, that's enough,' Roufos said, seizing the girl's arm and pulling her beneath him. 'Relax. That way it won't hurt.'

The door opened. He turned to see Maria Bekakou in an open robe, her hair loose over her shoulders, with a sheepish boy beside her.

'May we join you?' she asked.

'Why not? What about Rovertos?'

'He's with Paschos. Their girls were . . . reluctant. They're disciplining them.'

'Really. I'd like to watch that.'

'I wouldn't interrupt if I were you. Our lord and master has a short fuse.'

Tryfon Roufos nodded. It was extraordinary how much rage lay beneath Paschos Poulos's calm exterior. In some dark way it had driven his impregnation of his daughter Lia. Her disappearance had been both a blessing – what would Angie have said when the girl had begun to show? – and a curse. The people who were holding her had extracted millions of euros, which only increased Paschos's anger.

Maria Bekakou sat on the bed and rang her long-nailed fingers down the girl's back.

'She's a tense one, isn't she? Perhaps she's worried about what will happen to her father's job and the family home if she doesn't please us.' She glanced at the boy, whose head was hung low. 'It must be an epidemic. Priapos here can't get hard for more than a few seconds at a time.'

Roufos rolled off the bed and went to the wardrobe.

'Time to follow our leader,' he said, coming back with two pairs of handcuffs, a peacock feather and a narrow cane. 'These will help.'

Maria Bekakou laughed. 'Careful, you old swine. You're making them cry.'

The antiquities smuggler shrugged. 'All part of the fun,' he said, grabbing the girl's wrist. 'If you cry out I'll put golf balls, plural, in both your mouths.'

The young people kept quiet.

It was after five a.m. by the time the vehicles were all in place, Mavros having confirmed that on the deputy commissioner's phone. The two of them were in Lykos's van, with Akis, whose mouth had been taped again, Lambis Bitsos, Angie Poulou, and Cadres One and Four. The large BMW that the Fat Man had followed from Athens, a gold Mercedes and Rovertos Bekakos's Porsche were parked outside the pink house at the far end of the street. There was no sign of heavy security, suggesting that Kloutsis and his men hadn't yet been reported missing. But there was a green people-carrier near the other cars and it wasn't hard to imagine who that would have carried.

'Drive towards the house,' Mavros said to Lykos. 'No headlights.

Cut the engine about a hundred metres away and roll to a
stop.'

The young man nodded and started the engine. During the
short trip, Mavros glanced to his left and saw Yiorgos standing
by the rental Peugeot, which he'd manoeuvred into a blocking
position on the side street. Lykos cut the power and they coasted
towards the parked cars at the dead end.

'Remember, fire only in self-defence,' Xanthakos said, drawing
his weapon. 'We're doing this by the book.' He nodded to Mavros.
'Let's go.'

They got out, the VW's sliding door making more noise than
was ideal. It had been agreed that the deputy commissioner and
Mavros would lead the way, with Lykos, Bitsos and the fisherman
following. The two cadres would guard Angie Poulou at the rear.

Ducking behind the vehicles, Xanthakos and Mavros made it
to the entrance of the property. There was a chain across the
short drive, but no sign of any guards. They exchanged glances.
That seemed very unlikely. Then Mavros saw a brief flash to his
left. Aromatic smoke drifted across the low-level lighting in the
garden.

'Someone having a cigarette break,' he whispered.

The policeman looked away. 'There may be another one on
my side. Nothing else to do but—'

'Go and get them.' Mavros held up his thumb and two fingers,
counting them down. Then he moved away, crouching as low as
he could. There was a rock covered by a succulent and he made
it there without being spotted. He glanced over his shoulder and
saw Xanthakos behind the thick trunk of a palm tree. Looking
to the front, he made out the smoker. He was sitting on another
rock, this one bare, and the only thing in his hands was the
cigarette.

Mavros found a stone that filled his palm, took a deep breath
and tossed it towards the house. As the guard got to his feet, head
turned in that direction, Mavros rushed him, getting the muzzle
of the Glock beneath the man's chin before he could react.

'No noise,' Mavros hissed, taking the pistol and mobile phone
from the guard's belt and pulling the latter from the loops on
his trousers. 'Kneel down.'

Mavros tied the belt round the man's ankles, then taped his

mouth – Lykos had several rolls of the material. Then he took off the guard's shirt and lashed his wrists behind his back. Finally, he picked up the phone and turned it off, then put the pistol in his belt. Looking round, he saw the tall policeman across the driveway, one arm in the air.

'Secure, Telemache?' he whispered.

'He's not going anywhere. I've got his phone and weapon.'

'Phone turned off?'

'I'm not a complete idiot. There's one more guard inside, or so the *securitate* said. Probably in the kitchen, to the rear.'

Mavros turned and saw the other groups behind the cars. He signalled to them to stay where they were.

'I'll go left, you right—'

'And maybe one of us will make it.' The deputy commissioner moved away, shoulders lowered.

Mavros made it to the corner of the house. The electric blinds were tightly closed and he couldn't make out anything apart from lights in all the rooms. He followed the wall round and reached a swimming-pool surrounded by thick oleanders. There were loungers at the end nearest the house, a couple of which had damp towels on them. He tried the glass sliding door and, to his surprise, found that it opened. Stepping inside, he moved noiselessly across the stone floor. There was a single light above a pair of sofas. Gun in both hands, Mavros approached, but quickly saw that no one was lying on either. There were items of clothing on both furniture and floor. He crouched down and made out a female top, a brassiere, a pair of skimpy knickers and a single training shoe. The sizes suggested a girl or a small woman. Was Lia Poulou here?

He went back outside, intending to alert Xanthakos to the way in. There was no sign of the policeman, so he waved Bitsos, Lykos and Akis forward.

'What now?' the journalist said, standing by one of the sofas.

Mavros was pressing out a message to Xanthakos on the phone he'd borrowed from Bitsos earlier – they had all set their devices to mute. A few seconds later, he got a reply: 'In kitchen, guard down. Meet in hall.'

'Down?' Bitsos said over his shoulder, sniffing blood. 'Has he killed him?'

'I doubt it. I'll go first, then Lykos, Akis and you in that order, Lambi.'

Mavros opened the door as quietly as he could and crept forwards. A passage led to the main part of the house and came out into a large hall. The deputy commissioner was on the other side of a wide staircase.

'I haven't seen anyone else,' he said.

'What about the guard?'

Xanthakos smiled. 'He helpfully stepped outside for a piss, so he had the wrong weapon in his hand. He's trussed up nicely.'

Mavros told Bitsos and the other two to stay in the hall. He and the policeman headed upstairs, separating at the top. Mavros went left, putting his ear against every room door – they were all closed, except for a luxurious bathroom. A trail of clothes, this time male, led to a room on his right. He gripped the handle, took a deep breath and opened the door, swinging his pistol around. The room was empty, though the sheets on the king-size bed had been disturbed. There was a cloying perfume in the air. A suitcase full of women's clothing was on a collapsible stand. Maria Bekakou's?

He went into the corridor and headed to the door at the end. He could hear muffled noises before he got there, and then a sharp cracking sound. He pressed out 'Ready?' to Telemachos and got the OK. Counting to three, he turned the handle.

'Hands in the air!' he shouted, taking in Paschos Poulos and Rovertos Bekakos. Both were without clothes and aroused, the former holding a large purple dildo and the latter a whip dangling a single strip of leather. Two naked girls were on their fronts, their wrists and ankles bound to the iron bedstead.

'Drop those things,' Mavros ordered, 'and untie your victims.'

The men exchanged glances and did as they were told, fumbling with the ropes.

'I didn't know private investigators were allowed to carry weapons, Mr Mavro,' Bekakos said.

'And I didn't know lawyers were allowed to sexually abuse minors.' Mavros stepped forward, gun pointing at Poulos's groin and helped the nearer girl up. 'Go downstairs to the hall, there are friends waiting.' He handed her a gown from the floor. The other girl rolled away from the naked men and followed, wrapping a towel under her arms. Their faces were wet and there were red marks on their wrists and backs. Neither of them resembled Lia.

'Cover yourselves up,' Mavros said to the men, in disgust.

Poulos smiled. 'Not keen on the male form?'

'Where's your daughter, you piece of shit?'

The businessman reached slowly for his trousers. 'Shouldn't I be asking you that? My wife hired you to find Lia, didn't she?'

Mavros turned to the lawyer. 'Do you know where Lia is?'

Bekakos zipped himself up. 'If I did, I wouldn't tell a common criminal like you. Breaking and entering while carrying a lethal weapon is a very serious offence.'

'This is a police operation. Prepare to be arrested.'

At that moment, Paschos Poulos made a rush for the door. Mavros had no hesitation in shooting him.

The Son, who was working his way down the valley on foot and was only fifty metres from the top row of pink houses, heard the shot and stopped. He recognised it as coming from a pistol. The location was close to where he was headed. Checking his own weapons, he set off again, reaching the level of the rear garden walls. He remembered there was a path between the third and fourth houses. The fading light of the moon revealed it as he approached. He got to the pavement of Isiodhou Street, about twenty metres to the left of Omirou. In the distance he could see a car parked across the road, blocking it. Was he too late?

There was a tree with low branches on the garden to his right. The Son swung himself up and cleared a space between the leaves. He could see several people coming out of the house at the dead end. He was glad he had brought the Beretta sniper rifle with the ATN night vision scope rather than the tranquilliser gun. The only question was, how many people should he take down?

Then he saw Alex Mavros along with his other designated targets, as well as the bitch who'd slashed his ear.

This was going to be a massacre.

'It's OK!' Mavros yelled, after firing. He tied a sleeve torn from Paschos Poulos's shirt tightly around the businessman's upper arm and told him to press the rest of the garment tightly over the wound. Rovertos Bekakos had lost control of his bowels and was wiping himself with a sheet.

'Jesus Christ,' Mavros said, glancing down the corridor as Xanthakos pushed Maria Bekakou and Tryfon Roufos towards the stairs. The antiquities dealer didn't look at all happy to see Mavros. 'Come on.'

There was a crowd in the entrance hall. As Mavros was halfway down the stairs, a door to his left opened and the bent figure of Professor Phis staggered out.

'What's going on?' he demanded, eyes wide.

Mavros shook his head. 'Didn't anyone check the other rooms?'

Lambis Bitsos looked at Lykos, but both remained silent.

The cadres were at the front door, Angie Poulou between them. When she saw her husband, she rushed forward. He tried to back away, landing hard on his backside on the stairs. Mavros tried to put himself between them.

'How could you?' his client screamed at Poulos, slipping past Mavros. 'How could you hire that pig to kill me? Where's Lia? You know, don't you?' She looked at the young people who had been upstairs before glaring at him again. 'You disgusting pervert!' Her eyes shifted to the Bekakos couple. 'You're all child abusers, you . . .' She broke off and vomited over the banister, narrowly missing Epameinondhas Phis.

'All right, calm down, everyone,' Xanthakos shouted. He identified himself. 'We have transport to get everyone to police headquarters in Livadheia.' The Communist cadres glanced at each other. 'Assemble on the drive outside, please, and I'll allocate vehicles.'

Mavros pulled the tape from Akis's mouth as he passed. 'Didn't need you after all,' he said, touching Bitsos's shoulder. 'Lambi, keep an eye on Roufos, will you? I don't want him slinking off again.'

The journalist nodded avidly. 'He's got a big part in the scoop of my life.'

Mavros went outside and saw the Fat Man in the gateway. 'It's OK, Yiorgo. We've nailed the lot of them.'

'Really? The Son as well?'

Mavros froze. In the heat of the bust, he'd forgotten about the killer.

'Back inside, everyone!' he yelled. 'The Son, Telemache!'

It was too late. The first shot blew Rovertos Bekakos's head into a welter of blood, bone and brain. The second ripped through Tryfon Roufos's throat. A fountain of arterial blood arced through the air as he sprawled back on the steps. Paschos Poulos moved faster than anyone, getting back inside the house, closely followed by his wife, Maria Bekakou and Xanthakos. The Fat Man had taken cover behind the gatepost, while the cadres, Bitsos and Lykos ran towards the door. That left Mavros, who was on the ground crawling towards the rock where the guard had sat earlier, and Akis Exarchos. The fisherman stood in front of the main entrance, offering cover to the others.

'Get down!' Mavros yelled.

Akis did so, but not voluntarily. He was sent crashing back against the wall of the house by a shot that passed through his chest, killing him instantly.

'Fuck!' Mavros said, looking at Yiorgos. 'Stay there!'

'What are you going to do?'

Mavros called Xanthakos. 'What's going on in there?'

'The Communists have disappeared,' said the policeman. 'I think they've gone out the back to meet the comrade beyond the trees.'

'Can you see if the car's still blocking the far end of the street?'

'No, it's gone too. Bastards.'

'They have different priorities. So, what do we do?'

'Hang on, Poulos and his wife have disappeared as well. Has anyone seen them? Shit!'

Mavros groaned. Was there any way this could get worse, he asked himself.

He didn't have to wait long for an answer.

'Alex Mavro?' came a shout from down the street. 'Come out and I'll let the rest of them live. Come out now!'

'No!' the Fat Man yelled. 'Alex, no!'

Mavros lay back and checked his weapon. Then he ran through his options. The neighbours would presumably have called the police by now – sensibly, none of them had shown their face. Telemachos would find Poulos – how far could they have gone, the husband in shock from the gunshot wound? Yiorgos was armed, as was Bitsos, though Lykos's long knife wouldn't be much use against a professional assassin armed with a heavy-duty rifle. So, they could stay put and wait for backup – who would be shot to pieces by the Son – or he could save the day.

Stuffing the pistol into the back of his trousers, Mavros got up. He raised his arms as he reached the gate and smiled at the Fat Man as he stepped over the chain.

Then he set off down the street named after the ancient farmer-poet Hesiod.

# TWENTY-SIX

Angie Poulou had grabbed her husband by his injured arm and dragged him to the kitchen, before ramming a chair under the door handle and locking the door that led to the garden. Paschos collapsed against the fridge, cringing.

'Tell me why you did it,' she demanded. 'Tell me why you sent the killer.'

'I . . . no . . . aaaargh!'

Angie slowly released her grip from his arm.

'You . . . you hired that busybody Mavros. You . . . you should . . . have trusted me.'

'Trusted you? You like to put your pathetic penis in underage girls like those poor souls here. Is that what you did to Lia? Where is she?' Angie seized his arm again.

'No!' Poulos screamed, breaking off when there was hammering on the door.

'Mrs Poulou?' the deputy commissioner called. 'Please, let me in. Don't do anything you'll regret.'

'Where is she?' Angie repeated, taking the Son's pistol from beneath the back of her loose blouse and pointing it at her husband's groin. 'Tell me, NOW!'

'I don't know,' Poulos gasped, his eyes bulging. 'Honestly, I don't know. The . . . the killer was supposed to find her.'

Angela Poulou's shoulders sagged. 'Then there's no point in you living any longer.'

She lifted the weapon and pulled the trigger.

\*    \*    \*

Mavros heard the shot and wondered what had happened in the house. Then there was a noise closer behind. He turned to see Yiorgos following, his hands high and his belly pulled into an unusual shape.

'Go back, you fool.'

'Piss off.'

'He'll kill you.'

'Then my death will be forever on your conscience.'

'Oh, great,' Mavros groaned. 'This really can't get any worse.'

'Look, it's our killer,' Yiorgos said.

Mavros watched as a well-built figure came down from a tree and walked towards them, rifle slung over his left shoulder. The blonde-haired Son was pointing a pistol at them.

'Peel away,' Mavros said. 'We're still far enough away to make it tricky for him.'

'And I'm a tiny target.'

Laughing was unavoidable, but quickly curtailed.

The Son stopped about fifteen metres from them and raised his empty hand.

'Death does have its funny side,' he said. 'Though it strikes me I should be the one cackling.'

'What happened to you?' Mavros asked, staring at the bandages on his head and ear. 'The van Gogh look doesn't become you.'

The Son frowned. 'Van who?' He looked at Yiorgos. 'You, I take it, are the Fat Man.'

'The man's a genius.'

'A.k.a. Yiorgos Pandazopoulos, born 1943, member of the Communist Party, longstanding operator of a café on Adhrianou Street, organiser of illicit card games, mother Phedhra deceased 2003—'

'All right,' Mavros said, 'you've made your point. No doubt you have even more on me. But you're wasting time. The cops will be on their way.'

'You and I will be well on *our* way before they get here, Alex Mavro. You, Fat Man, bring us a car. And don't try anything smart. I'll be holding this –' he brandished the pistol – 'to this busybody's head.'

'Do what he says, Yiorgo. Please.'

His friend turned reluctantly away.

'And take that pistol from above your arse, Fat Man,' the Son called. 'Put it down slowly on the asphalt. That's right. Now, fuck off.' He walked up to Mavros and felt behind him. 'What are you, unidentical twins?' He put the pistol into the pocket of his utility jacket. 'Who was that man giving cover in the doorway?'

'Akis Exarchos. A fisherman from Kypseli.'

'I thought I recognised him. He was the lunatic who ran into me when I was trying to take out the ecologists.'

Mavros heard the Fat Man's Peugeot start up. 'Didn't you bring your tranquilliser gun this time?' A thought was stirring, but it wouldn't come to the surface of his mind.

'No,' the Son said, grinning slackly. 'But I've got my fish hooks.'

Mavros swallowed bile as he remembered the Father and Son's favourite torture method. 'Whoever's employing you has obviously had enough of Poulos and his gang of Hades-worshipping child abusers and set you loose on them.'

'Something like that, I imagine.'

'But aren't you meant to be finding Lia Poulou?'

The Son glanced at him, then pressed the muzzle of his Glock against Mavros's head as the Fat Man drove up.

'Out!' the Son ordered. 'And be grateful I didn't turn that gut of yours into a sieve.'

'Fu—'

'Go, Yiorgo,' Mavros interrupted. 'I'll be all right.' The Son nudged him into the driver's seat and sat next to him.

'I don't know where you got that idea, Alex Mavro. You aren't coming back from this trip.'

'Listen to me. There's a man in the house who knows where Lia Poulou is. Wouldn't you like to find her? For me it's a question of professional pride.' Mavros had almost finished turning the car. 'For you, no doubt there's money involved.'

The blonde man thought about that. 'All right. Who is this man?'

'Paschos Poulos, of course.'

The Son stared at him as if he were simple. 'Her own father? He put down the cash for me to . . .' He broke off.

Mavros returned his gaze thoughtfully. 'Yes, he paid for you to find her, but I don't think he intends for her to live.' He pulled up in front of the chain and stopped the engine. 'How do you want to do this? I can phone the policeman inside and get him to send Poulos out.'

'Go ahead.'

Mavros did so, explaining the situation.

'Forget Poulos,' Xanthakos said. 'He committed suicide.'

Mavros remembered the shot. 'How did he get a gun?'

'It turns out his wife was armed. He took it from her.'

Mavros remembered the fury in his client's eyes and wondered if that was the true story.

'What's happened?' the Son demanded.

Mavros told him, then the thought that had been tormenting him finally surfaced. 'Wait, someone else knows where Lia is.' Faces flashed before him – the turncoat Angeliki; the black-clad cadres sent by Tatiana Roubani, Lykos's Communist MP aunt; and the young ecologist himself, who had supposedly taken Ourania to a safe place.

'Telemache?' he said, 'Send Lykos out. Tell him his only chance of escape is if he comes with us.'

The Son put the Glock back against Mavros's head. 'What is this?'

'We've all been played for fools. Lykos, the ecologist, kidnapped Lia Poulou, probably with the backing of his aunt. I'm sure you can think of a way to make him talk.'

They watched as the young man walked slowly from the house, knife in hand.

'Drop it!' the Son shouted, then stiffened as Angie Poulou appeared at the door. She ran to catch up with Lykos, only stopping when the Son fired a shot that ricocheted from the drive in front of her. 'Stay there, bitch. This time I really will kill you.'

Mavros raised a hand to discourage his client and she took a step back.

'You drive,' the Son said to Lykos, getting into the back seat. 'That way I can shoot either or both of you before you do anything stupid.'

Moving to the passenger seat, Mavros looked at the young man. He seemed to be in control of himself, but the rapid blinking was a giveaway.

'Where to?' Lykos asked.

Mavros laughed. 'Good try. Go to the end of the road – I wonder where your friendly cadres have disappeared to? – and turn right. We're going to where you have Lia Poulou stashed.'

'I don't know what you're talking about.'

'Which is also where you took Ourania yesterday, isn't it?' Mavros opted for hard ball. 'Have you been fucking them?'

'No!' Lykos exclaimed, glaring at him.

'Eyes on the road,' the Son ordered. 'No, you haven't been fucking them but, yes, you've stashed them?'

Lykos took a deep breath. 'All right, I'll take you there.'

The Son stroked the back of the young man's neck with his pistol. 'A wise decision.'

'Was it you or your aunt who set this whole thing up?' Mavros asked.

'My aunt.'

'I can't imagine it was approved by the Communist Party leadership.'

'I don't know. Probably not. She was so angry about the amount of Olympic Games contracts Poulos A.E. obtained and the huge profits the bastard was making. I was already fighting the company over the pollution and the deaths down here.' Lykos turned right and headed for the shore. 'Taking his daughter seemed the best way of getting to him, but he managed to get a media blackout applied. That actually suited us. He paid plenty for us to keep quiet. We've enough to campaign for years now.'

Mavros was watching him closely. 'How did you get Lia to sound so natural on the phone after you'd snatched her?'

Lykos laughed lightly. 'We didn't snatch her. She came willingly. Her idiot father thought she came to Paradheisos with him because she was interested in the company town. We inducted her into the cult of Demeter and Persephone, as well as educating her in ecological matters. She's a smart girl – she'd done a lot of research on both issues.' He glanced at Mavros. 'Good, eh? The bastard's own daughter was working against him. Then again, I don't blame her. He's the one who was sexually abusing her.'

A police car roared past them, lights flashing and siren wailing.

'Where are the girls?' Mavros asked, thinking of his client again. What had happened between her and Poulos at the last?

'A place called Chrysso, a few kilometres below Delphi.'

'Are they being well looked after?'

The young man swallowed hard. 'Em, you have to understand. Our worship of Demeter is based on a cult that predates the pantheon of the Olympian gods. For fertility to return to the land, substitutes for Persephone must be offered up.'

'What?' Mavros said, his flesh creeping.

'They should still be breathing,' Lykos said, turning on to the coast road towards Kypseli. 'They're beneath the surface of the earth, but the ritual requires they stay alive as long as possible for the most beneficial effect.'

'They'd better still be breathing,' Mavros said, 'or I'll put a hole in your windpipe.' He looked over his shoulder. 'Don't tell me you worship the ancient gods too.'

The Son smiled emptily. 'I don't worship anything. If you're referring to the pomegranate seeds I put in my victims, I was told to do that. I even have some in my bag for you.'

Mavros was again forced to face up to the proximity of his own death. He'd been lucky the Son had taken the bait over Lia Poulou. That didn't mean he wouldn't finish with Mavros when she was found. He wasn't the kind of man who would forget being beaten two years earlier.

'Where's the Father?' he asked, searching for a weak point.

The Son looked out the window as they passed through Kypseli. 'He's happy enough. Doesn't get out much.'

'He's dead, isn't he?' Mavros saw the killer's gaze harden and knew he was on target. 'Old age, illness, accident, suicide or murder?'

The muzzle of the Glock was jammed into the back of Mavros's head.

'You've got a big mouth, dick,' the Son said. 'What do you think of this? The old man kept a file on your brother.'

Mavros felt a wave of nausea break over him. The long-lost face flashed before him as it used to, lips creased in a soft smile. The Father told him he hadn't tortured Andonis. But even if he hadn't been lying, he might have heard from fellow torturers who knew his brother's fate.

'I thought that would shut you up,' the Son said, with a callous laugh. 'After we find the girl, I'll consider telling you what the

Father knew. You won't be able to do anything with the information in the seconds before I kill you.'

Mavros swallowed hard. 'Tell me now,' he said. 'Please.'

The Son sat silent, pistol in hand, as Lykos took the turn for Itea and headed away from the fume-covered bay. The first grey of dawn was eating into the darkness behind them. Mavros was determined to make the most of his last hour on the surface of the earth, but he had no idea how.

# TWENTY-SEVEN

Brigadier Nikos Kriaras stepped out of the helicopter that had landed on the concrete circle outside the hospital in Dhistomo. A portly officer in dress uniform stepped forward to meet him, introducing himself as the commissioner of the Viotia police. Within seconds, they were in an unmarked car, heading for Paradheisos.

'Your deputy would appear to have an inflated opinion of himself,' Kriaras said, as they entered the defile between the mountains.

'Telemachos Xanthakos is a capable officer,' the chief said neutrally.

'He has presided over a botched operation that resulted in several deaths. Is it true that he kept you in the dark about it?'

'He kept everyone in the dark – the first the Paradheisos team knew was when neighbours reported gunfire.'

Kriaras looked ahead to the pale blue sea and the dark clouds from the HMC plant. 'He was insolent when I called him. As far as I could understand, Paschos Poulos, Rovertos Bekakos and Tryfon Roufos have all been killed—'

'The first by his own hand.'

'Apparently. And a local fisherman was shot too.' The brigadier turned to the commissioner. 'Not that he's of any importance. But you'll understand the press will be down here in droves if they discover that such a leading businessman, not to mention a member of the Olympic Games security committee, has died. I will require absolute obedience from you and all your officers. No one must talk, not even to their families.'

The commissioner raised his shoulders. 'Paradheisos is a small town. I don't see how you can stop the residents gossiping.'

'I don't see how they will know the identities of the dead.'

'Maybe they won't. But Telemachos . . . Deputy Commissioner Xanthakos told me that several other people were involved and most have already left the scene.'

Nikos Kriaras was shaking his head. 'Very lax. You'll be lucky to escape with your pension intact.'

'Me?'

'You're in charge, aren't you? Anyway, that's for later. Now I need to know the whereabouts of the private investigator Alex Mavros.'

'The last I heard, he had been abducted by a sniper known as the Son.'

Kriaras gave him an icy stare. 'Your deputy didn't tell me that. Do you have officers in pursuit?'

'No. Xanthakos thought that would endanger the captives even more.'

'Captives, plural?'

'Yes. One of the Ecologists for a Better Viotia was also taken – calls himself Lykos.'

The car turned into the first street and went to the pink house at the far end.

Kriaras got out, ignoring the policemen at the gate. Then a woman in creased linen clothes turned towards him and he felt his jaw drop. Angela Poulou's mouth was that of a demon with filed teeth and the look she gave him almost liquefied the contents of his bowels.

The sun was still behind the mountains when Lykos drove up the road from Itea to Delphi, but there was plenty of daylight. The valley was a huge forest of olive trees and the great shoulder of Parnassos stood up in front of them, the dots of white on its lower flank marking the modern town of Delphi. Chrysso, their destination, was a few kilometres nearer.

Mavros turned to the Son. 'The man you decapitated in the

ancient stadium up there – were you given that modus operandi or did you pick it yourself?'

'I always choose the method of dispatch.'

'You cut the man's head off?' Lykos said, sitting bolt upright.

'Yes,' the Son said, with a smile. 'He was another Hades worshipper – had a mini-statue in his house.'

'Vangelis Gilas, a *phylax*.'

Mavros had been following the exchange. There was something off about the set of Lykos's lips.

'That name's familiar,' the Son said. 'How do you know him?'

'He was in the cult that my partner Angeliki turned out to be involved in, along with Poulos and Bekakos.'

Mavros narrowed his eyes. 'Your cult worships Demeter and Persephone, yes?'

Lykos glanced at him. 'The pre-Olympian religion had no Hades figure. The Mycenaeans worshipped goddesses and priestesses controlled the rituals.'

'Really? So who's your priestess?'

Lykos didn't answer, his eyes on the ascending road.

The Son put the muzzle of his Glock against the back of the young man's head. 'We need to know that, kid. You might be leading us into the jaws of a very big trap.'

'I . . . I can't say. My tongue will be torn out.'

The Son laughed. 'What do you think a bullet at point blank range will do to it?'

'I . . . my aunt.'

'Tatiana Roubani?' Mavros said, amazed. 'So she was killing two birds with one stone – pressurising Poulos and finding a sacrificial victim.'

'He may have been misled,' the Son said, 'but the Father always told me the Communists were godless.'

'My aunt . . . she has her own way.'

Mavros looked round at the Son. 'Maybe you should give me a weapon. Who knows how many crazy cultists might be waiting for us?'

'I don't think so. As I've already proved, I can cope very well with poor odds.'

'The people in Paradheisos didn't even know you were there,' Lykos scoffed. 'See how you like it when . . .' He broke off as the Son replaced the pistol with a combat knife, its point drawing a line of blood beneath the ecologist's hair.

'You'll give me plenty of cover, won't you?'

Shortly afterwards Lykos drove into Chrysso, then immediately turned left up a dirt track with only a few houses on it. A minute later, he pulled up by a ruined farm building.

'They're . . . they're in the outhouse,' he said, trying to lean away from the knife.

'Let's move before the natives start gathering,' said the Son, putting the Glock in his belt and shouldering the sniper's rifle. He removed the knife-point from Lykos's neck long enough for them both to get out, and then grabbed the young man around the upper chest, the blade against his throat.

Mavros followed them past shattered stone walls and collapsed roof beams. In what would have been the livestock shed, there was a long heap of earth, with the edges of a corrugated iron sheet beneath it. On the earth, at regular intervals, were three small terracotta figures of women with their arms raised. Two shovels stood against the wall.

'Dig,' the Son ordered, stepping back. 'Both of you.' He took out his pistol.

Mavros and Lykos did as they were told, the young man removing the figurines carefully, bowing his head to each one. The earth wasn't compacted, so it didn't take long to clear. They took opposite ends of the metal and lifted it up.

'What do you see, Alex Mavros?' the Son said.

'Two girls in white robes with a small marble statue between their heads.' Mavros jumped down and struggled to loose the ropes on the victims' wrists and ankles. Strips of cloth had been tied tightly around their mouths. Their eyes were closed, their faces pale and their skin cold. At first he thought they were dead, then Ourania's eyelids flickered and opened.

'I need that knife,' he called. 'At least one of them's alive.'

There was silence, then the blade dropped point down into the earth by his foot. He cut the ropes and gags, helping Ourania to sit up. She coughed and asked for water in a croaky voice.

'Hold on while I get Lia up,' Mavros said, turning to the other girl. Her lower abdomen was swollen and her bladder had voided.

'Lia? Wake up.' He put two fingers against her throat and got a weak pulse. 'Lia?'

Suddenly she shook violently and opened her eyes. Her hands went straight to her belly and cradled it. 'Are we . . . are we safe?'

Then Mavros understood. She was pregnant, presumably by her father. He pulled her and Ourania up, their legs as unsteady as new-born lambs', and asked Lykos to help them out. He did so reluctantly, the Son's pistol on him. The girls stood on the opposite side of their grave, Mavros climbing out and supporting them. They trembled at the sight of the heavily armed man.

The Son pointed at Lia. 'You're the one.' He moved his gaze to Mavros. 'All right, I've fulfilled my original commission. Unfortunately for you, I've since had new orders. That's why I killed the people in Paradheisos. You're last on my list. Come on.'

Mavros squeezed the girls' arms. 'Hold on,' he said, 'you can't leave them with Lykos. He'll just bury them again.'

'Not my problem. Come *now* or I'll shoot the pair of them.' The Glock was aimed at Lia's burgeoning belly.

Mavros moved round the piles of earth, then realised the girls were being pushed after him by Lykos.

'Stop!' the Son ordered.

Lykos kept shoving until they were all close, then burst out between Lia and Ourania, one of the spades aimed straight at the Son's throat. Mavros thrust his shoulder against the young man and he fell to the left, smashing his head against a stone. The spade missed its target by only a few centimetres. The Son got a shot off, but it passed through the gap that Lykos had just made.

Mavros turned to comfort the girls, looking over his shoulder. 'Don't kill him,' he said. 'He wasn't on your list, after all.'

The Son glared at him. 'Are you sure of that?'

'Yes.'

'You're right.' The assassin cocked his ear. The sound of a helicopter could be heard in the gorge. 'Here comes the airborne cavalry. Well, Alex Mavro, it seems I owe you, if not my life, at least some part of my anatomy. And obviously I can't leave them alone in case that little scumbag comes round. So, although our business isn't finished, I'll let you live.' He grinned. 'That should really piss Kriaras off.'

'Nikos Kriaras?' Mavros said, his jaw dropping. The cop was a dubious operator, but he'd never put him down as a murderer by proxy. 'Jesus.'

'For what it's worth, I think the job started off with him doing favours for his friend Poulos, but as time went by that friend became more trouble than he was worth.'

Mavros watched the Son move towards the VW bus. 'I don't suppose you're expecting me to thank you.'

'No.' The Son threw his weapons into the front seat and climbed in after them. 'And I don't suppose you're expecting me to say this.' He laughed cruelly. 'Your brother's alive. And we'll meet again.'

With that he slammed the door, started the engine and drove away in a cloud of dust.

Mouth dry, Mavros raised his arms and waved at the helicopter, encouraging the girls to do the same. It could have been that he felt he owed the Son, multiple murderer though he was, the opportunity to get away, but what he really cared about was keeping him alive and at liberty so he might lead him to Andonis in the future.

The helicopter circled and then came down in a bare field fifty metres away.

Waiting for Kriaras and the tall figure of Telemachos Xanthakos, Mavros spoke softly to the girls. He told them everything would be all right. As for himself, he knew that he would be unable to rest until he found Andonis, which was doubtless the Son's intention. And there was no guarantee that his brother really was alive. He might have been in Hades' halls for over thirty years, the Son exacting the kind of revenge to be expected of a hardened hunter cheated of his prey.

The sun finally cleared the mountains of Viotia and Mavros blinked back tears. He hadn't only saved two innocent girls; he had raised his beloved brother's ghost, invisible and intangible though it remained.

# EPILOGUE

'What a staggering waste of money,' the Fat Man said, as the Olympic Games closing ceremony got into full swing.

'Mm,' Mavros said. He was sprawled on the couch in Yiorgos's *saloni*, a bottle of Amstel in one hand and a copy of Seferis's poetry in the other.

'Don't you agree?'

'What?'

'And those tossers can't even sing in tune.'

Mavros looked at the screen, but he couldn't even raise a moan. He was thinking about Lia Poulou. She should have been at the Olympic Stadium with her parents, but instead her mother had taken her to a clinic in London. He was sure she would return without a fetus in her womb, not that he blamed her or Angie. His client had given him a generous bonus. He'd wanted to ask about her husband's suicide, but he didn't really care. The world was a better place without Paschos Poulos.

'For the love of Lenin!' the Fat Man yelled, as fireworks exploded around the arena.

Mavros didn't react, unable to get the stricken face of Lia Poulou from his mind. The girl had mentioned Demeter frequently and seemed still to be under the sway of what had been drummed into her by Lykos and Angeliki, even though they had turned out to be worshippers of different cults. He hoped Lia would get over that.

As for the others, Maria Bekakou had been charged with child abuse, Telemachos Xanthakos having witnessed her with the under-fourteen in Tryfon Roufos's room. So far, she hadn't talked. Mavros was sure a deal would be done and her silence ensured. He remembered her meeting Brigadier Kriaras in the brasserie. The Father's and Son's details were in a secret police file. Mavros had tried to publicise their involvement in the gangland case when he'd first confronted them, but no newspaper would print the full story. Kriaras, perhaps under command from his political masters, had obviously brought back the younger enforcer, but he had played a dangerous game. The Son wasn't a man to cross.

'Come on,' Yiorgos said, chinking his bottle against Mavros's. 'At last the Games are over.' He nodded at the blank screen, all the lights having been briefly turned off. 'What's up with you, Alex? You found the girl, most of those paedophile bastards are worm-fodder, we're in the money . . .'

Mavros sighed. 'Do you think Lia Poulou will ever be the same again? Do you think her mother will?'

'At least that bastard Poulos can't torment them any longer.'

'True. And maybe the aluminium plant will be cleaned up.'

The Fat Man looked dubious. 'Maybe.'

'What are the comrades saying about Tatiana Roubani?'

'That her resignation was due to ill-health and her service to the party has been exemplary.'

'My father will come back to haunt her.'

'Is that right? Don't tell me you've become a Hades worshipper too? Typical Greeks, eh? They couldn't even agree over which defunct deities to worship.'

Mavros thought about the rival cults. Lykos had been keeping quiet, as had Angeliki, who had been picked up by the police in Thiva; she had taken refuge with a friend after escaping from Kypseli. They would be the scapegoats, sent down for long terms for the kidnapping of Lia Poulou. At least the girl had collapsed joyfully into her mother's arms when they were reunited, failing to notice the disaster area that was Angie's mouth.

'One of the cadres must have given the cops the location of the girls' grave. Otherwise, how did Kriaras know to direct the helicopter there?'

'Good for whoever it was,' Yiorgos said. 'They were pawns.'

'They could have hung around at the denouement.'

'You think they'd have stopped the Son? I still don't understand why he didn't kill you.'

Mavros looked at his friend. 'He wants me to suffer. Saying that Andonis is alive was the perfect way to achieve that.'

'So you don't believe him?'

'It doesn't matter if I believe him or not. I can't let it lie.'

The Fat Man lumbered over to the TV and turned it off. 'What are you going to do?'

'Exactly what the Son wants – pursue him.'

'But you said it before – he's protected.'

Mavros smiled grimly. 'And I know who's protecting him – or was. Plus, Kriaras added my name to the list of targets. I'm not going to let him get away with that.' His phone rang. 'Hi, Lambi, what's up?' There was the sound of loud carousing in the background.

'Come down to the coastal strip,' the journalist said. 'I'm having a ball, not to mention several lovely young ladies.' Bitsos had written up a huge story about Paschos Poulos's death, although some of his copy had been struck out by his editor, under pressure from the politicians, and more delayed till after the Games. 'I'm enjoying my new-found hero status.' The journalist hadn't been reticent about highlighting his role in the case.

'Have a good one,' Mavros said, cutting the connection. The idea of Bitsos pawing young flesh, admittedly over the age of consent, wasn't enticing. Besides, he couldn't help thinking about the losers – Akis Exarchos, who had sacrificed himself, probably because he couldn't live with having turned traitor; Ourania, who had told her parents she couldn't live in Paradheisos any more; and Lia – how would she grow up into any kind of normal woman? And what about the Son's victims? The burned man had been identified as a high school literature teacher, who'd made the sole mistake of worshipping the Olympian gods – as had the beheaded man at Delphi and the mutilated female professor in Trikkala. They had been killed to put pressure on Lia's kidnappers, but Lykos and his aunt hadn't buckled.

Then there was his own family. They and Niki had spent a frightening couple of days before he was able to tell them the danger was over. He didn't think the Son would do anything to them now that he had Mavros well and truly hooked. At least Telemachos Xanthakos had come out of the case well. They were in touch and he hoped he'd see more of the unusual policeman.

'So you're meeting the mad woman tomorrow,' the Fat Man said.

'Do you mind?' Mavros had called Niki when he got back to Athens and she'd agreed to have lunch with him. His name had been prominent in Bitsos's articles and she'd congratulated him on saving Lia. There had been warmth in her voice.

'I suppose you're going to move in with her,' Yiorgos said, heading for the kitchen.

'It's a bit early to say, Fat Man. Even if I do, I'll still be round here all the time to sample your pastries.'

'Speaking of which.' His friend reappeared with a mound of honey-drenched filo.

'What on earth is that?'

'Don't you recognise it? Look, I even made the temple.' Yiorgos pointed at the side.

'You made an edible replica of the mountain overlooking the HMC plant?' Mavros said incredulously.

'Yes. There's even a tunnel going down to where you were imprisoned.' The Fat Man grinned. 'And at the bottom, I put a miniature figure of Hades.'

Mavros shook his head. 'And what about Demeter, the Green Lady?'

'She isn't in season, you fool. I'll do her next spring.'

Spring and fertility, Mavros thought. It had been a nightmare for Lia Poulou, but perhaps things would turn out better for Niki and him – if she took him back.

'Here,' said Yiorgos, handing him a plate. 'Eat your portion of Viotia.'

Mavros obliged. Paradheisos hadn't lived up to its name and the Olympian gods were long gone, but the Fat Man had made his own version of ambrosia – even if the pomegranate seeds on the top were a flourish several kilometres too far.

# ACKNOWLEDGEMENTS

**M**any thanks to Kate Lyall Grant and her excellent staff at Crème de la Crime for turning this one round quickly. Great jacket, people, and best review ever, Kate! And to my peerless agent Broo Doherty of Wade and Doherty for devotion well beyond the call of duty.

Just after I finished this book, my traitor body presented me with a third bout of cancer. Yet again, Drs Haris Katsifotis and Miltos Seferlis and their superb team at the Polykliniki Athinon saved my posterior or thereabouts. They really are my heroes. My sister Claire braved Omonia Square at night to keep me company in hospital, while brother Alan provided essential music and related magazines.

My friends did their utmost to keep me going. Victoria Crosses to Robert Wilson, Julia Wallis Martin, John Connolly and the dedicatees. I'd also like to acknowledge the moving support I received from Facebook and Twitter friends, many of whom I've never met in the flesh. Paul Johnston and Alex Mavros have their own pages on the former, while you can follow me at @Paul1Johnston on the latter. You know it makes sense. My website www.paul-johnston.co.uk also provides information about this book and the rest of my, ahem . . . oeuvre.

Finally, my deepest love to Roula, Maggie and Alexander. Long live Kloutsis.